MY HUNDRED DAYS OF WAR

A MALCOLM MACPHAIL WW1 NOVEL

ISBN 978-94-92843-02-9 (Trade Paperback edition)
ISBN 978-94-92843-03-6 (e-book edition)

First published in the Netherlands in 2018 by Esdorn Editions

Cover design by JD Smith Design
Interior design and typesetting by JD Smith Design

Cover photographs acknowledgement: Library and Archives Canada/ Ministry of the Overseas Military Forces of Canada fonds: *An explosion taking place in a house in Cambrai.* October, 1918 (a003404), *Canadian ammunition column passing through recently captured village.* September, 1918 (a003081), *Detachment of Canadians passing through Cambrai.* October, 1918 (a003405)

This book is a work of historical fiction. The names, characters, events and dialogue portrayed herein are either the product of the author's imagination, or are used fictitiously, except where they are an acknowledged part of the historical record.

www.darrellduthie.com

MY HUNDRED DAYS OF
WAR

A MALCOLM MACPHAIL
WW1 NOVEL

DARRELL DUTHIE

Esdorn
Editions

Also by Darrell Duthie in the
Malcolm MacPhail WW1 series

Malcolm MacPhail's Great War

PART ONE

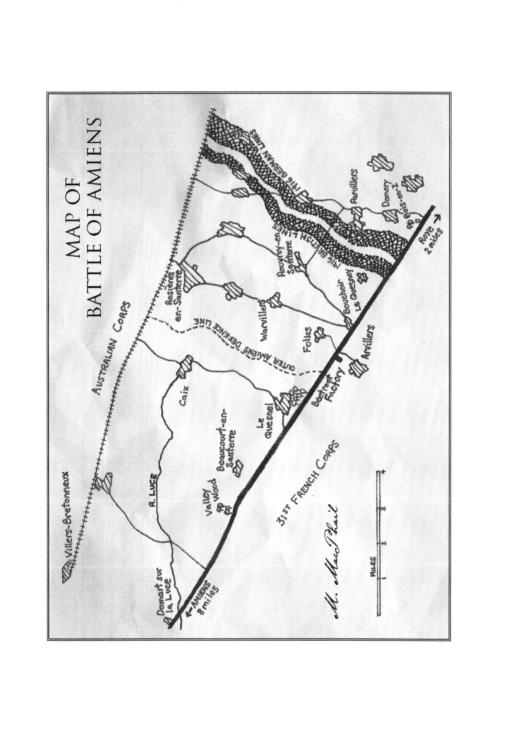

CHAPTER 1

9th of August, 1918
Quarry near Domart-sur-la-Luce, France

It is an axiom of mine that nothing good ever comes from being woken in the middle of the night. Since 1915 I've had few reasons to reconsider that wisdom.

'Sir, wake up,' said the voice. And then more urgently, 'Wake up. Wake up, sir.'

I was groggy. Comatose actually. At least I *had been* prior to this voice buzzing irritatingly in my ear. Its owner was shaking me roughly by the shoulder.

'Smith, what time is it, for Christ's sake?' I mumbled.

'It's almost four-thirty, sir. There are new orders.'

'In the morning?'

'Yes, sir, in the morning.'

I groaned and rolled over to my other side. I'd been running from a broad-shouldered Fritz with huge red eyes and a bayonet that could have skewered an elephant.

'Can't you deal with something by yourself?' I growled.

That was a little unfair. I regretted it the moment the words left my mouth. "Disparage in haste and repent alone," said my mother. In my defence, I'm seldom at my best at four-thirty in the morning, and Smith was what you might call something of a morning person. I've never had much tolerance of morning people, so I suppose I had a chip on my shoulder long before he started to shake it.

It didn't help that my trusted assistant looked in fine form. His uniform was clean and neatly pressed, his sandy hair combed and proper. Smith was always in fine form, even at four-thirty in the morning. That's what made him such an invaluable fellow to have around, that and his unfailing good humour – *and* the fact he spoke German. At this particular moment, I could have shot him. I hadn't slept much recently. Not since the 4th really. On that day, in a beautiful château in Dury, France, itself a dreary village tucked away behind the shell-marked ruins of Amiens, General Lipsett told me we were going on the offensive against the Imperial German Army.

'I'm sorry, sir, the colonel has asked for you.'

'Whatever could be so important?' Wearily, I hoisted my legs onto the ground and began to dress.

'New orders just came in, sir.'

'Yes, I heard, Lieutenant. But what on God's green Earth have new orders got to do with me?'

'We're going into action, sir. They're sending us back in.'

If I hadn't yet been fully awake, I was now. I sat up erect.

'What do you mean they're sending us back in? You must be joking. We were only put into reserve yesterday afternoon! And we're heading back to the front again?' I was incredulous. 'We've been going pell-mell for weeks, we've had no sleep for two days. We were in the thick of it all day yesterday. And they want to send us back in?'

'Yes, sir. We're to attack later this morning.'

I frowned. 'Great. To whom do we owe this stroke of genius?'

'I'm not sure, sir, the orders came from Corps headquarters.' Smith's voice was studiously neutral, much like Holland the entire war. Smith had no Dutch blood in him I was aware of, his parents having emigrated from Germany. In 1918 that was reason enough to keep a low profile.

I, on the other hand, had no German blood in me, and I was never one to shy from speaking my mind, especially when it was running on fumes. 'Bloody idiots,' I croaked.

When I reached Lieutenant-Colonel Hore-Ruthven, the senior staff officer in the division, he was rocking back and forth on his heels, staring at a map and looking like he hadn't slept a wink in the past week. Normally, Hore-Ruthven was a model British officer. This morning, however, the colonel's short greying hair was tousled, his tie was undone, and a length of shirt protruded gawkily out from underneath his olive-green tunic. It was as if I was watching an older version of myself in the mirror, all except the hair: mine was brown. But this was Colonel Hore-Ruthven and such sloppiness was unheard of.

'Good morning, Major MacPhail,' he said with a sigh, when he saw me. 'You've heard the news?'

'Yes, sir,' I replied. 'I'm dumbfounded, Colonel.'

He smiled weakly. 'We all are, Malcolm. I sent a wire to Corps HQ and they confirmed it. We're to go back into action. Someone at Fourth Army Headquarters didn't approve of the 32nd Division replacing us. So we're heading back in and they're pulling out. The plan is to resume the advance sometime after 10 a.m. The orders are being written as we speak. It's all a bit up in the air.'

What was also up in the air was a noticeable Scottish lilt, and that was remarkable; the colonel, Scotsman or not, typically sounded like he'd learned his English from the same tutors as the King. It was another foolproof sign he was close to the end of his tether.

Anxious to hear what my own role was to be, I said, 'You sent for me, sir?' I yawned – a loud lazy eruption that made it sound as if I'd awoken from deep hibernation.

'God damn it, MacPhail. We're all tired. Pull yourself together man. It's only thanks to the general that you're not in front of a court martial today. That's a thought that may keep you awake.'

I bowed my head. 'Yes, sir. Sorry, sir,' I mumbled.

'Fine,' he replied, and threw me a pointed glance before continuing. 'Now then. General Lipsett is meeting later with the commander of the 8th Brigade. He wants you to accompany him. But before you do, I need to know everything about the enemy positions around Folies. We have to prepare. Frankly, we don't have a lot of time. Our orders are to take the village and move beyond it to Bouchoir.'

His finger went to the map and moved down the Amiens-Roye road to the southeast, first to Folies, then a mile further, to Bouchoir. Both were miles inside enemy territory. I tried to concentrate on what

Hore-Ruthven was saying, '… above all, Major, we need to keep the momentum going…'

It didn't really need saying; since yesterday we were smashing down Kaiser Wilhelm's door. Knowing a thing or two about Willy and his army, it wouldn't do to let up for a single, solitary moment – not if we were to make the breakthrough that might end this blasted war.

Back at the modest tent that passed as home and intelligence headquarters for the 3rd Canadian Division, I was fully awake and apprehensive. All this haste, the sudden last-minute changes – none of it bode well on the eve of an attack. Too many attacks had ended in disaster for less. That wasn't the well-informed intelligence officer in me speaking, nor even the cautious lawyer, but rather the weary warrior. After 43 months at the front, you pick up a thing or two.

The tent was pitched in a corner of a lime-stone quarry near the ruins of Domart-sur-la-Luce, together with the rest of the Advanced Divisional Headquarters. Even in the moon's pale glow, the grey walls of the quarry weren't exactly scenic, but it was reasonably safe from Boche guns. My thoughts were elsewhere. The prospect of an impending battle has a rare way of focusing the mind.

A soft, flickering yellow radiated from a gas lantern gently swinging back and forth on the ceiling, casting small shadows that flitted across the canvas before disappearing. Smith was seated at our rickety wooden table under the lantern, on an even more rickety wooden chair. He was hunched over, valiantly punching away at the round metal keys of a little Corona typewriter, in a two-fingered dance you get rather adept at when you've done as much of it as he has. He looked up when I opened the flap. 'Did everything go alright, sir?' He'd obviously not seen my face, or he wouldn't have asked.

I slumped down on the edge of my cot and exhaled: somehow the tent's flimsy walls held. 'Splendid, just splendid,' I replied, clearing my throat. 'We're to attack Folies. We've got four or five hours to prepare and almost no time to reconnoitre. There's near zero coordination with the other divisions, the men are exhausted, and there's not nearly sufficient artillery in range for a decent barrage. To top it off, most of the tanks are destroyed or broken-down. So, Smith, it's splendid all round.' Tiredly, I shook my head. This was shaping up to be an altogether worse morning than usual. 'And to think I was so full of optimism going to bed last night,' I said.

'Folies…,' Smith said thoughtfully, sensibly ignoring most of what I'd said. He pulled a large map over onto the table, '… that's two miles past Le Quesnel. But we haven't even taken Le Quesnel, sir?' He looked puzzled.

I shook my head. 'No, we haven't. According to the colonel, 4th Division sent a battalion in to capture it right around the time you woke me. I expect it'll be a couple of hours before we hear anything.'

While I'd been whining about being turned out of bed, another group of men had more serious worries. They were running across the treacherously flat fields fronting that farming village, hoping not to rouse the ire of the machine guns hidden everywhere, the ones which had stymied us yesterday. It was a thought that put a missed nap into a healthy perspective.

'Once they take it – *if* they take it – we're to pass through the 4th Division units and resume the attack,' I added.

'Hmm,' said Smith, still scrutinizing the map. 'The good news is there aren't many prepared positions. All of the old Somme defences are further back.' He was referring to the trenches, wire and other defences from our early-1916 lines. Smith hadn't been around to remember that battle, although I sure did after two months convalescing in a hospital. Field-Marshal Haig had blown through a quarter million men in six months for a few miserable yards of mud. They called it the "strategy of attrition". Smith may not have remembered the Somme, but he remembered all too well when the field-marshal tried the same trick again last year at Passchendaele, near Ypres. We both made it out, but the overall result was gloomily similar.

'Yes, that's exactly what I told the colonel, Smith. The machine-gun nests are the biggest problem, and the Boche have spent all night reinforcing. With all this screwing around, they've gained another five or six hours, so it's anyone's guess how it looks,' I said, a little gloomily.

'Very true, sir,' agreed Smith. 'We're fortunate the Germans will be equally confused. After all, they were as good as routed yesterday. And their reinforcements will have travelled all night.'

I nodded. Smith had hit the nail on the head; if there was one small mercy, the Germans were in a worse spot than we were.

'It's ridiculous, Smith,' I moaned. 'Is there no one in this army who knows or even cares that the division spent hours marching into reserve last evening, while the 32nd marched forward? And less than twelve hours later we're doing the reverse? It's sheer bloody madness. It's hard enough to win this war, without this sort of incompetence.'

Smith bobbed his head understandingly, concentrating on the papers in front of him. Any scent of controversy was anathema to him. He wasn't going to jump into a beehive just to comfort me. In another age, he would have been in the diplomatic corps instead of the army. However, eighteen years into the twentieth century there was precious little demand for diplomats; most countries with a dispute preferred to fight it out.

An hour or two later, a capped head pushed its way through the tent flap, interrupting our work. I'd been busy. There was a lot of detail on the maps and photographs, and a massive stack of prisoner inter-rogations. It was dawn and bright sunlight silhouetted the soldier as he entered. For a fleeting instant, it gave him the appearance of some rough-hewn angel sent down to inspire us. His message proved less inspiring than his entrance.

'The general is asking for you, sir,' said the soldier. His eyes blinked as they struggled to adjust to the gloom. I quickly donned my cap and fastened my belt, slinging the lanyard of the revolver around my neck, and made to follow him. Then, on an afterthought – call it a premonition – I turned and scooped up the battered tin helmet from the cot.

'Good luck, sir,' said Smith. 'Oh. I forgot to mention, this came for you.' He stood and handed me a letter. Reading my mail would have to wait. I tucked it away. Given the contents, it was as well I did.

Major-General Louis Lipsett was waiting at the top of the quarry, his hand drumming impatiently on his thigh. A tense looking Major Duguid was beside him. Behind them stood an idling staff car. Lipsett gruffly acknowledged my salute and waved me aboard. It was one of those big, boxy, Crossley staff cars that possessed all the streamlined grace of a small house on wheels. Even so it was crowded. There were two other officers propped in beside the driver in the open-air front seat. The major slid in beside me and the general in the back, closing the door as he did so.

'I'm sending in the 8th Brigade,' Lipsett announced. Whenever the general threw the conventions of English nobility or common politeness to the wind such as, "good morning", I knew it was serious. 'And I'm moving headquarters to Valley Wood.'

'From what I recall, sir, there's not much shelter other than trees. I passed through it twice yesterday, not long after it was captured.'

'Then we'll camp under the damned trees,' he snapped. Lipsett might have been only a few ranks under God, he was never one to let a little danger stand in the way. Woe betide the officer who thought otherwise.

Just after nine we reached a row of tall beeches which marked the western boundary of Valley Wood. There, a group of officers had collected, leaning on their canes awaiting our arrival. Valley Wood stood amongst flowering grasslands in a long vista of fields of swaying grain. High above, a thin veil of cloud sealed off the sky colouring it a misty grey, but it was bright, the air already warm, presaging another hot day. Four or five cars were parked haphazardly in the grass next to the trees – a couple of small Fords for the junior staff, a big Crossley for the general, and a smaller one for the brigadier. Small knots of officers and orderlies sat cross-legged on the ground or perched on the leather and wooden trunks doing double duty as furniture. The whole scene resembled not so much a headquarters as a picnic.

'Ah, General Draper,' enthused Lipsett, as he greeted the weathered-looking brigade commander. I shuffled over to listen, remaining a few respectful steps behind, in time to hear him say: 'The 75th Battalion took Le Quesnel at five-thirty. They and the 87th are currently dealing with Quesnel Wood. Our orders have changed, Draper. The division is to continue the advance.'

At the sound of a loud motor approaching I turned. It was a steel-plated box on wheels with a few helmets and the dark grey barrel of a Vickers machine gun protruding out the top: an armoured car from Brutinel's Brigade. Brigadier-General Brutinel had gathered two dozen of them, a score of lorries with Newton 6-inch mortars and sixty-odd motorcyclists. Since their remarkable debut during the spring offensives when they helped hold it all together, they'd earned themselves a fearsome reputation. A tall, thin officer jumped adroitly down; it was Brutinel himself.

When I looked back, Lipsett and Draper, and a major from the brigade, stood in the field of knee-length grass, seemingly unperturbed by the noise and the dust from the car, deep in conversation. Draper was gesturing in the direction of the front. Brutinel was striding energetically towards them. He'd been in the fight all day yesterday, not that you'd guess. I felt worn out just watching him.

'We're off to a late start this morning, Malcolm – even by your standards.' It was Major Duguid. With Duguid you never quite knew what was serious, and what was not, so deadpan was his expression. However, a twinkle in his eye gave him away.

'I'm keeping my fingers crossed,' I replied. 'Yesterday, we rewrote the text book on successful surprise attacks. Unfortunately, today, it appears we're tackling the chapter how *not* to follow them up. 'Mark my words, Archer, it'll be grist for the mill, for you historians.' Duguid had once confided he was a bit of an amateur historian.

Duguid smiled nervously. He knew that only the great victories made the history books – those and the great defeats.

Draper and Brutinel were taking their leave of General Lipsett. It had been a short conclave. I saw the two of them clamber aboard the armoured car and roar down the road in the direction of Le Quesnel.

Before long I heard the unmistakable crunching of boots on the march. A long twin column of soldiers stepped into view from the direction of Amiens, bayoneted Lee-Enfields resting on their shoulders. It was the first of the brigade's battalions, the 5th Canadian Mounted Rifles – more than a thousand men strong. Soon, the 4th CMR would follow in their footsteps. Lipsett made for the coterie of officers in front, motioning me to follow. I overheard their commander explain they had orders to assemble on the far side of the wood. Lipsett politely told him their new orders were to push on. If they weren't already on edge, the sight of the divisional commander here to greet them personally must surely have quickened their blood. The attack was only hours away.

'MacPhail?' enquired the general, over his shoulder.

'Yes, sir.'

'I want you to accompany the 5th CMR. I need someone to keep me informed. And, if need be, coordinate with the French. I'm sending a couple of runners with you.' He turned to face me. 'A lot can go wrong, Major. I'm relying on you to ensure it doesn't.'

The picnic for me had come to an end. To make matters worse, I hadn't eaten.

Last evening, the sky to the east had flared red and orange, resonating to the deep thump of explosions as the Germans frantically blew their ammunition dumps and all the material that risked being overrun. The explosions had long since ceased, as had the enemy's panic. Now he was reinforcing.

With trepidation, I stared down the road in the direction of the German lines. I could hear gunfire. It was either that or my stomach. I put on my helmet.

CHAPTER 2

9th of August, 1918
Arvillers–Folies junction on Amiens to Roye road, France

The bullets whined into the embankment beside me, not two arms lengths away, causing a violent staccato of dust puffs that briefly lingered, swirling above the dry earth.

'Oh, *damn*.' Belatedly, I rolled to the bottom of the roadside ditch.

'Keep your head down, sir,' puffed the winded soldier I landed on.

He rubbed his already grimy chin with an even grimier hand. 'They're in the sugar beet factory, sir.' He motioned towards the collection of large wooden buildings not 500 yards away on the right of the road. A sign *La Râperie* was visible. Based on my modest French, his translation was plausible enough. I didn't doubt him for a second when it came to the location of the enemy guns. They had a straight shot along the road, and our attack here was going nowhere so long as they did.

'Who's in charge?'

'That would be me, Major. Sergeant Kearn,' volunteered one of the half-dozen soldiers who were huddled together, warily eyeing the road. Squat, with more hair in his moustache than on his head, his commanding brown eyes really left no question who was in charge.

'You've got yourself a real problem, there, Sergeant.'

'Don't I know it, sir,' he replied. 'The Boche have got another of their machine-gun nests in those buildings. We just finished taking the one down the road.' I let it pass, but as information goes this was completely superfluous; it was 4 p.m. and I'd been ducking machine gun fire ever since we moved into action an hour ago.

Two of the privates let off a quick volley before sinking back under the lip of the embankment.

The sergeant cocked his head, visibly irritated, and barked, 'Cease fire. We need to get closer. All you're doing is attracting their fire.' He turned back to me, rolled his eyes in bemused exasperation, as if to say "boys will be boys", and said instead, 'It's so bloody flat here, sir. There's not much cover. We've got to find a way around.'

'What about the French, then? It's on their side of the road. If they were to attack from the flank…' I left him to draw the obvious conclusion. The Amiens-Roye road, which we were worming along, marked the southern boundary of the Corps' operations. To our right, the French 31st Corps was supposed to be moving in unison. Only the French were nowhere to be seen.

'They've been held up. They're stuck at the rail line as far as I can tell.'

'That's a lovely spot to be,' I said, wiping the sweat from my brow. It was a hot day. All this running and diving wasn't helping. 'It does explain why I saw Germans moving around Arvillers. Apparently, the Boche still hold the town.' I pointed at it, a few rooftops poking from the horizon to the right of the factory, visible even from here.

'Yes, sir, that's correct. Unfortunately Arvillers is in the French sector. But if they don't get a move on and take it soon, we're going to have a devil of a time getting down this road.'

One of the machine guns in the factory opened up, reminding us there were more immediate concerns than the devil. Across the road a squad of soldiers made a hurried dive for cover. From the direction of Folies, out of sight, but less than a mile to our left, there was the rattle of more gunfire. 'The boys from the 4th CMR must be attacking, eh,' said one of the soldiers, excitedly.

'It's your call, Sergeant, but if I were you, I'd send one of these lads back to fetch a tank or two. There are a couple in the woods at K.15.a,' I said. Helpfully I pointed out the coordinates on his map. That was before I realized how absurd it was; the small copse of trees, this side of Le Quesnel, was a ten minute walk along the very road we'd just come down. Were it not for my abbreviated night's rest, advancing senility might have been a real concern.

'Yes, a tank would be just the ticket, sir,' said the sergeant, nodding thoughtfully. Like most NCOs, he left the philosophizing to others and sprang instead into action. At law school we would have debated the issue. The private whom he assigned the task clearly hadn't been to law school, either. He wasted no time scampering back down the road at record speed, a feat probably inspired by the water-cooled MG08s currently inhabiting the beetroot factory.

It couldn't have been more than ten minutes before the roar of an engine, and a chorus of rattles and clanks, confirmed the success of the private's mission. Shortly, the two noisy beasts grumbled into range, spewing smoke, fumes and an aura of invincibility. *My God they were ungainly machines.*

Ungainly or not, I'd long since turned from a disdainful sceptic into a strong supporter, if not an outright admirer. Partly that had to do with Turner, a cheerful tankman I knew with a stupendous taste in Scotch and an endless faith in these newfangled contraptions. It could also have been that after three-and-a-half years of war, only the pig-headed stuck by their ways. I was trying my best not to get that sticker. But mainly it had to do with my observation that when you were facing off with your pop-gun of a Lee-Enfield against a band of trigger-happy Prussians shooting 550 rounds a minute, having a tank in your corner was a real life saver. These two were Mark V Stars, the most modern tank in the field. The small group of Mounted Rifles looked at each other, smiling broadly. They were in high spirits. I suspected that 500 yards to the southeast the mood was more sombre.

One of the soldiers crossed himself. On the sergeant's signal, they rose together and made a sprint for the rear of the second tank as it passed in a cloud of thick dust and petrol fumes.

'Hold down the fort, sir,' yelled the sergeant, as he left, leaving me with a feeling of being the sole single man at a dance for couples. I knew very well Lipsett hadn't sent me here to take on machine-gun nests. He wanted information. And, if need be, steer things in the right direction. Regardless, I was soldier enough to feel a twinge of shame as I watched them move away at a fast gait in the wake of

14

the landship. I pushed the thought out of my mind. There were more important matters to attend to.

From my breast pocket I retrieved a tattered leather notebook and the stub of a pencil. I scribbled a few lines: a message for headquarters – if I could find one of those accursed runners.

Down the road, the rat-tat-tat of the machine guns erupted in full fury. The bullets bounced off the lead tank in a frenzy of metallic pings, sharp clangs, and the occasional whistle, as a piece of lead ricocheted wildly to one side. It was the sort of cabal a party of six-year olds might make after too much chocolate cake, all hammering away together on an xylophone; were it not that these were Germans, and they were squeezing their triggers for all they were worth.

Then a deep *BOOM* shook the air. One of the tanks' 6-pound guns was answering back. The machine gun fire tailed off. The tank gunner was either incredibly on form, or the Germans were urgently reassessing their position. I guessed the latter.

I took a last glance through my Lemaire field glasses at the two tanks. They plowed into the central building, its timber boarding snapping like matchsticks. A party of soldiers followed closely behind. One of them suddenly grasped at his leg. Three of his companions began shooting into the factory until they too charged out of sight. If the Germans had any sense, they'd have pulled out. I tucked the glasses away, rose from the ditch and hurried toward the same copse of trees that had sheltered the two tanks. There I hoped to find the battalion commander, Major Rhoades, and some means of communicating with headquarters. In the first critical hours of an attack, we were always on edge. And from what I could see we had a serious problem on our right flank.

The last week had passed in a blur. What I didn't suspect when General Lipsett told me were to spearhead a bold surprise attack near Amiens, was that it would take place only days later. If I was surprised, the Germans must have been flabbergasted. Yesterday, we'd blasted a massive hole in their lines eight miles deep. Between the Australians and ourselves, we'd captured and killed thousands. Everyone was still savouring the heady brew of victory. But there was unfinished business – the decisive breakthrough which might just break the stalemate of this war, once and for all.

'Ah, there you are, Major MacPhail. Good news at Folies. The 4ᵗʰ CMR are meeting little resistance and getting ahead fast,' said Major Rhoades, when I caught up with him. He was preparing to leave.

'B Company is attacking the sugar beet factory, along with the tanks. I think you'll soon be able to move down the road on Bouchoir,' I told him.

'Excellent.'

'The only problem is to the right of the road, on the French side. The Boche still have Arvillers. I'm going to head back to the beetroot factory to keep an eye on the situation. I don't suppose you have a phone or wire here?' I asked, 'Or even a runner? I need to warn headquarters.'

'No, but there's a brigade captain around somewhere. He should be able to help. Let me know what happens at Arvillers, would you? Our whole right flank is in the air.'

The major had *that* right; air was the only thing separating him and the right side of his battalion from a German counter-attack.

Two steps out of the wood, and who should I run into, but Jarvis, the brigade intelligence captain, along with a suspiciously familiar face following close behind. 'Captain,' I said, making no attempt to keep the annoyance off my face, 'I might have known you were the one that pinched my missing runners.' Sheepishly, the private looked away, clearly unaccustomed to first being pinched, then being accosted about it.

Jarvis, with the benefit of three pips on his shoulder – it was the new fashion, stripes and pips on the cuff were far too inviting for German snipers – feigned surprise. But my crown beat his pips. 'I didn't realize they were yours until later, sir. By that time we were ducking fire.'

'Don't worry about it,' I said. I handed him the note I'd written. 'It's critical I send this along. Can you do that?'

'Of course, sir. I'll send it to Brigade HQ with my report. There's not much shelling, so I'm hoping the signallers will get a wire up here before long. Then we won't need the runners.'

'Just so you know, Jarvis, Major Rhoades intends to move on Bouchoir. However, our right is wide open. Unless the French show up promptly, I think we should send a few platoons across the boundary to help them out and to guard our flank. If the Germans get wind of it they'll smash us. It's all in my message, but if you have a chance, you might whisper it in the Brigadier's ear. A little repetition never hurts,' I said. What I didn't say, but was thinking, was that in the turmoil of the attack the likelihood my scrawled message would set off a light-bulb at brigade HQ was slim.

He left almost immediately. There are few things that reduce the propensity for needless chit-chat as much as an ongoing battle. I let him keep the runner.

When General Lipsett first asked me to join his staff, way back in December 1916, I must admit to having felt a palpable sense of relief. Lying in a hospital bed, while my health and shoulder recovered, my mood had steadily darkened; I knew a return to the trenches was imminent. The general's offer of a cushy staff job had come as a godsend. Or so I thought for a few glorious weeks, before reality set in. For staff jobs in Lipsett's army were almost as hazardous as manning the front lines. Later, when he assigned me to the intelligence staff, I'd jumped at the chance. But the last ten months had proven even more harrowing. I didn't delude myself that today would be any different.

Entering the cavernous factory hall, the tank-sized gap in one wall was the most obvious sign of recent fighting. Underneath a tri-pod-mounted MG08 was a small mountain of brass cartridges. The tanks had already left, the MGs were silent, and a few pigeons were settled into the rafters far above my head, peaceably cooing – celebrating, I'm sure, their narrow escape as a supplement to Fritz's rations. In the air hung the sharp smell of gunpowder and the stench of death.

The smartest Germans had cleared out when the tanks first appeared. Those that had not, lay sprawled on the concrete floor. I didn't see any of ours.

Absentmindedly, I fished the envelope Smith had given me from my tunic. The chocolate brown, 3-cent postage stamp with the profile of a vital looking King George V was stamped Calgary, July 20th. Nearly three weeks ago. I recognized the handwriting. It was my father's. Usually he wrote a line or two, but never an entire letter.

Dear Son,

I hope this finds you well and coping with all that we read about in the newspapers. Your mother and I are so very proud of you. There's never been a major in the MacPhail family before! We pray that this war will end soon.

I'm afraid I must trouble you with some bad news, on top of all that you're going through. Your mother didn't want to burden you, but I knew that you would want to hear.

She has been hospitalised. She was bringing in the laundry last week and suddenly, out of the blue, she collapsed. I saw it happen from the kitchen window. It was a terrible shock, as you might imagine. Apparently she suffered a heart attack. The doctors tell us her heart is very weak, which was a considerable surprise. You know how energetic she always is. However, she's recuperating rapidly and she says she feels weak, but otherwise fine. She sends her love. Unfortunately, it's impossible for the doctors to predict how things will progress. The worry, of course, is for a recurrence. They can happen rather quickly and without warning. When she returns home she'll need to keep off her feet, so it will keep me very busy! We both wish you were here, but please don't worry, everything is fine now. You have enough concerns where you are...

I read on, but my eyes kept returning to the top of the page. I didn't think of home much anymore. When I did, it was the fantasy place where life was quiet and peaceful and an ocean away from the troubles here.

My mother was always so fit and vital. If anything, I'd always figured my father was the weaker of the two. They'd need some help around the house and dealing with the doctors. Perhaps I could apply for leave. I'd ask around when I got back to headquarters. Once the offensive was over, we ought to be up for leave. The colonel would know.

Sergeant Kearn found me some time later as I sat on my haunches. I was crouched over one of the bodies, examining the German military pass I'd found in a pocket. 'Back so soon, sir?'

I looked up. 'Yes. The attack went well, I see.'

'Thanks to the tanks, sir. Without them it would have been another story. Have a look, sir.' He pointed to a pile of full packs and a sagging pyramid of neatly rolled field-grey greatcoats stacked beside one of the steel beet-receptacles. 'They're all recent arrivals,' he added. 'Must have moved in during the night.'

'Yeah, they're reinforcements alright. One hardly needs a greatcoat around here.' The sergeant grunted. He was so drenched in sweat he looked like he'd swum the Channel.

'Sir! There's a big group of Boche moving out of Arvillers.' The squad corporal was calling.

Quickly, I moved over, and gazed through the hand-sized hole he'd turned into his own personal O-pip. Even without my field glasses they weren't hard to see. There were a lot of them. They were heading southeast, towards their rear lines. 'How many do you count, Corporal?'

'Close to three hundred, I'd say. They must be pulling out.'

'Any sign of the French?'

'Not a wink, sir.'

I frowned. The Germans I knew didn't retreat on a whim.

Within half an hour, an explanation of sorts presented itself.

CHAPTER 3

9th of August, 1918
Beetroot factory near Bouchoir, France

'We've almost taken Bouchoir,' announced the soldier. He was the tallest of three who shuffled into the factory. His arm hung limply in a rough sling and he had an ugly gash on his temple. The other two were equally battered. I looked at my wrist. It was a quarter after five in the afternoon. We were making good progress.

'Sir, they *are* retreating. I can see vehicles. A lot of them. They're being loaded with crates. Yes, sir, they're pulling out for sure.' The corporal's voice trembled with excitement.

That cinched it. I was afraid the Germans would hit us in the flank. But with our men at Bouchoir, the garrison at Arvillers was so nervous of being surrounded themselves, they were the ones doing the fleeing. If only they didn't have a last minute change of heart.

Hastily, I scribbled out a message and tore it from my notebook. We had to move fast.

'Well done at Bouchoir,' I told the threesome. They were sitting awkwardly on the edge of a packing crate catching their breath. I handed one of them the note. 'The dressing station is just down the road. Take this with you. It's a message for Major Rhoades. Make sure he gets it, it's very important.'

Now I'd have to hope Rhoades, or somebody else, would get my message and act. If the French weren't going to secure Arvillers and our flank, we had to. This was a golden opportunity. Only yesterday General Lipsett had gone out on a limb for me, and I wasn't about to disappoint him.

After pacing a while, I sat down on the packing crate vacated by the three Mounted Rifles. Developments were heartening, astounding really. Despite everything, the bungled start, the lack of surprise and coordination, the planning on the fly, we'd made almost four miles today. It was a huge advance by any standard – save that of yesterday's astonishing gains. We were in sight of the British trench lines as they were prior to the Somme battles of 1916. Only the more I considered it, the less cheery I became. Since 1916, we'd spent two years fighting, and we were only back to where we started. At home (I winced at the reminder) we called that running in circles; it was the story of my war.

Today's battle was a long way from won. From the direction of Bouchoir I could hear the unmistakable thud of shells falling. It was then that a crowd of soldiers barged noisily into the hall, rudely interrupting the pigeons as their cooing reached an irritating new crescendo. I was glad for the interruption, especially after hearing why they'd come.

They were a platoon from C Company, led by a Lieutenant Rutherford. Under his direction it transpired they were less of a crowd than I at first supposed. The lieutenant spoke softly, but the platoon formed up in orderly fashion and were listening intently. They'd been ordered to clear Arvillers. *Someone was reading my messages, after all.* Rutherford gave them their final instructions.

'I'm Major MacPhail,' I said, as they prepared to leave. Rutherford was of medium height, with very short-cropped hair, and a clean-shaven, earnest look that seemed at odds with the job he'd been given, not that any of us looked like born warriors, with the possible exception of my good friend Benoît DuBois. I guessed Rutherford was only a couple of years younger than I was. 'I'd like to accompany you, Lieutenant, if you don't mind? I'm rather anxious we sew up the right flank before the Germans decide to waltz on through.'

He looked surprised. And I don't think it was because I mentioned his battalion's 4000 yard exposed underbelly. I'd been where he was, so I could commiserate; staff officers were not renowned for their eagerness to dive into the action. 'As you wish, sir,' he politely replied.

Quickly, I trooped out with them before I changed my mind. I had few illusions my presence would make any difference and the idea of going into combat had all the pent-up excitement of preparing to jump off a cliff. I just didn't relish having to face General Lipsett and tell him the day's attack had failed at the very last minute because of a huge gap in the line which I'd seen, and done nothing about.

From somewhere a tank materialized. We filed into two columns behind it. Almost immediately, we turned right off the main Amiens-Roye road and headed south down a narrow, dirt track towards Arvillers, whose shell-torn habitations we could plainly see.

We had just passed the tiny communal cemetery on our left when there was a harsh crack. We all ducked – the sort of involuntary re-action that's about as useful as swatting a mosquito once it's already sucked you dry. But no one fell, or grasped a limb in pain. 'It came from the village,' I said.

Rutherford must have thought the same, for he nodded. 'You told me they were pulling out, sir?' He was a sight calmer than I would have been, had the roles been reversed.

'They *were* pulling out. I'm sure of it. There must be some stragglers,' I said guiltily.

Rutherford was taking no chances. He banged his palm twice, very hard, on the tank's hatchway, and after a hurried exchange with its commander, turned to his two NCOs.

I fingered the rifle I was holding: a German M98, standard fare for half their army and a good rifle, especially out here in the open. I'd snatched it and a black leather satchel of five-round stripper clips from the factory floor, there being no surplus Lee-Enfields on hand for divisional staff out for a jaunt. My Webley revolver aside, I always felt better with a rifle in my hands, even if the sole choice was a German one. It was a lesson I'd learned in the trenches – along with the impor-tance of keeping your spare socks dry. I worked the action to chamber a round.

We edged forward to a country intersection where another dirt lane crossed ours at a right angle. Rows of simple wood-frame houses lined both sides of the road ahead. They were pressed together side-by-side, their doorsteps ending on the dusty lane that ambled onwards in the direction of what I knew must be the church and the village centre. Several of the houses missed broad swathes of their rooves and all were deserted. The white slatted shutters on the windows to each side of the doors were hermetically closed; their owners evidently banking, against better judgement, on a war-time etiquette long since passé. A larger two-story building, one of its walls emblazoned with DUBONNET in rounded white capitals, held up the remains of a neighbouring house which looked as if a giant wrecking ball had smashed down the middle.

It was there, above the "T", and through a gap in the building's thatched roof, that I saw a flicker of movement.

'Get down,' I shouted. 'A gunner. The warehouse ahead. Attic.'

Rutherford glanced quickly. 'The Lewis gun, set it up there,' he yelled, pointing at the crumbling brick wall a few steps ahead. 'Sergeant Cook, you take left. Richardson, you're right.'

Three-quarters of the platoon melted away, to encircle the village, leaving me with the lieutenant, six others, and a couple of Lewis gunners.

The tinny TUF-TUF-TUF of a machine gun opened up, shattering the calm of this balmy summer evening. Much as the troops at the beetroot factory had done, the enemy gunner was pointlessly directing his fire at the tank. It responded almost instantly. As a female, it was armed with Hotchkiss machine guns. From the turret on its right side, two of them ripped into action, the sound of pistons thrusting back and forth at an impossible speed.

Then I heard the slower, deep cadence of the Lewis gun. The hole in the building's roof widened like an ink blot. After two thousand-odd bullets had turned the T into a gaping hole, the firing petered out. 'You two, check it out,' Rutherford instructed.

From the end of the lane, to our left, came a single shot followed shortly thereafter by the crackle of rifle fire. A two-story red brick building was visible in a stand of trees. Silence followed. Cook's squad had dealt with the erstwhile sniper.

'We were lucky,' said Rutherford. 'I don't think they were completely prepared when they saw us coming. I suspect you're right, sir, it's a rear-guard action.' And to the others, 'Let's go. Quick as you can. Before they have time to prepare any more surprises.' The two-man

Lewis gun squad hurriedly began collecting their pans of ammunition.

We moved down the street in two single files, hugging the houses to each side, while the tank roared boldly down the middle; not that there were many other options for an eleven-foot wide, thirty-ton steel behemoth.

Within minutes the street ahead of us opened up onto a humble dirt square dotted with trees, behind which the ruins of a church were visible, a half-turn off to our right. Almost directly across the square, two hundred yards away, was an elegant one-story building of white stone and red brick with a grey roof, atop which a black, red and white Imperial flag and a regimental pennant hung listlessly – the local *Mairie* prior to its reincarnation as a German headquarters. In front of the city hall were two improvised sandbag emplacements. They were fully manned, as soon became evident.

The Germans started firing the instant the tank rumbled into view. Ahead of me, Rutherford had his field glasses out, squeezed up against the wall of a house, staring down the street and into the square. I knew he was searching for Sergeant Cook's squad. They ought to be entering the square from the left at any minute.

Shards of plaster and wood flew from somewhere above our heads. I grabbed at Rutherford's belt and yanked him down. There probably weren't many sharpshooters at a headquarters, but even a cook might get a lucky round off, now and again. I could hear at least a couple MG08s firing. Each one of those could put hundreds of 7.92mm slugs into a target 2000 yards away. And it only took one.

'Watch yourself, Lieutenant,' I said. 'Don't worry about Sergeant Cook. He'll be there. But even with the tank, it's suicide trying to advance from here. We need to hit them in the flank.'

He looked thoughtful and then it came to him. 'Richardson,' he said.

I nodded. 'Exactly. Go. We'll draw their fire.'

'You lot, keep them busy. I'm going to get Sergeant Richardson,' Rutherford shouted to the others.

Another burst of machine gun fire turned the parched yellow road into a swirling maelstrom of dust and deadly ricochets. Belatedly, I realized what I'd got us into.

The Lewis gunners set up across the road in the shadow of a large house. I signalled for the soldiers behind me to move forward. We did so on our bellies. I took rough aim at the sandbags and the distant figures which seemed little more than specks, really, shot a couple of rounds, and wormed forward. The others were doing the same. The tank was halted a few yards ahead, right at the edge of the square. Its machine guns were spraying a deadly fusillade at the German positions.

Rutherford, bent low, raced up to the back of the tank. Then he sprinted around the corner into the square where he was lost to our sight, heading in the direction of the church.

The Boche were giving it everything they had. And that was a lot. I guessed they had two or three machine guns, and from all the grey assembled, at least fifteen to twenty rifles. A group of them appeared to be manhandling another machine gun into place.

The tank was firing, we were firing, and I could tell from the way the Germans were pivoting left to right that Sergeant Cook's squad was also firing. With both sides hunkered down, the only ones making any real progress were the munitions manufacturers.

I squinted through the rifle's sights, lined up with a dot of grey and squeezed the trigger. Miss. We weren't getting anywhere like this.

'Cover me,' I yelled to the soldiers. When they all began firing, I picked myself up and scrambled across the road in a mad dash to the back of the tank. It had to move forward or we risked getting completely chewed up, cover or not.

Suddenly, as I climbed up the back, banging desperately on the riveted iron plates to get the crew's attention, two blasts went off behind the German sandbags. Rifle grenades!

Peering over the top of the tank, I saw the troop of olive green and my heart leapt. The Germans saw them too, but they were too late. Off the Germans' left flank, Rutherford, Sergeant Richardson and his squad of ten soldiers were letting loose at near point-blank range. They'd circled around and were firing along the façade of the *Mairie,* straight into the line of defenders. The white handkerchief came too late, but for a handful.

'Well done, Lieutenant,' I said to Rutherford, when it was all over, thankful that it was. Incredibly, we'd suffered no casualties beyond a leg wound to a young private and a few scratches here and there. Our right flank was secure.

The *Mairie* held a few surprises. The first was that it turned out to be not just any headquarters, but a divisional headquarters of the 1st Reserve Division no less. That explained the stiff last-minute resistance and the large convoy of vehicles we'd spotted earlier. As we mounted the marble steps leading up to the double oak doors, we were met by three meek looking Germans with their hands in the air. There was little taste for resistance left. With their generals long since safely en-route to their next plundered French château, the remaining denizens of the headquarters staff seemed only too amenable to a hasty surrender. I can't say I blamed them.

Under Rutherford's direction a dozen men fanned out, several returning almost immediately with dishevelled and harried-looking Germans driven at bayonet point. The bayonets hardly seemed necessary.

The second surprise came when we entered the main hall. As we stood there, a private pushed forward an older looking Fritz in a NCO's uniform carrying a large metal box. Approaching Rutherford, he bowed curtly, clicked his heels and ceremoniously handed it over. Judging by the audible grunt, the *Zahlmeister* seemed relieved to be rid of it. I couldn't help thinking the man was a decade or two too old for the army. But when I saw how Rutherford tensed as he took hold of it, made an awkward half-step backwards, and set his legs wide apart, it dawned on me that the box was heavy.

Normally, such a box would be secured by a thick padlock, but the lock was already off and lying on the table beside us. Rutherford eased the box onto the table top. With both hands he carefully opened the lid. At which point he began to chuckle and I soon saw why. Inside were stack upon stack of blue bank notes and a small mountain of silver coins – the division was going to miss its pay this week. It was by far the most money I'd ever seen.

'Well, Lieutenant, it may finally be time to think of your retirement.' Rutherford smiled. 'I wouldn't know what to do with it all, sir.'

The same could be said of our next discovery: an entire roomful of stacked wooden cases, each containing a MG08 machine gun, greased and in mint condition.

'Phew,' I whistled, after pulling the lids off a half-dozen crates. 'I'm glad they didn't get around to unpacking these.'

Neither of us was enthralled by our other trophy, a large pigeon carrier containing hundreds of cooing birds.

While there was no shortage of guns, cash, or pigeons, the same couldn't be said for edible food. I guessed food was one of the first things they'd loaded to move – German generals having an unusually fine nose for strategic priorities.

Rutherford began detailing two-thirds of his platoon to various locations around town. He was understandably determined not to let the Germans sneak up on *him*. Then he and I plunked ourselves down to sample what rations we could find. Neither of us was especially disappointed when a soldier in horizon-blue tromped noisily into the *Mairie*. Fashionably late, the French had arrived.

The local Fritzs were either dead, on their way to the prisoner cage, or had fled hours ago, but the French were taking nothing for granted. There was a whoosh of shells as their barrage came thundering down south of the village, in alarming proximity to where we now stood. Rutherford and I looked at each other. It was time to depart. When one of their officers appeared, we both knew what to do.

'*La ville c'est à vous*,' I pronounced with a flourish, thinking this was exactly the sort of formal handover of the keys to the city the French would appreciate. Secretly, I was pleased at my ability to string five words of French into a coherent sentence. Benoît would be thrilled.

'*C'est plutôt un village, monsieur, mais merci quand même* (It's more of a village, sir, but thanks all the same),' said the *capitaine*, without so much as a trace of humour.

Even he had to smile, however, when we showed him the guns. Even more so when he glimpsed the contents of the cash box. His eyes widened when I opened the lid. I couldn't help noticing how his hands clenched together. Gifting it to the French Army was not one of Rutherford's more inspired actions, I thought grumpily. How big an understatement that was, I would only realize much later.

Rutherford, his platoon, and the tank, tore off to Bouchoir to tackle their second village of the day. I headed back to the beetroot factory.

The August evenings were long and it was still light when I shuffled into the hollow confines of the darkened hall. Major Rhoades and his staff were assembled there, having set up their battalion HQ. I told them the news from Arvillers and handed over my brief report for headquarters. There was a message awaiting me.

I chose a spot on the floor and slumped down with my back to one of the huge metal urns. In the days when ordinary machines were used for ordinary tasks, they were for shredding sugar beets. These days, most such equipment was dismantled, shipped off to the Krupp factories and melted down to make artillery barrels. It surprised me the Germans hadn't got around to it here. Of course, they'd had more pressing concerns on their minds of late. I unfolded the message.

2nd CMR TO RESUME ADVANCE TOMORROW. WILL ATTACK LE QUESNOY-EN-SANTERRE 4.20 A.M. PLEASE OBSERVE AND ADVISE ON PROGRESS. SIGNED, L.COL. H-R., 3DIV.HQ.

CHAPTER 4

10th of August, 1918
Bouchoir, France

It might have been three o'clock in the morning, the Râperie was humming with the sort of activity it hadn't seen since the pre-war years, and maybe not even then. We were pressing the attack, while there was still time – at least I hoped there was.

Three full companies of the 2nd Mounted Rifles had debussed here in the past few hours. General Brutinel had offered them a ride forward in his armoured cars and a screen of motorcycle machine gunners to protect them. Tumbling over themselves to accept, the Rifles didn't bother to consider that the drivers were going non-stop for three days. Arriving intact at their destination was hardly a foregone conclusion. My qualms aside, the battalion arrived unscathed. Before long they were marching off to the outskirts of Bouchoir, from where they would attack Le Quesnoy in little more than an hour.

'Lights,' ordered Rhoades. The handful of lamps scattered here and there were promptly extinguished. Someone had heard something and I moved outside with the others. Enemy bombers had been overhead all night. Listening, I could hear their droning to the north. There'd been nary an enemy aeroplane in the sky on the eighth, but by the tenth the Germans had emptied their aerodromes and sent them to Amiens, making up for lost time. There were a series of thumps, one followed in rapid succession by many others. On the horizon, a series of speckled glows flashed and then faded.

'1ˢᵗ Division is taking a real pasting,' said a young lieutenant, fresh from the reinforcement camps.

'Someone is always taking a pasting in this war, son,' said Major Rhoades, quietly.

I headed off to Bouchoir, to observe the attack.

I reckoned I was halfway there – it ought to have been an easy one-mile walk straight down the Roye road – when I heard movement. Not that movement was unusual; the road had bustled with activity earlier. But it was nearing half-past three, the troops were in place and the road was deserted. The only sounds I'd heard until now were the crunch of my own boots, the creaking of my gear and the soft flutter of a bat overhead as I strode along. This new sound had drifted in from the ink dark fields to my right. Our troops were already at Bouchoir, readying themselves for the attack. They certainly weren't skulking through the fields, heading in the direction of our rear lines. I presumed the French had moved on through Arvillers and were holding our right. But what if they weren't? What if the Germans were slipping through to hit us in the flank, just as we prepared to launch the assault?

Cautiously, I stepped off the road into the thigh high grass. I knelt down on one knee and listened, leaning forward against my rifle.

There was a group, for sure. The grass rustled. I heard something snap as one of them stepped on a stick. There were probably five or six. They were coming in my general direction. I figured they were 50 yards away, which gave me a minute or two at most.

Crawling forward into a dense tuft of grass I lowered myself onto my stomach. Painstakingly, I eased the bolt on the rifle upwards and back, then paused to listen. The crunching came closer. Slowly I eased the bolt forwards and down till there was a soft click as it locked into place. Loaded.

I lay it on the grass within easy reach and pulled out my Webley revolver. Cocking it, I placed it too on the dry stubble. Then I put my hand in my haversack and rummaged around. *Damn it…* I hadn't taken a single Mills bomb, or even a bayonet. Beyond throwing my respirator that left with me with seven rounds, one cocked and ready in the rifle, and six in the Webley. There wouldn't be much time to reload the rifle at close quarters, but thank heavens for the revolver. The Webley was hopeless at long range, but up close it packed a hefty punch. I'd have to make every round count.

Peering down the rifle sights, I was startled as the first shadowy figure stepped into sight, passing only a few yards in front of me. Then, in a crackle of grass, two more appeared behind him, even closer. My finger was tight on the trigger. I swallowed. *Where were the others?* If they popped out on top of me I was done for.

Then one of them said something. It wasn't loud, but it changed everything.

'Hold your fire,' I shouted, my heart still madly pumping. 'I'm Major MacPhail. From HQ. I'm coming out.' Very slowly, and very deliberately, I rose to my feet. Two soldiers in Brodie helmets stood ten feet away, rifles pointed in my direction. The patrol congregated around me. There were six of them, led by a lieutenant.

'Am I glad to see you,' I said.

Nervous rows of white teeth emerged. The lieutenant said, 'Good thing you called out, sir. What are you doing here?'

After I explained, I had some questions of my own. 'What's your story? You're coming from the direction of the enemy lines.'

'We were out looking for the missing Light Horse men, sir. I'm Lieutenant Logie.'

'Light Horse men?'

'Yes, sir. Five of our mounted scouts. They went after a fleeing Boche ammunition column, yesterday afternoon. Captured it too, shot the lead horses, and took 20-odd prisoners. But they got caught by a machine gun and only three made it back. The other two were missing. They sent us to find them.'

'And did you?'

'One. But he was already dead.' Logie looked downcast. I could sympathize; with death all around it was the lone soldier that really hit home. 'The stupid thing was, sir, there was a whole squadron of Imperial cavalry from the Scots Greys resting nearby. They could have easily handled it. But they refused to do anything.'

'Why not?'

'Oh, they mumbled something about it being in the French sector. It's not as if the cavalry has shone in this war, sir,' he said. 'You'd think a target like that, served up on a silver platter, would be too good to resist.'

'Bureaucrats on horses,' I muttered.

'Yes, sir. That's what we thought, too.'

We shook hands and parted ways. He was anxious to get back to battalion headquarters and I needed to get to Bouchoir.

Approaching Bouchoir I heard bursts of gunfire. Surprised, I looked at my watch and saw that it was shortly after 4 a.m. I'd spent the best part of an hour walking a mile and the 2nd CMR had apparently gone in early. I hoped that was a positive sign.

I stuck to the road and as I passed out of the village, spotted a group of soldiers huddled behind a hedge. From ahead sounded a lengthy burst of machine gun fire. It was close enough I could see the flashes pricking through the darkness.

'Shit,' I heard one of the soldiers say. As I joined them, I saw it was a sergeant. He saw that I was a major and nodded politely.

'And?' I said. 'How's it going, Sergeant?'

'We made it undetected almost halfway to Le Quesnoy, sir,' he explained, 'but we ran into a trench system. We wanted to get as close to the village as possible and try for a bayonet charge, but it looks like we'll have to do things the hard way.' If a bayonet charge was the easy way, I wasn't terribly inclined to ask what he had in mind. Sometimes healthy ignorance trumps curiosity.

'So, do you think we'll make it?' I asked.

'The problem is A Company,' he said. He pointed down the road. 'The Heinies have got a host of machine-gun nests. We're taking a helluva battering. They told us we'd have a tank in support, sir?'

A private piped up. 'The captain told me to tell you they're both broken down.'

The sergeant stared at him, with an expression halfway between surprise and annoyance. This was news he was hearing for the first time. I groaned, not meaning to, although they both heard me.

'Don't mind me,' I said. 'Early morning.' With the benefit of hindsight there were a half-dozen more helpful things I might have said. However, as with everything else in this war, there was no point in looking back, only forward. And one thing I was well prepared for was a stock of quips for my next encounter with Turner from the tank corps – assuming he made it. The last couple of days had been tough on tankers.

Then I asked, 'Does anybody back at headquarters realize those two tanks didn't arrive? They're unreliable, but you know better than I, Sergeant, there's nothing like a tank to run through an MG nest.'

'I don't know, sir,' said the sergeant. He glowered at the private with a gaze that could have shot down the Red Baron. 'The captain may know more, but he's with B Company at present.' He pointed northwards. From that direction came sharp bursts of gunfire and the dull pop from a Mills bomb.

'Well it's high time somebody told them,' I said. I looked at the private. 'I want you to go to Brigade and fill them in. Tell them it's urgent. And don't be shy about asking for new ones.'

'Yes, sir.'

'And mention my name. I'm Major MacPhail from the divisional staff.'

'Move it, Bedford,' growled the sergeant. 'It's just down the road, so I'm hoping your legs are more developed than your brain.' The private set off at a sprint.

'Nincompoop,' said the sergeant.

I gazed in the direction of Le Quesnoy. If we could make another four miles along this road, we'd be through the old Somme battlefield and the key junction of Roye would be ours for the taking. Then, with miles of open terrain ahead and no prepared defences, the German line would be shaking at its foundations. But first, there were four miles of tough ground, beginning with this tiny village.

The sun's rays were dancing precociously over the curvature of the earth, waiting to make their leap onto the fields that spread before me. Already, here and there, shrubs of knee-length grass or a tree stood out, visible as dark jagged forms against a dark grey sky growing ever paler. Leaving the sergeant and his platoon, I moved north, skirting the motley assembly of age-old farm buildings that marked Bouchoir's eastern edge. It was approaching 5.10 a.m. Within ten rotations of my

Borgel's second hand it would be sunrise and with dawn the challenges multiplied exponentially. The grassy fields in the direction of Le Quesnoy didn't look much different than the pancake flat prairies at home. Lacking tanks and artillery it was not ideal terrain for an assault. And definitely not against an enemy, forewarned and entrenched.

The attack was indeed well underway. The going was tough. I watched from a shell hole as the 2nd CMR pushed steadily from trench to trench. Within an hour, the first of the battalion's soldiers reached the collection of farmhouses known as Le Quesnoy.

Later, arriving at battalion headquarters in Bouchoir's ruined church, the mood was upbeat. When I asked about tanks, I saw in the captain's flushed face the answer I was hoping for. 'Brigade sent us two replacements, sir,' he said. 'We should be through those machine-gun nests in no time. Once we are, the 1st CMR will move on to the old British trenches.'

And so said, so done. The inevitable German counterattacks were beaten off with a rain of rifle and Lewis gun fire. Around nine-thirty, a runner came with news that the French, with their left flank secure, had seized the major transportation hub of Montdidier to the south. The very same 32nd Imperial Division, with whom we'd played musical chairs a day earlier, was already passing through.

They were to continue the attack on the tiny settlements of Parvillers and Damery, only a mile further, but on the far side of all the old trenches. Pockmarked by shell holes, lined with thick hedges of rusting barbed wire, the ground was going from bad to worse. The big question was, were we too late? Had the enemy taken advantage of all those precious hours we'd wasted?

But we were going into reserve, so it was time to head back.

The division had encamped to the vestiges of a war-torn château near Beaucourt. Fortunately I was able to beg a lift from one of the armoured cars for most of the seven mile trip, emulating the Rifles' fearless example. It was either that or spend half a day walking.

Exiting Colonel Hore-Ruthven's make-shift office – preoccupied, he had hurried me through my report – I smelled something good. There were few things that wouldn't have smelled good after days on half-rations of bully beef and biscuits. A possible exception was horse, for I'd seen their torn and blackened carcasses strewn by the roadside all the way back.

I followed my nose. Unfailingly, it led me to a modest room at the rear of the building. After poking my head tentatively through the open doorway, I smiled; the divisional staff were lunching in a congenial atmosphere that surely owed everything to our most recent orders.

As I entered, a broad-shouldered, bearded giant in a captain's uniform threw me a cursory glance. Ignoring me, he turned back to his companions.

'I told you,' he boomed, in a thick *Québecois* accent. 'A little food on de table and he'd be back. And 'dis is de best meal we've had in a week.' He said it loudly, though not quite as loudly as the accompanying laughter.

'Thanks, Benoît,' I said. 'Hello all. Nice to see the war hasn't kept you from more important matters.'

There were seven of them, including DuBois and his superior Paul Tibbett, as well as Lieutenant Smith.

Tibbett waved me over. 'Come have a seat, Malcolm,' he said, and they squeezed together like so many school boys to make room on the narrow hardwood bench. I'd never been much for church, but it distinctly resembled a church pew. Seeing as how a German unit had bivouacked here only days before, I had a sneaking suspicion it was. Little could surprise me when it came to our foe.

I stared enviously at their crude earthenware plates heaped with some delicious stew. DuBois was watching me, his face unable to contain his amusement.

'Go ahead,' he offered, indicating the casserole on the table; 'We weren't hungry, anyhow.' Normally I'd have a retort at hand, but my stomach had taken the reins and it was preoccupied with more important matters than fending off petty barbs.

'So the Aussies kept pace?' I was saying. Lunch was over, and I was sitting with Smith and Tibbett in what was once an elegant anteroom, which presently resembled an open-air ruin. Smith was filling in the blanks from yesterday, explaining what had happened elsewhere while I was dodging bullets and beetroots on our southern boundary.

'Yes, indeed, sir. They had a lot more casualties than on the 8th but they advanced 3 miles. 2nd Division also had some tough going, near Rosières, but the Corps made an average of four miles along our entire front.'

'All things considered, quite a success,' I concluded. 'You know, I'll admit I was apprehensive after that wake-up call of yours, yesterday.'

Smith smiled. 'You always were somewhat of a worrier, sir.' Tibbett nodded vigorously.

As I pondered this, a 250-pound Benoît stormed into the room. One false step and he'd have taken out a supporting wall which, given the state of the place, could have brought the whole château down with it. 'Mac! 'Aig is here!' he cried. Field-Marshal Haig was endowed with most of life's lucky charms, but a name pronounceable by my French-Canadian friend was not one of them.

I frowned. 'What do you mean, Haig's here?' I said calmly. I was thinking that Benoît was as sleep deprived as I was. 'In spirit he is, I'm sure,' I added. Then I chuckled mean-spiritedly.

'*Non*, he's really here, Mac. Come and have a look outside.' I went with him.

Sure enough. A mere glance at the sleekly groomed chauffeur cooling his heels at the entrance was all the evidence I needed. We went out to take a look. The gleaming Vauxhall staff car proved it beyond a reasonable doubt.

'What the hell is he doing *here*?' I said uneasily, my lunch coming back to haunt me. The Commander-in-Chief of the Empire's soldiers on the continent – the British Expeditionary Force (BEF) – was not one to make unexpected house calls. Not without good reason – and those were the sort of reasons that led me to dive for cover.

'Your guess is as good as mine, Mac.'

'You don't want to hear my guess, Benoît. Every time the field-marshal and I have crossed paths this year has been the harbinger of trouble ahead. This bloody war just keeps getting worse.'

'Harbinger?' DuBois looked at me quizzically.

'A sign, an omen…'

'So why didn't you just say that?'

36

'I'm trying to expand your English vocabulary, Benoît.'

Benoît sighed and then shook his head. 'I don't see what you're so worked up about. They tell us what to do, and we do it. You know how it is, Mac.'

'My mother had a heart attack,' I blurted out. I wasn't planning on telling him, but I had to tell somebody, and somehow it jumped out.

I could see he was shocked. Benoît was never one to hide his emotions. While it might be a tired generalisation to attribute it to the French side of him, I loved him for it. 'A heart attack. Is she all right?' he finally said, his face twisted in concern.

I nodded. 'The last I heard she was fine. I know my father's terrified she'll have another. I wish I was there so I could keep an eye on things, though. Make sure the doctors are on their toes.'

'Perhaps you can ask for leave?'

'Yeah, I thought of that. There's a possibility for compassionate leave, isn't there? Ryerson from the 58th applied for it. What happened with him?'

Solemnly Benoît shook his head. But then he brightened and looked up. 'Ask the general. He's crazy about you.'

Now I shook my head. 'Only two days ago Lipsett saved my ass from years of penal servitude. Besides which, we're in the midst of the most important offensive of the entire war. I doubt he'll want to ship me off home right in the middle of it. I could jump up and down on the field-marshal's toes and he'd probably still want to keep me.'

'You could try.'

'Stomping on the field-marshal's toes?'

Benoît groaned.

I shrugged. 'I suppose so. But pray this war ends soon, Benoît.'

He crossed himself. Despite the kindness of his intentions, it was an act my mother would have shuddered at. She made a point of carefully correcting anybody who made the fatal error of writing *Mc*Phail instead of *Mac*Phail. What greater horror could there be than someone thinking we were Catholic? 'If there's anything I can do?' he said.

'One thing. I hope you still have that bottle of Scotch tucked away,' I replied.

37

Benoît ignored me and I saw him stiffen. 'You mentioned the field-marshal,' he said.

I glanced towards the entrance. Behold: it was the man himself, radiating vim and vigour. Field-Marshal Haig occupied the landing at the top of the stairs like some newly crowned Pontiff from 13th century Avignon. Victory was a reinvigorating tonic it seemed – even for a field-marshal. Benoît would no doubt underline the novelty aspect of it all, recent victories having been few and far between. Of course, the sort of victory that would get me home risked slipping out of our grasp with all the back-slapping and handshaking that was going on.

Haig was putting his cap on, effortlessly giving it that rakish tilt he always achieved, whilst saying his good-byes to General Lipsett. From the smiles all around, and the way Lipsett was preening his hair with a hand in response to the field-marshal's words, I presumed it must have gone well.

A group of officers milled around, gamely trying to look busy, watching circumspectly. Haig shook the general's hand. Then he swaggered down the steps like he owned the place. There wasn't an aide in sight. Awkwardly we came to attention.

'A very good afternoon, gentlemen,' he said in a kindly tone, to which we all politely mumbled a reply and saluted.

Upon seeing me, the field-marshal hesitated and then stopped, his blue eyes lingering for what seemed an eternity. 'I'm glad things worked out for you, Major,' he said.

'Thank you, sir,' I replied. 'I'm very grateful you interceded on my behalf.' And I was. When a member of the General Staff accuses you of insubordination (and a colonel had less than a week before) endings don't tend to be happy. Miraculously, in the wake of our attack, the field-marshal intervened and the charges were dropped.

Politely he nodded. 'You should thank your general. Louis spoke very convincingly of your contribution to this victory. As I told him, it would be a shame to lose the services of a good officer. Best of luck, Major.' He went through the motions of a salute and headed for his car.

'Ah, gentlemen,' said General Lipsett, 'you may as well be the first to hear.' He'd slipped down the stairs to the gravel path as we watched the Vauxhall roll away. Half his staff was gathered, most still star-struck, if not outright shell-shocked, at this impromptu visit. Thanks in no small measure to the field-marshal, most of us had more experience with the latter than the former, not that I would ever dream of saying that – not anymore. 'The Field-Marshal was so kind as to pay us a visit. He especially wanted to congratulate the division on account of the difficult task we had to carry out. He desired me to convey his appreciation to all ranks.'

'That was most gracious of him, sir,' said Tibbett. Benoît was rolling his eyes.

Myself, I was still trying to piece it all together. There was no denying Haig's message was a thoughtful gesture. Exactly the sort of thing great soldiers did – I gulped at the thought – to boost the morale of their troops. However, I couldn't help recalling the last time the field-marshal did something similar, less than a fortnight before Passchendaele, on the eve of losing sixteen thousand men and spending four weeks in Hell. For the life of me, I couldn't figure out what the fly in the ointment was on this occasion. There were few places Haig could send us that were more important than here. Though, with the German defences stiffening, and High Command paralyzed in a torpor of elation, I feared we'd fall into the same old futile slugging match that had defined the war. Perhaps that was the plan.

'MacPhail, I trust you kept that infamous wit of yours in check with the field-marshal?' said Lipsett, skilfully applying a firecracker to my meditation.

'Oh yes, sir,' I replied. 'Thanks to you, sir, I've become the most witless officer in the entire army.'

His eyes widened but he said nothing. Lipsett was a good soldier, and a fine man, and I'd have followed him pretty much anywhere. And anywhere it might be, for general or not, he had to follow orders just like the rest of us.

'Did any of you happen to notice Haig's boots?' I asked the group, once Lipsett left.

They shook their heads.

'They were as dirty as mine. Filthy even. The field-marshal is a lot of things, but filthy is not one of them. He's been touring more than the 3rd Division today,' I said ominously.

The faces looked on in bewilderment – *MacPhail spouting off once again...*

Wearily, I explained. 'We might be out of the action this afternoon, but don't count on it lasting long, that's all I can say.'

The grins vanished.

CHAPTER 5

11th of August, 1918
Beaucourt-en-Santerre, France

'Are you absolutely certain that's what he said?' I asked.

'Yes, sir, they're to hold the line at all costs,' replied Smith. I was staring at a particularly sorry specimen from von der Marwitz's Second Army. Smith's words notwithstanding, the soldier was wrapped in a blanket, and from the sorrowful way he was clutching it to himself, I was fairly certain he wasn't the stoic infantryman von der Marwitz had in mind when he'd issued his order.

Fortunately, I didn't have to worry about him crying out in English; he didn't appear to understand a word. Although he'd learn soon enough where he was heading – a POW camp across the Channel. So I didn't hesitate in talking openly with Smith. Even if the lad did pick something up, it would be of little use to him there.

'That their generals are worried is a good sign,' I said. 'Still, this order is going to make things even more difficult. He's not the first one to tell you that, is he?'

'No, sir. Four new German divisions have been identified moving into our front alone, and virtually all the prisoners are repeating the same thing. Their generals are laying down the law. They're not to surrender. They're not to retreat. They're to hold where they stand.'

'Easy enough for some Prussian aristocrat to say,' I grunted. 'With a family history of three centuries of military conquest and a *von* in front of his name. Especially when he's miles behind the lines in his own private château, holding a looted cognac in one hand and a cigar in the other. It's almost enough to make me feel sorry for these poor sods.'

'I don't, sir. Feel sorry for them, that is. The Corps lost more than two thousand men the day before yesterday and we thought we got off lightly. The ones doing the shooting weren't any different than this "poor sod", as you call him.' He glared at our prisoner. Either I'd vastly underestimated Smith's ability to terrify, or our prisoner's command of English was better than I thought, for the poor sod looked inclined to crawl under the table. Beneath his modest, unassuming exterior, my young lieutenant was showing himself to be a real firebrand. The war was having its effects on all of us – those who were still around.

I let out a deep sigh. 'Yes. But you have to concede, Lieutenant, they're simply doing what they're told.'

'That may be true, sir. However as long as they're staring down a gun sight, with one of us in it, I'm hard pressed to feel much sympathy.'

I let it go. I'd lost too many friends to have my heart in the discussion. And I didn't like the sounds of the enemy's stiffened resolve one bit. Only a day or two earlier, the prisoners were flocking into our arms, dejected and demoralised, their army wavering on the brink of collapse. Today was the eleventh, and only the fourth day of the offensive. How quickly the tides of war could shift.

Within the hour, came word that our headquarters was to move two miles eastwards to Le Quesnel. In a staff car loaded down with boxes I soon learned why.

'We're to relieve the 32nd Division, starting this evening,' said Major Duguid, who was squeezed in beside me and two others. He was invariably well informed so I listened carefully. 'The Brits got completely chewed up and spat out.'

'Chewed up in less than one day?' I said, not able to restrain my astonishment. 'An entire division? How far did they get?'

'Perhaps a thousand yards, on average. A little further near the road. They failed to capture Damery or Parvillers, although they're at it again today.' It was not at all what I hoped to hear. At this rate it was going to take weeks to go four miles, by which time it would be pointless.

Duguid was spared the need to comment further by our arrival at the Château le Quesnel. It was a large, three-story affair in elegant white stone, with a curving driveway and a dark gabled roof. Like everything else in this part of the world, it looked distinctly worse for wear – few buildings were immune to four years of war with Fritz as a long-term tenant. We were swapping places with the 32nd. I couldn't help thinking a bigger bed seemed a poor exchange for what we were getting ourselves into. And that was before I saw the accommodations.

'Show me the maps, Smith,' I said. We'd settled once again into our office in the château, glad to be back above ground. The draughty, humid underground caves which ran underneath the château and the village, where we'd been assigned billets tonight, were not my idea of a cozy place to bed down. Even if they were lit. Somehow this vast complex of tunnels, built in 1886 (according to a plate affixed on the wall), was illuminated by electric light. Instead of revelling in minor miracles, I concentrated on the maps. The rough lay of the land was already familiar to me, but tomorrow's plans might require a miracle of a different sort, based on what Smith and Duguid had just told me.

12th of August, 1918
A dug-out 900 yards northwest of Parvillers, France

General Lipsett had determined that an attack on Parvillers was the most promising approach, and I concurred. Not that he'd sought my seal of approval, or even my advice – a soft poke at my ego, though by this summer of 1918 it had seen too many battles to kick up much of a fuss. While the general may not have needed reassurance, I found it comforting I'd come to the same conclusion as he had; little else about the map was comforting.

Yesterday, Smith and I had spent an hour studying it, bent over like wizened elderly men, tracing with our fingertips the varicose veins of blue and red lines that marked the old British and German trench systems. The German line, in red, was a maze three or even four trenches deep, riddled by saps, communication trenches and concrete bunkers, all of it surrounded by waist-high belts of wire and manned by the newly arrived 121st and 221st Divisions. The Corps' intelligence summaries said the elite Alpine Corps had joined them.

For the most part we held the old British trench line. However, in the north of our sector near the recently captured village of Fouquescourt, and a little below it at the southern tip of Parvillers, we'd forced our way into the German trenches themselves. It wasn't a roll of the dice that had made Lipsett decide to enter the fight here.

The plan was to push down through the Boche's own trenches. They ran from north to south as in much of France. Lipsett, the tactician, was at work. A more devious mind than mine might call it breaking and entering, but we were doing it through the side door. As a result there was a chance we'd manage it in one piece. Once in, we could move south and steadily flush the enemy out of the heart of his defences, the very ones the Borders Regiment officers had described as "impenetrable" yesterday afternoon. Inexplicably, the 32nd Division had knocked at the front door. Little wonder they'd got nowhere.

Step by measured step. That was what had served us well in the past.

'You're not an easy bunch to find,' I said, greeting the lieutenant at 42nd Battalion headquarters. Headquarters was no more than a deep trench in the ground next to the road to Parvillers, sheltered by a handful of rusty corrugated steel sheets lying haphazardly on top.

'We're trying to keep a low profile, what with all the shelling, sir,' he replied. To the north there were plumes of smoke and I heard the concussions. The German 5.9s and heavy 8-inch howitzers were pummelling Rouvroy. It was yet another sign the Boche were regaining their footing. They'd moved in fresh guns to replace all those they'd lost. 'Welcome to the Black Watch, sir,' said the lieutenant.

'Well, I'm feeling rather lucky I made it,' I said. I looked again towards Rouvroy where the bombardment was coming down heavy.

The lieutenant nodded. 'If truth be told, we're lucky to be here as well, sir. Our guides from the Borderers last night didn't seem to know their left from their right, let alone which one of their frigging units we were to relieve.'

I grimaced sympathetically. He was frustrated. He'd probably been up the entire night as a result. 'You're not the only ones complaining,'

I said. For the first time I could remember, every single battalion was bemoaning how the Brits' had cocked up their own relief. If there was one thing units could usually be relied upon to get right, it was their ticket out. 'They were anxious to leave, I expect,' I said.

The lieutenant was in his mid-thirties I estimated. Old for his rank. He had an uncanny alertness to him, accentuated by piercing eyes, softened just a touch by fair eyelashes and the wisp of an equally fair, neatly-trimmed moustache.

'What's the latest?' I asked.

'We're bombing down the trench lines. We went in at three-thirty this afternoon with two companies.' I stole a glance at my watch: an hour ago.

He continued. 'And so far, so good. It's all close quarters fighting and the Germans aren't taking it lying down. But we've got every bomb we could lay our hands on. When they run out it'll be back to the rifle and the bayonet.'

'Any counter-attacks?'

'One. There'll be more, count on that. The Boche are dead-set on holding this. Luckily the Patricias are going to attack a little to the south in an hour or two. They think they've found an opening.'

'That's good,' I said. 'The more places we hit them the better.'

'Hoyles!' In the small space, the shout was redundant. The CO, Major Ewing, was requesting his lieutenant, which reminded me I hadn't even asked him his name. 'Excuse me, sir,' Hoyles said politely.

He disappeared from the dug-out soon after. It was the last I was to see of him. The next day I heard he was killed an hour later, doing a reconnaissance. Later still, I learned that Lieutenant Hoyles had been a barrister – like me. Unlike me, he'd been so eager to get here, he'd taken a demotion from captain to do it. That's one of the few advantages of starting as a private; there's not a lot of room for demotions.

I stayed at battalion headquarters for four hours. Long enough to know that the Black Watch and the PPCLI were getting the job done. As it happened the fighting went on for five hours more. Most of it at close quarters, sometimes as close as the hard steel of a bayonet or a knife. And by the end of it, we were only approaching the village – where the Germans were digging in. The offensive was grinding into ever lower gear. I should have known not to put too much reliance on miracles.

13th of August, 1918
Le Quesnel, France

Overhead, one of our aeroplanes came tumbling steeply out of the western sky, the familiar blue-white-red roundels adorning each wing. Roaring after him were four… five… six enemy planes. His engine screamed and the airframe shuddered as the pilot fought to regain control. I knew nothing about flying, but I could see his speed was too high, his dive too steep. The enemy planes followed in a gentler arc, nipping at his heels, hunters driving their prey before them: four high and lazy, two close and hungry. They buzzed over and flew east, towards Rouvray, the chase continuing. But then our man disappeared as the horizon and the plane merged into one. The Germans began to climb. Soon they vanished into a bank of clouds. I hoped it wasn't an omen. I walked down the driveway and into the château.

'Listen to this,' I said, wiping my brow for the fourth time in ten minutes. 'The first stage of this Battle of Amiens is over, and one of the most successful operations conducted by the Allied Armies since the war began is now a matter of history.'

But Smith appeared as uninterested in the Corp Commander's special order as the Germans were, so I spared him the unabridged version. Actually, the Boche in our sector didn't seem familiar with either the abridged or the unabridged version, and certainly not with the part that said the battle was over. They were still going all-out, in a desperate attempt to rewrite the history.

As to Smith, he was preoccupied. He was trying to break our prisoner – naturally, in the nicest possible way. Which, when I thought about it, was exactly how Smith was, no matter what he pretended otherwise.

'*Ich bin Französisch*,' pleaded the dark-haired soldier in field-grey. '*Ich kom aus Elsass.*'

Before Smith could reply, I raised my hand as if to say stop. It was the only way to get a word in edgewise. 'Maybe he's telling the truth, Lieutenant, and he *is* French. The 42nd were insistent he went out of his way to help them. He showed them which way to go in the trenches to reach their objective. He even repaired and put into action one of the enemy machine guns. There aren't many Boche who would do that. On top of which, if he is from Alsace, he's almost certainly French.'

'Yes, French,' said the prisoner, nodding vigorously. His English vocabulary expended in one short burst, he continued in French; '*Oui, monsieur, je suis Français. Tout à fait Français.*' Sheets of sweat were pouring down his face. Today was stiflingly hot, so it wasn't entirely nervousness.

Smith looked at me dubiously and then shifted his gaze back to the prisoner. 'But what if he's really German, sir?'

'If it helps, Smith, it's always a risky decision giving somebody the benefit of the doubt. Invariably a time arrives when you're wrong. Naturally, when you're as wise and experienced as I am, that doesn't happen often,' I said. I wasn't able to keep a straight face long enough to finish and Smith wearily shook his head as if he'd heard that line before. 'If it works out, it feels good, though,' I concluded. Generally, I tried to avoid this kind of sermon, but I could see Smith was searching for an excuse. I saw no reason not to give him one, but he'd have to make the decision.

Smith was thinking it through and the prisoner was watching. I left them to it.

The Battle of Amiens might be over, but the one for Parvillers was raging.

14th of August, 1918
Maison Bleue (800 yards north of Parvillers), France

'They need to press harder,' said General Lipsett.

We were sheltering behind a couple of the tall plane trees that lined this road, as they did half the other roads in France, just outside the tiny hamlet of Maison Bleue. Lipsett was not the kind to loiter around at headquarters – regardless how charming or safe it might be – when the action was elsewhere. Today he'd asked me along. We still hadn't taken the village. If he was impatient about it, he didn't show it, certainly not in a way I could see. I suppose he knew it had been a tough slog.

Down the road was Blucher Wood, which we'd cleared yesterday. From there the road curved round to the southwest and on to Parvillers, 500 yards further. From our vantage point we could see the first row of houses, with an orchard peeking out behind, due south across the fields.

'The Boche don't appear to hold the village in much strength, sir. Perhaps they're pulling back,' I said cautiously, lowering my field glasses.

The taut line of the general's mouth relaxed. He lowered his glasses as well. 'Which is why we need to crack the whip, MacPhail.' The general was not exactly the whip-cracking sort, so it was with a certain degree of curiosity that I followed him to the battalion headquarters of the 49th.

The handful of battalion officers, including the commander, took the surprise arrival of General Lipsett in stride. They were used to adapting; they'd put the regimental band to work as stretcher bearers only yesterday.

The general and the colonel secluded themselves in a corner.

Colonel Weaver had only just returned from a reconnaissance. Whether it was that, or simply a strongly worded suggestion from the general, Weaver quickly decided to push out some patrols towards the village. The general holstered his whip. Not long after, the two of us set out for our next destination: 7th Brigade headquarters.

Hearing the guns open up, the general cocked his head. 'What's that?' he asked, his step slowing a beat.

'Our heavies and the 60-pounders, sir. While you were speaking with the colonel, Captain Hale reported that the Germans were massing in Schwetz Wood. So the battalion requested artillery support. They're quick off the mark, I must say.'

'They should be. I didn't arrange a brigade of field guns and extra batteries of those 6-inch naval guns for show alone, Major.'

Two hours later, to my surprise, I was back with the lads from Edmonton at the 49th Battalion headquarters, *sans* general and *sans* whip. In their stead I'd brought Major Meredith, the brigade major from 7th Brigade, and Major Duguid. This trio of majors, arriving together, did manage to upset the normally unflappable battalion staff. It might have been Duguid's opening line that set off the sirens.

'Why the hell are you pulling back?' Duguid demanded of the first officer he saw. His dark eyebrows were bristling. Duguid was here on behalf of the GSO1, Lieutenant-Colonel Hore-Ruthven. I couldn't have worded it better myself. I watched as the captain's confident lines melted away.

Colonel Weaver had noticed our entrance too. We'd blown in with all the subtle unobtrusiveness of a platoon of *sturmtruppen*. 'The Princess Patricias reported they met your boys in Parvillers, sir, and the village was as good as ours. But your D Company is pulling back,' I said testily. I was here on behalf of the major-general.

'AND, as a result, the Boche think we're retreating, so they're counter-attacking. The Patricias have landed in a wasp's nest, sir,' added Meredith, on behalf of the brigadier-general.

'Christ almighty,' cursed Weaver, on behalf of himself.

His gentle round eyes were drawn, and the friendly, neighbourhood grocer's face had taken on the look of someone kicked in the ribs. 'We *didn't* order them back. Of that you can be certain. Leave it to me, gentlemen.' And he turned and began consulting with his staff. Three minutes passed and a runner sprinted away. 'I've ordered our patrols forward,' he said, 'to re-establish contact with the PPCLI.'

He left to the forward area a few minutes later to monitor the situation himself. A couple of generals were momentarily none too pleased with Lieutenant-Colonel Weaver. We stayed long enough to hear that the patrols at first went well, but the Germans beat them off when they attempted to get back into the village. Worse, the Patricias were in retreat.

The verdict back at Brigade HQ was unequivocal. 'What a fuck-up,' I overheard one of the officers say. 'The Patricias report they lost four officers and 35 other ranks.' What the officer didn't say, but I knew, was that the Germans would be digging in again. *God damn it.*

The heat was wearing on all of us and the men were exhausted. Capturing Parvillers – again – would have to wait for tomorrow. The momentum was leaking out of this offensive as surely and as quickly as the air from a bicycle tire with a nail stuck in it.

CHAPTER 6

15th of August, 1918
Schmitt Trench, Damery, France

I wasn't where I imagined I would be. I was a mile to the south of it to be precise. Not at Parvillers where Benoît's old battalion, the Royal Canadian Regiment, was storming the village, but at its neighbour, Damery. Colonel Hore-Ruthven had sent me here well before dawn, presumably at Lipsett's instigation. I should have been pleased – out of harm's way and all that.

Events, however, were taking an unexpected turn at Damery.

Lieutenant-Colonel Foster had just returned from his early-morning reconnaissance with a scout captain, by the name of Strong, and two snipers. The colonel had had a bad night from all the Boche shelling and machine gun fire. And now he was planning on doing something about it.

'We located the machine guns in front of the village,' announced Foster to the few officers present. Resting his map precariously on the side of Schmitt Trench, he began pointing them out with dramatic jabs of his index finger. 'Here's what we're going to do, gentlemen. We'll split C Company in two. I'll take all the rifle grenadiers, some bombers and two Lewis guns and we'll move due east. Young, you take the rest of the company and loop around to the north. I want you to enter the village from the orchard so we can hit them in the flank.'

Captain Young nodded. Young had stumbled in from a dressing station only five minutes earlier – a visit occasioned by the Boche saturating his company in a shower of gas and high explosive last night.

Breathless, a soldier scrambled into the trench and headed for Colonel Foster. 'Lieutenant Churchill is dead, sir. A machine gun got him,' he blurted out. The other officers sighed and shook their heads. It was hard to tell whether they were upset or simply weary. Likely both.

Colonel Foster stared in my direction, obviously sizing me up. I had recognized him straight away, but failed to see any spark that the recognition was mutual. We'd been at Passchendaele in a dreary bunker named Waterloo Farm, the success of the first day's attack was hanging from a string and Foster was being ordered into action, so it wasn't altogether surprising he didn't remember me.

In any event, I had no trouble believing he'd had a bad night. The colonel's eyes were glazed over and the bags underneath rivalled most observation balloons. However, I spied a trace of sunshine lurking underneath the glumness, so he must have liked what he saw. At six foot two, 200 pounds, and having spent most of my war near the front, I figured I looked more like an infantryman than a staff officer.

'I realize it's not exactly your role, Major, but would you mind terribly coming with us? I don't have many officers left. In fact, I've had sixteen casualties in the past few days and I could really use an extra man.' Now I understood; it wasn't my burly posture, leadership qualities, or fighting experience that had attracted the colonel – he was looking for a pulse.

'Of course, Colonel,' I replied. I tried to keep the edge out of my voice. All that nonsense about going into battle being like riding a bicycle... well... it wasn't like that in my experience; few ever died peddling their bicycle.

The 52nd Battalion were recruited from the bush country of western Ontario, all big tough men who clawed out a living in the vast outdoors: miners, prospectors, lumberjacks. Colonel Foster was from British Columbia, but otherwise he fit in well; he climbed mountains in his spare time. It didn't seem particularly opportune to mention that I wrote legal articles in mine. My Labrador might have felt as I did, thrown in amongst a pack of wolves. Fortunately I hadn't shaved. With a reassuring click, I fixed the bayonet on my rifle.

Almost immediately we moved out. Foster sent the grenadiers to the left, and the rest of us headed in attack formation straight towards the main trench fronting the village.

Disconcertingly quickly we were spotted. A Maxim to our left opened up with its telltale TUF-TUF-TUF, followed by others. 'Keep your heads down and return fire,' shouted Foster, which we did. Foster didn't seem nonplussed in the slightest by this turn of events. Only then did I catch on that our role was to draw the enemy's fire. *Great.*

I took a hurried pot shot with the Lee Enfield and ducked down. No point in being reckless when you're bait.

But then Foster, throwing caution to the wind, raced 50 yards ahead to the ruins of a small building, accompanied by a corporal. At first, I was puzzled by this until it dawned on me that he had an unencumbered view of the German positions all down the left side. Perhaps I'd jumped to conclusions. At a fresh burst of fire I planted my head in the earth.

THUD. THUD. THUD. From our left came the sound of rifle grenades going off.

The party of grenadiers were coming to our aid. The machine gun fire abated. Spirals of smoke and the scent of gunpowder now sullied the morning air.

The colonel's corporal reappeared with a message. 'Send word to Major McCagney to stand to with his company,' he said to a runner. 'When the situation permits, he should follow Captain Young through the orchard.' Reinforcements sounded promising, I thought.

A split-second later I heard, 'Oh, shit.' It was the soldier next to me. 'They're counter-attacking, sir.' I spun around to follow his view.

Sure enough, a German bombing party was running down the trench in our direction, their grey helmets bobbing up and down in sequence like a party of ants on the trail of fresh bread. But the Germans weren't after bread, they wanted to root out our grenadiers, holed up in a sap, halfway between our position and theirs.

The fire from the remaining machine guns tailed off. The Germans had been firing from all along the length of their trench towards us. But to avoid hitting their own men rushing past, they'd taken their fingers from the triggers. It gave us an opportunity.

Lieutenant-Colonel Foster had returned and he saw it too.

'Gentlemen, let's take the fight to them,' he said, and swiftly explained to the squad what he wanted.

In file, we raced off down the German trench northwards, to intercept Fritz's gang. The bombers were in the lead. At each zig-zag and every dug-out, they tossed a couple of grenades to clear the way, barely pausing to wait for the explosions. It was all about speed and shock. The rest of us followed, shooting into the dug-out entrances and mopping up the stragglers they'd missed.

My heart was pumping. Combat was always like this. The heightened senses, the blood coursing uncontrollably, the prospect of action dulling the mind.

'Heinie!' If it hadn't have been for the shout I would have missed him. It was a figure in field-grey, a mere twitch of movement on the periphery of my vision. He was emerging from a dug-out only a few feet away, his rifle and bayonet extended. He was gathering speed and I was square in his sights. 'Don't think. Act. Get him before he gets you,' my old instructor had drilled into us. It may sound like common sense, but there wasn't a battle since when I didn't hear his words ringing in my ears.

I turned and lunged in one fluid motion. My left foot was extended and I bent into it, thrusting my rifle forward with everything I had. I did it exactly as Sergeant Mills had instructed, during those endless drills with jute bags full of straw hanging lifelessly from a rope. Dismayed, I felt my thrust shudder to a halt. Which was when I looked down. My bayonet had slid clean into his chest, all the way to the hilt where it now rested. The tip of his bayonet was buried in the fabric of my breast pocket. There was a simple explanation: he was short, and I was not.

He gurgled, a trickle of blood running from his mouth. Then he went quiet and slumped. The full weight of him hung inertly from my rifle, his arms drooped awkwardly, like those of a cloth doll, limp at his side. I saw only red and felt rage. Relief would come later. I pulled at the rifle, but the bayonet was stuck. Something to do with his weight and the angle. Soldiers were rushing past me. There were shouts ahead. And more bombs. I let my rifle sag. His body collapsed to the trench floor, my rifle still protruding from him like a Roman spear. I stepped

53

on his chest with a boot near the entry wound, grunted and wrenched it away. The rifle came free and I ran after the others.

'Well done, Major,' said Colonel Foster, when it was over. My hands were trembling. I nodded.

Victories were like that: everybody turns out to be a hero. The colonel, however, was not done for the day.

'We've taken the line. Seven machine guns in all. Now on to the village,' he said. He was not one of those officers who counted his blessings and went to ground. I can't say I blamed him. The attack was going well and there was no substitute for striking when the iron was hot. It was a proverb not everyone in the British Army embraced. I couldn't help thinking this whole Amiens show had been a huge success, but also a huge missed opportunity. With a few more Fosters at the helm we might have broken through completely. Hell, with a few more Fosters, we wouldn't have been going into year five of this damn war.

Around eleven, we stood together, smashed and desolate buildings lining the four sides of the dusty field that I took to be the village square. Captain Young was reporting. 'We made it through the orchard, sir,' he told the colonel. 'There were a few machine guns to deal with, but when we hit them in flank, they ran like rabbits.'

'A splendid effort, Captain. And if I'm not mistaken that's B Company coming up behind you,' said Foster, having all but shed his early morning dourness. 'I want you to take a few men and mop up around town.' He was fingering the ragged hole in his sleeve, with apparent fascination. Apparently he'd had a close shave with a bayonet too, an hour ago. Foster's pistol had dealt with the matter.

'I hate to ruin the party, Colonel. There's something about this that doesn't feel right,' I said.

It was the kind of comment that typically brought down a barrage of sarcasm from those who knew me. But Foster didn't, and he responded with seriousness. 'What do you mean, Major? MacPhail, wasn't it?'

'That's right, sir. Well, all the prisoners we've interrogated since Sunday… that's what? Four days?' I said. In my head I counted them off again to make certain, 'Yes, four days. For the last four days all the prisoners have told us – to a man – they're to hold the line. They're to hold it at *all costs*. I'll grant you, getting through the trenches wasn't easy, but they cleared out of the village awfully fast. In my experience, your average German soldier is about as tenacious as a tick, so when his superior officer instructs him to hang on at all costs, he certainly isn't going to make tracks when he sees a spot of olive green. More likely he'll double down. And there's one other consideration; the Boche artillery is back in strength and on form. After last night I guess needn't tell you about that, Colonel.'

Foster looked uncomfortable. 'What exactly are you saying, Major?'

'What I'm saying, Colonel, is that I think this is a ruse… a trap. I believe the Germans are pulling back so we move into the village. Then, at a time of their choosing, probably when they think we've moved everyone in, they'll pound us with their pre-targeted guns and launch the counter-attack.'

Foster was thoughtful. I was conscious of soldiers moving around while I watched him, my flanks in the air. Then he smiled. It was not a response one of my wild-eyed theories had ever elicited in the past. 'Well, why didn't you simply say so, Major? I think we'll simply let them have it…'

A noise that some – by whom I mean the clods at divisional headquarters – might uncharitably call sputtering, bubbled up in me. 'No, sir, I didn't mean it like that…'

Foster winked. 'Oh, don't worry, Major. I'm not about to hand back what we just spent the whole morning fighting to take. No. I think we'll push on a little further, get out of the village, and *then* dig in. Perhaps we have the beginnings of a ruse of our own.'

I grinned. A man after my own heart.

It took less than an hour for Captain Young to report back that the village was cleared and almost immediately he and C Company were sent packing. They were assigned a line directly east of town, ending at the cemetery – a landmark most infantrymen liked to avoid.

I walked with Foster along a small path to the northeastern edge of Damery, where he found the shambles of a barn to set up his headquarters. The barn wasn't much, but the view made up for it. The buildings of Fresnoy were directly opposite us, those of Goyencourt only 2000 yards and a half-turn to our right. The land to the east was flat, slowly descending into a hollow of sorts, before rising again to the two villages. If there were any attackers, we'd see them from a long way off. Of course, the reverse held true as well. But it was pointless dreaming up new problems; the really tough ones have a way of popping up all by themselves, and our day wasn't over by any measure.

The colonel's plan had merit, I thought, as we made our preparations. He spread his three companies out in a line of outposts from north to south, to cover the easterly approaches. It was across those empty fields that the Germans would come, and we were waiting. Damery was deserted.

The wait proved to be short. We had scarcely settled in before the Germans revealed their hand. As so often was the case, it was preceded by a pounding from their artillery.

The first dull thud sounded around one o'clock, closely followed by a fleeting whistle overhead and almost instantly a sharp crump, as the round buried itself somewhere in Damery; a shower of shrapnel or high explosive that would have killed anyone within twenty feet. A field gun, likely dug in near Fresnoy or Goyencourt, I guessed. From there, they'd have a clear line of sight. The whizz-bangs fired high velocity shells every infantryman learned to fear. *Whizz. Bang.* They were so fast there was virtually no warning; by the time you heard anything, your fate was in Lady Luck's hands.

More field guns opened up, and then came the deeper boom of the howitzers, the dark, smoky plumes of their shells rippling overhead. Finally, the heavy machine guns began chattering, arching a deadly spray of lead across. Fritz was putting his best into it. But of course we were long gone.

Foster nodded appreciatively. 'It appears as if you were right, MacPhail.'

I nodded. Perhaps I hadn't been just a pulse.

The barrage went on for ten minutes, maybe longer. Suddenly the colonel asked, 'Major. Can I borrow your field glasses?' He must have seen something.

Without a word I handed them over.

He grabbed at them impatiently and stared in the direction of the two villages, slowly rotating from left to right. 'There they are,' he murmured. 'Have a look for yourself.'

Everywhere small groups of soldiers had appeared, many with machine guns. They were moving towards us. Some were running, as if speed alone would win the day, while others poked cautiously from bulge to depression, neither providing any cover worthy of the name. They'd been counting on the barrage to do its work.

'Fire when ready,' said Foster. 'Pass it on.'

The Germans returned fire, but they were too exposed. Our piquet line of outposts was weakly manned, but we had command of the ground. Within minutes, the fields lay littered with corpses. Still they came, their numbers thinning as they approached until even the most reckless of them recognized the sheer futility of it. They fled and sought shelter as best they could.

The gunfire petered out and the wisps of cordite and smoke began to dissipate in the breeze. The midday sun beat down relentlessly. It might have been just another lazy August afternoon in the French countryside were it not that since 1914, carefree August afternoons had been consigned to history.

I looked over at the colonel, who had my glasses again, scanning a wide arc in front of his HQ. He was frowning. 'They'll be back,' he intoned, a note of resignation in his voice.

I grimaced. 'Yes, sir. That's what I'm afraid of as well.'

It took them less than two hours. The clang of a single bell from a church tower far behind the German lines rang in the half-hour; it was thirty minutes past three. A new German bombardment began exploding in all its fury.

'Gas! Gas!'

We fumbled to don our box respirators. With their goggled rubber mask, and a corrugated tube leading to a filter box in a haversack strapped to the chest, they were anything but graceful. The oblong-shaped filter boxes bore an uncanny resemblance to DuBois' hipflask, albeit on a smaller scale – DuBois being a thirsty man. As much as I hated wearing one, the masks worked a charm. Assuming you got it on in time, there was no reason for concern. But I'd always loathed the gas so I was nervous.

The Germans were firing green cross shells; gas mixed with high explosive in a single round in the hope the latter would mask the former. It was a tactic that worked all too often – last night again, for instance, as Young and his company could attest. Obscured by darkness, the explosive charge provided a diversion and the gas crept up unseen until it was too late. Last night's shelling was a big reason why Foster had felt the need to draft me in. Today, however, there was a decent westerly so the gas was blowing up above our heads, out of Damery and back towards the Boche. Poetic justice in my view.

'I've never seen such heavy machine gun fire,' whispered the colonel. Agreeably I nodded. Truthfully, I was more anxious about the alarming number of shells coming down on the eastern side of Damery, and frighteningly close by. Our platoons to the north would be taking a beating. Evidently, Fritz still clung to the belief that we were occupying the village, which was extremely fortunate. Had his sights been set a hundred yards to the east, there's no telling what would have happened.

I'd seen a lot of bombardments recently, but this was the first time I'd been on the receiving end and I was not revelling in the experience. Normally, fifteen minutes passes in the wink of an eye, but in a bombardment every minute can seem interminable. But finally it ended. When it did, we shifted to a better vantage point behind the barn's concrete foundations and looked east.

I felt a hard knot tighten in my stomach as I stared through the glasses.

A staggering host of soldiers was assembling. From Goyencourt and Fresnoy, and regions beyond, their ranks were swelling. Long twisting lines, four rows deep, were snaked across the horizon from north to south. Already they were moving towards us in full marching dress, complete with packs and rolled blankets on top, as if they had miles to go. The Boche were counting on a breakthrough.

'Uh oh,' I muttered. 'There must be three battalions out there.' I wiped my brow.

'More,' Foster said firmly. He'd found his own field glasses and was studying the scene. 'I estimate two thousand men... no... maybe closer to twenty-five hundred.'

'And we have, what? Four or five hundred?' I asked, trying not to sound discouraged. I hadn't expected an answer and I didn't get one.

There was a shout from the pair of soldiers beside us: 'Here they come.' Under the circumstances the warning was understandable. It was also completely pointless – an ostrich with his head in the sand wouldn't have missed the tidal wave of field-grey bearing down upon us.

Foster stood serenely, gazing forward, his hands clasped behind his back. A minute or two passed, and I was on the verge of asking him if he was all right when I realized the reason for his calm.

The answer came in a thunder of noise. The grasslands erupted into a bubbling cauldron of explosions. Smoke filled the warm air, and everywhere tufts of earth were churned up and flew skywards, like so many splashes in a downpour.

Foster had alerted the artillery. And the artillery were letting the Hun have it.

I turned and he saw the shock on my face. A wry grin lit up his. 'After the last attack, I sent a message to Brigade, to forewarn them. I expect the French are helping out too.'

I whistled. 'Well done, sir.'

He bowed his head, ever so slightly and turned back to the devastated farmlands of Picardy.

The massed ranks, so regimented and intimidating, were shattered. Corpses carpeted the fields with such abundance the fields themselves had taken on a greyish hue. It was a chilling sight. Near the road linking Fresnoy to Goyencourt, the falling shells were drawing an impenetrable curtain to the Germans' rear. The only way out was to advance. But to advance was to brave the fusillade of rifle and Lewis gun fire of the battalion. Hundreds of them pushed on desperately towards Damery.

I'd given up observing. Instead I was working the bolt of the Lee-Enfield. The fear of being engulfed by the horde at our doorstep added extra urgency to my actions. The Boche vanguard was almost upon our foremost outposts. While I was several hundred yards back, that was a shot I could make. As I popped out the clip and reached for another, I saw Foster and a platoon of men in tow. 'Sir?'

'Their officer was shell-shocked and they were pulling back, so I went to retrieve them,' the colonel explained. And then another head appeared. It was the scout captain, Strong, from this morning.

Foster tugged at his helmet and greeted him warmly. 'Formidable timing, Captain. 'I need you to get over to D Company. See that they move up to support C and shore up our right. I'm going to take this platoon and any remnants here at headquarters to help Major McCagney on the left.' Presumably "remnants at headquarters" referred to me and the three privates beside me: not the leftover crumbs from lunch. Even so, Foster was truly scraping the bottom of the barrel.

McCagney's men were pushed out in a line well away from town and the thirty-five rifles we brought were received with open arms, speaking figuratively; B Company had their hands full. Row upon row of Germans were advancing fast, less than 200 yards away.

'You three, come with me,' I instructed the three privates from headquarters. We sprinted to a ditch where four others lay on their bellies, shooting for all they were worth. It was a stroke of luck this morning's salvage party had found an old British small arms dump.

200 yards. 150. 100. Relentlessly, the Germans advanced, even as they dropped. The ones that made it stepped over their comrades who lay in macabre mounds of bodies, stacked two or even three high in places. We were going to be overrun...

'Oh, damn,' I cursed, as my finger slipped off the metal guard onto the trigger. The round bore into the dirt. Hurriedly, I wiped the sweat from my palm onto my chest. A couple of feet away, the head of a man beside me listed, his helmet tipped off and his forehead came to rest on the lip of the ditch. I aimed and fired. There were casings and dust flying everywhere, heavy explosions sounded further off, gunfire rattled. The air was heavy with acrid-smelling smoke. I focused on breathing.

My next shot didn't miss. Nor did the one after that. This had little to do with marksmanship. More about keeping a cool head – thus the breathing – and shooting until the ten-round magazine was empty, which was very quickly.

The two I blasted with my Webley revolver fell headfirst into the trench next to me. The bodies were piling up. Their foot-long bayonets, which had looked so menacing when they were pointed at me, tumbled harmlessly to the ground. Crazed, I raised the revolver to shoot again, but there was nothing. I jerked my head from left to right. Still nothing.

'We did it, sir,' said one of the soldiers. 'We beat them off.'

'That was close,' I gasped. 'You fellows okay?'

'Yes, sir,' they replied. They were hunched down, catching their breath like me.

'Sir, they're pulling back.'

The advance parties of Germans were confused. They were taking fire from ahead and from both sides. I watched as a group of twenty or so tentatively raised their hands in the air.

'It's our Lewis gunners, they wheeled around to the left and the right,' I said excitedly. 'They're shooting at them from the flanks.'

The sight of their comrades surrendering was contagious. Other groups raised their arms. Further back, bewildered and confused, the groups that remained were scattering and scrounging for what little cover there was in the grassy undulations.

When the kilts came flying into view, they were a sight for sore eyes. A wild cheer went up from our lines. It was the 43rd Battalion, the Cameron Highlanders. Shouting, their bayonets extended, the Camerons charged at the remains of the German onslaught, scattering the attackers that remained. The counterattack was broken.

CHAPTER 7

16th of August, 1918
Le Quesnel, France

'More than thirteen hundred enemy killed or wounded,' whistled Tibbett. 'That must have been quite a battle.'

'And 250 prisoners,' I added. 'Yes, it was a real battle, that's for sure. It may have turned into a rout, but I was on pins and needles for most of it, I can tell you that.'

'From the prisoner interrogations it appears the Boche threw in four battalions when they counter-attacked – an entire brigade,' said Smith.

'I believe it. They just kept coming, row after row after row of them. They certainly weren't expecting much resistance. I think our Colonel Foster threw a real spanner in the works,' I said, grinning. Then more soberly; 'I've never seen so many dead and wounded in one place, not even at the Somme.'

Captain Cunningham spoke up. 'That's a beating they won't soon forget.'

'I wish that were true,' I replied. 'But to think the Germans lost Damery and its wood, and had hell and damnation brought down on their heads simply because they gave the colonel such a rough night...' There were chuckles. 'Surely there must be a useful lesson in there somewhere; maybe on the importance of letting a man get a decent night's sleep...' Pointedly I looked at Smith.

Smith looked away. He appeared to have something in his eye.

'If they had interrupted the colonel's dinner I might have understood,' said DuBois. Understandably that brought even more chuckles. Benoît's appetite was legendary. Almost like mine.

'Anyhow,' I continued, 'with Damery in our hands, the Germans started to withdraw from the Bois-en-Z. The French captured it a few hours later.'

DuBois was beaming. I presumed it was with pride. 'And the RCR secured Parvillers,' he said. Since he'd taken to quoting the intelligence summaries verbatim, his English was improving in leaps and bounds.

'It shan't be long before the French take Roye, then,' piped up Tibbett, his own choice of language firmly anchored in the 19th century. It earned him a little good-natured ribbing. For once, I remained on the sidelines. I was still bagged after the past week.

However quaint the language, Tibbett's way of thinking was modern enough. The broad corridor of trenches that passed to the west of Parvillers and Damery continued south to the Amiens-Roye road. It was there, athwart the road, that the Bois-en-Z loomed above the surrounding fields, the pivot to the defences of Roye, itself only a tantalising two and a half miles southeast. A forest so named for its distinctive shape, Bois-en-Z was atop a 100-metre high hill. With its gradual sloped sides, slit with trenches and fortified by wire and machine guns, it commanded the approaches to the town as surely as any fortress in centuries past. The Fort Garry Horse had charged the hill to certain death, mere days ago. Another futility in the war's long list of futilities. The French had also thrown themselves at it, to no avail. But the pivot was now broken. The French were moving on Goyencourt today and Tibbett's prediction was by no means a stab in the dark.

Later, when we were packing up to leave – at long last the division was going into reserve – my eye caught sight of a book in the boxes, bound in black along its spine. I took it out.

'Here's something you really need to read, Smith.' And I threw the bundle onto his lap, trying not to smile.

He read the title. 'SS 135 Instructions for the Training of Divisions for Offensive Action. Hmm. Is it any good?'

'Guaranteed to put you out like a light,' I said. 'I happen to know one of the authors, a captain by the name of Montgomery. That's how I came by it. His book's certainly invaluable if you're having trouble sleeping.'

'I'll keep that in mind, sir.'

Thus, unceremoniously dismissed by my own lieutenant, I went back to preparing the move.

17th of August, 1918
Beaucourt-en-Santerre, France

I stood near a window, or what passed for one, in the well-ventilated confines of Beaucourt's old château. Dressed in my shirt sleeves, I had my woolen tunic off and one of the sleeves turned inside out. I was scratching at the seams with my fingernail.

'Don't tell me you have lice, Malcolm.'

Wearily I glanced over my shoulder. It was Tibbett. Both he and DuBois had been promoted in my absence – for the counter-battery work they'd done at Amiens. Which had been excellent, no question. In fact, I'd never heard the infantry speak so well of the artillery. Yesterday evening we'd all shared a congratulatory drink to celebrate their promotions and then I conked out. I had some catching up to do, sleep-wise.

Nor had Tibbett's promotion gone unnoticed in the deepest echelons of the division's administration. This led to my current predicament: sharing a room. Some clerk, in a flash of brilliance, decided what could be better than putting two majors together. Tibbett and I got along fine, especially since he'd shed his haughty airs. Still, I wasn't convinced I was prepared to spend day and night with him.

In the trenches, your fellow soldiers are often the only thing ensuring you put one foot in front of the other. I'd come to discover that it was no different behind the lines at headquarters. Take Tibbett. He and I hadn't exactly gotten off to a flying start. Actually, he struck me as precisely the sort of stuck-up English twit for whom the term "army surplus" was invented. Who knows what he first thought of me, but it couldn't have been pretty. Only after he'd really gotten stuck in the mud at Passchendaele and I'd plucked him out did we have a meeting of the minds. You might even say we were friends. I could say categorically that I relied on him, and he on me. On the Western Front that meant a lot.

'No, Paul, I don't have lice. Thank heavens. I've just been terribly itchy the last couple of days. What with this accursed heat and all the time I've spent in the trenches, I thought I'd best have a look. Woolen tunics leave something to be desired when you're running around in a heat wave.'

'I'm glad to hear it, Malcolm. I'm not sure Colonel Hore-Ruthven would have understood. Traditionally, divisional staff are held to higher standards of hygiene.'

I moaned. '*Traditionally*, divisional staff aren't cavorting around all day on their bellies in the front lines, either. And certainly not in the blazing heat.' It came out a little sourly.

'No,' he agreed, 'I suppose not.'

I took another look at my tunic and grabbed a fresh one from my chest. For eight months old it didn't look nearly as fresh as it ought to have. It had cost me a fortune.

'Have you heard any news?' I asked, as I buttoned up. 'I rather expected there'd be another big push.'

'It keeps getting delayed. I'm not sure why. There were only a few local operations. The French are pushing ahead, as you know, and the Aussies straightened their line. Oh, and 2nd Division took Fransart yesterday.'

'Yes, I heard.'

'I think the Battle of Amiens is well and truly over.'

'So it would appear,' I said.

He looked at me. 'I thought you'd be pleased?'

'I am. A little disappointed we didn't make it further. I really believed we had a chance to break this war wide open, Paul.'

'And now we're back to the hard slogging? Yes, I see what you mean. But in all honesty, Malcolm, they'd grind us to bits in no time the way things are going. It's taken us a week to get as far as we did in the first few hours on the eighth. Be thankful we're out of it for the moment.'

'Don't worry, I am. I'm pleasantly surprised I must say. After the field-marshal's visit, I assumed he'd have us bashing our heads on some impregnable objective by now.'

'Well, you'll have an opportunity to ask him yourself. He's visiting 7th Brigade, tomorrow, for a march-past.'

'Really? He's visiting us again?' For a man with 60 divisions under his command we were receiving an untoward amount of attention. I hoped that was because we were seeing an untoward amount of action, not to mention winning an untoward number of battles. The alternative didn't bear thinking about.

18th of August, 1918
Valley Wood, France

It was fine and warm, and a few greyish clouds were sailing dreamily overhead. This morning I'd mustered up my courage to go to Colonel Hore-Ruthven and ask for leave.

He listened sympathetically, nodding at all the right moments. When I was finished he leaned back in his chair, his fists clenched together in careful consideration. Then he lowered them and his face had a rueful gentleness to it. 'I'm sorry, MacPhail. I can imagine how badly you must want this. But I'm afraid it's simply impossible. The general reiterated only yesterday that he needs every man he can get. He's convinced our next assignment will come very soon. There's no way he'll allow his intelligence officer to leave. Not now – no matter how compelling the reason. I'm sorry. I truly am. Let's hope this whole thing ends soon. By the spring they say we should have a fighting chance.'

I didn't protest. There was no point going to the general. That would only make me look deceitful, sneaking behind the colonel's back. Hore-Ruthven was a hard taskmaster, but an honourable man and if that's what the general had told him, the general wasn't going to change his mind just because I was doing the asking. I think the colonel did feel bad, for he insisted on giving me a four day pass. As of tomorrow I was on leave.

For the moment, however, I was standing again in the grasslands at Valley Wood. A hastily erected parade ground had sprung up between it and Hamon Wood to the west. Without the stresses of an impending attack, my immediate future looked brighter than it had in a long while. I was relaxed and wearily resigned to my fate. Which, however I looked at it, was vastly improved compared to my last brief visit here.

Near the road the engineers had constructed a modest reviewing stand. Judging by the number and shine of the many staff cars parked nearby, an impressive contingent had shown up to inspect the 7th Brigade's four battalions.

Earlier I'd run into Major Ewing and a lieutenant of the 42nd and we chatted briefly. Colonel Weaver of the 49th also greeted me with friendly enthusiasm; he'd obviously got past the sorry circumstances of our last encounter near Parvillers.

I was standing in the bleachers, along with the other less exalted guests, including most of the divisional staff. The bleachers consisted of the rough ground with grass to our knees, to either side of the reviewing stand. Apparently we were expected to stake out our own couple of square feet to stand on; an experience similar to the gold rush, I imagine, as everyone rushed to seek out a vantage point to observe the worthy souls lining up on the reviewing stand.

'Look at that,' I said, whistling, as we watched the dignitaries arrange themselves. The man I had in my sights was familiar to anybody who'd so much as glimpsed a newspaper in the past year. He was short; portly in the sense of prosperous well-being, and balding – that is except for the fierce tangle of white guarding the northern approaches to both his eyes and his mouth. The white, walrus moustache that covered his mouth was not so much a tangle as an entire forest; it was so big I feared the soldiers on march-past were going to have to make a detour just to get around it.

'Premier Clémenceau,' exclaimed DuBois. 'Who's that beside him?'

'I don't know, but he looks French, too,' I said. 'You tell me.' From his uniform it was blatantly obvious he was a French general. With his cap momentarily off, he fitted my imaginary picture of a French detective; dark black hair, waxed oh so carefully to the right, flat pointy ears and piercing eyes capped by expressive thin eyebrows, epilated only this morning. An equally dark moustache, curling playfully upwards at each end, watched over taut thin lips.

A little churlishly Benoît said, 'I don't know, or I wouldn't have asked.' It didn't matter, I'd hear the full biographies later.

'Just trying to keep you on your toes, Benoît. What about him, then?' I asked, motioning at the hatted fellow in a dark three-piece suit next to the general. 'He's definitely not French. Not a soldier, either.'

'Pfff. No idea,' said Benoît.

Major Meredith from brigade headquarters had been following our discussion. 'The minister of munitions, perhaps?' he said with a wry grin. 'Here to complain about our excessive expenditure of bombs and small arms ammunition?' I knew what he was getting at. We'd had some painful instances recently where our attacks were stymied by a shortage of munitions.

I smiled and shook my head. 'No, Meredith. The minister is a balding chap by the name of Churchill. I'm sure he'll try his best next time.'

'No. No,' said Tibbett quietly, ignoring the three of us. 'That gentleman is Lord Derby, the British ambassador to France.'

'Ah,' we responded in chorus. How he knew that was a mystery. Though he'd once told me his family was well-connected, so presumably they moved in the same circles as the lord.

Tibbett appeared frustrated by our response. 'Come on, surely you must know him. His name is Edward Stanley,' he prodded. Meredith stared blankly. 'His father, Frederick Stanley, was Governor-General of Canada.' Puzzled, I kept looking, trying to connect the dots.

He looked at DuBois, as if for salvation. DuBois looked back, as if needing salvation. 'He was the one that donated the Stanley Cup,' offered Tibbett, finally.

And like that, the seas parted, and the faces cleared. Hockey's great trophy. *Why hadn't he simply said so in the first place?*

Trumpets and drums announced the inspection was to begin. The regimental band of the 42nd had seemingly been relieved of stretcher duty, for I saw it parade proudly into sight with the others.

At the head of each battalion, the regimental banners were flapping softly. I couldn't help noticing that the pole of the PPCLI's crimson standard was heavily bandaged, although its bearer was doing his best to camouflage the fact, embracing it with his forearm as if his life depended on it. It seemed a pointless precaution; a bullet had shattered it at Parvillers. The Patricia's rivals, its sister battalions, found it a source of considerable merriment, which was naturally where I heard about it.

I peered to my right in time to see Benoît straighten up. I was glad I wasn't standing behind him; he was large enough when slouching. Now it would have been like trying to peer over Mont Blanc. His old unit, the RCR, came marching into position. Myself, I was more interested in the Black Watch and the 49th. I'd spent a lot of time with them recently and I scanned their ranks in search of familiar faces.

A studiously erect Brigadier Dyer led the dignitaries along the assembled lines, with Premier Clémenceau and Field-Marshal Haig in the advance guard. I could see the two got along. Haig was a touch taller than Clémenceau and altogether less dowdy than *Père la Victoire* (Father Victory). I soon lost sight of them as they passed along the ranks.

The uniforms were sharp and the men surprisingly so. With all the pomp and circumstance it was easy to forget how heavy the fighting had been. On the other hand, perhaps that explained the straight shoulders. God knows we'd done enough drill to last a lifetime, but that look of fierce pride… well, that came only from success on the battlefield.

As the party trooped back onto the podium for the march-past and the sergeants screamed their orders, we went back to our who's who.

'What about the guy with the scrambled eggs on his hat beside Lipsett and General Rawlinson?' Meredith was asking. I'd seen the gold braid hat too, but couldn't place him either.

Duguid could. 'That's the Major-General, General Staff, Sir Archibald Montgomery. He's chief of staff of the Fourth Army and Rawlinson's right-hand man.' I took a closer look.

'Any relation to Captain Bernard Montgomery?' I asked, thinking back to the opinionated young staff officer I'd met at Passchendaele last October, and his quintessential manual on offensive operations.

Duguid looked at me as if I'd asked the time in German. 'No idea. Never heard of the fellow.'

'Just thought I'd ask,' I said. 'It's a common enough name, I suppose.'

'He's the one responsible for sending the 32nd back into reserve, and us into battle on the 9th. I imagine you recall that debacle?' said Duguid.

'Do I ever. The worst decision of the entire attack,' I said. 'So it was him? But General Rawlinson approved the order for us to go into reserve in the first place? And Montgomery works for Rawlinson?'

'Montgomery doesn't seem to think so,' said Duguid. 'But Montgomery was the one that countermanded the order, all right. Took a piece out of General Webber at Corps HQ, too, for "aiding and abetting" Rawlinson, if you can believe it. He seems to think the Fourth Army belongs to him.'

'Christ almighty,' I thundered, 'it's hard enough trying to win this war without self-important blockheads throwing obstacles in the way. We might have broken through completely were it not for that harebrained decision.' Sheepishly the others looked away.

'One other thing you might be interested in knowing, Mac…' said Duguid. He began to inspect his fingernails.

'Well out with it then. I haven't all day.'

'The attack's been called off.'

I never saw so many heads turn so fast. 'Really?' I said.

'The field-marshal…' He glanced over at the podium with a look that suggested he was afraid our commander-in-chief might overhear. Which wasn't much of a concern, as Haig was a hundred feet away in conversation with Lipsett and Rawlinson. 'He convinced Marshal Foch to call it off.'

'That is news. Are you certain?'

'As certain as I can be.'

'He's learning at last,' I muttered under my breath.

'What's that?' asked Tibbett, who was listening attentively.

'Oh, I was just thinking. High Command are not what you'd call quick learners,' I said. 'I was afraid we'd be back to smashing ourselves against stone walls like at the Somme and Passchendaele. You have to give Haig credit, he's finally figured out when to call it a day.' The others were silent, but nodded thoughtfully.

'And you're off to Blighty, I hear,' said Tibbett.

Startled, I eyed him suspiciously. 'That got around awfully fast. Yes,

I have leave. But no, London's a little far. I've only got a four day pass, so I thought I'd head to Paris instead.'

'It's supposed to be nice this time of year.'

'A lot nicer than when the Germans were shelling it, if that's what you mean.'

DuBois smiled mischievously. 'He's only after the women you know.' Predictably, our half of the bleachers exploded in laughter, and I grimaced along with them.

Up on the reviewing stand the dignitaries were also sharing a moment of good cheer. It was a rare gathering of the high and the mighty near the battlefield. But as I looked at them, it dawned on me there was a very conspicuous absentee. The man who had probably done more than any other to ensure the startling success of the Amiens attack was nowhere to be seen. Where was our Corps Commander? Where was General Currie?

CHAPTER 8

19th of August, 1918
Paris, France

Emerging from the bustling Gare du Nord into the streets of Paris felt like stepping into another world. Not that the signs of war weren't everywhere. Soldiers of every hue and nationality crisscrossed the vibrant tableau in front of me. The city teemed with a life and a frivolity I'd half forgotten. And crossing the street, stepping out from the city's famous taxi cabs, and careering around them on bicycles of every description, were women. Benoît was right about that. There were a lot of women in Paris. And compared to where I'd been this entire eighteenth year of the century, that made for a pleasant change.

Early this morning I took a train from Amiens along the very rail line our offensive had secured. Only hours later, a little dazzled, I stepped out into the City of Light. I'd been here before, of course, long ago – so long ago that I often wondered whether my memories were really memories, or simply an elaborate fiction I'd dreamt up to where I could flee to escape my miseries.

The hotel, however – a recommendation of the well-travelled divisional chaplain – was every bit as tattered as I remembered Parisian hotels to be. Older, wiser and with a far thicker pocketbook than I had then, I made the same decision I had years ago. I dumped my tote and headed for the door. It wasn't worth wasting time to find something else. Besides, it was the lap of luxury compared to where I'd been sleeping these past few months.

After the German advances in the spring, the Boche had taken to shelling the city with a long range beast of a cannon, capable of shooting more than seventy miles. The war had truly reached Paris. But now I saw few signs of that, nor the huge craters left by their shells. Life had returned to a normality of sorts. After crossing the Seine with the domed grandeur of Les Invalides looming before me, I came to the bustling thoroughfare of the Quai d'Orsay. There I paused, watching as a cavalcade of shining cars passed by, pennants flying. And in one of them, suddenly, appeared the face of the French detective, the general who'd accompanied Premier Clémenceau to the march-past at Valley Wood.

I turned to the small gnarled man beside me, whose right sleeve hung listlessly at his side, and asked who it was. '*Le Général Mordacq, Monsieur,*' he replied. Which meant little to me, but his next words did: '*Le chef du cabinet militaire.*' He was Premier Clémenceau's right hand man.

That evening, approaching the hill of Montmartre on my way to see the dancing clubs of Pigalle about which I'd heard so much, I entered the Place de Clichy. I could hear the excited buzz from afar. Curious, I crossed the street and soon came to an illuminated café that announced itself as Le Wepler in bright red letters. The sultry August air was infused with cloying perfume, tobacco smoke, the smells of food and the heady scent of unadulterated amusement.

Ostentatiousness may have passed from fashion in war-time Paris, but Le Wepler would have none of it. I eased along the sidewalk tables, gawking at the sight of flashy uniforms and well-tailored suits; at their female companions whose outfits left precious little to the imagination. The sidewalk was crowded with onlookers. Laughing couples were searching agitatedly for an empty table. I eased my way through the throng. A shriek and chorus of giggles from the large table near the entrance caught my attention. A French officer was stretching casually across the table to return a magnum of champagne to its ice bucket, water dribbling from its bottom. Beside him, the pretty girl with crimson lips around whom his right arm was draped, was dabbing at her slender sequined legs with a white serviette, admonishing him good-naturedly. Her two scantily clad companions were watching, champagne flutes held to their lips, looks of exaggerated delight on their faces. A huge silver platter heaped with oysters dominated the centre of the table.

The man was curiously familiar. Somehow, across the crowded terrace he sensed I was staring, and his eyes rose to meet mine. Embarrassed, I looked away, as if I'd intruded on an intimate moment. An elderly waiter in black with a white apron stood in my path.

'*Je peux vous aider, monsieur?*'

To his offer of assistance, I asked if the gentleman near the door was famous, for I thought I recognized him.

'*Ah, non, monsieur,*' he said with a knowing smile. '*Il n'est pas célèbre, mais il est bien connu ici. C'est le capitaine Madelot.* (No, not famous, but well known here, it's Captain Madelot.)'

The scene kept returning to my mind, and as I strolled back towards my hotel not long after, it came to me; the man was the *capitaine* from Arvillers. Rutherford and I had handed over the village to him, together with its well-endowed Mairie.

Life appeared to be treating him well. Remarkably well, when I thought about it.

20th of August, 1918
Paris, France

'Mac! Is that you?' I looked up to see an olive clad officer barging between the tables, smiling broadly, an arm raised in the air in greeting. I waved to him. It was Major Malcolm McAvity, once of the 3rd Division, and now of Corps HQ. He headed up the Corps intelligence section. 'I thought it must be you,' he said, as he approached, his friendly face bathed in sweat. 'Hey, it's great to see you!'

'Sir Malcolm! What a surprise. What brings you here?'

'Same as you, I expect: leave. Webber gave me a couple of days off. I just arrived. You know I can't even remember the last time I had leave, let alone in Paris. What a coincidence finding you here!'

I was sitting tucked away in a shady corner of the crowded terrace outside the Café de la Paix, resting my feet and my mind after a busy morning. Whether my choice of establishment was some parapraxis or not – not that I had any delusions about the likelihood of peace anytime soon – or simply that I'd spied a table emptying up, it was an inspired decision. Judging by the astonishing assortment of military headgear, from the distinctive pill-box French Képis, in all the colours of the rainbow, to the slouch hats of the Aussies, the allied armies in France were well represented. And that wasn't a bad thing; there was no more jovial soul than a soldier on leave.

McAvity asked, 'What are you drinking?' and pointed at the bottle.

'Does it matter? You'll be wanting some, regardless, I expect,' I said, with a grin. I waved to the waiter to bring over another glass. McAvity shook his head – he was long since inured to my quips – and pulled out a chair.

'It's from the Bordeaux,' I explained, as I poured him a generous measure of wine. McAvity sniffed at it with curiosity, and must have smelled something he liked for he said, 'They're paying you too much.'

'Oh, I wouldn't say that,' I replied. 'You should see the hotel I'm in – Le Terminus.'

'As in, end of the line?' he asked, laughing. I nodded. 'So whatever few francs you're saving on your dead-end hotel, you're wasting on wine?'

I raised my glass. 'It's all a question of priorities, Mac. A lucky thing for you too,' I said. 'Cheers!'

Thoughtfully McAvity sipped at the wine, then leaned back in his chair and sighed as if the worries of the world had just lifted from his shoulders. He had lines in his cheerful round face I didn't remember. The last month had been hard on all of us.

'Any news?' I asked.

He shook his head. 'Not much. Your division is shipping off to Arras tonight.'

'Arras? Really?' I pondered this unexpected development. We were moving north to our old stomping grounds. We'd spent most of last year there.

McAvity looked up. 'Oh, yeah, there was one other thing. Currie is absolutely steaming. You lot had a march-past with half the High

Command attending and your General Lipsett didn't see fit to invite him.'

'Yes, I wondered about that,' I said. 'The 7th Brigade was on parade. Haig was on hand. General Rawlinson, too, as well as the French premier, the British ambassador, and a lot of others. At the time I couldn't figure out where the devil Currie was. It was as if the guest of honour hadn't shown up. But you know, it's not at all like Lipsett to step on toes like that. There must be some explanation.'

'Well, on the strict QT, Currie is livid. He went the very next day to do his own march-past with your brigade.'

'He didn't miss a great deal,' I said, feeling oddly guilty – it was my division after all. I'd always liked Currie, even if to the men his stilted ways were occasionally as inspirational as a wet sock. Old "guts 'n gaiters" certainly beat the pants off most of the BEF's tired collection of brass hats.

'Easy enough for you to say,' said McAvity. 'You know Currie's a little insecure, what with all the sniping he gets. Being snubbed is just the sort of thing to send him off the deep end. It doesn't help that Lipsett's always been so well connected. And he's English. The general probably thinks Lipsett is currying up to Haig and the others to snatch his job.'

'I'm pretty sure he's not. Lipsett's a good man and a good general. I don't know him intimately, but trust me; that sort of conniving is not his thing,' I said firmly.

McAvity grunted. 'I'll let you convince General Currie of that.'

21st of August, 1918
Paris, France

Right as I was deciding whether to abandon the soft sagging mattress, which was too short and too lumpy by far, and simply sleep on the floor, a loud banging on the door interrupted my deliberations. There were voices. '*Excusons-nous, monsieur,*' said one. And then another, much louder: 'Mac, it's me. Let me in!' The second one I recognized.

The first was no doubt that dim-witted paraplegic who manned the front desk, the same one who had mercilessly waved off my complaints about the bed.

'Look, I know we agreed to get an early start with our sight-seeing, McAvity, but this is ridiculous. It's just past three in the morning. And careful with the door. It almost blew down earlier.'

'Sight-seeing will have to wait, Mac,' declared McAvity, as he elbowed his way past me. I closed the door on the sallow-faced moustache cowering meekly behind.

McAvity crinkled his nose and shot his head from left to right, taking in the ten square feet of dilapidation I currently inhabited. 'You weren't kidding about this place. It stinks.'

'And you haven't even tried the mattress yet,' I said. 'Perhaps that goblin who you roused from his slumber could find you a room? I'm fairly sure it's not full.'

McAvity ignored me. 'All leave has been cancelled,' he said.

'ALL leave?'

He nodded vigorously. 'All leave. I had to forward an address where I could be reached. I received the message an hour ago. I was to pass the word on to any others I came across. So naturally I thought of you.'

'There was no reason to be so damned considerate,' I mumbled. My earlier good cheer at seeing him had evaporated as quickly as an open bottle of rum in a company mess.

He removed his cap and began rubbing the top of his head. 'What are you moaning about? I was barely here a day. Look, Lipsett's going to be needing you. You must know that, Mac,' he said.

I groaned and nodded. 'Give me a minute.' As I dressed, I called over my shoulder, 'What's it all about do you think?'

'I don't know,' he responded, 'but the whole Corps is to move in haste to the area of Arras. You know what that means.'

'Yeah, fortified trench-line after fortified trench-line. And somehow I don't think High Command is moving us for a change of scenery.' On an afterthought I asked, 'Are you sure you couldn't just forget you ever saw me?'

'Move it along, MacPhail,' he growled. He held the door open, and brusquely waved me through as I'd seen military policemen do. 'If you don't keep dawdling we can catch the early train.'

PART TWO

CHAPTER 9

22nd of August, 1918
Hautecloque, France

Hautecloque was a long, long way from the elegant boulevards and smart cafés of Paris. Other than the obligatory church standing forlornly amongst a smattering of modest brick and stone houses, the tents, huts and requisitioned buildings of the Corps HQ were the sole attraction – not that they were attractive, only it was there that the reason for my hasty recall would shortly be revealed. There wasn't a Café de la Paix anywhere in sight. If my suspicions were correct, that was entirely appropriate.

The swallows were out in force as the sun eased ever lower in the western sky. A gentle breeze tickled the leaves of the trees lining the narrow road to the village. War hadn't touched little old Hautecloque, but I had a feeling Hautecloque would soon touch the war.

General Lipsett, Colonel Hore-Ruthven and I had made our way to this pinprick on a map, not far from the outskirts of Arras, to attend a meeting of the divisional commanders. Awaiting us was the tall portly figure of Lieutenant-General Sir Arthur Currie, our renowned Corps Commander. Leaning on his cane, his jowls sagging as much as the rim of his dowdy cap and the paunch of his belly, the general's eyes were fiercely alert. While he may not have looked like anybody's idea of an accomplished general, appearances deceived.

'Welcome, Louis,' he said to Lipsett, as the two shook hands. I watched intently for any signs of tension between them but saw none. Perhaps McAvity had exaggerated it all, not that a level-headed guy like McAvity was the type for that. The colonel and I saluted and Currie nodded in return. 'Good evening, MacPhail. It's a pleasure to see you. You look in fine form.' The general and I knew each other from long ago.

'Good evening, sir,' I replied. Uncharacteristically, I left it at that. I'd resolved to keep my ad-hoc rejoinders to a minimum when speaking with the brass. Less danger from friendly fire.

They were all here, all four divisional commanders, accompanied by one or two from their staff, plus a handful of officers from Corps Headquarters, including McAvity.

Currie was never one for meandering preambles. Tonight he meandered less than normal, taking a straight shot to the subject at hand. 'Gentlemen. Thank you for coming. I expect you are all anxious to hear why I summoned you at such short notice. We are to force the Drocourt-Quéant Line. The Corps is going to break the hinge of the Hindenburg system,' he declared.

The room went silent. Uncharacteristically silent. A long stilted silence in which my brain whirred through the implications and the others were lost, deep in thoughts of their own.

Major-General Watson of the 4th Division spoke up. 'If I'm not mistaken, that's one of the strongest positions the Boche have,' he said. Then, as if to underline the seriousness, added, 'It's supposedly impregnable.' Watson had the reputation of being a trifle rash, so that he should be the one mentioning this was worrisome. There wasn't a soldier in the army who didn't know that the Hindenburg Line was the German equivalent of the Great Wall of China.

'You're not mistaken, David, their defences are strong. But not impregnable,' said Currie with a grim smile, and made as if he wanted to continue. But then it seemed as if the whole room had something urgent to say.

It was Batty Mac of the 1st Division whose words cut through the melee. 'When is the operation to begin?' asked General Macdonell, in his sing-song Scottish lilt.

'The morning of the 26th,' replied Currie. I shook my head in disbelief. We were to tackle the infamous D-Q Line. If I remembered anything from the hours spent studying the maps, the Germans had three lines of defence arrayed in front before we even reached it. And there were a mere three days to prepare. To make matters worse, the entire 4th Division was still in Amiens, along with much of the divisional artillery.

'It doesn't give us much time,' protested General Macdonell, echoing my own thoughts. 'We had four weeks to prepare for Vimy Ridge, and this is at least the equal of that.'

On the facts of it General Currie should have conceded defeat. Instead, he rubbed his chin and his eyes focused on Macdonell. 'High Command believes the Germans intend to collect and reorganise their forces behind the Hindenburg Line. We must do everything to prevent that. Maréchal Foch is determined to maintain the momentum of our offensive. I have great faith in you and the men of this Corps. Time is short, but flush from our victory at Amiens, I'm convinced we are ready for this task,' he said.

I stifled a groan. I suppose if it hadn't been Currie doing the talking I wouldn't even have made the effort. The general's rhetorical embellishments aside, he appeared confident. When he revealed that the 2nd and 3rd Divisions would be leading the assault, the groan bubbled up anyhow.

23rd of August, 1918
North of the Scarpe River and 2 miles east of Arras, France

We were staring southeastwards from across the Scarpe River, no raging torrent fed by the snow-capped peaks of the Rockies, but a modest stream like every river in this part of France, its waters flowing gracefully westwards to Arras and beyond. And like every river in this part of France, its strategic importance far outweighed its humble dimensions. Beyond the Scarpe to the southeast, no more than a mile distant from our vantage point, was the modest rise of Orange Hill. A ridge really, its formidable defences blocked the path eastwards from

Arras. For a short time – it was only a month ago I realized with a start - we had thought this was to be where our offensive would come. We'd planned how to storm that very hill down to the smallest, most excruciating detail. But then we were secreted south, in haste, to the great show at Amiens. Now we were back to do it for real and a whole lot more if General Currie was to be believed.

The Arras-Cambrai road headed east from Arras into enemy territory. It was straddled by two hills, like twin towers guarding a castle gate: Orange Hill to its left and Chapel Hill to its right – the 2nd Division was to tackle that. Behind Orange Hill and further to the southeast, I saw the third major obstacle looming, the conical peak on which rested the village of Monchy-le-Preux. The town dominated the torn-up land as surely as it had the communiqués the last few years. During the offensive at Arras in the spring of 1917 – at the same time we'd stormed Vimy Ridge – the hill had become ours. And the Newfoundland Regiment had held it against bitter counterattack. But in the spring of 1918, as the German offensive smashed forward, the defences here had melted, as they had in so many other places. The well-organised old British frontline in front of Monchy was now only another hurdle on the route to the D-Q Line. Close behind it was the old German front line, and then the Fresnes-Rouvroy Line, all three strewn with wire, trenches and machine-gun nests. And then there was the Wotan-Stellung: the Drocourt-Quéant Line. The German name made it sound even more ominous.

'It appears General Currie has once again found us the choicest assignment,' I murmured. General Lipsett was off my right flank and naturally he heard. Normally my choice of words would have led to a sarcastic rebuttal, a skirmish no major in his right mind should ever engage in with a major-general, or a stiff rebuke. Today, Lipsett only grunted noncommittally. 'Be thankful the general convinced Field-Marshal Haig to call off the Amiens offense, MacPhail. Here they may be less prepared.' Then he turned to the others.

'Gentlemen,' he began. Brigadier Draper of the 8th Brigade and his four battalion commanders, including the very same Major Rhoades from the 5th CMR – who I knew rather well by now – were listening attentively. 'As you can see our sector is a challenging one. The reason I've taken you here is to see the lay of the land for yourselves. And what we must do is devise a plan to take Orange Hill and Monchy without losing the best part of a brigade doing so. I await your suggestions.'

As the others began discussing it amongst themselves, I ambled over to the captain from the 51ˢᵗ Imperial Highland Division, now temporarily part of the Corps. He'd come along as a guide. 'I realize you fellows are supposed to be looking after our left on this side of the river, but what do you think?' I asked. 'You've been here for a while.'

The captain, a dispirited looking chap by the name of Gillespie, with lines under his eyes deeper than most slit trenches, said, 'Aye, it's a fearsome sight, sir,' and shrugged wearily.

'Word has it you Scots were a great warrior nation before they invented whisky,' I said. 'You've been gazing at those hills for days, Captain. Surely you must have noticed something? Other than the fact they're not exactly the Highlands.'

At the mention of whisky and the Highlands Gillespie perked up. His gloomy eyes assumed a fiery, startling, intensity. Then it occurred to him I was joking. 'Yes, sir,' he said, with an easy smile. With that the Gaelic flood-gates opened.

Captain Gillespie had noticed the odd thing or two. What was most interesting were his observations about the south bank of the Scarpe, the land to the north of Orange Hill and Monchy. It would be on our far left as we attacked. 'It's broken ground, sir. It affords a lot more cover than anything further south. And their defences seem less organised there.'

'Really,' I said, suddenly enthralled by what the laconic Scotsman had to say. I fumbled with my field glasses. 'Perhaps you could show me? Hang on, I'm going to call over the brigadier.'

General Draper heard me, and must have understood a little Scottish himself, for all five feet nine inches of him, hastened over. I could have sworn he was shorter, but Smith – who'd looked it up in the brigadier's service record – had settled the matter. Stature aside, Draper demonstrated a well-tuned sense of the challenges for his brigade. He instantly appreciated the significance of Gillespie's words. As for Gillespie, I don't think he'd ever felt so much at the centre of events. Certainly it's not every day you have a brigadier-general and four battalion commanders hanging on your every word.

I left them after a bit and returned to General Lipsett. The general's right foot was resting jauntily on a small boulder, while he stood erect, sweeping from left to right with his field glasses. It might well have been a fox hunt if you ignored the shell-pocked desolation, the fields burnt by the summer sun, and the abundance of concrete bunkers – as well as the absence of a single creature, save those in a *Stahlhelm*.

'And?' he asked.

'I think General Draper has the beginnings of a solid plan, sir,' I said.

Quizzically he raised his eyebrows. He looked over at Draper and the commanders encircling Gillespie, then back at me. I explained what Gillespie had told us and what Draper had repeated to his officers. I didn't mention my whispered interventions; the brigadier was a proud man.

'Very good,' he said after a pause. 'I like it. It's a shame we won't really surprise them, MacPhail. Not like at Amiens.'

'That's true, sir. The Germans know full well something awaits them. And they may already have taken some identifications. I'm afraid we have to assume they're aware the Corps has moved from Amiens, despite all the secrecy. There is one small thing, though,' I said cautiously. 'It just might help tip the scales.'

'I'm listening, Major.'

'Hopefully the Boche don't know the Corps is coming, but they do know something is. However, what they don't know is *when*.' Lipsett had a puzzled look, which was unusual. Typically a report to him felt like scaling a rampart, with the general peering down ready to sever my ropes at any misstep. Benoît always said I was imaging things.

'Of course, they don't,' Lipsett said. 'No one knows *when* we're coming. Not even I do.'

'What I'm trying to say, sir, is while the Boche may not know the day, or the exact time, they do have a pretty good idea based on what we always do. It's no coincidence they start shelling us from about 4 a.m. on. Their trenches are always well manned by early morning. What if we were to go in earlier, sir? In the middle of the night. When they're not expecting it.'

The general looked thoughtful. 'You realize, MacPhail, night attacks are atrociously difficult to coordinate? It would be an awful risk.'

'But would it, sir? Of course it would be challenging for the lead battalions, although we've done our share of fighting in the pitch dark of late. It's not as if we're not accustomed to it. However, if we could catch the Boche sleeping... well, that might make all the difference.'

'You know, MacPhail,' said Lipsett, speaking very slowly and deliberately for an Irishman, 'you might have something there.' I could tell from the ways his eyes lit up he was excited. 'I'm going to have a word with General Currie.'

24th of August, 1918
London Cave, Arras, France

'I tell you, it smells like a schoolroom down here,' I said again.

'It's the chalk,' said Tibbett. 'All the walls are chalk. Just like the white cliffs of Dover. Although I'm not convinced you can actually smell chalk, Mac.' Tibbett was a physics graduate so I took him at his word, even if I didn't immediately see how physics applied.

We were moving into our new Advanced Divisional Headquarters in London Cave, part of the huge network of caves and tunnels that I was learning ran deep under much of Arras. It was definitely more picturesque than what I'd seen up above. While the city wasn't exactly razed to the ground, it did seem that every time I had a fresh glimpse of it, the more it resembled a building yard.

Today had been another hot day. It was with a marked degree of relief that Tibbett and I entered the cave system just after three to be met by a welcoming wall of cool still air. It didn't smell particularly fresh, but away from the heat of the city streets and the steady fall of German shells, it was a fine place to be. Clambering down the steps, we reached a tunnel and began walking in an easterly direction. Away from the crash and thud of the shelling it was spookily quiet.

Tibbett had a map in hand. 'Listen, Paul, I know you're not much with directions but this tunnel has only one direction,' I said. That sounded smart for all of thirty seconds. Until we reached the junction with five gloomy passageways to choose from. 'On second thought,' I said, 'you may be right.'

'Be prepared, Malcolm,' said Tibbett, a little primly. 'Always be prepared.' It was no doubt a little pearl of wisdom he'd picked up in the boy scouts, not that it was bad advice. Deep down Tibbett was a good-hearted fellow and I'd learned to accept his stilted manner. I strained occasionally to keep my mouth shut, though.

Conversationally, I said, 'It's astonishing how big this place is. Incredible. There must be miles of tunnels down here.'

Tibbett slowed so I could come up abreast of him. 'There were more than twenty thousand troops quartered here, before the battle of Arras last year,' he said.

'Twenty thousand. Really?'

I held out my arm as I walked, my fingertips tracing the lines of the cold, rough-hewn wall. As I came to another of the yellow electric bulbs fastened in the stone, I retrieved it. The lamps showed us the way well enough, but laboured to light the dark crevices high above. From the ceiling, drops of water fell onto the floor at intervals with an audible *plop*. 'Careful,' I said to Tibbett, spotting a sleek patch. I motioned him away from the centre of the passage. 'I bloody near fell on my ass already. We don't want you wounded before the action even starts.' Tibbett snorted, unsure if I was jesting. I wasn't.

We walked for what seemed like miles, although it was probably closer to one, passing a modest kitchen and a small alcove for prayer carved into the tunnel wall. There were more and more troops as we went on. All ours, all from the division. 'So where are we, Paul?'

He studied the map for an instant. 'We're almost there. London Cave is roughly 2000 yards from the city and about the same distance to the front line.'

The front line. Down here I'd briefly, mercifully, forgotten about it. That didn't happen much these days. It's a little difficult to forget when you're always in it, I thought grumpily.

'So what do you make of our odds, Paul?' I asked. 'It's all fine and well to talk about the D-Q Line, but it's essentially one massive 10-mile-wide fortified swath, most of it before we even get to the D-Q. I saw some aerial photographs yesterday.' I shook my head. 'The Germans have had their best engineers working on these defences for months, or even years.'

'I don't know about that,' Tibbett said, 'but we have more guns at our disposal than we've ever had. Two-thirds of the heavies will be on counter-battery work. It'll be bigger than Amiens. You remember the barrage at Amiens, Malcolm?'

I nodded. It was a spectacle I'd not soon forget. 'Yeah, I remember. You just make sure you and DuBois do your best,' I said. It was a needless reminder, the kind of thing mothers are prone to say. The same kind of thing that gives them the reputation as nags. I didn't mean to nag, but I was worried.

25th of August, 1918

Benoît said dubiously, 'The *hinge* of the Hindenburg system?' I could see he was struggling with the strategic import of this attack. However, not so very long ago, I imagined he'd been out climbing trees in the eastern townships of Québec. That wasn't much of a background for a military strategist. On the other hand, it might just have been my convoluted explanation.

He looked tired. Almost as tired as I felt. We'd been at it non-stop, all the endless preparations and details. To my dismay I heard ZERO Hour was pegged for 4.50 a.m. Apparently Currie wasn't convinced of the merits of a night attack. And knowing Lipsett, he'd have me in the advance parties.

'Here, have a look,' I said, beckoning DuBois over to the table. I pulled out one of the large scale maps that lay underneath the trench map Smith and I were studying. I put my finger on a spot near Neuville-Vitasse, a village a mile east of Arras. From it I slowly traced a line down eighty miles to the south. 'That's the famous Hindenburg Line. And that's where the Boche will make their stand,' I said. 'Do you notice how it curves out easterly from Neuville-Vitasse, and then turns sharply to head south? And right where it turns, it's intersected by the D-Q Line coming from the north, which is really just an extension of the Hindenburg system running up to Belgium. Look, it's a 'Y' shape where they connect. That's the hinge – there, at that junction. If we can break through where the two lines come together we'll be behind the strongest defensive system the Germans have, and all their positions to the south, and even to the north, will be threatened. We'll be able to push forward on all sides.'

I could see DuBois scrutinizing the map and he nodded. 'So, what you're saying, Mac, is they're throwing us at the strongest point on the Western Front?'

I began to hem and haw at this bastardization of my words. But then I threw up my hands and said, 'That's one way of looking at it.'

Benoît crossed himself. He wasn't even particularly religious. Nor was I, and it was probably too late to make a credible conversion.

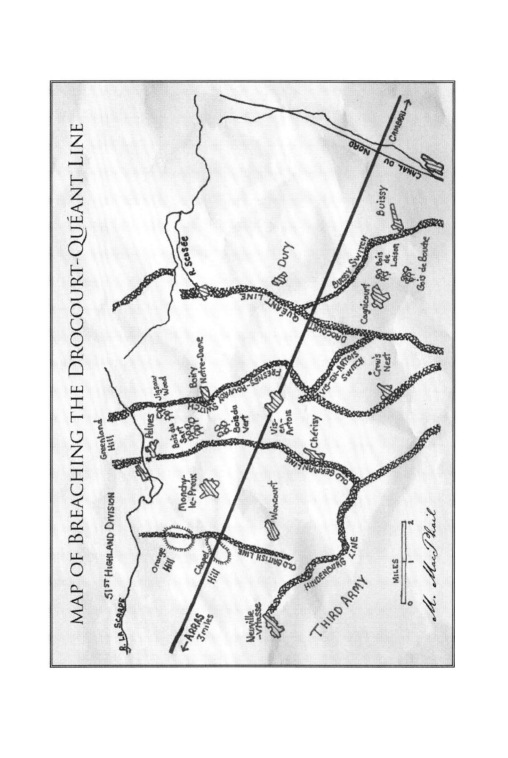

MAP OF BREACHING THE DROCOURT-QUÉANT LINE

CHAPTER 10

26th of August, 1918
Near Orange Hill (3 miles southeast of Arras), France

How often had I sat in a miserable hole getting absolutely drenched? We'd had the occasional light shower the past couple of days, but now it was driving down with a vengeance and I was soaked through to my woollen trunks. Water was pouring off the rim of my helmet from all sides. Earlier I'd glimpsed the moon – it was just past full, but presently nature had drawn the curtains. Thick billows of cloud moved over a couple of hours ago and with them driving rain. As a result it was very dark. I don't think I could see a trolley length ahead, although the rain appeared to be easing up. If we didn't lose our way, at least the Germans would be as blind as we were. That was fortunate. From the intelligence we'd gathered, there were three full divisions lined up against us, and more in reserve. Lipsett had received the news with his usual mask of imperturbability.

A red-cheeked officer pushed his way past the squad of soldiers next to me in the trench. 'How are you, sir?' he inquired. 'I have a jot of rum for you, if you'd like? We're to assemble soon.'

'I'm fine, Lieutenant. Thanks,' I said. But then I reconsidered and downed it in a hasty gulp that left my throat glowing. Liquid courage. There was a time in the beginning when a jot of rum was the only thing that slowed my trembling enough to get myself over the parapet.

Thankfully, I discovered a hidden courage, though it might only have been fatalism. I'd discovered that too. 'Best of luck,' I said to the lieutenant. He nodded and moved on.

Thoughtfully I fingered the letter in my breast pocket. Of course I'd instantly recognized the beautiful, looping handwriting. Not like mine, which bore an uncanny resemblance to Egyptian hieroglyphics according to my fourth grade English teacher. She hadn't meant it as a compliment. My mother was upbeat, full of small news, trivial things like how the Jones were painting their fence Dominion red after the *Calgary Daily Herald* trumpeted the victory at Amiens. She had enclosed the article. Normal odds and ends about life at home that should have brought a smile to my face. She breezed over her own condition. But my father had scribbled a few lines at the bottom. Reading between them I knew he was concerned, and so was I. This was no time to be preoccupied, however.

I was with the 2nd Mounted Rifles who had begun forming up next to the light railway, roughly a mile from Orange Hill, and well into No-Man's-Land. The men seemed eager. Beside me I saw nervous smiles after one of them poured his upside-down helmet into his water canteen from a height, an act carried out with great drama and an astonishing amount of water.

The rain had tapered off. I stared into a black abyss. There was a thud, then a deafening roar. The ground trembled and the sky lit up as if someone had switched on an electric light. More than 700 hundred guns were firing in near unison. The attack was on. It was exactly 3 a.m.

Currie had decided to send us in early after all.

'Come on boys. Let's go!' urged the NCOs, waving the troops forward. Eastwards. Always eastwards.

We approached the hill from the north. Further north, and even closer to the river, the 4th CMR was passing through the lightly rolling terrain, by-passing Orange Hill and heading for Monchy, two miles distant. Ahead, German SOS flares of double red spiralled up into the sky, out from the explosions that rippled over the hill. Their retaliation when it came landed far to our rear. The few guns that had escaped the counter-battery fire were shelling our front line. Only we were gone.

Moving at a fast trot, to keep pace with the barrage's hail of iron and high explosive, we came to the enemy's first line of wire and trenches, the Halifax Line, the British trenches of early 1918. There was the sound of scattered rifle fire. A brief burst from a machine gun, visible as pinpoints of light flickered low to the horizon. Then the platoons of B Company wheeled off to their right to head down the trench, to root out the Boche in his first line of defence. This was the plan; to turn their positions at Orange Hill and Monchy from the side. The 5th CMR had drawn the unenviable task of what was almost a frontal assault, passing immediately to the right of the hill.

We pushed on up the gentle incline. 'That's it,' said the young lieutenant at my side, 'That's Invergordon Trench.' The lead platoon, murky figures not ten feet from us, began rushing forward to storm the second line.

The barrage had done its work admirably. The coiled loops of glistening wire were mangled and torn. Huge gaps were visible. The trench's occupants were either dead or gone. Together with the lieutenant and his platoon, I jumped into the darkened trench. The rest of C Company followed and we headed southwards. I knew the timber clad walls would bring us along the crest of Orange Hill. We were moving fast, hoping to catch any defenders unaware.

The barrage thundered on eastwards, thrashing all before it like a hundred giant flails, the rest of the battalion in its wake, the next trench system only 500 yards further.

A rattle of gunfire sounded from ahead. Mainly I heard the thump of my boots on the trench mats and my own quick breathing. I'd fixed bayonet when the others had, and in the darkness nicked my finger. It had bled profusely for a minute leaving my right hand sticky to the touch. If I could get through the charge with only a bloody finger I'd be happy. The trench made a sudden turn and we arrived at a junction.

To the right, it curved to follow the ridge line southwards. To the left, it split again into two, with both branches heading eastward to the hill-top. The squad stood poised, waiting. The lieutenant looked at me. It was a question. To which I answered by pointing right. That's where the defenders would be, gunning for the 5th CMR as they ascended the southern slope of the hill. The German support lines and the regimental staff would be at the hill-top. We could worry about them later.

The lieutenant nodded and waved us right, like a baseball coach as we rounded third and made for home. I went with the lead squad.

The trench was of a standard British design, with some unmistakeably German touches here and there, like concrete steps leading down to a dug-out. The trench zig-zagged its way further southwards until, rounding a corner, we came face-to-face with five machine gunners. Fortunately, it was not entirely face to face; they were gathered in a sand-bagged alcove, fiddling with an ammunition belt, their backs to us, their gun facing downhill.

Five feet away, I brandished the Lee-Enfield menacingly at my hip, ready to plunge it at the first one that moved. 'Hands in the air,' I shouted. Naturally, I said it in English, but even to a high-school drop-out from some hamlet in Bavaria, the meaning was crystal-clear. Beside me, a handful of others were gathered, ready to finish anything I couldn't. Prisoners either went willingly or not at all. There wasn't much appetite for offering second chances these days – nor first ones, for that matter.

This crew chose wisely and with alacrity the hands shot up. They looked surprised, which itself was hardly surprising, blasted out of their beds half an hour ago and already facing a cluster of hard-looking types with bayonets who'd turned up from behind. A stream of soldiers in the trench filed past, ignoring the drawn faces now eyeing me nervously.

The lieutenant appeared. 'Atkins, you take them,' he ordered. 'When we have a few more you can escort them back to the divisional cage.'

'So far so good, Lieutenant,' I said. Lipsett had been adamant we quickly secure the hill if we were to take and hold Monchy. 'What do you say to securing the hill-top?' I asked. He agreed. Before long the lieutenant was able to report to his colonel that the battalion had itself a new headquarters, in a dug-out near the crest of Orange Hill. Up until a half hour before, it had belonged to a regiment of the 214th Infantry Division. They'd fitted it with electric light, of all things.

It was there, only a few minutes after four a.m. that a runner appeared. 'We've taken Jericho and Jerusalem Trenches, sir,' he said, addressing the colonel. 'We're cleaning up the last of them now.'

The battalion commander looked pleased. 'Congratulations, sir,' I said. 'Shall I send a runner back?'

'Yes, good idea. But you won't need to send a runner, Major,' he said. 'Flash Brigade HQ,' he instructed the signaller. 'We've captured Orange Hill. Send white over white over white.' The crucial first stage was complete.

By 6 a.m. it was past dawn and brightening fast, despite the smoke that lingered. I was anxious to know how Major Rhoades' 5th Mounted Rifles were faring. They were to continue and breach the hill-top fortress of Monchy-le-Preux. Small parties of the 2nd Mounted Rifles had already gone south to establish contact, but hadn't yet reported back. I wasn't surprised. No one ever knew what the hell was going on during a battle. Of course, the principal reason Lipsett had sent me here was to ensure that he did know, so I had my work cut out for me.

I carried on along Invergordon Trench and was soon confronted by large squads of soldiers moving across the southern slopes. 'Are you fellows with the 5th CMR?' I asked one bunch.

They laughed dismissively. 'No, sir, we're with the 1st CMR.' Which was logical enough when I thought about it. They were passing through to help press the attack on Monchy; the 5th would veer right while the 1st would encircle it on the left. But where in God's name was the 5th CMR?

I calmed down a little when I came upon a mopping-up party bearing the beaver-embossed badge of that battalion. They were south of the hill, heading eastwards. 'We had a stiff fight at the beginning, but we made it past,' one of them told me. 'We captured a few trophies along the way, didn't we, boys?' he said, addressing his mates. 'Yeah, a couple of trench mortars, two field guns and at least half-a-dozen heavy MGs, Major,' piped up another.

Eventually I tracked down the battalion HQ, but Major Rhoades had left. The staff said the assault on the town had begun. Pleased with the news but frustrated at not finding Rhoades, I left almost immediately. I began picking my way across the shell-torn fields and abandoned trenches in the direction of Monchy, hoping to run into him.

Closer to the village, I caught sight of a huge wooden cross on the otherwise near barren slope of the hill, fashioned from the trunk of a single tree. Its smooth lines were scarred and pocked by bullets, but its humble majesty was undiminished, a totem pole of the faith that dominated the western approaches. With any sense the French would have erected it on the other side of town; to ward off the demons from the east. Buried in the hill, and virtually underneath the cross, I stumbled upon a simple but sturdy German dug-out. The roof was reinforced with lengths of logs, like a frontier cabin, but it was empty. I checked carefully, wary that I might be running ahead of the battalion. From the direction of the village sounded a series of explosions.

I quickened my pace and took the rifle from my shoulder. Monchy was never going to be easy – that I knew. And as if to illustrate, ten feet on, two soldiers from the battalion appeared, heading for the rear. Both were wounded.

'What happened?' I asked, as they drew abreast of me.

'Gibbs and I got hit by some flying shrapnel, sir. The Hun are shooting pineapples all over Monchy.'

'And the attack?'

Uncertainly they shrugged. But their faces brightened as a file of almost fifty prisoners, a sour looking Boche officer in the lead, approached under guard.

'Rutherford,' I heard one of them mumble to the other. They both grinned. For some reason I didn't make anything of it. I gave them some water before moving on.

Further up the hill I spotted the first of the villages' squat and ruined stone houses. Columns of smoke and the crump of explosions came from ahead. Perhaps that's why I almost missed the pill-box. But in some well-ingrained instinct, or sense of self-preservation, I spotted something off to the side and my brain made the connection. I dropped to the ground.

I waited for the shots, but they didn't come. Then they did. But they weren't aimed at me as I expected. A phalanx of our men were storming the pill-box. I rose to my feet and rushed to join them.

By the time I arrived – a distance of maybe forty yards – it was over. The soldiers were rounding up a platoon of the enemy, more than thirty of them.

'It's a strong position,' I said to one of the men. 'Four machine guns too, I see. They could have held us up for a very long time here. Well done.'

The soldier pointed at a young officer who'd appeared. 'It's the lieutenant's second pill-box of the morning, sir,' he said. 'He captured the one at the crucifix by himself.'

'Did he now?' I said. I turned towards the officer. To my surprise I recognized him. 'Rutherford! Lieutenant Charlie Rutherford,' I cried.

'Hello, Major MacPhail. I didn't expect to see you here.'

'Yes, it's a long way from Arvillers, that's for sure. Congratulations are in order, though. You've just singlehandedly opened the door to Monchy.' I paused, a thought coming to me. 'You realize, Lieutenant, this was supposed to be a 3rd Division effort? The general is a big believer in teamwork. Now I'm somehow going to have to explain it was all a solo action…'

Rutherford looked away, embarrassed.

It turned out I actually underestimated what he'd done. The entire bastion of Monchy-le-Preux, with its clear views to east and west, fell within less than thirty minutes. When the confirmation arrived, I couldn't help but think back to what I'd overheard one of Rutherford's young soldiers saying earlier; 'Sort of makes you wonder why we all don't go home. Leave the war in Lieutenant Rutherford's hands…'

As suggestions go it had some real merit. But I knew something the private didn't; this was only just the beginning. General Currie's sights were fixed on a fortified line far to the east.

CHAPTER 11

27th of August, 1918
Bois du Sart (2000 yards east of Monchy-le-Preux), France

I had one clip left and maybe five rounds in the rifle. That made fifteen. It wasn't a lot. If I'd kept my wits about me earlier this morning I would have been more economical with my ammunition. Although that's easier said than done when there's a gang of Boche headed your way. But at least I had the Webley and a bayonet.

A lieutenant suddenly appeared in our midst. Dick Ineson of D Company. He was a piano stringer by trade. I don't know any other piano stringers, not having a piano myself, although if I did I can't imagine inviting Ineson in. He had a huge white bandage plastered to the side of his face and his head was wrapped in a matching white turban, a wound from an hour or two ago. He should have been in a hospital bed. 'Listen up men,' he said in a muffled tone. 'I have yesterday's special order from General Currie: "I desire to congratulate all concerned on the magnificent success achieved this day. It has paved the way for further success tomorrow. Keep constantly in mind Stonewall Jackson's motto: Press Forward."'

The grimy looking private beside me mumbled, 'Who the hell is Stonewall Jackson?'

'A Confederate general in the American civil war,' I answered. Then, sheepishly, I realized why nobody likes know-it-all lawyers. Which, on reflection, is why I don't generally spread the details of my old profession too widely. That's one concern piano stringers don't have.

The private reflected on what I'd said. 'He must have been quite a general, sir.'

'Well, I don't think General Currie respects Stonewall because he was accidently shot by his own men,' I replied. That notion seemed to amuse the private. He excused himself and edged over to a few of his mates. I needn't have worried that I'd left him with the wrong impression, for only minutes later I heard one of them jokingly ask the platoon sergeant when they could "press forward" again.

'I know you,' I said, examining the sergeant more closely. His face was brown and leathery, the result of a hard life lived outdoors. He carried himself with a casual ease that suggested he'd seen it all before, which he likely had. 'You're Clarkson, aren't you? I remember you from Lens.'

'Yeah, I was there alright, sir,' he replied gruffly. He didn't mention remembering me. I didn't dwell on it. I guessed his tone had everything to do with the fact that he'd been up all night, marched four miles from Orange Hill, fighting since five this morning.

'I thought so,' I said, and meant to continue.

'The Hun,' the sergeant bellowed. 'They're coming again. Another counter-attack.'

One of the Lewis guns opened up. I looked out through the brush. A long line of them stepped onto the fields from the trees behind. A swarm of grey was intent on one thing – pushing us out of the Bois du Sart, dead set on preventing an advance of a single yard further. Their generals knew all too well what was at stake.

The day before, the battalions of the 7th Brigade had passed through Monchy and continued the fight into the swathe of trenches and rusting wire that was the old German line, immediately east of the village. It was the second obstacle to overcome before the D-Q Line. They had had a tough go of it, not least because they beat off a succession of counter-attacks well into the evening.

This morning in a cold driving rain the attack resumed. It had been broiling hot the entire summer, but the moment we launched an attack, it began to pour. I was with the 58th Battalion out of central Ontario. I'd just moved up to the wood, captured only fifteen minutes earlier, to see what the problem was. As was so often the case in this war, there wasn't a single problem, but several. The life-threatening one was streaming towards us from Jigsaw Wood via Hatchet Wood, less than a thousand yards to the northeast.

'Put up some covering fire,' yelled Sergeant Clarkson to his squad. 'Our patrol is being driven back.' A small group of soldiers, their tin hats easily visible to the naked eye, was pulling back from Hatchet Wood. The land was broken and uneven from years of fighting, treacherous from the morning's rain. A light drizzle still fell. Long grass had grown in the desolation. The patrol knelt and returned fire before scrambling back another few yards towards us. They took the last few yards at a sprint.

A road passed along the northern side of the Bois du Sart. From that direction, and from the fields in front, the enemy came. There was a whistle and some cracking noises, tree branches tumbling down. Further off I heard the unmistakable TUF-TUF-TUF of a barking Maxim.

I fell to the ground beside Lieutenant Ineson and a handful of others. The Lewis gunners were putting a new pan on their gun. I yanked out my Webley and pushed open the cylinder to double-check: six rounds, it was fully loaded. I holstered it again and raised the Lee-Enfield. It was five minutes past seven and the day's attack was already two hours underway.

'Let them have it,' roared Ineson, as the first *stahlhelms*, foliage wrapped around their helmets, rose up from the grass and began an imprudent rush from 200 yards away.

This time I aimed carefully. Every bullet had to count. I exhaled in relief as I saw one drop, and then another. And then a miss. Not too quickly, I told myself. *Concentrate.* I worked the bolt back and forth and squinted through the sights looking for a fresh target. I heard the Lewis gun chattering away. There was a stench of gunpowder and smoke in the air, and a smell I couldn't place but likened to fear. I held my breath again an instant, then gently squeezed the trigger. They were dropping like flies but even now the first of them were entering the wood, a short sprint away. I clipped in my last magazine. The soldiers beside me were fidgeting. They'd stopped firing, seemingly ready to take to their heels.

Sergeant Clarkson roared, 'Let's get 'em, boys.' He rose to his feet, his bayoneted rifle protruding before him. My heart was beating. I rose and followed. So did the remnants of D Company.

We rushed at the oncoming figures in the trees. There was a burst of shots tightly spaced. Sergeant Clarkson shuddered, came to a halt, then sank awkwardly to the ground. His head slumped onto the forest floor. To my right another soldier crumpled away. I screamed in rage and quickened my step. Beside me I heard the shouts of others. We tore into their lines shooting and thrusting, and wildly thrusting again, like madmen. The survivors, only a handful, fled eastwards. Few made it far.

When it was over I sank into a pile and my breathing slowed. The red mist that had enveloped my brain lifted, like dew on a warm summer morning. 'We did it, sir,' breathed the private, lying beside me. For a precious moment I closed my eyes, inhaled deeply and heard silence.

It didn't last long.

I was hardly back on my feet before a soldier came stumbling into our midst. 'They're into the wood, sir, below us in the southeast corner,' he panted. He was reporting to Lieutenant Ineson.

'They're going to surround us,' I told the lieutenant. 'They've got the road and Tusk Trench on the left. Now they're coming from the right.'

'We're running out of options,' mused Ineson. While I pondered what possible other options there were, another runner approached. 'B Company is counter-attacking from the south,' I heard him say. Whether a counter-attack on a counter-attack could be called a counter-attack was a question almost as difficult to answer as how this bloody war started in the first place. But the news was welcome.

Ineson ordered a handful of the riflemen, and two Lewis guns, to hold fast in this corner. The rest, including me, set out through the ravaged underbrush to drive the Germans out. Close to the centre of the wood we came across the first of them. There was a rapid succession of shots and the Germans dropped. Rifles to our shoulders, fingers tight on the trigger guards, we pushed carefully on.

One moment Ineson was moving forward, five paces to my left. The next, his head whipped violently back. The lieutenant slumped to the ground. There was no need to look further, although I did. It was a scene I would not forget.

More shots rang out, and the rest of the company advancing in a rough line through the trees, now abandoned any attempts at cover and moved rapidly through the brush. By seven-thirty the Germans were beaten. If there were any prisoners taken I didn't see them.

When the gas shells began to fall in the Bois du Sart, I left. A cynic might have made a connection. Of course that wasn't it; I'd been through too much with the men of the 58th to abandon them without good reason. I needed a telephone, or a runner, or anything to contact headquarters. I wasn't here simply because I could hold a rifle, I reminded myself.

Halfway down Poodle Trench I spotted a familiar face. 'Jucksch,' I said with astonishment. 'It's you.' He stared at me, first puzzled, then the recognition clicked in – I'd tagged along on a now famous raid of his many months before.

'Major MacPhail! I didn't expect to see you. You were assigned to HQ?' I saw him glance at the rifle I was holding. It was an accoutrement most officers did without.

'I am,' I said, 'only General Lipsett feels uneasy when I'm not out leading the advance.' And then, lifting the rifle to explain, added, 'And I feel a lot better doing that when I'm carrying one of these.'

He smiled. 'Welcome. We can sure use another man and another rifle.'

'I'm afraid I'm just passing through,' I said. 'I see you made major. Congratulations.'

'Thanks,' he replied. 'They made me second in command of the battalion.'

'Ah, then it's fortunate I ran into you. Your men in Bois du Sart are holding fast, but they're in bad shape. They've had a lot of casualties. And you've got a nasty problem in Jigsaw Wood from what I can see. The Boche are pouring in reinforcements. It's a shame we couldn't hold it yesterday.'

'Yes,' he agreed. 'It's been see-sawing back and forth all morning. The Boche keep regrouping and sending in new counter-attacks. They've got a lot of MGs. Pelves is also a problem.' He said something

103

else, but his words were lost in the sound of a large blast from the direction I'd just come.

The small village of Pelves was on the southern bank of the Scarpe, less than a mile to the north. From the aerial photographs, I knew it harboured a battery of field guns. Its surrounding trenches had a clear line of fire across the rolling fields. Apparently they were taking a toll on Jucksch's battalion.

'Pelves, you say. I wanted to ask about that. Our left hasn't kept up as you probably know. The problem is the enfilade fire from across the river. This morning the Imperials finally went in to take Highland Hill, which would solve the problem. But I don't know how it went.'

Jucksch sighed. 'We'll cross our fingers. I don't see how we're expected to push on to Boiry this way, not with our left in the air. We're dangerously exposed, MacPhail.' I nodded. It was precisely why I needed to find a telephone, and fast.

'Actually the orders are not just for Boiry, Jucksch. The division is to crash the Fresnes-Rouvroy line, and push beyond it.' Jucksch was a determined man, I'd seen that before, but his expression buckled when he heard this. 'Look at it this way,' I said, 'at least they've left Berlin for tomorrow.'

Walking back across the fields westwards, towards the ruined hill-top citadel of Monchy where I hoped to find a brigade headquarters, I stumbled a few times on the uneven ground. The grass concealed ancient shell holes amongst the many fresh ones. In the distance was the shell of a burned-out tank. We only had a handful. Torn and tangled wire hung from double and triple lines of fence posts. In the trenches, a few men were going about their business here and there. Outnumbering them were the bodies, sprawled grotesquely on the trench floors or caught on the wire. Mainly they were theirs, but there were plenty of ours, too. There'd been no time and no one to clear it up. It was a wonder we'd made it through this mile of horror. And I knew the worst was to come – it was a long way yet before we reached the D-Q Line.

As the morning progressed, the rain stopped. The skies, etched a uniform hazy grey, brightened. I squinted as I clambered down into the dank gloom of a large dug-out, built into the hill on the fringes of Monchy. A wooden sign outside announced it as belonging to the *Infanterie-Regiment nr.363*. The war had moved on, even if the signage hadn't. The signallers had strung a field telephone line here this morning. I was in luck.

Lipsett was out at the front, so I spoke with Colonel Hore-Ruthven. 'The 51st took Highland Hill, but they lost it again,' he told me, when I asked about our sagging left.

There was a long silence on the line, during which I smacked my knee with one hand and cursed under my breath. Finally, I said, 'So it's up to us, sir... as usual...' Hore-Ruthven let it pass, and I continued. 'Well, sir, on this side of the river we're going to have to do something about our left flank. Can't we send in the PPCLI or the 49th? Even another heavy bombardment of Pelves would go a long way. At least the Boche would be preoccupied with something other than shooting at us.'

The line crackled, although it could have been my head playing tricks. I stared at the German gas mask hanging on the wall opposite, awaiting his reply. I felt a little dizzy. It had been a long time since I'd eaten. I couldn't remember the last time I'd slept.

'I agree it's a dicey situation, MacPhail. I'll speak with General Lipsett about it.' I pictured him furrowing his brow. Knowing the colonel he'd arrange something.

'Oh, and one more thing, sir. We're running up against new regiments. They're from the 35th Division, moved in last night from Douai, according to a prisoner. Apparently, it's sheer chaos on their side. We are getting ahead, Colonel, but we're paying a terrible price.'

I heard what sounded like a sigh. 'I know, Major. I know.'

With the call completed, I moved outside and climbed up to the Observation Post. From there, at the peak of the hill, was a stunning view to the south and east. On any other day you might have called it pretty. A group of men stood in front talking. A well-turned out officer and two civilians were gazing south.

'The 2nd Division is moving on Chérisy and Vis-en-Artois and is to cross the Sensée River. Then they're to break through the

Fresnes-Rouvroy line,' the officer was explaining. The civilians were war correspondents, writing in their notebooks. I took out my glasses and looked for myself.

From a ridgeline under Monchy the land to the east fell away into a shallow dale. On the maps it was drawn as a maze of blue trenches and a veritable forest of wire, with the two villages and the river behind. Even at two or three miles there was no mistaking the ferocity of the battle. White and black puffs speckled the valley. When the wind eased for a moment, there was the sound of gunfire.

For some reason my eye caught sight of a lorry closer by, passing Monchy and slowly winding its way along on the tree-lined Arras-Cambrai road, our vital artery. Men, material, food, ammunition. Everything two divisions in battle required had to move along that single road. Vaguely I heard a boom in the distance. As I watched, the lorry disappeared in a ball of flame and black smoke, the charred remains crackling on for minutes. Small arms ammunition. The liaison officer was pointing north. He realized it too; the shell had come from Pelves, or across the Scarpe – our open left flank.

Whatever I might have hoped after Amiens, the Germans weren't played out by a long shot. The way the casualties were piling up, the real question was: were we?

CHAPTER 12

28th of August, 1918
Near Boiry-Notre-Dame, France

Today was a day for unfinished business: Pelves, Jigsaw Wood, Boiry-Notre-Dame, and the last major hurdle before the D-Q Line, the Fresnes-Rouvroy Switch. Lipsett was throwing in all three of the division's battered brigades. There were to be no excuses.

'It makes sense, MacPhail,' said "Dangerous Dan" Ormond tugging at his ear. It was hard to fathom how the man did it, but he looked as if he'd marched straight off the parade ground. Only I knew for a fact he'd been going non-stop for more than two days, and it was a little before 7 a.m., with a long day ahead. I suspect he was rather less awed by my appearance than I was by his. He did, however, see something in my idea for the attack.

'When I spoke with General Lipsett, he told me he could give you the entire divisional artillery for the barrage,' I added. His nickname notwithstanding, the 9th Brigade's commander was not the kind to court danger unnecessarily. This information appeared to please him, for he nodded thoughtfully. I knew Ormond from when he was a major and I was a lowly private, and our battalion was swimming in a cloud of gas in the mud of Ypres. Now I was a major and he was a brigadier-general. While that's akin to the difference between a muskrat and a bear, Ormond was responsible for the main thrust of the attack. He was smart enough to know he could use all the help he could get – even from a muskrat. It didn't hurt that General Lipsett had sent me.

'A thousand yards is a narrow, not to mention dangerous front to put four battalions through,' he said. 'Although it's true their artillery fire is scattered…'

'Exactly,' I interrupted excitedly, 'and their machine guns are the real threat, sir. If we can take a lot of them out of action with the barrage, we can pierce their defences, take Boiry, and roll up the Boche line from the rear.'

Ormond looked at me a little peevishly. 'Yes, I'm not a complete fool, MacPhail.'

'No, sir,' I mumbled, studying my boots.

'You're right, though,' he mused. 'The 49th is going into Pelves…' He paused, glancing at his watch. '… Right about now. And then Dyer's going to tackle Jigsaw Wood. It would definitely help if we outflanked the Boche on his right.'

I nodded. Yesterday, Hore-Ruthven had been true to his word. The Princess Patricias had battered their way towards Pelves, but ran out of bombs and were forced to withdraw. Then our batteries of 18-pounders, arrayed on the far slope of Orange Hill, pulverised the village into the evening. There were reports the Germans had pulled out. We'd soon see.

'Well, it appears as if you've convinced the general,' said a voice sometime later. It belonged to the brigade major. He smiled thinly which, as it turned out, was the sugar coating on his message. 'Would you mind following up the attack in the field? The general wanted me to ask. We lost our own intelligence officer yesterday afternoon.' I gave the response expected of me. Sometimes I'm my own worst enemy.

Back at brigade HQ it had all seemed so simple. That was another irrefutable rule of war; the further away you are, the easier it seems. Now, viewing the rows of wire, trenches and machine-gun nests that made up the Fresnes-Rouvroy Switch, I had a bitter dryness in my mouth. This was *virgin* soil; no allied soldier had set foot here since 1914. I tucked the field glasses away and turned at the sound of feet.

A platoon of the 52nd Battalion, the same lads who had stormed Damery, were arriving. They'd only just made it, and I could see they were exhausted. They collapsed in the grass.

'Where are the rest of you?' I asked their lieutenant.

'Only 220 men answered the battalion roll call this morning, sir,'

'220. That's a single company, not an entire battalion, lieutenant.'

'We lost a lot of men yesterday. All the units are mixed up, so I expect we'll find some more, but that's what we have.' He shrugged, a gesture halfway between resignation and defiance. 'We'll make the most of it, sir.'

A lithe-looking captain approached. 'Young, I'll be damned, is that you?' I said in astonishment. 'After that show two weeks ago at Damery, I didn't expect to see you again so soon. Although we do have another hostile village that needs capturing…'

Captain Young gave me a friendly salute. 'So I hear,' he said. 'Nice to see you, Major. You're becoming our lucky charm, sir. I'm glad you're here. We can sure use an extra man.'

I moaned. 'That's the first thing everyone says, when they see me,' I said. 'My plan was to accompany the follow-up companies, only I see there's so few of you left, there aren't any.' It wasn't that I dreaded the idea of going in with the assault. I was supposed to be keeping our commanders advised on the battle's progress, not beating recalcitrant Württemburgers away from their MG08s. It looked as if I was going to have to do both.

'Fix your bayonet, Major,' Young advised, and I complied. It was the sort of practical advice best not ignored. This time I took more care.

After a lot of rain in the past several days, the morning was warm and bright. There was no reason to think this would be anything other than a picture-perfect day in the French countryside. Until 11 a.m., that is. Then the barrage came thundering down, the roar of the artillery and heavy machine guns put an angry end to any misplaced daydreams.

The men rose and rushed along the narrow dirt path eastwards, across the fields towards the smoke. Earth was flying and fire flashing, but the lads of the 52nd had a vigour and determination I wouldn't have thought possible. Behind us, thick plumes of white and black and showers of dirt erupted as the German guns responded. Who knows how many those guns had killed or wounded in the past two days, but Ormond was right; their coordination was off. Our gamble might just work.

Crossing a small dirt road, Boiry Lane, we came to the first swath of wire. We were going to encircle Boiry from the south and east. The 58th Battalion would follow in our footsteps, then repeat the stunt at Artillery Hill, a little north of the village. The wire belonged to the Fresnes-Rouvroy Switch. It ran southeast across the Scarpe, thus diagonally across the Corps front until it intersected the D-Q Line at an angle a mile or two below us.

Every vale and peak in this rolling country had a military significance. Even the rawest of recruits soon understood that when a Hun was peering down from a height, you didn't want to be in a hollow next to him. Which was why Boiry and Artillery Hill were our next objectives. They rose above the terrain to the west, higher even then the Bois du Sart and the Bois du Vert. The machine guns they concealed had ruthlessly beaten off our attacks yesterday. However, before we could reach them, we had to brave their fire and breach the wire and the rest of the Fresnes-Rouvroy Line.

'Thank God. The wire's cut,' a private exclaimed to no one in particular. We moved quickly through the first row of fence posts and made for the second.

There we came to a soldier sprawled on the ground, moaning loudly and clutching his middle. His helmet was beside him where it had fallen in the grass, his auburn hair even redder in the midday sun. The boy's youthful freckled face was pale, contorted in pain, a dark glistening blotch widening over his stomach.

'It's Rusty,' I heard one of our group say. 'It looks bad,' whispered another.

'Let's go boys,' commanded the sergeant. 'Keep moving. Before the barrage ends.'

Every head in the squad turned and stared as we moved by, but we didn't halt. A few mumbled well-meaning words of encouragement. We all knew they were likely futile.

Ten feet on, I heard him cry, 'Oh, Mum, Mum…,' a plea of desperation that pierced the very marrow of my bones. The pain had become too much to bear.

Then there was a harsh rattle of a distant machine gun, another immediately after. Were we going to meet the same fate as the lads yesterday?

'Keep low,' shouted Young.

I ran abreast of him bent over, keeping a low profile. 'It came from Boiry way, I think,' I said.

'I thought so too,' he responded and plunged ahead.

To the south was more gunfire. Two privates exchanged ominous looks. 'The 116th,' I said. 'They're on our right.'

Stepping through the torn tangles of the last row of wire our lead man went down. A harsh rattle sounded from in front. Perhaps a hundred yards away, a lone gunner's helmet peaked out atop the sandbagged parapet of the trench: Edward Trench. A slit in the sandbags was spitting fire. I dropped to my knee, and fired off a quick shot, then another. More soldiers were collapsing. I fell prone.

Around me others did the same. 'Outflank them,' roared Young, crouching behind a fence post. A smattering of men, one party going left and the other right, made a mad dash forwards before diving to the ground amidst a burst of gunfire. 'Where the hell is Edmonds?' shouted the captain.

Beside me it turned out. I hadn't noticed earlier, but unlike the rest of us the private to my right was carrying a Ross rifle with scope. The Ross rifle is longer and sleeker compared to the muscular Lee-Enfields and I hated it with a passion. I'd damn near died when mine had jammed in the mud of Flanders back in 1915. At the first opportunity, I dropped it in the mud and scooped up the Lee-Enfield of a luckless British Tommy. But that was long ago, back when I believed the war would be over by Christmas. Much later, when cynicism had taken root, I was assured the Ross was a highly accurate weapon. A scout sniper related that he could put a .303 round in a bulls-eye at 600 yards with a Ross. Naturally, I didn't believe him. Until today, when young Edmonds pulled the trigger. Through an opening no wider than the palm of my hand, he put a bullet in the German gunner. Or at least he must have, for the firing abruptly ceased. The company rallied and rushed the trench.

'Watch out for others!' I shouted as I dropped into the trench. No one answered. In the long moment that followed I sensed something was amiss.

A log dropped on my helmet with a loud clang. I reeled backwards. Dazed, I made to turn. An entrenching tool was rewinding back above his head, the sharp edge of the shovel hanging menacingly in the air. I kicked. A hard, desperate kick with my heel. It hit him midriffs and he stumbled backwards. His arm fell and the shovel clattered onto the wooden duckboards. Winded, he glared at me, his helmet tipped a little off centre, the finger of a dark moustache holding up his lip. In his eyes I saw a madness, and a twinge of fear, too. I pulled out my Webley and fired. He sagged into a heap.

Looking around, other small skirmishes were ending, most in the abrupt retort of a revolver shot or the thrust of a bayonet. There were only a half-dozen of them. Within minutes the trench was ours. I removed my helmet – now bearing an indentation the size of a moon crater – wiped my brow and breathed a sigh of relief. It might just have been tiredness. I was dead on my feet and my head felt like a crushed peach. B Company had moved through in the wake of the barrage, but this lot had survived unnoticed, and emerged the moment we came along. The fog of war had nearly done us in.

'Major?' Young was beckoning. 'I'm considering a change of plan. Instead of sending a company into the village, I want to take the battalion behind Boiry and surround them. What do you think?'

I thought about it for a second. 'Good thinking,' I said. 'Leave a few riflemen and a Lewis gunner or two to keep them busy, surprise them from the east.' He needn't have consulted me; it was his show and his battalion, but Young was a smart officer.

We walked another few hundred yards and then wheeled left into the shattered village. Not far behind I saw the lead company of the 58th. They would swing further around the village and move north to envelop Artillery Hill and its thickets of machine gunners.

The barrage had been cruelly effective. Pieces of stone littered the road as we cautiously entered the village. Most of the small stone houses exhibited ragged holes. There wasn't a German in sight, yet I could hear the clatter from their machine guns.

'Let's root them out,' said Young. After a hurried exchange, we split into small groups to comb the town for the remaining defenders.

With a handful of privates, my party surprised four. They were raking the gentle western slope leading up to Boiry. A single shot in the air proved sufficient inducement for a show of hands.

I caught up with Captain Young not long after, near the remains of the church where tens of Germans were being herded into file for the long march back to the divisional cage. Whilst talking to him another bedraggled party of Germans appeared. 'That's the last of them, sir,' reported the corporal who was shepherding them along. 'They heard us coming and threw in the towel. We didn't have to fire a shot.'

When the message from the 58th arrived to say they'd taken Artillery Hill, I slumped down in the shadow of a house to write a short report and eat the apple I'd found on one of the Germans. I don't think I've ever tasted anything so delicious. I must have dozed off.

With a start I opened my eyes and grasped for my revolver. Someone was nudging my arm. 'Sir,' said the corporal. 'It's alright, sir. The captain asked me to tell you we're to be relieved. The 4th Imperials will take over our positions tonight.'

I smiled at him and he smiled back. Despite everything we'd taken the objectives. Had I known the Brits would turn up well after midnight, in a wild driving rain, and I would spend half the night marching six miles back to the battalion's new digs, I might have kept my emotions in better check.

CHAPTER 13

29ᵗʰ of August, 1918
Château de Duisans, Duisans, France

'What on Earth did you run into, MacPhail, a tank?' said General Lipsett, when he saw me stumbling in his direction early the next morning. The general was cradling a cup of tea in his hands, conversing with Captain Cunningham on the steps of the imposing white stone château we had occupied in my absence. At the general's words, Cunningham's features assumed a smirk the size of Big Bertha. I think he was still a little sore about the corner bed in London Cave I'd gone to so much trouble arranging for him – the one under the dripping ceiling.

'A shovel, sir.' I removed the battered disk of tin that masqueraded as a helmet and placed it under my arm.

'So that stretch with the Australians a while back has turned you into a proper *Digger*, after all,' Lipsett said. 'I might have known.'

It was a weak joke, even by my standards, but any witticism I might have fired back was mired in a No-Man's-Land between sleep deprivation and a raging headache. I simply grimaced and stood wavering on my feet.

'It's all right, Major. Get some sleep. We'll talk later,' said Lipsett.

Later happened sooner than I might have hoped. I managed a few hours of blissful oblivion before being roused by a zealous orderly.

From his depressingly neat uniform, he hadn't seen any action beyond the parade ground. He was new, one of the first batches of conscripts – not that that excused him. 'Keep your pants on, lad,' I snarled. 'Once we have you in the front line, you'll have plenty of opportunities to impress the general.' He stared at me with popping eyes and a flush to his cheeks. I felt a slight pang of guilt.

Lipsett looked up as I entered his office, if you could call it that – it was big enough to house a battalion or two, maybe even three; the battalions were not what they'd been three days before.

'It's quite a place, sir,' I said, taking in the elegant cream wallpaper and elaborate oaken wainscoting. Behind the general's desk was a stone fireplace that was crying out for a couple sides of beef to roast. If it hadn't been August and stiflingly hot, I would have offered to fire it up. Not that there were any sides of beef at hand. And Lipsett, for all his Irish roots, wasn't really the sort for an impromptu barbeque.

'Yes it is,' agreed the general. 'You'll be interested to know, MacPhail, the architect is the very one that designed the Abbey of Mont St. Eloi.'

I stared up at the massive dark rafters far above our heads. 'Luckily for him there's not much repair work needed, sir. He can concentrate on the Abbey.'

Lipsett permitted himself a watery smile. But this was no exaggeration on my part. The magnificent Abbey of Mont St. Eloi, from a time when men had built things of beauty in France rather than destroying them, had been reduced to two skeletal towers of stone in a barren wasteland. St. Eloi wasn't far from Duisans, where we were settling in. Peering due north from the village, which bumped up against the western boundary of Arras, I'd even glimpsed the Abbey's towers in the distance as I arrived and felt a cold shiver.

After a moment, Lipsett asked, 'How are they holding up?' I presumed he was referring to the Germans.

'The first day they were clearly caught off guard. They thought the Corps was still near Amiens. But by the second, when their reinforcements began to arrive, they fought for every foot. And by the third…' I took a deep breath. From Lipsett's pained expression I saw that he understood. 'After Amiens, sir, I hoped we'd crushed their will to fight. But unfortunately I didn't see much sign of that. Their machine gunners remained at their guns even when it was patently hopeless.

Enemy or not, it was difficult not to admire them. That being said, we did find one group who were chained to their guns. Either way, through devotion to duty or fear, they put up a stiff fight.'

Lipsett considered what I'd told him. 'General Ormond was very complimentary about you,' he said, finally. Mildly surprised I raised my eyes to his. 'There was some initial confusion whether we were talking about the same man,' he added.

I opened my mouth to respond, then saw that familiar twinkle in his eyes. I should have known better.

'You did fine, Major,' he said.

'Thank you, sir. And how did the rest of the division fare yesterday?'

'We took Boiry and Artillery Hill, as you know, as well as Pelves and Jigsaw Wood, and pushed our right ahead, but not quite to Haucourt. As to the 2nd Division, they had another gruelling day, I'm afraid. Despite a terrific effort they didn't make it more than a few hundred yards. They fought off a score of counter-attacks. But the attack on the D-Q Line won't be long in coming.'

'I suppose the division's work must be considered a success, then, sir,' I said softly.

'Five and a half miles through deeply entrenched terrain,' exclaimed Lipsett. 'We completely shattered two of their divisions, and part of a third. 1600 unwounded prisoners, many more dead and wounded, almost 300 machine guns, 60 mortars and artillery pieces. *And* we took the Fresnes-Rouvray Line in our sector. The division did itself proud, Malcolm.'

'And our casualties, sir?'

'2700,' he said. 'Most of them from machine gun fire.'

'It's a heavy price to pay.'

'It is. And you're probably wondering if it was worth it?'

Not for the first time Lipsett had taken the shortcut. When it came to what I was thinking, Lipsett always seemed a track length ahead. I nodded.

'You probably don't know this, but the German High Command ordered a partial withdrawal up to 10 miles in places, the night following our initial attack. So in addition to smashing some of the enemy's toughest positions, we've gained a lot of ground for the armies to each side. In fact, Field-Marshal Haig even called personally this morning, with his congratulations. He told me our battle here was, and I quote: "The greatest victory which a British Army has ever achieved."'

Predictably, Benoît had his own twist on this news when I told him. 'And to think it wasn't even a British Army, Mac. It was the 2nd and 3rd Divisions.'

'Which is why Currie should seize the opportunity to transform each division into an army,' I said. 'He'd be a field-marshal in no time. Just think, Benoît, you might even make colonel. It has quite a ring to it, don't you think? Colonel DuBois of the Third Canadian Army? Of course, you might have to shave.'

'Ah, you're just jealous, Mac,' he said. 'And you should be, with that baby face of yours. Real men all have beards didn't you know?' Second language or not, Benoît could handle himself fine. That reminded me of something else.

'I don't know what it is about Lipsett, Benoît. Whenever I see him, I always seem to end up on the receiving end of his humour. One moment he's telling me I did fine, and the next he's shipping me off to 1st Division as a liaison officer, in a day or two. In case you didn't know, they're the ones who are supposed to crack the D-Q Line. So you can imagine what that's going to be like. It's almost as if he doesn't want me around.'

Benoît slowly shook his head. '*Sacrément*, Mac, whining again? Are you still too dumb to realize the general is your biggest fan?'

'Easy enough for you to say. I'm the one he breathes fire on.'

Benoît sighed. He sounded exasperated. 'Why do you think he's always ribbing you? All the men love him, but it's you he picks on. Heaven knows why, but he respects you, and he likes you. I think he even appreciates your cynical view of the world.'

'I'm not so sure *that's* true,' I said cautiously.

'Of course it is. You say things he'd like to, but he's a general. And he has *etiquette* to follow.' I could almost hear the guillotine in Benoît's voice; he wasn't exactly an admirer of the army hierarchy, let alone the English class system. I looked sceptical. 'He's saved your bacon more than a few times, Mac. Do you really think he would have got Field-Marshal 'Aig to intervene for just anybody, back when Colonel Wexley-Wigley wanted you locked up because of your big mouth?'

'Whatley-Wigham,' I said, correcting him. 'No. Perhaps not,' I admitted. For all his simple *bonhomme* manner, Benoît had a percep-tiveness about him that never ceased to amaze me.

DuBois shrugged. 'You know, Mac, if it had been me, I would have left you to rot.' At this thought he started to chuckle.

I decided to keep the other mysterious bit of news under my hat. Smith had revealed that three military policemen had come calling in my absence… looking for me.

30th of August

Temporarily far from the action, I felt better than I had in days. We'd earned ourselves this respite. The 1st Division and the 4th Imperial Division had taken our places (our own 4th Division was still making the move northwards). They were to slug through the remaining 2000 yards to a spot where the attack on the D-Q Line could jump off. After the battering we'd gone through, a rest for the division was no idle luxury. Rest, reinforcements and replaced equipment were the order of the day. Even the perilous state of my own equipment had not escaped notice.

'Major MacPhail?' At the mention of my name I looked round and saw the AA & QMG himself, the divisional quartermaster. He was beckoning to me.

'Yes, sir,' I piped up, rising to my feet. I was sitting next to Smith in a large room at the back of the château, where much of the staff was hard at work, even as the sun waned lower.

'I'm told you're needing a new helmet, Major MacPhail,' said Lieutenant-Colonel Gibsone. He was brandishing a spotless dark green model, with a leather strap so new I could smell it.

'Thank you. I am, sir,' I replied.

'I have more than a million rounds of small arms ammunition to replace, and fifty other things, but an urgent request for a new helmet for Major MacPhail came in.'

I was puzzled that my equipment inadequacies should be so widely known, particularly as I hadn't filed any such request myself. But upon seeing the sprightly expressions of those around me, all of whom were watching closely, it became abundantly clear.

'Keep a close eye on this one, Major,' said the colonel, with a wink. 'We've got our hands full keeping the boys in the field in equipment, let alone the headquarters staff.'

'Yes, sir,' I said, as he left.

I took a closer look at the Brodie helmet. It was new, and at nearly 1 ½ pounds every bit as heavy as I remembered. On the front, in black stencilled letters, was written "Digger MacPhail". In the event I hadn't grasped this subtle humour, there was a shovel with a cross through it drawn on top. 'Hilarious,' I muttered. This seemed to amuse the rabble to no end.

'It was DuBois' idea,' confided Tibbett a few minutes later, edging over.

'I might have known,' I replied.

'Have you heard the news?' he asked. '1st Division rolled up the Vis-en-Artois Switch and took Upton Wood. And the 4th Division, Remy and Haucourt. The Imperials even captured Greenland Hill this morning.'

Inwardly I smiled at his description of the 51st Highlanders, conscious of the irony that Tibbett himself was a Brit, and the Highlanders Scottish. 'They took their bloody time at that hill,' I said. 'They're only two days too late.'

Tibbett fiddled with his spectacles, then stared me full in the face. It was the kind of directness he usually tried to avoid. 'Are you feeling all right, Malcolm? You don't seem yourself.'

I shrugged. 'A lot on my mind. Some days, Paul, I wonder whether any of us are going to make it home. It's not terribly conducive to good cheer.'

'There's no reason to be so glum. The war's going better than ever. The Australians moved towards Péronne this morning. Word is they'll attack soon.'

'Really? If they can manage that we'll be across the Somme.' Péronne and the heights in its lee, Mont St. Quentin, were 25 miles south and crucial to crossing the river. I wondered if my old chum Dan Banting of the Australian Corps was brooding over how best to accomplish that.

'Yes, and the Kiwis took Baupaume. The Third Army are also moving forward, as are the French. We're attacking almost daily. For once we're truly taking it to the Boche.'

I nodded. I knew that from Lens to the north of us, down to the Marne River, the Allied armies were exerting a merciless pressure. 'It's the strategy of a hundred punches,' I said. 'Marshal Foch wants to pummel the enemy everywhere. You read about *"Tout le monde à la bataille"*? Well, this is it. Uncertain where the next blow will fall, Ludendorff's reserves will be pinned down. And every so often we throw a few well-timed blows to the gut when he's not expecting it.'

'And that's where the Corps comes in? The punches to the gut?'

'So it would seem.' While I didn't mention the risk of us taking some heavy uppercuts while going for the gut – ask Goggins who went down in the fifth against our own George Baker – I *was* thinking it. That probably didn't contribute to my humour. Three letters from home hadn't helped. Nor did my orders.

'Are you sure?' DuBois asked, a second time, as if he couldn't believe what he was hearing. I could scarcely believe it myself.

We were in the back garden of the château, lazing on the cool grass near a tree, under a sky coloured a deep purplish black. The general had loosened the reins tonight, and while that might have seemed an open invitation to enjoy myself, I was thinking of tomorrow. I was off to the 1st Division. If all went well the attack on the impregnable switch line was to begin the day after, on September 1st. And Lipsett, planning ahead, wanted to know all there was to know – in case we were called upon, again. It was hardly an idle concern. In the distance I heard the steady pounding of our heavy howitzers, even now beating paths through the wire. An aeroplane, one of our scouts, droned over.

I shook my head. 'Yeah, I'm sure,' I replied. 'No more wine. I've got to have my wits about me tomorrow.'

Unburdened by such concerns, Benoît tipped his head back, emptied the bottle and tossed it on the ground beside another. The wine was of the sort charitably known as plonk. I'd had mouthwash that tasted better. And it didn't leave a red stain in my mouth. But then mouthwash wasn't delivered six bottles at a time, by a delicate, blonde beauty in a daringly short dress on a bicycle, all of which presumably accounted for Benoît's enthusiasm. Tibbett was partaking of a fresh bottle. The reason for his enthusiasm was less obvious.

'Paul, you really ought to have taken up drinking when you could have plundered the treasures in your father's cellar, rather than learning to drink this botch,' I admonished him. He'd been a teetotaller up until last spring, not that you would have guessed these days.

Tibbett grinned wildly, his pale grey eyes rolling unsteadily before they focused on me. It was as sure a sign as any that the wine had taken its toll. A few pale hairs under his nose, glistening from the drink or the heat, made a mockery of the moustache he was determined on growing. Try as he might, Major Paul Tibbett was never going to look like a soldier. And as I'd gently tried to tell him, he needn't make the effort. His talents lay elsewhere. He was certainly the smartest chap on the divisional staff. His perceptiveness earlier this evening had surprised me. Even DuBois, who'd been my best friend in the army forever, hadn't picked up on my mood.

'Have some nut cake,' I said. I passed over the rectangular tin, decorated in the colours of the Union Jack, with a red Maple Leaf on it for good measure. God knows where my parents had found such an abomination, although I suspected it was all the rage back home.

Benoît helped himself to a generous piece and passed it on to the others. 'It's tasty,' he offered, still chewing on a bite that could have fed a small French family. He put an arm around my shoulder. His eyes had assumed a cold soberness, his thickly accented words were soft, meant for my ears alone. 'You're with our old division tomorrow. You take care of yourself, Mac.'

CHAPTER 14

31ˢᵗ of August, 1918
A dug-out between Neuville-Vitasse and Wancourt, France

I was a mile east of Neuville-Vitasse, a small village three miles southeast of Arras, better known for its name than its sights, not least because it was here that Field-Marshal Paul von Hindenburg had begun the dreaded fortified line which bore his name. The result was a sight that was anything but attractive. However, since the 2ⁿᵈ Division had so rudely intruded, the first several miles of Hindenburg's line were no longer his. Since then its cavernous dug-outs were as popular amongst the Corp's well-tailored set as any *estimanet* on a hot summer day. A little after 9 a.m. Captain Patterson of the 1ˢᵗ Division greeted me outside the imposing concrete dug-out they had claimed as an Advanced Divisional Headquarters.

Patterson had a pleasant, relaxing manner to him. His rosy cheeks, thin fair eyebrows and sparkling eyes made him look as if he wouldn't hurt a fly. Only later did I notice the coloured pip of a Military Cross on his tunic, just going to show that first impressions are not always to be relied upon. 'Welcome back to the *Old Red Patch*, Major,' he said, saluting.

Not having ever met Patterson, I found his greeting remarkably cheery, not to mention astute. I hadn't expected anybody other than DuBois to make the connection between me and the division in which

I'd served for more than two years. Evidently, there were excellent reasons why Patterson was the divisional intelligence officer.

'Thanks, Captain. It's good to be back. Forgive for me for saying so, but you seem in remarkably good cheer. I hadn't expected your section of the front to be a walk-over?'

'Oh, it's not,' he assured me solemnly. 'But we received some good news, Major, not long before you arrived. The 8th Battalion managed to capture Ocean Work, right before dawn.'

'That is good news. So there are only a couple of strongholds left before you reach a favourable jumping-off line?'

'That's right. And the attack has been postponed by a day – to give the heavies a chance to clear more of the wire. So hopefully we can tidy up the rest in the interim.' Seeing as how the rest included a particularly nasty fortified bluff called the Crow's Nest, overlooking the D-Q Line from the west, I made no attempt to spoil his mood and I kept my mouth shut.

The day passed quickly at Patterson's side, and with news that the 4th Imperial Division had made its ground and taken Eterpigny on our far left, I was beginning to think the captain's enthusiasm was infectious. My own enthusiasm waned after I read McAvity's latest scribblings from Corps HQ.

'Have you seen this?' I said to Patterson, waving the intelligence report in front of his nose.

He shook his head, and glanced at it briefly. 'More new reinforcements, eh? Exactly how many divisions have the Germans sent here?'

'Oh, it must be fifteen or sixteen by now,' I said. 'I'd guess von Below is in a state of mild panic. His army is being stomped upon. But look which ones he's sent to face you.'

Patterson held up the sheet again. 'The 1st and 2nd Guards Reserve, and the 3rd Reserve Division, it says.' He looked at me quizzically.

'Well the first two are elite units, Captain. Prussians mainly. You know what they're like. In fact that bloody 1st Guards Reserve has followed us around the entire Western Front. Though I'm pleased to say they've come away with a bloody nose or two to show for it.'

'That's reassuring,' said Patterson.

Soon he returned to his papers and I to mine. New divisions or not, there was nowhere to go but ahead. At a certain moment, the divisional commander appeared. He waved me over to meet him.

Major-General Macdonell, a stiff looking man with a bushy white moustache and white hair cropped to within an inch of his head, was as close to a living legend as anybody in the Corps, perhaps even in the entire BEF. He greeted me with friendly enthusiasm, 'Welcome, laddie. Anytime Lipsett's done with you, know there's a home for you here.' According to Patterson, Macdonell was born in Kingston, but he had a Scottish streak in him that was simply itching to come out. And whether it was a Scottish trait or not – I thought not – Batty Mac also had a predilection for cavorting in full sight of the German snipers, for that's how he came by his nickname. Understandably, Patterson was a *wee bit* nervous when he had to accompany the general on his frequent trips to the front.

Around 4 o'clock, a frenzy of excitement broke out in the dug-out and virtually the entire staff hurried outside. Following them, I was in time to see a big Crossley pull up nearby. From it emerged a familiar figure resplendent in red tabs, and a nose so steep the end was lost in his moustache.

It was General Sir Henry Horne of the First Army. It was his army we were in, so he had more than a passing interest in what was occurring here. With the exception of our brief but bloody outing with Plumer's Second Army at Passchendaele, and our recent show at Amiens in Rawlinson's Fourth, we'd been with Horne for almost two years. That showed as Sir Henry greeted Macdonell and his GSO1 with a casual ease. Amidst the salutes and handshakes, I overheard the words "St. Quentin", or their nearest approximation as spoken in the King's English. The three of them disappeared inside, and I turned to Patterson: 'Mont St. Quentin?'

'Yes, sir, the Aussies took it. If they can hold it, we'll be across the Somme in no time. The Boche will be hightailing it back to the Hindenburg Line.' It was, I hoped, an accurate précis of the situation. For if we could pierce the D-Q Line, a retreat to even those vaunted defences might provide little comfort.

1ˢᵗ of September, 1918

The next day brought more welcome news. The 15ᵗʰ Battalion success-fully captured the purported Rock of Gibraltar, otherwise known as the Crow's Nest. Not encountering any crows, the Highlanders did run up against 350 Germans, a third of whom were left where they fell. The survivors joined the divisional POW cage, accompanied by a booty of more than 80 machine guns. Assuming we could hold the line against the flurry of counterattacks, we were in a fine position for the assault.

Macdonell, to my dismay, decided to visit all three of his brigades. Patterson and I dutifully tagged along. Happily, it proved less harrow-ing than I feared. Until, that is, we reached the simple headquarters of Brigadier-General Frederick Loomis, commander of the 2ⁿᵈ Brigade.

Loomis was back from visiting his battalions and he still wore his helmet. It was so tight on his head that the black leather strap risked leaving a permanent indentation in his chin. The brigadier was a red-head, a fact I ascertained by observing the ginger-coloured moustache and matching eyebrows visible under the metal rim of his headgear. In itself a man's hair colour doesn't say much. But in retrospect, the old saw of redheads and tempers should have come to mind. However, in discussion with Macdonell, I noticed nothing of a fiery temper, merely a driven officer still basking in the glow of success; they'd seized Ocean Work and the last uncaptured section of the Fresnes-Rouvroy Line.

I turned to Patterson. 'So what do you think,' I asked quietly. 'Can we not only smash the D-Q Line in a day, but also make the Canal du Nord?'

Patterson grimaced. 'You're thinking of that operations order I showed you earlier?'

'Yes, and I can see from your face what you think. I thought the same myself,' I said. 'I don't know whose idea this is, but making it through the D-Q Line seems more than enough to chew off in one day.'

'It'll be a challenge for sure,' replied Patterson, diplomatically. Out of the corner of my eye I noticed that General Macdonell had moved over to a group of junior officers. From the nervous laughs and glowing faces, they were visibly flattered by the attention. Loomis had disappeared.

'A challenge? To storm the D-Q Line and all its support trenches, then move four and a half miles and secure the canal bridges! We've spent four years barely keeping our head above water and suddenly some general thinks we can move mountains. The Canal du Nord isn't a challenge, it's lunacy!' Then I saw General Loomis. He was staring at me, five feet to starboard. Barring total deafness it was a fair bet he'd heard me.

Patterson, whose face was glowing a robust red, stuttered through an introduction.

Loomis said, 'MacPhail, eh?'

'Yes, sir,' I answered.

'Your name rings a bell.'

'I was with the division, sir. The 10th Battalion. The Fighting Tenth.'

'The 10th you say? That would put you in my brigade, yet I see a 3rd Division patch on your shoulder?'

'Well I *was* with the brigade. Until December of 1916, sir. I was wounded at the Somme, you see.'

Loomis remained impassive, his unblinking eyes boring into me. He made as to remove his helmet.

I fidgeted, but then drew breath, and returned his stare. 'Yes, sir. As I was recovering, General Lipsett visited and asked me to join his staff in the 3rd Division…' Loomis said nothing. I felt the colour coming into my cheeks. 'He knew me from when he commanded the 2nd Brigade,' I explained.

'And what is it, *precisely*, that you do now, MacPhail?'

'I'm in the divisional intelligence section, sir.'

'Ah… that would explain it,' he said, his voice rising. 'The good major from intelligence feels he has a superior grasp of our strategic position,' he announced to the small group standing nearby. 'So you believe you know better than the General Staff how to conduct the war, Major?'

It was the voice of the schoolyard bully. Billy Watkins had done it to me for the best part of a year, and I'd had twenty-odd years to mull over what I ought to have said to Billy, but didn't. I can't think of any other explanation why I reacted so rashly.

'In my experience, sir, the amount of gold braid on a planner's cap is rarely correlated with the success of his plan.'

'Is that so?' Loomis was frowning.

'Yes, sir. That's been my observation.'

Loomis tossed his helmet on the table with a loud clank. 'With an attitude like that, it's a lucky thing you're not in my outfit, MacPhail,' he said very slowly. His tone wasn't without a certain cold menace.

'I can't disagree with you there, sir.'

Loomis shot me a look that made a German bayonet look blunt. He may be a bloody brigadier-general, I thought, but I hadn't exactly been picking my nose this war – whatever he insinuated to the contrary.

Patterson, all too aware of the tension in the air, spirited me away with some vague, but well-meaning excuse, and Loomis went back to Macdonell. To think, not so long ago, I'd firmly resolved to watch my tongue; only my tongue, less conscious of the dangers and ignorant of my resolution, sometimes exhibited a will of its own. So be it. At least I had a major-general watching my back – if Benoît was to be believed.

Plus I had other things to worry about; tomorrow the battle for the Drocourt-Quéant Line would begin.

CHAPTER 15

2nd of September, 1918
Between Cagnicourt and Buissy, France

In battalion headquarters an easy quiet reigned, broken occasionally by a few words of conversation, or a joke to lighten the spirits. It was well past midnight and soon enough the battalion would be making its way to the assembly points. Of the strings of barbs and concrete blockhouses that lay ahead no one spoke a word, but we all knew. On the dug-out steps slouched a runner in kilt, staring east out into a dark windy night lit only by the flashes from the falling shells, both ours and theirs. In the distance there was a roll of thunder. A wooden wicker cage of pigeons took up most of the signaller's table and the five of us – the signaller, a captain and a lieutenant from the battalion, as well as Patterson and myself, sat back from it, leaning on our chairs with the backs resting against the timber supports. Two candles on the table cast a warm flickering light that reached even the furthest recesses of the dug-out. It was cozy.

'The CO should be back soon,' offered his deputy, a captain from St. Catherines.

Patterson replied. 'I hope so. The general wanted me to pass along a message before you go in.'

'It's all a question of luck, Patterson,' I pontificated. 'You're obviously down on yours or we wouldn't have missed him by five minutes.' The others smiled half-heartedly.

Into this serenity came the scream of a shell. Before I could even register what it was it grew to a horrifying crescendo. There was a rush of air, then a crash, thud and flash, followed by pitch darkness. And silence.

I blinked. The smell of cordite and smoke was overpowering. I felt a pigeon brush past my cheek in a whirlwind of feathers, chirping madly or whatever it is that a pigeon does. There was a long scratch followed by the flicker of a match across the room.

'Is everyone all right?' said someone, the battalion captain I presumed. The table was in shatters and the corporal and the lieutenant lay prone on the ground. Both lifted themselves at the sound, and there were murmured assents. From behind me, the doorway to Germany, I heard, 'Yes, sir.' Somehow, the runner had made it too.

'Well, Major,' said a voice from the gloom. 'You have a worrisome way with generals, but no one can fault *your* luck.'

I'd been telling myself the exact same thing for years.

Not long after 5 a.m. came dawn, and right before dawn, came ZERO hour. The assault on the vaunted Drocourt-Quéant Line had begun. The massed guns roared in unison. The sound and weight of the Germans' own scattered bombardment instantly overwhelmed by the greatest barrage of the war. Shrapnel for the trenches and HE for the wire. Any infantryman could tell you the difference. It certainly didn't take an artilleryman to explain why shrapnel, and not high explosive, was the ammunition of choice when the soft ranks of the enemy soldiers were being targeted.

To many at divisional HQ the sound of the barrage was a relief – finally it was on. The night had brought report after report of fierce hand-to-hand fighting across our front. The Germans were pushing back for all they were worth.

After thirty minutes came the first update. 'The 15th Battalion reports large numbers of prisoners filing back,' said a signaller.

'Good news,' I murmured to Patterson. 'The wire must be cut. So many prisoners, and this early – it's an encouraging sign.'

Patterson cocked an eyebrow. 'I want you to look at this,' he said, and beckoned me over to the huge map draped on the conference table.

Astride the Arras-Cambrai road heading east, the 4th Division had finally arrived and their starting positions were carefully drawn along a long, two mile-wide front; a mile to the north of the road and a mile to the south of it. Further north, and immediately to their left, was the 4th Imperial Division. But something about the map was odd. 'What happened?' I asked. 'All three divisions were to attack?'

'Plans changed. The 4th Imperial's commander reported he could only attack with a single brigade. His losses were too heavy. So Currie had to shrink their front and expand the 4th Canadian's.'

I grunted. 'Nothing ever goes to plan, except maybe the plan to plan for anything,' I said.

'That about sums it up,' agreed Patterson.

Further south of the road, and abutting the 4th Division, was 1st Division ground. There, the German defences took the form of an "M". Four major trench systems, one after the other, all converged in a five mile radius. The first was the Fresnes-Rouvroy, running south from where my own division had broken through near Boiry. From it, at an angle, ran the Vis-en-Artois Switch to the southeast. After two miles it was joined by the Drocourt-Quéant line coming from the north. As if that weren't enough, there was the Buissy Switch. A mile and a half back up the D-Q Line, right where it crossed the road, the Buissy system jutted off to the southeast. The *Old Red Patch* had made it through the first two in the last four days. But that wasn't what Patterson wanted to show me.

'See here,' he said tracing an oval on the map with his finger. 'There are three or four belts of wire in front of the main D-Q trench. Then there's the secondary trench preceded by another two lines of wire. And finally, there's the support trench in front of Cagnicourt with yet more wire. And I can't even begin to count the number of machine-gun emplacements. So I grant you, Major, it is good news. But I find it a wee bit early, as the general likes to say, to break out the firecrackers.'

'And to think I'm always the one accused of being dour,' I said. Patterson grinned uneasily.

Not too much later the grins flashed for real.

Line after line of trenches and wire, deep dug-outs and tunnels, redoubts and pill-boxes; Hindenburg had ordered it be held at all costs. It was a national lifebelt. It had taken Germany's best engineers, the efforts of an army of Russian POWs, and the lives of many of them, two years to build. And we carried it in an hour.

I felt almost giddy when the news arrived. Which made it all the worse shortly thereafter. For as it turned out, my battle was only just beginning.

'Major, if you would,' said General Macdonell, waving me over. 'I urgently need you in the field. Every officer I've got is out, and it appears our right may be faltering. We're at the support line and Cagnicourt. But if we don't take the Bois de Loison and the Bois de Bouche... well...' Macdonell frowned.

So much for being General Lipsett's eyes and ears, I grumbled to myself, as I picked my way through the shattered Drocourt-Quéant defences. Scattered everywhere were coats in field grey, rifles, all manner of kit, and bodies... sometimes one or two sprawled in a trench, but more often than not thick bunches of them. They were mainly Germans and I took note of the numbers on their regimental ensigns as I stepped around – habit, I suppose. Soon there were more than I could count. As I pushed on, I spotted more and more of our own men, from the 15th and 16th Battalions, lying motionless.

A hundred yards from the second trench a score of bedraggled Fritzs was heading to the rear under the careful watch of a bleary-eyed soldier. On my left, I could make out the buildings of the small village of Cagnicourt. Ahead, the ground was flat. Fields sloped gently off to the southeast, where little more than a mile distant was a hill, standing fiercely on guard. It was the Bois de Bouche. To its left was the smaller Bois de Loison. From the higher ground to the right I heard rapid bursts of machine gun fire. They were strafing the ground in front of me. I stooped to snatch up a rifle, but then I saw something better: a Lewis gun.

Reaching the third and final support trench in a clumsy sprint, I was surprised to see it filled with men. They were from the lead battalion, the 16th Canadian Scottish – this took no particular insight on my part as their shoulder badges shouted it in brass letters. 'Where's your commander?' I asked when I reached them. To which I received a flurry of responses. But it was the outstretched arms, pointing east, that gave me my answer.

I found Lieutenant-Colonel Peck in a shell-hole 200 yards further on, together with a piper. I was glad to find him. Almost as glad as I was to get myself out of sight of what seemed like half a company of machine gunners.

'Hello, sir,' I said, breathing heavily. 'My name's MacPhail. General Macdonell sent me. He's very concerned about our right flank.'

The colonel pulled thoughtfully at one handle of his well-endowed moustache, his eyes resting for a long second on the French-grey patch on my arm, and an even longer second on the Lewis gun over my shoulder. 'The general has good reason to be concerned, Major. We're taking a lot of fire from our right, and the field guns are shot out. It's getting desperate.'

'I expect the Imperials will be coming up shortly, sir,' I said, by way of encouragement. 'The 57th Division have a regiment who are to follow us in, and then break right to cover our flank.'

'Well it won't be the Munsters,' he replied.

'The Munster Fusiliers? Yes, that's the regiment I meant, sir. What do you mean?'

'I think they were lost when they got out of bed this morning, Major. And it hasn't gotten any better as the day has progressed, I'm afraid. They've cost us an immense amount of trouble. Not only have they mixed up hopelessly with our own troops as we tried to advance, they even bombed the 15th Battalion's HQ.'

Incredulous I stared at him. For once I was at a loss for words. After close to four years of war that wasn't something that happened very often. I always figured I'd seen it all.

'That's right, at the Crow's Nest,' Peck continued. 'Now you may think that's two whole map blocks before the enemy line, and you'd be right. But the Munsters *mistook* it as a Boche dug-out. No, Major, I don't think we'll be waiting for the Munsters' assistance.'

Fog of War I was familiar with, but this was an entirely unexpected twist. I'm not sure von Clausewitz ever realized how thick the fog could be. As I considered this, a grumbling trio of tanks in a fog of their own approached. There were loud cheers from the men. If there was one thing that could put run to a Boche machine-gun nest, it was a tank. I'd seen that more than once at Amiens. Provided they avoided the enemy field guns, the tank was an intimidating weapon. If you thought about it from the viewpoint of an infantryman, pulling futilely at the trigger as 30 tonnes of steel, and spitting fire, ground inexorably towards him, it was understandable. However, having roared to the rescue, these tankers now appeared content to provide moral, if not material support. The tanks stood rumbling where they were.

Then I saw something I'll never forget. The stocky — more accurately, outright pudgy — lieutenant-colonel stood up, and took off across the field towards them in an ungainly trot, his kilt flying. Spellbound, we watched as bursts of machine gun fire tore at Peck's heels. Reaching the first of the tanks he waved his cane in the air like a mad sorcerer, cursing and pounding on the tank, all the while gesturing to our open right flank.

By some miracle he made it back intact. The tankers, however, listened neither to orders nor reason, nor even the clanging of Maxim bullets on their iron sides, for they lingered only briefly before turning tail and disappearing from view. But Colonel Peck's example was contagious. His battalion, with the piper blowing madly in the lead, along with the 15th Highlanders who were now to press the attack, began pushing forward in quick rushes. Grimly determined, with jaws set, they rushed ahead as more MGs stuttered into action. They knew full well many of them wouldn't make it, but they went anyhow. No one at home would ever understand. But I did. And I went with them.

The morning air was filled with the harsh rhythmic chatter of machine guns, theirs to the right, and ours behind. Ours were firing off pan after pan to cover the advance. Painfully, methodically, we crossed the grassy ground in short sprints and climbed the incline to the wood. With an extra 28 pounds in my arms I was panting, regretting whatever stupid impulse had led me to salvage this unwieldy Lewis gun. I'd fired one once or twice, although when I was in the trenches we'd never had enough of them. Thanks to Currie we did now, but whether I could get the bloody thing pointed in the right direction when it came down to it, was a fair question.

We entered the Bois de Bouche in artillery formation, single file. 'Oh Christ,' I muttered to myself, remembering my promise to Macdonell. I'd promised him I'd keep him informed. Only in two hours I hadn't sent a single message, and now I was swept up in the attack. The general's mood was probably as black as the Earl of Hell's waistcoat. It was just as well I didn't understand Gaelic – the general's cursing was as famous as he was.

The Bois de Bouche, like most woods in France – except those long since shelled into a landscape of matchsticks – had a rough tangle of undergrowth. It seemed a foregone conclusion that our progress was likely to be slow. Ten feet in, matters got worse.

'TUF-TUF-TUF' reverberated from in front. A couple Highlanders crashed to the ground. The whole line behind them, including me, went weaving into cover where we could find it.

'Are you intending to use that thing, sir?' asked the soldier behind me. While it was embarrassing he should ask – I was the major, after all – it wasn't an unreasonable query.

Over my shoulder I barked, 'I'll cover you. You boys find a way around.' I went down on both knees, and then eased onto my belly behind the tree where I was sheltering.

'Right, sir,' said the private. In a rustle of leaves he slunk off with a handful of his mates. Quickly I manhandled the tube-like barrel of the Lewis gun around to where I guessed the Germans must be. Fortunately it had a bipod. I rested it as straight as I could amongst the roots of the tall chestnut.

'TUF-TUF-TUF' sounded again and this time I saw the flashes. I heard shouts. I grasped the stock and twisted it round to line up with where I'd seen the gunfire. And I pulled the trigger.

The gun had a kick you wouldn't believe, and like any machine gun, it pulled up. I'd forgotten. As I let my finger slacken, foliage began to fall. I hadn't hit a thing; I'd only alerted the Boche to my presence.

Clamping the wooden stock firmly against my shoulder, I peered over the sight, determined to get a round on target. Only I had to press my head to the ground when a long burst of bullets began chewing up the tree trunk, a foot above. When they let up, and without really aiming, I squeezed the trigger again, a long volley that roared in my ears.

Frustrated, I pulled myself up, pointed the gun in the general direction of the MG nest, and pulled the trigger once more. The Hun must have had the same idea. This time their rounds covered me in a thick coating of dirt and a large heap of tree splinters. The next burst they'd have me.

The sad thing was, I almost didn't care. This war was going to get us all. I guess I was blessed I'd made it this far. A lot of others hadn't.

The loud thud of a Mills bomb pulled me out of it. There were rifle shots.

'God damn Heine,' I heard someone exclaim. And then, in my direction: 'We got 'em, sir.'

'Well done,' I enthused, and I scrambled to my feet and rejoined them. The first soldier I saw I patted on the shoulder in a gesture of thanks and relief, and offered him my canteen. He took a long thirsty swallow and bobbed his head in acknowledgement. Then tilted it to one side and spit a stream into the pit where five Germans lay crumpled over their gun.

Our file regrouped and pressed on further into the wood. The Highlanders moved with a certain recklessness and vicious desperation, their faces bone-weary, their eyes hard and cold. The wood was packed with enemy gunners, but the advance steam-rolled ahead in a wild melee of bombs and bayonets.

Exiting the eastern side of the Bois de Bouche, the platoon I was with almost stumbled upon an enemy party moving up as reinforcements. Hastily, the Germans threw their hands in the air, a mixture of fear and resigned acceptance written on their faces.

'One minute they're fighting like madmen, and the next they're surrendering in shoals,' said Maxwell-Scott, the company lieutenant, sidling up to me. 'But we've taken the wood.'

'Yes, and a bloody good thing too,' I said. 'Without it, all the morning's gains would have been for nought. General Macdonell will be mightily relieved. Only where is our support on the flanks? We're still out on a limb here.' The Imperials were nowhere to be seen. And the left was also deserted, save for some Boche gunners who were sending a hail of fire our way.

'The 14th should be up at any moment. They were already past Cagnicourt. I don't know what's keeping them. But I'm sending a runner back to HQ. Do you have anything, Major?' Before I could respond, there was a whoosh and a shell exploded in the wood behind, closely followed by others.

'That didn't take them long,' I muttered. 'We need some reinforcements.' Which, other than the news that we'd taken the Bois de Bouche, was more or less the gist of my message for General Macdonell. We pushed on a few hundred frantic yards east of the wood, and hunkered down, hoping for the sight of troops on either flank, but saw none.

We were taking fire from all around. Finally I said, 'We're going to have to move.' Beside me a corporal patted down his helmet in anticipation. 'Where's the lieutenant gone to?' I asked.

'He fell five minutes ago, sir,' he replied. I winced. There were almost no officers left.

'Well, let's get a move on. Staying here is going to get us all killed.'

Less than a mile east of the Bois de Bouche, down a long descending slope and up another, was the heavily wired line of the Buissy Switch – the last trench system we faced. I could see it from where I stood and I was glad it wasn't the Highlanders' objective. My platoon broke right, keeping roughly parallel, and headed for their own objective, the railway embankment.

Halfway between the embankment and us was Queer Street, a communication trench that extended at right angles from the Buissy Switch. It ran alongside a road heading back west to the D-Q Line. We'd have to cross both the trench and the road, and then another 500 yards, to reach our destination.

I took a deep breath and let the air seep out very slowly. It wasn't the distance that was intimidating. My Gram could have crossed it in five minutes – without her cane. But across open fields with little cover, and bullets coming from three sides of the compass, it seemed hellish long. Luckily I'd had the good sense to offload the Lewis gun onto a willing soldier. By the way he grabbed it, he had a better idea how to handle it than I did.

We moved in small sections, desperate 50 yard rushes, with those behind laying down a covering fire. Rush, fire, repeat. The grass-grown lip of Queer Street Trench was a welcome beacon and we piled into it, expecting a fight. However, No. 4 Company had beaten us to it. And there were others.

'We're 3rd Battalion, sir,' they explained. One shrugged in puzzlement when I inquired whether the general had sent them. Regardless, they were a blessing.

Accompanied by one of their companies, we reached the railway embankment and dug in. A Major Kippen from the 3rd Battalion set about organizing an outpost line with a handful of rifles and a few Lewis guns. Scouts were sent out to watch the flanks.

It was an hour or two later, past 3.30 p.m., when Kippen waved me over. A runner squatted next to him. I did the same. 'Good news,' he said. 'The rest of the Highlanders made contact with the 14th. They've come up and they're starting to work their way down the Buissy Switch. So our left is secure.'

'And the Imperials?' I asked. He shook his head.

'Perhaps I should head back, and see if I can find a telephone…' I began.

'Aeroplanes!'

Both of us swung round. They came as a flight of black specks from the south. At first they seemed to move slowly, but as they approached, their speed increased. Until they were almost upon us.

'Hun!' shouted someone, unhelpfully. Smith, whose knowledge of aeroplanes was nothing short of encyclopedic, had remarked that even I ought to be able to spot a Fokker triplane. He wasn't wrong.

They came in low and we all ducked involuntarily. With a loud droning they buzzed over, one after another, like a flock of malignant jet black crows. More than twenty all told. Their guns were silent, no doubt awaiting the many targets they'd find up by the Arras-Cambrai road in a minute or two.

A Lewis gun began to rattle. The planes swept on. However, now the Boche opened up. Whether it was the Lewis gun, or simply the boost to morale from seeing planes of their own, an entire battery of machine guns in the Buissy Switch, and off to our right, took the embankment under fire. And I heard the unmistakeable bang of their 77m field gun – the one I'd seen being set on the road not long before.

The Boche had been shooting at us all day, but for some reason this appeared to infuriate the men. Every rifle and Lewis gun along the embankment began firing back. The next few minutes were chaos.

There was a shout. 'Look lads, Lieutenant Lewis got the field gunners.' Momentarily forgetting the old wisdom regarding curiosity and cats, I pulled myself up the embankment, with my elbows, to get a better look. Through the field glasses I spotted the gun. The crew was down alright. *Yes!* Then someone took a crowbar to my arm.

I felt a searing pain halfway between shoulder and elbow. Dust billowed up all around me and belatedly I heard the Maxim's telltale beat. I slid back down the embankment and placed the palm of a hand against my left arm. It was wet and clammy. I twisted it to look better and saw it coated in blood. I struggled to get to my knees. Suddenly the hunger, thirst, and fatigue hit me like a hammer, and I began to sway. I reached out to the gravel to steady myself.

'I'm hit,' I must have said. I remember thinking that at least I'd been there when we stormed the famous D-Q Line. Then everything faded into black.

CHAPTER 16

3rd of September, 1918
Cagnicourt, France

At the sound of shelling I woke, confused. Until I noticed the left sleeve of my tunic. It had been cut open and a white dressing was wrapped around my upper arm. I wiggled my fingers, then moved my hands. They were fine. In my arm I felt a dull throbbing pain.

When I first came to, not long after I collapsed, I remembered staring down my body and to my great relief saw my boots. I'm not sure what I was expecting, as my feet hadn't been anywhere near the action. It was a fear I've had ever since I helped out our first CSM, poor Tom Atkins, back in '15. He was a rough old geezer, like every company sergeant-major I'd met, before or since, with a harsh bark for anyone who stepped out of line, which is all too easily done by a young private. But not unkind. He was so tough and gnarled we thought nothing could stop him, until a Fish Tail landed in the trench beside him. It took me a long time to get over the sight – that rock of a man, still alive, two bloody stumps hanging where his legs used to be.

'What time is it?' I asked. Someone had removed my wristwatch. I was curled up against the embankment, had nodded off now and again, only to be woken by the flashes, thunder, and shaking of another Boche bombardment. Other than the sentries, who were warily looking east, watchful for any signs of a counter-attack out of the Buissy

Switch, most of the men were doing the same. They had their rifles resting against them as they dozed. I'd found a Lee-Enfield of my own, and with a grunt I lifted it up from where it had fallen. Bad arm or not, I might need it.

'Half-past one,' replied the man beside me. 'I don't know whether you heard, sir?' I shook my head. 'We're to be relieved.'

And those were the most relieving few words I could have imagined.

Within an hour we began straggling back in the dark towards the dug-outs of the once impregnable D-Q Line. There I slept for a few hours until dawn. After a sober breakfast, consisting of dry rations and water, I made east – no longer the intimidating walk of a day earlier – until I hit the road from Cagnicourt. I turned north on to it, in the direction of the village. At Cagnicourt was an Advanced Dressing Station, I was told. It wasn't difficult to find.

Immediately east of the village, in a crook in the road, was the triangle-shaped plot of the communal cemetery. The Germans, being Germans, had built a deep dug-out underneath it. Once we'd taken it, the medical corps had put in their claim. For a medical post, the location struck me as mildly ominous.

Fortunately, after I'd navigated the steep stone staircase and the scrutiny of a sergeant from the medical corps who peppered me with questions and probed at my arm, I heard that I had little to fear.

'So. That's that,' said the orderly, putting away his scissors and a roll of gauze. 'It's a good blighty, sir.'

'Well, that's a relief,' I said. 'I wouldn't have wanted a naughty one on my hands.' Naturally I knew very well what he meant, but I was feeling better. The cup of hot tea had helped. As did the fact the pain was subsiding.

The orderly frowned – in fairness, I imagine his was not the most humourful of professions. 'No, sir,' he said, 'what I meant is your wound is a good one. That's often the case with the machine guns. The bullets go right through. The only worry is if they hit an organ or a bone. However, in your case, it looks fine. I've cleaned the wound and redressed it. So you're ready to go. You'll be sent to Arras, although I'm not sure when that will be. We've got a lot of serious cases and of course they have priority for the transport.'

After spending hours sitting fitfully outside the dug-out entrance on a small wooden stool in a field full of apple trees and stretchers, I was beginning to wonder how low a priority I was. The stretcher-bearers had stopped risking the treacherous climb down below, to avoid the casualties landing prematurely in the plots up above. So the field was filling up. I watched as an olive green Ford pulled in. The side of the road was occupied by three field ambulance cars that were being loaded. The Ford simply stopped beside them. The door opened and an officer, who seemed vaguely familiar, stepped out. I squinted, and then I recognized him.

'Smith!' I shouted. Smith looked over and waved. He stepped carefully around the two rows of stretchers guarding the approaches to where I sat.

'What in heaven's name are you doing here?' I said, aware that despite the pain, I was sporting a grin that went from here to Calais. It shouldn't have mattered, but I was thrilled to see a familiar face.

'I'm glad to see you, sir,' he said, and saluted. Exactly as he should, although I would have settled for a hug, even if that wasn't the army way. He was staring at my arm, which hung limply by my side.

'Don't mind that,' I said. 'It looks worse than it is. They tell me I'll be fine. However did you find me?'

'We got word you were wounded. Lieutenant-Colonel Peck from the 16th Battalion phoned Colonel Hore-Ruthven this morning. He said he'd seen you not long after you were hit. So the colonel asked the ADMS to find out where the dressing stations were. After that it was merely a question of spending some time with a map. This seemed logical. So here I am.' Smith could be a bull-terrier when he had something on his mind. I knew how smart he was, yet he never ceased to amaze me.

'And you travelled here just to see me?'

'Not entirely, sir. We're to relieve the 4th Division and General Lipsett wanted me to go over the ground. I thought I'd take a small detour.'

'I'm happy you did. Come have a seat.' With my uninjured arm I pulled over a stool. Soon I was explaining all that had happened. And soon after that I was asking the same of him.

'We did it, sir. We smashed the D-Q Line, exactly as General Currie intended.'

'When I saw the boys in action, I never had any doubts,' I said. 'The D-Q was everything we feared. There were some dicey moments... but the men wouldn't give up. What happened on the left?'

'The 4ᵗʰ Division had a lot of heavy fighting, as well, sir. They didn't make it quite as far the 1ˢᵗ Division, but they still managed to crack the line and take Dury and Villers-lez-Cagnicourt. Dury was a veritable fortress. The Brits had it easier, but they also broke through.'

'And the Canal du Nord?'

I could see from his expression that not everything had gone according to plan. 'General Currie sent Brutinel's Brigade tearing down the road towards Cambrai and the canal,' he said. 'We hoped to seize the Marquion Bridge. Of course, the armoured cars had to stick to the road. With the Boche shooting over open sights, they didn't get far. The morning air patrols reported that the Germans are blowing the bridges.'

'Too bad,' I said. 'It was a gamble worth taking, though.'

Smith nodded. From the expression on his face, I could see he was disappointed. I wasn't surprised, but I did share his disappointment. We'd done what no one would have held for possible a few short weeks ago. But I found it hard to bask in the glow of victory. That wasn't simply because a 7.92mm bullet had torn a hole in my arm. We'd smashed Hindenburg's line, only a huge new obstacle had already presented itself: the canal. That was enough to put a damper on anyone's spirits.

'The air patrols did report one other thing,' said Smith slowly. A cautious smile appeared on his face. 'They couldn't see a single German between here and the canal. It appears they pulled out last night. Also, the Third Army took Quéant and Pronville south of us without as much as a fight. The Germans are withdrawing to the outposts of the Hindenburg Line, all along their entire front. Between the Aussies at Mont St. Quentin, and what we did here, they had no choice. They're in full retreat.'

'The hinge of the Hindenburg system,' I murmured.

'What's that, sir?'

'Oh, just thinking. The generals actually got it right. Perhaps all our sacrifices did achieve something.'

A bespectacled sergeant appeared, a red cross prominently displayed on his sleeve, clipboard in hand. 'Major MacPhail? Your transport has arrived,' he said, and pointed at a horse-drawn wagon emblazoned with an even bigger red cross. 'We have room for one more man. It'll take you to the light railway, sir, and you'll be in Arras before you know it.'

I rose to my feet. Smith made to salute, but before he could, I grabbed his hand and shook it. 'I'm not sure when we'll see each other again. Take care, and good luck, Lieutenant. Who knows, GHQ may find someone besides the Corps to assault the canal.' Naturally, I meant it well, even if the odds of that happening seemed as slim as me being sent home. But I wanted to end on a positive note.

CHAPTER 17

4th of September, 1918
Arras, France

Medical Officer Major Andrew Pierce was a man who, by all appearances, took great pleasure in his work, even if his bedside manner needed some polishing. He'd conjured up a needle the size and shape of a pencil and was flicking it with his finger in front of my face. 'This might sting for a second. A tetanus shot,' he cheerfully explained, before ramming it into my backside.

I groaned and curled my toes into a ball. I would have screamed had there not been an entire dressing room watching and listening.

'You're an extraordinarily lucky man, Major,' he proclaimed, as I struggled to pull up my pants with one hand.

'So everyone keeps telling me,' I said, a little cantankerously.

'Tell me, what were you doing when you were shot?'

'I was looking through my field glasses, I believe.'

'Yes, that would explain it. Your wound is on the underside of the arm where I wouldn't generally expect it.'

I must have looked puzzled for he felt compelled to explain. 'See,' he said as he raised his arms to simulate holding field glasses to his eyes. 'The skin and any fat naturally sinks when you raise your arms, and then tightens when they're lowered to your side. The angle of the wound is all wrong if your arms had been down.'

'Ah,' I replied.

'What did they tell you at the dressing station?'

'That I'd live. And to take a seat.'

Pierce pulled a grimace. 'Well there's little time for hand-holding at the dressing stations in the field. Nor here for that matter. But with the attack winding down it's fortunately not as hectic as it was. In actual fact the bullet only pierced the lower flesh of your arm.'

'So, it's a scratch?' I said interrupting.

'No, it's a little more than a scratch, Major. Moreover, I'm positive it doesn't feel like one. Your good fortune is that it wasn't somewhere else; half an inch higher and it might have hit the brachial artery. However, it didn't, and it's a clean wound. I expect you'll be back in the thick of it in no time.'

'Suddenly my luck feels like it's running out,' I said.

Pierce smiled sagely. 'I'm sending you to the Corps Rest Station to recuperate.'

'That sounds relaxing, but why don't you keep me here?'

'This is only a dressing station. For the walking wounded. We'll keep you here until we have a full lorry.' Pierce was not simply a talent in medicine, but also logistics.

Filling the lorry took longer than expected, which was surprising as both the dressing and waiting rooms were busy, although it gave me some time to take in the surroundings. The *Ecole des Jeunes Filles* was a collection of brick buildings, closely adjoining one another, in the centre of Arras. While the piles of brick and timber outside testified that the school hadn't escaped the wrath of the German long-range guns, the medical corps had transformed it into an efficient operation. Entering a long rectangular room, each patient was funnelled to several rows of wooden benches to ponder his fate, before eventually being summoned to a dressing table. There, a doctor or an orderly, together with a clerk, examined the injuries and made a diagnosis. The "lucky" ones, like me, were sent to a Rest Station, or back to their division. Those less fortunate went to the Casualty Clearing Station at Mingoval for further treatment.

I was ushered past a YMCA refreshments table where I happily availed myself of a drink, and into another building where three benches and a space for stretchers made up the waiting room. There were a few lads on stretchers, but most were sitting, as was I, with a bandage around their head, or bound tightly around an arm or leg. A couple were so trussed in white they could have passed for mummies, were it not for the awful moans they exuded. Their war was temporarily over, if not permanently.

There was a loud commotion as a soldier barged his way unceremoniously through the door clearly marked "exit". Behind it the lorries and motor ambulance cars were assembled. 'Ah,' boomed a deep heavily-accented voice. 'I thought I would find you here – *avec les jeunes filles.*' A huge bearded man in the uniform of a captain stood in the doorway, gaping.

'Benoît, you need glasses, there isn't a young woman in sight,' I said, as he charged down upon me.

Benoît looked ready to clap me on the shoulder until he remembered what I was doing here. Instead he seized my outstretched hand in a vice-like grip.

'Ouch,' I mumbled.

'Oh, sorry, Mac,' he said, releasing it. 'I thought it was your other arm that was injured.'

'It was,' I said, shaking my hand. 'But now I can go back to the front of the line.'

Benoît smirked. He had what you would call a jovial face, although now a dark cloud passed over, his brow furrowing as it was wont to do when the subject was serious. 'I was really worried, Mac, when I heard,' he said. 'I even prayed for you.' That was one of the things I really liked about DuBois. He wasn't too much of man to admit his feelings. Someone else would have cloaked it in some dispassionate euphemism such as, "we were all concerned". Not Benoît. He always said it like he thought it.

'You shouldn't have been,' I said. 'Concerned, that is. You know me, I can look after myself.'

'Not as well you think, my friend,' Benoît replied. It was the apparent seriousness with which he said it that surprised me.

'I didn't think you'd have time to be making sick calls. Shouldn't you be out with Tibbett looking for enemy batteries to bombard?'

He shook his head. 'We're moving into the line tomorrow at noon. We're at the canal bank. But the attack is over. *Pour le moment.*'

'Any signs someone else gets to cross the canal? Reinforcements from the First Army for instance?'

'Ha!' he exclaimed. 'No. 'Orne and 'Aig think they're on to a winning team. There's already talk of plans being made.' That's another thing about Benoît, he was never going to master the English "h" and, come to that, he was almost as cynical as I was.

'How is your mother?' he inquired.

I rocked my head from side to side. '*Comme si, comme ça*, last I heard.'

'I think you should ask Lipsett about that extended leave, Mac. He gave Cunningham a ten-day pass to go to Blighty.'

'Did he now?' I said, rubbing my chin.

And then my name, concealed among thirty-odd others, was called out.

The Corps Rest Station in Agnez-lès-Duisans exhibited none of the architectural details, and even less of the luxury of the Château de Duisans where I'd been six short days ago. Duisans was only a few miles down the road. I'd been assigned a tent, together with three other officers. While on the surface it may have lacked the grandeur of a château, my quarters were more than comfortable. The company was fine too: two disarmingly polite young lieutenants from the 7th and 14th Battalions, and a gregarious captain from the rowdy but decimated Van Doos, "*les vingt-deux*", the 22nd Battalion of Montreal.

The first night I twisted and turned in my cot. The air was cool and strangely quiet, only once disturbed by the penetrating drone of an enemy bombing machine. Yet in my head battle raged. Shells plummeted down with a whistle and a crash. In the background was the incessant chatter of the Maxims, searching us out as we raced across the grassy fields.

By day peace reigned, and that made for a pleasant change, and one I was all too willing to embrace. I had a lot of time to sleep and to think. Both of which were welcome. I hadn't engaged in much of either this summer. Three square meals a day were also nice, as was an occasional hot bath.

The biggest disappointment was the absence of any sisters. Once

I'd felt a nagging guilt even joshing about women. But my wife had been dead for more than four years, four years in which I'd barely touched another woman. Many men had. Many of them even had wives or girlfriends back home. But even in the alcohol-fuelled frenzy of leave, I'd never been tempted. Well, tempted, of course, but never so tempted that it overcame the inhibitions that clung to me like wet socks in a winter trench. In my memory she was so beautiful. The tattered picture I still carried in my billfold hardly did her justice. Yet when I thought of Kathryn – to my shock – I realized there was so much about her I never knew. Without the photo I would have had trouble describing her. It all seemed so long ago – a life time – and our marriage didn't survive a year. So much had changed since then. The entire world really. I definitely had.

Mainly I read the newspapers, and I thought, and I chatted with the others. My arm ached at times. Less than my conscience, although the letters from home were upbeat. I tried to console myself with the fact there was little I could do. But Benoît had held out the promise of leave; even three weeks would give me time to make the long journey to and fro, and still have a short visit.

By the third day, time was wearing heavy on my hands. By the fourth I was thinking of the Canal du Nord. So when one of my roommates, Lieutenant Field, sought to satisfy his curiosity, I was prepared. Only he asked the very question I didn't have a ready answer for.

'Do you think we'll be able to force the Canal, sir?'

I looked at him. He was a handsome looking fellow of twenty-one, with fair skin and the vestiges of a youthful exuberance, except when he walked. He shuffled along with his cane like someone four times his age, his leg pierced in two different places by bullets. 'I don't know, William,' I replied, truthfully. 'We'll try, of course.'

In retrospect, I might have devoted more attention to the canal. But a week before, it was twelve miles distant, ten of which were honeycombed with trenches, wire and fortifications, manned by what turned out to be fifteen enemy divisions. Call it pragmatism. Making any sort of progress in this war was usually a question of one painful step after another, much like Field's gait.

Field persevered with his questions: 'They say the Germans have flooded the banks.'

'Yes, I heard. North of the road. The marshes will make the approach even more difficult. Also, as far as I can remember, the far side is high ground. And quite heavily wooded. Which is ideal for a defender with a machine gun. Then there's the small issue of getting across the canal.'

'The engineers were already busy with bridges,' said Field, who despite his limp leg, was proving himself to be quite an optimist.

'True, but I suspect putting a bridge across a forty-yard stretch of water, while being peppered by machine guns and whizz-bangs, will prove challenging.'

Field nodded thoughtfully. Watching him I made my decision.

An hour later I informed the orderly: 'I've decided to return to my division.'

'Your arm is healing well, sir, but it's not a hundred percent by a long shot. The front is not the best place for a full recovery. Besides, you've only been here a few days. I'd strongly advise against it.'

'I'm on the staff for Pete's sake. Most days lifting a pen is the extent of my exertions.'

He screwed up his face in suspicion. 'We don't get a lot of staff officers with bullet wounds,' he said.

'Right, well. I was stupid,' I said. 'It won't happen again.'

He threw his hands up. 'As you wish, sir. I can't force you to stay.'

I'm sure he thought I was mad. But I had my reasons.

149

CHAPTER 18

10th of September, 1918
Vis-en-Artois, France

'You'll never guess who I met when I arrived back?' I said. 'The Minister of Munitions, Winston Churchill.'

A head turned in the front seat. Without looking I knew it was Tibbett's. The others wouldn't have a clue who I was talking about. Sometimes it seemed as if Tibbett and I were the only ones who bothered to read a newspaper, now and again. On the other hand, Tibbett's family probably shared a box with the minister at Ascot. He came from that sort of milieu. 'Churchill! What was he doing here?' he asked. I suspect he regretted missing the opportunity, and telling his wearisomely *hautaine* father about it most of all.

'I'm told he arrived a day earlier, having flown over the Channel, if you can believe that. Then he followed it up with a grand tour of the Drocourt-Quéant line, with General Lipsett as his guide.'

'Astonishing,' said Tibbett, 'that a man of his stature would take such risks.' Naturally, Paul was referring to the flight, not the tour.

There was a moment of silence, till Benoît said, 'If he was here last week I would agree with you.' And naturally Benoît was referring to the battle. How those two could work together mystified me.

To avoid any unpleasantness I piped up again, 'General Lipsett

150

introduced me to him. He was very complimentary about our victory. And curious about the battle. He saw the dressing on my arm.'

'What did you tell him, sir?' said Smith.

'That it was hard won,' I said grimly. No one said a word.

I was with the rougher half of the divisional staff, squeezed into one of two staff cars that were poking along the shell-pocked road towards Vis-en-Artois. Sensibly, Lieutenant-Colonel Hore-Ruthven had gone ahead with the general in the big Crossley. Oddly, I was happy to be back, and pleased with this little excursion; it might provide an ideal chance to broach the idea of leave with the general. I'd try to have a word with him once his obligations were fulfilled.

The honour guard of plane trees (*platanes*) that had once dignified the road were reduced to sorry stumps, and only a super-human effort on the part of the engineers had kept the road itself passable. We slowed to a crawl as a lorry ahead edged around the wreck of another, its metal skeleton burned and twisted. The land looked as if a giant rake had shorn it of anything green, leaving only brown dirt, holes and trenches, the debris of war: wooden ammunition boxes, spirals of torn wire, and rails from the light railway, bent as if they were mere paperclips. The salvage crews were already toiling away. As always there were the horses, untold numbers of them rotting in swarms of flies which proliferated when the showers passed. The horses were the last to be buried.

I turned away from the window and sighed. 'What's this all about, anyhow?'

'General Lipsett is making an address to the 4ᵗʰ Mounted Rifles.'

'Yes I know that. But since when does he invite his entire divisional staff to be on hand?'

There were shrugs.

At Vis-en-Artois the 4ᵗʰ CMR had been busy. Well outside the village, where the shells periodically still fell, the battalion had cleared a patch of ground and erected a flag pole. The Red Ensign was flapping madly in the wind. Arrayed behind the flagpole, the battalion stood in a matrix of ordered rows and columns, their NCOs curtly marshalling the ranks while the officers mingled amongst them, anxious to please their superiors and the divisional commander.

Another Patterson, this one a lieutenant-colonel, and the 4ᵗʰ

CMR's CO, was all charm when he greeted us as we pulled up. From the lingering glance he threw me, as I exited the car, I had a feeling he recognized me. I wasn't mistaken. After he returned my salute he said, 'Hello, Major. The last time I recall seeing you was when we shared a barn together near Ypres, in July.'

'Yes, sir, I remember it clearly. When your battalion was sent to create that little diversion ahead of the Amiens show.'

'Yes, indeed. It was a hectic week,' he replied. Which, I thought, didn't cover it by a long shot. I'd spent a lot of time with his men – enough to see one of his company commanders, and a good man, killed; it was just as well Patterson didn't bring that up. Likely, the colonel was only doing what all of us did to keep going, locking the bad memories far away.

'Welcome back, Major,' he said.

'Thank you, sir,' I replied. 'I'm happy to see you and the battalion in more festive surroundings.' In the light of later events, it was a stupid rejoinder. It made me wonder why the hell I was an intelligence officer – I certainly had no inkling what was coming. Not that the colonel did either.

It wasn't long before the colonel and General Lipsett made their way forward to address the troops. Lipsett looked tired and drawn walking across the wet grass. It wasn't like him. He had a way with the men, a concern for them that they readily saw. They reciprocated with an outpouring of enthusiasm which in turn gave a visible bounce to his step. Not today. Overhead, the clouds were darkening – the next downpour was coming our way.

Colonel Patterson said a few words of introduction. Then Lipsett began to speak, his voice strained and tinny against the wind.

'I have just received an order this morning,' Lipsett bellowed, 'to report to the 4th Imperial Division.' My head jerked upward. *That couldn't be true.*

'I cannot express to you the great disappointment I feel on being forced to leave the 3rd Canadian Division, which I have commanded for two years and three months.'

I was stunned. General Lipsett leaving us. It was unthinkable. He was the man who had brought us so far. So many battles we had fought and won under his leadership: Vimy, Hill 70, Passchendaele,

Amiens, Arras and the D-Q Line. Time and again he'd chosen the right path, ensured we were prepared to do what was asked of us. I couldn't imagine a 3rd Division without Lipsett.

And there was me. But for the general I might very well be lying near a battlefield in one of those tiny dirt graves marked by a wooden cross. He was a hard taskmaster, for certain, but no harder than he was on himself. I knew a few brigadiers – the lazy ones – who would cheer his departure. They'd suffered his rebukes. For all my whining to Benoît, I hadn't. I knew that.

'For the general, boys!' Colonel Patterson was shouting. 'Hip-hip-hurrah, Hip-hip-hurrah, Hip-hip-hurrah,' roared the ranks.

Later that day I was summoned to the general. His office at the chateau had been replaced by a dark corner of a deep dug-out at Aden Mound, where the ground rises to the Vis-en-Artois Switch. A simple table served as his desk.

'I wanted you all to hear it from me at the same time,' Lipsett said, when he saw me. 'That's why you were all invited.'

I nodded. I think my mood was plastered on my face, for he quickly continued. 'No need to be so glum, Malcolm. Life goes on. And so does the war.'

'Yes, yes it does, sir.'

'Let me show you something.' He stood and unfolded a map of the Western Front. I walked around the table to stand beside him. The front line was drawn in red. It curved in a gentle arc down from Ypres in the North, to past Reims in the south. Two bulges were prominent. The first was a huge bump facing the coast between Ypres and Lens; the Lys Salient left after the German spring offensives had threatened an enemy breakthrough to the coast. The general pointed at this now. 'As a result of what we've done here, his position has become completely untenable. There are strong indications the enemy intends to withdraw completely from the Lys Salient.'

'And this is us,' I said, putting my finger on the second deep indentation, this one bulging eastwards, just under Arras.

'Indeed. You surely know the Seventeenth Army opposite us has withdrawn. And their Second Army further north has as well. What's more, since the capture of Mont St. Quentin by the Australians, and our own success here, the Eighteenth and Nineteenth Armies to the south are also in retreat. So you see, Major, the Germans have lost all their gains from the spring offensives. The war may go on. But thanks to our efforts the enemy is firmly on the defensive.'

'Don't get me wrong, General, I'm as happy as the next man that we're taking it to the Boche. I'm just sorry you won't be here to see us through it.'

'So am I, Malcolm. So am I. I would have wished it otherwise.' Lipsett looked wistful. I debated whether I should ask him the reason for his transfer. But I knew it wouldn't accomplish anything other than satisfying my own morbid curiosity. It was painful enough for the general. That was plain to see. Besides, I figured I knew anyhow. I thought back to what McAvity had told me in Paris about how rankled General Currie had been. As to leave... well, I'd just have to ask my new commander.

The general brightened. 'There's one final piece of advice I'd like to give you, MacPhail. A good soldier never offers up an undefended flank.' It was classic Lipsett. Cryptic to the end.

I grinned. 'You mean I should watch what I say, sir?'

The glimmer of a smile passed over his face, and he offered me his hand. 'It's been a great privilege to have had you under my command, Malcolm. I wish you the best of luck. I'm very sorry I can't take you with me.'

I shook his hand, then took a step backwards, and gave him the sharpest salute of my entire life. 'Thank you, sir. For everything. And good luck with your new command.'

CHAPTER 19

11th of September, 1918
Aden Mound, near Chérisy, France

'Fifty-two divisions,' laughed Smith, shaking his head.

I looked up. Smith was a pleasant chap, always ready with a smile and a friendly word, but he wasn't exactly the sort to stand up and shout retorts during a performance of the Dumbells. So to see him laugh aloud, while the entire dug-out craned their necks to see what the commotion was about, was unusual enough for me to put everything aside.

'What's so funny?' I asked.

The tears weren't quite running down his face, but my worthy adjutant was clearly amused. 'This, sir,' he said, passing me a few sheets. TRANSLATION OF DOCUMENT FROM GERMAN GENERAL STAFF it read. 'It was captured on a Boche officer not long ago.'

I thumbed through the pages. 'And where should I be reading?'

'About two-thirds of the way through,' he said. 'According to the German General Staff, sir, no less than fifty-two Canadian divisions have been identified since the war began. Fifty-two!'

I smiled weakly. 'They must be in more of a fuddle than I thought. Fifty-two divisions. That's quite a step up from four. Either their math skills are slipping or they've taken to drinking schnapps instead of water. Mind you, with a few like Captain DuBois storming their trenches, you can forgive them for seeing double.' And then on an afterthought, I added: 'Or wanting a little schnapps.'

Smith glanced furtively around; no one was paying us the least bit of attention.

'Our new commander is to be a Canadian,' he whispered.

'Well, Smith, last I looked we were in the Canadian Corps,' I whispered back.

'Yes, sir, but I hear that's why General Lipsett was transferred.' His voice took on a conspiratorial tone. 'The powers that be didn't want an Englishman anymore.' At this revelation I paused for a moment.

Eventually I said, 'I always thought of the general as Irish, part Canadian even, but be that as it may, I wouldn't believe everything you hear.' And then I related what McAvity had told me at the Café de la Paix, and what I'd observed myself at Valley Wood. 'So you see, Lieutenant, it's simply an ordinary squabble. Our General Currie has many admirable qualities, but he's too thin-skinned for his own good. It's a damn shame, though, if you ask me. Lipsett is the best thing that ever happened to this division. With everything that's going on in this war, you'd think the army would have more pressing matters to attend to.' It was an opinion I had occasion to revisit early the next day.

12th of September, 1918
Neuville-Vitasse, France

The Corps Headquarters near Neuville-Vitasse was everything you wouldn't expect a Corps Headquarters to be. It was a dump. Not literally, of course, although with all the jetsam of battle still scattered around appearances were suggestive.

The sunken road we'd been driving on widened at a certain point. A semi-circle plot of gravel and dirt appeared where vehicles could pull off the main thoroughfare. Preceding it, a proliferation of tents and wooden Armstrong huts were ranged along the track, all under camouflage netting.

Two open-topped Vauxhall D-types were parked to one side. Clusters of officers from the Corps staff stood in the open in animated conversation, several of them holding papers and maps. Behind this busy scene, hugging the contours of the muddy pitch, ran a high grassy embankment of the kind you might see at the shore, where the dunes meet the beach. An astounding number of ramshackle wooden and corrugated steel structures protruded from it, each harbouring dark entryways into the embankment itself. The entrances faced east, thereby belying their provenance. The Germans had burrowed extensively here, with a whole series of tunnels and dug-outs for their staff, right at the head of the Hindenburg system; that is, until the boys from the 2nd Division unceremoniously rousted them.

Stepping from the car, I almost tripped over three bicycles lying in a tangle on the ground. Their owners were casually lounging on their sides on the embankment, helmets off, smoking cigarettes and awaiting the next signal to be sent.

'Ah, there you are,' I cried out, as I surveyed the scene. I was pondering how I was supposed to find McAvity in this ugly warren of Boche ingenuity, until I saw the good major clamber up and out of a dark hole in a mound. The mound bore an uncanny resemblance to an enormous anthill. While I felt the temptation to quiz McAvity about this, I suppressed the urge, especially after I noticed the stiff looking worker ants who marched up after him.

McAvity gave me his hand. 'Hello Mac,' he said with an engaging smile. 'Listen, we'll talk later. These gentlemen accompanying me are looking for you. They seem desperately anxious to talk to you. It was a lucky thing you decided to come when you did.' I shrugged it off, but shortly thereafter came to rue his choice of words.

McAvity turned and I could see them better. There were three of them, an officer, and two other ranks. None of them appeared to have as much as a spot of dirt on them, which was odd – sort of like spotting camels at the North Pole. I saw something else, too. Around their caps was a thick red cover. They weren't from the general staff, so they could be only one thing: *Redcaps*, otherwise known as military policemen, or just plain *Cherrynobs* to the troops.

'Major MacPhail?' inquired the officer, a captain.

'That's correct. And you are?'

'Captain Clavell of the military police.'

'What can I do for you, Captain?'

'We've been trying to catch up with you for a rather long time, sir,' he said, his eyes narrowing. His tone suggested impatience, and verged on irritation. It was the accusing ring, though, which got under my skin. McAvity had sensibly taken his leave.

'Yes,' I said, 'fighting a war can be frightfully inconvenient at times. I find you're never quite sure if you're going to make your appointments.'

His thin lips puckered together. He looked at me as if I was speaking an ancient Swahili dialect.

I sighed irritably. 'Captain, if there's something you want to ask me. Please ask.'

He lowered his voice. 'It's a delicate matter, sir. Perhaps there's somewhere we could talk in private?' Off to my right I saw a dark hole and was ready to point in that direction when I saw Lieutenant-General Currie emerge. Not wanting to unnecessarily trouble the Corps Commander, I waved in the direction of the embankment, out of earshot but not far from where the signallers were still enjoying a mid-morning break from the work and the rain.

'Have a seat gentlemen,' I said, and sat on the sole tree stump within twenty feet. Helpfully, I motioned to the grassy incline beside me. It was still moist.

Clavell looked down his nose, which wasn't hard to do given its Eiger-like slope, and sniffed, 'Thank you, sir, we'll stand.'

'As you wish.'

My parents would have been appalled at my behaviour, rather like when I was ten and left my babysitter, Mrs. Malone – a nasty piece of work if ever there was one – cooling her heels on the front porch for ten minutes while my mother finished doing her hair. Were it not January, and a blizzard, I don't think she would have been nearly so mad.

Normally I had no quibbles with the MPs. Others did, although I never understood why. They were doing their job like the rest of us, and ever since they'd dedicated themselves to traffic control, our reliefs and attacks went a lot smoother. It wasn't as if I was in any trouble myself. However, something about Clavell grated at me. Despite my crown to his pips he deported himself as if I ought to be deferring to him and his powers, which he held like an invisible truncheon over my head.

'Sergeant, take notes, if you please,' he ordered, and the sergeant extracted a large notebook from the front pocket of his tunic and cocked his fountain pen. 'Now then, Major. I understand you were present at the capture of Arvillers on August 9th this year.'

'Yes, I was. You might even say I helped capture it.'

'Ah, yes. And that would have been with a platoon under the command of a Lieutenant…' He looked across at the sergeant, who seemed accustomed to this, for he swiftly came to the rescue.

'Rutherford. Lieutenant Rutherford, sir,' said the sergeant.

Clavell bobbed his head knowingly. 'Quite. Rutherford. That was the name, indeed.'

I brightened. 'Oh, now I understand. You want to ask me about the commendation I wrote for him. He's a remarkable officer, the lieutenant.'

'No, no,' interrupted Clavell. 'This is a separate matter, entirely. I believe there was very a substantial booty captured at Arvillers.'

'Yes, there was. Probably a hundred and fifty machine guns, all new and greased in their packing cases. Some money, too. Even a whole wagon of carrier pigeons.'

'Hmm,' said Clavell, puckering his lips. 'I recall that from your report.' He twiddled his fingers at the sergeant, who looked to the lance-corporal, and the lance-corporal, after rifling through a brown leather case, produced a few sheets of paper. I'd been puzzling about the corporal's role, but now it came to me; he was the portable filing cabinet.

'If you've read my report already, Captain, I fail to see what the point of all this is.'

'Shortly, you will, Major. Shortly you will,' he said, and flipped through the pages of what I presumed was my report. 'It says here you found a considerable sum of money in a large steel box.'

I nodded. 'I suspect it was the divisional pay. The box was full to the brim with German banknotes and coin, and a little French money. I've never seen so much.' By now I was grinning at the thought of it.

'And you write here that you turned all this booty over to the French Army? Including the money?'

'Yes, that's right,' I said. 'The French arrived shortly after we did. As it was their sector, we turned the whole mess over to them, pigeons and all. Rutherford was anxious to get back into the action.'

Clavell paused, and puckered his lips again. Then the truncheon fell. 'The French acknowledge receiving the pigeons, Major. However, they have no record of any money.'

In the silence that followed my mind whirred madly away, and Clavell just stared at me with cold unmoving eyes. I didn't know where to begin.

'Surely, Lieutenant Rutherford can corroborate what I've just told you?' I said at last.

'Rutherford, yes...' Clavell said slowly. 'Unfortunately Lieutenant Rutherford has been sent to England on leave. He's to be awarded the Military Cross. Of course, there's no question that he's involved. But, regardless, we can't talk to him at present.'

'Well what about the French captain then?' I stuttered. 'The one we turned everything over to. He would know. Capitaine...' My words trailed off. Then, as I remembered the scene and the words of the French waiter outside Le Wepler, it came flooding back to me. 'Madelot. Yes, that's it. Capitaine Madelot. Surely you can just ask him. M, A, D...' I began, and proceeded to spell out the rest.

The sergeant, an older man than Captain Clavell, with two wound stripes on his sleeve, spoke up. 'The major's right, sir. We could speak with this Madelot and clear up the whole matter straight away.'

Peevishly, Clavell shook his head. I had a feeling the sergeant would receive an earful later. 'Interrogating French officers is strictly a matter for the French army,' said Clavell. 'No, I must rely on the response I received through official channels. And it states very clearly, the French army did not record receipt of *any* German money at Arvillers.'

'Well, if it's a matter for the French, why are you here?'

'Because, sir, when charged with the care of public money – in this case what was captured from the enemy, and which therefore belongs to the Crown – embezzling the same is a serious offence. Punishable by penal servitude if I'm not mistaken.'

I gasped and got to my feet. 'Whoa, one moment, Captain. Let me get this straight. The French say they know nothing about this money. You're unwilling to investigate when I provide you with the name of

160

the officer whom we handed it over to. You're too lazy to go and ask Rutherford yourself…' The captain began sputtering at this, but I held up my hand. 'No, I'm afraid you'll have to hear me out for a minute, Captain. So, unwilling to ignore what is blatantly obvious, you'd rather badmouth me. As it happens I spotted Capitaine Madelot at a Paris nightclub, not that long ago, living the life of Reilly. If you had any sense you might deign to suggest to the French to look into that.'

'A Paris nightclub, you say…' muttered Clavell. I could tell from the expression on his face I'd just handed him another "fact" with which to beat me. What I couldn't figure out is why this captain, whom I'd only just met, seemed to be bending over backwards to incriminate me.

So I asked him. 'I don't ever recall meeting. Have we?'

'No, sir. But as chance would have it, your name came up in a very illuminating conversation I had with my uncle, when I was last on leave.'

'And who is your uncle, Captain?'

'Colonel Whatley-Wigham.'

I took a deep breath, and puffed out it in a blast; the kind that could blow down a tree. *Of all the rotten luck.* It was the very same stiff-necked bundle of gold braid who'd almost had me up before a court martial. That was only at the beginning of August – until General Lipsett convinced Haig to intervene on my behalf. Now I knew precisely what I didn't like about Clavell: his family tree.

Captain Clavell's mouth curled upwards. 'Yes, indeed. I will continue my investigation, Major MacPhail. Make no mistake about that. In the meantime, I'm afraid I must insist the sergeant and corporal accompany you back to your quarters so they can inspect your belongings.'

The inspection naturally turned up little more than my souvenir disk of tin and a serious shortage of wearable uniforms. I think the sergeant felt bad about it, for when they left he said, 'Don't worry, sir, I'm sure this is a small misunderstanding. Knowing the Frenchies they've probably just mislaid that cash box.' Not that that provided much consolation. I was fairly certain, having thought about little else on the trip back, the answer to the missing cash box lay with Madelot and his outlandish lifestyle. For the moment, however, barring a sudden change of heart by Captain Clavell, I was in a bit of a fix. While the tortuous workings of the army bureaucracy were always a favourite target for derision, it was obvious this was no laughing matter. I wasn't so naïve not to realize I was slipping into a sinkhole; one I might have trouble getting out of.

CHAPTER 20

13th of September, 1918
Arras, France

Friday the thirteenth had never held any particular associations for me, certainly nothing to do with luck, bad or otherwise. Mainly I found it a day like any other. In the past, to suggest differently would have led to a mocking reminder from me that we were living in a modern time and had learned a thing or two since the Dark Ages. Only since 1915, for the life of me I can't imagine what I'd been thinking; the Dark Ages had returned with a vengeance. Older, wiser and a shade more cynical, I wasn't any more superstitious than I'd ever been, even if today's circumstances warranted it; our new general was to assume command at 10.30 a.m. It was Friday, September 13th, 1918.

Early this morning, along with eight or nine divisional staff officers, I departed the dug-outs of Aden Mound – otherwise known as the Advanced Divisional Headquarters – for Arras: the Rear Divisional Headquarters. A couple of years ago I might have joked there was never any shortage of headquarters in the army, just brains to fill them. Having been in one myself for longer than I dared admit, I'd felt a curious need to reconsider.

Even in the shell-ravaged streets of Arras' city centre, the rear HQ was definitely the nicer of the two. Partly that had to do with distances. Whereas the Germans could shell our advanced HQ with almost any variety of gun they fancied, thanks to our attack only the long-range howitzers and naval artillery could reach Arras. Although they still did – with regularity. The occasional whistle and sudden crash of a shell, that echoed in your ears and reverberated in your chest, was long part of *la vie quotidienne* (everyday life) in Arras. Neither the civilians who remained, nor the soldiers who bivouacked here, found any of this remarkable.

L'Hôtel Dubois de Fosseux was located at 14, Rue Marché-au-Filé, not far from the Grande Place. And despite four years of Boche shelling, which had reduced the Grande Place to a quarry of stone, the Hôtel Dubois de Fosseux was largely intact.

An elaborate white limestone, two-story tribute to Louis XV, topped by a steep attic covered in blue-grey tile, the building's façade was embellished by elaborate stone carvings beside the door and the upper windows, and decorative strips of pink stone. Its wrought iron balconies and elegant French windows spoke of another age, one before Kaiser Wilhelm's hordes, or the British army – whose presence here for nearly 1500 days didn't add to the ambiance. All the same, I was impressed. Inured to Boche dug-outs, it didn't take much admittedly.

The building was arranged in a rectangular horseshoe, and its three sides looked out onto a cobblestone-paved courtyard where cars could arrive and their occupants disembark. This is where I stepped out, along with a handful of others from the division. The remaining staff were already loitering on the front steps.

'So, who's it to be, our new commander?' I asked Major Duguid. The conversation in the car had been frightfully unenlightening, so I jumped at the chance when I saw him. Duguid usually knew a thing or two, and the formal handover was to come in less than two hours, although General Lipsett had already departed to his division. If I had my druthers I would have chosen to be somewhere else myself. This rigmarole was decidedly not my cup of tea. There were already five hostile balloons up, their aeroplanes were out in force, and there was a lot of movement on the road from Douai. There was plenty to do. Of course, the illusion of free choice was the first of many illusions I'd abandoned over the years. A sergeant at Camp Valcartier had soundly beat *that* idea out of me way back in the autumn of '14.

164

Duguid cleared his throat. 'I thought you knew. The Division's new commander is Brigadier-General Loomis.'

A deep silence followed. 'Loomis...' I said, aware I was colouring a particular shade of green familiar to those who knew me well.

Benoît noticed. 'What's wrong, Mac?'

'Oh, nothing. What makes you think there's anything wrong?'

He stared me down until I relented. It didn't take long.

'I met Brigadier Loomis a couple of weeks ago. We didn't exactly have an immediate rapport.'

Benoît clapped his hand on his brow and shook his head. '*Tabernacle*. Don't tell me you've pissed off another general?'

'Well, I might have done,' I said cautiously.

Benoît sighed. 'I thought you learned your lesson by now, Mac. You're not exactly Canada's answer to Talleyrand, so when in doubt say nothing. You hear me?' It was probably sound advice, even if it wasn't the response I was hoping for. Benoît's unbridled optimism was renowned, as was his endless repertoire of Québécois curses. So to hear his sombre assessment, laced in profanity, left me in little doubt what kind of day it was going to be.

Breezily, I replied. 'I didn't realize you took such an active interest in diplomacy, Benoît. I always imagined you being more interested in Napoleon than Talleyrand. Or perhaps Big Joe Mufferaw? Another man of action not words. Big Joe was a lumberjack, too.' DuBois wasn't really a lumberjack, although half the division thought differently, for which he probably had me to thank.

Benoît wearily shook his head. 'It's your funeral, Mac.'

'I wouldn't worry,' I said. 'Loomis has had a lot on his mind of late. Even more so with his promotion to divisional commander. And he'll be a major-general soon. Besides, it was a trivial matter, anyhow. Everything and everyone will be new to the brigadier, so I expect he'll have totally forgotten about me.'

'Ah, Major MacPhail, wasn't it?' said General Loomis. I was standing in a reception line. The general was shuffling along with Lieutenant-Colonel Hore-Ruthven, being introduced to his new staff officers. Until they got to me. Apparently I didn't need introducing. To my ears Loomis sounded crotchety. I saw the colonel raise his eyebrows ever so slightly. They went up even more when the general spoke again.

'I'm going to be making some changes, MacPhail. I'd like to speak with you afterwards.'

I swallowed. 'Yes, sir,' I mumbled. Loomis moved on without as much as a second glance.

To each in turn, the general spoke briefly. When he was done he and the colonel left the room. The regimented ranks of the staff disbanded into little groups. Everyone was anxious to exchange first impressions. Except me. Ignoring the questioning look on DuBois' face, I walked over to the open doors and out on to the balcony overlooking the courtyard.

I gripped the railing and stared out at the pallid bleakness of Arras under a sky shaded grey. The air was cool and I took a deep breath. *Make some changes.* That's what he'd said. *I'm going to be making some changes.* So much for the possibility of leave. My mother would be in her grave a decade before Loomis consented to that. Worse, if Loomis did plan on dismissing me, I had very good idea where I'd end up. There was one place where experienced officers were always in short supply: the infantry battalions. And I would arrive right in time for the attack on the Canal du Nord.

Then there was the matter of Captain Clavell. Deep down, I think I'd secretly assumed my new divisional commander would put in a word for me, to cut through the bureaucratic thicket. As General Lipsett surely would have done, but as General Loomis surely would not. "Guilty as charged". In my brief time in practice I'd heard that often enough. It took on a whole different meaning if you were the one in the docket.

Involuntarily I shuddered.

'It's a dreary sight, isn't it?' Whipping my head around, I saw the general. He was standing in the doorway.

'Oh yes, sir,' I agreed, as he walked over to me.

He placed his cap on his head, and then lowered his hand to the railing. Turning, he examined me with the same cold unsmiling eyes I remembered. 'By the by, what did you make of General Lipsett's transfer, Major?'

As questions go this one possessed all the dangers of a midnight romp into No-Man's-Land. Unlike that, there were no places to hide. I shrugged. 'I thought it was very unfortunate, sir. He's an excellent general and the division flourished under his command. No reflection on you, sir.'

Loomis nodded agreeably. 'I concur. General Lipsett is an outstanding general. I'm well aware of the boots I'm stepping into.' He turned away as if he'd seen all that he needed to see. He looked in the direction of the city. 'You're admirably loyal, MacPhail, I grant you that. I value loyalty. I must tell you, though, my first instinct was to replace you immediately when I saw your name on the list of divisional staff. In my old brigade I had a rather competent intelligence officer. He had no reservations, or ignorance, about how the chain of command works.'

Taking Benoît's advice I said nothing.

'I demand a total team effort, Major.'

'Well I'm not an *einzelgänger*, sir, if that's what concerns you.' Loomis looked puzzled, so I added, 'A lone wolf, sir.'

'An ayezelganger,' he said, and repeated it again. It didn't sound any better the second time. 'That's interesting. You chose to use a German term. General Lipsett told me you were quick on your feet. As did Colonel Hore-Ruthven, just now, for that matter. Both spoke very highly of you, in fact.'

'I'm relieved to hear it, sir.'

'Taking that into consideration, I've decided to defer judgment, and to keep you… for the moment… in your current position. I'm going to allow you a period in which to prove yourself. A probation as it were. You're familiar with the concept?'

Impulsively I said, 'Yes, sir. Don't screw up or I'll be off to jail.' Quickly I added, 'I was a lawyer, sir.'

'Well, so long as you don't let *that* go to your head. I demand that all my men, and particularly my officers, adhere strictly to order. Please remember that. Although I can assure you, Major, jail won't be the alternative. Do I make myself clear?'

PART THREE

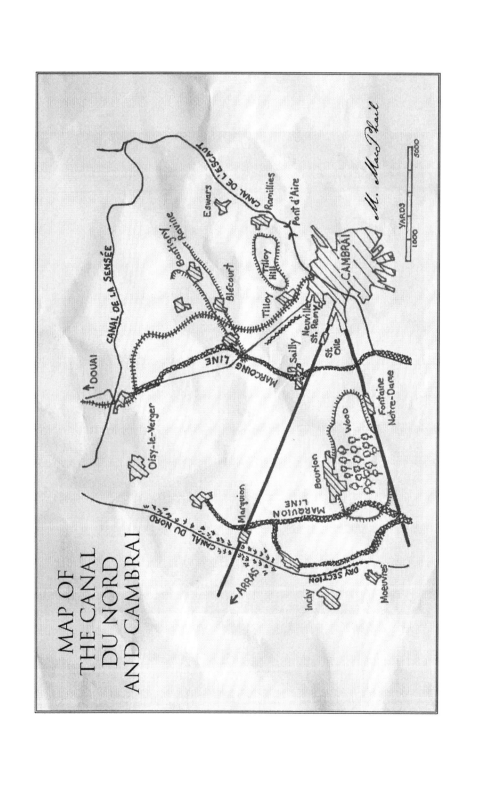

MAP OF
THE CANAL
DU NORD
AND CAMBRAI

DOUAI

CANAL DE LA SENSÉE

Bantigny Ravine

Eswars

CANAL DE L'ESCAUT

Ramillies

Pont d'Aire

Blécourt

Tilloy
Hill

Tilloy

Neuville
St. Remy

CAMBRAI

Sailly

MARCOING LINE

St.
Olle

Oisy-le-Verger

Fontaine
Notre-Dame

Wood

Bourlon

MARQUION
LINE

Marquion

CANAL DU NORD

ARRAS

DRY SECTION

Inchy

Moeuvres

YARDS

1000   5000

M. MacPhail

CHAPTER 21

15th of September, 1918
Canal du Nord, France

The wind was blowing a harsh and piercing gale in my face. I scarcely felt it, nor did I really notice the roar in my ears. It was exhilarating.

The French countryside was inching by, a quilted patchwork of greens, yellows and off-browns, striped by meandering country roads. And then I caught sight of Arras. The curving streets and open squares of the city were reduced to a *maquette*, the kind we painstakingly constructed before every battle. I spotted the Cathédrale, prominent in the model town of small grey building blocks, a holed and crippled version of what it had once been, but proud and defiant all the same. The belfry and the town hall resembled not so much themselves as a jagged mountain of stone.

We were climbing.

I peered down at the little roads, the pinpricks of things I recognized. I was astonished how my nervousness had all but evaporated. In the short time that my attention shifted from my nerves to the sights, we were well on our way. It felt peculiarly safe up here in the emptiness of the sky, in this ungainly contraption, with a comforting quilt-work of clouds stretched above.

Once Arras passed underneath, the ground assumed a uniform brown colour. Shell-holes and trenches dotted the landscape. We flew on and I saw the darker zig-zag patterns of the trench systems running from north to south, edged by broad belts of wire easily visible from above, one after another. I shook my head. To think we'd made it through all those.

'Look,' Captain Catchpole shouted. Startled, I pivoted round in my seat. As the "observer" I was seated backwards with a fine view of our tail. He dabbed his finger downwards repeatedly, as if he were typing out Morse code for the hard of hearing.

Below was the Arras-to-Cambrai road. We were crossing in a north-easterly direction. I could see all kinds of miniature vehicles moving along, and the slower moving shapes of horses. Astonishing really. They looked identical to the toys I'd played with as a child.

The leather, fur-lined headgear I was wearing was warm enough, the goggles which I'd awkwardly wrestled with on the ground fit fine. I felt a tap on my shoulder and craned my neck around again. 'The Canal du Nord,' shouted Catchpole.

'All right. Thanks,' I bellowed in response, the plane already banking to the right. I saw the flooded marshes beside the waterway, the village of Oisy-le-Verger off to the left on the far side of the canal. It was from those heights that the Boche were pouring down machine gun fire. Between that, and the shelling from the artillery to the north, my division, holding the line, was suffering almost two dozen casualties a day.

The shelling was due to our unenviable position. After weeks of battle, and despite the softening resistance, the rest of the First Army north of us, and the entire Third Army to the south, were still miles behind. So that left us trying to keep our heads down in this hazardous salient, a nose wedged into a beehive that was anything but deserted.

The canal itself was surprisingly modest. Anything looks modest at 4000 feet. But with a swamp to navigate, no bridges, a traverse of 40 feet, and a high eastern bank bristling with wire and manned by Maxims, crossing it was not for the meek or the mild. And the canal was flooded. That much was abundantly clear, even if you were as short-sighted as Tibbett. No wonder 2nd Division had concluded the canal was impassable. They'd reconnoitred extensively and reported that perhaps a platoon could make it across; the platoon would need to be good swimmers.

Catchpole kept the plane well to the west of the canal so I could easily see it over my right shoulder, and we began tracing a path southwards. That put us at less risk from the Maxims, although to a field gun the extra range hardly mattered. Fortunately they had no interest and let us be.

Roughly two minutes, and three miles later, we buzzed again over the Arras-Cambrai road, this time approaching from the north, and I spied the shattered remains of the bridge at Marquion. There was no hope of getting anything across that. While the engineers were feverishly preparing all manner of material, bridging the canal under fire would be more of a suicide club than joining the tanks.

Then I picked out the first two German trench lines: the Canal du Nord Line and the Marquion Line. Both paralleled the canal. Two to three miles further to the southeast, the darkly wooded mound known as Bourlon Wood appeared. Taking that commanding position would be a necessity in any plan. Beyond the wood, 2000 yards past the third and final line, the Marcoing, lay the occupied city of the Frankish kings, Cambrai, nestled in the valley of the River Scheldt (Escaut).

Cambrai. It had been in German hands for almost the entire war. And to the wet and weary troops there was a palpable excitement when talk turned to Cambrai. This was the first major city conquered by the Hun we had encountered, and imaginations of its grandeur flowered. Tantalizingly, it sprawled virtually on our doorstep, crying out for liberation. Even my driver to the aerodrome had enquired. 'If we take Cambrai, sir. That would definitely change things wouldn't it?'

I assured him it would. I didn't point out that there were several intimidating obstacles strewn in our path – one of which was the reason for my early morning ride. The private was right, though. Taking the city would complete the work we'd done at the D-Q Line. Cambrai was not only well behind the Hindenburg system, which still barred the path of the Third and Fourth Armies to the south, it was a major transportation hub. Haig and Foch were understandably keen to break the enemy's lateral communications, and capturing Cambrai would do precisely that. A rail line linked it with Douai to the north, and to St. Quentin and points southwards. In addition to which a tangle of roads converged in the city, tying north with south, and the Western

Front with the east, and Germany. Denied them, there was only one direction open to Ludendorff's legions.

Seeing the town on the far bank, and something else, I tapped on Catchpole's shoulder. I pointed down.

'Sains-lez-Marquion,' came a shout. I gave a thumbs-up and motioned that we should descend. Catchpole nodded and pushed his stick forward. The nose fell and we plummeted downwards in a buzzing whine, the unfastened leather straps of my flying helmet flapping wildly.

What I'd seen was a lock. More important than the lock was what was to the south of it – nothing. The canal bed was dry. This was the unfinished stretch of canal.

In addition to the absence of water, the banks looked lower in this section, although I did see generous helpings of wire. From below I heard the sudden rattle of gunfire.

'What are they shooting at?' I hollered in the captain's ear.

Two holes appeared in the lower wing.

I'd forgotten the west bank here was still in German hands. XVII Corps had been in a fierce scrap for days and the enemy had ruthlessly repelled all attempts to reach the canal.

By now we'd passed the village of Inchy and were coming up on Moeuvres. Abruptly, at the locks, a thousand yards south of the hamlet there was water in the canal. 'Okay, take us up,' I roared ahead. 'I've seen what I needed to see.' The motor revved higher and we began to climb.

'Hardly the St. Lawrence is it?' said Catchpole as he eased us into a lazy turn in the direction of Arras. Catchpole was a Canadian. Almost a third of the RAF aircrews were.

I was taking in the scenery, reflecting on what I'd seen, when the black spot above and to our rear, caught my attention. The damned thing was getting bigger, coming closer and descending fast. I couldn't see any insignia from this distance, but I did recognize something of the shape, and how it was flying – like a bird of prey. A svelte-looking biplane painted in dark colours. As it swallowed up the sky between us, I noticed its lower wing was shorter than the upper, giving it a formidable air: a Fokker D VII.

'Captain, there's a plane behind us. I think it's a Fokker,' I shouted at the back of Catchpole's head. He nodded to show he understood. Then he jerked around to look for himself. After a brief moment he turned back, the motor's revolutions eased off, and we flew on – a couple of old folks, dressed for church, out for a leisurely Sunday drive. Then he yelled over his shoulder.

'1000 yards,' he said. 'Tell me when he's at a thousand yards.'

'1000 yards. Right. Will do.'

I squinted at the enemy biplane and tried to remember everything I'd ever learned on the musketry range. Judging distance is never easy. Up here without any landmarks, I was struggling. In everyday life a thousand yards isn't terribly far. With the naked eye you can make out moving figures at a thousand yards. So when details like the under-carriage and the struts on the wings began to emerge, I estimated he must be close to that.

'He's there. 1000 yards behind us,' I shouted. In the unlikely event he'd been dozing, I drummed on Catchpole's shoulder. 'Captain!'

Captain Catchpole nodded deliberately, so I knew he heard me. He seemed to slowly count to twenty, or it might have been two hundred if my heartbeat was anything to go by. Either way, it was an eternity as the black plane bore down upon us at a terrifying speed. No mistake about it, it was a Fokker all right. In an Old Joey, a Fokker on the warpath makes you feel like a tiny grey field mouse alone on a freshly harvested field with a Horned owl screaming down on you.

What I couldn't figure out, was why the Fokker wasn't firing. The Heine pilot was less than a thousand yards away and I knew from bitter experience that a machine gun could shoot much further than that. I wondered if I should be doing something other than staring fate in the eye. I pulled energetically at the Lewis gun and, after some fumbling, lined it up. But of course we were wobbling, and the Fokker was wobbling too. The only thing I saw with any clarity through the big metal sight was grey nothingness. Images of me blasting off the tail of our craft with a careless pull of the finger came to mind. I concluded I had as much chance of landing a shot on our pursuer as I did of hitting General von Below at the lunch table. So I held my fire. That's one thing I learned in the infantry, no sense wasting ammunition; you never know when you'll get any more. And the aeroplane in green and black camouflage, much closer by now, still wasn't firing either. We were being reeled in like a plump bass. 'Hang on,' shouted Catchpole.

The motor suddenly whined harder, Catchpole pushing the throttle all the way forward and we banked sharply to the left. Despite his warning it caught me off guard, and I was thrown to the side, temporarily powerless to regain my balance.

'What the hell,' I cursed. Out of the corner of my eye I saw the Fokker still descending and racing forward on his old course.

Catchpole couldn't have heard me, anyhow. The RE8's engine was at a fever pitch. With the wind and the pressure I could barely hear myself think. As we pulled through the sharp turn I lost sight of the enemy biplane. Soon, however, I found myself able to shift around in my seat so I could see.

In the brief instant it took me to spot him, I realized he too had begun to turn – towards us. And I saw something else. Amidships, above his engine and ahead of the cockpit, two holes were spitting orange fire. When they lined up with our path, we were in trouble. And that couldn't be in more than a second or two.

Then Catchpole yanked up the nose. The Fokker was still diving. I heard the heavy Vickers machine gun stutter into action. We were flying dead at him, no more than 200 yards away, maybe less. I could hear the engine of the hunter and the harsh consonants of his own machine guns. His turn was all but complete. The tick-tick-tick staccato of the Vickers erupted again. The Vickers could shoot a round 4000 yards. Eight of them every second. This was a long burst.

A hiccup came from the Fokker, and then a sickly cough, followed by a clunk. The propeller's rotations slowed as if they were churning underwater. Black smoke poured from the mottled cowling, and there was a flickering of flames. With that the biplane lost its momentum, tilted forward like a drunken sailor, and fell into a long arching dive. It passed just beneath us, and I turned and watched it in a mix of horror and morbid fascination as it plummeted to Earth, a dense plume of smoke marking its descent. The time ticked away till it hit ground. In my mind it was as if the whole world went quiet for an instant. After a pause there was a small flash. I took a deep breath and then looked ahead. I realized I was shaking. I don't think I was cut out for aerial combat.

Catchpole had his thumb in the air.

CHAPTER 22

16th of September, 1918
Aden Mound, near Chérisy, France

'So there really is only one way we *can* cross the canal,' I concluded.

General Loomis asked, 'The dry ground between Sains-lez-Marquion and Moeuvres?'

'That's right, sir. And I expect the Germans are well aware of that. Although they may think we'd be daft to do so given the defences. I suppose that's what we'll have to hope.'

The general frowned. He knew as well as I did that there were three divisions lined up across the canal with another five in reserve. And hoping the Germans believed we were of sound mind and a conservative nature was not what you would call a well-prepared plan – not in my estimation, and certainly not in Loomis'. From the little I'd seen of him he was a stickler for details.

'I wondered about XVII Corps,' I added. 'They're opposite that stretch now, still fighting the Boche on the western bank. If we're to crash the canal, then we can't do that with them in the way.'

He nodded. For a brief instant I thought he might smile. I don't think I'd ever seen him smile. It turned out to be a feint. 'Well, Major, that's one problem that *has* been solved. General Currie has arranged for us to side-step southwards. The Corp's southern boundary is now at Moeuvres. The intention is to leave the Germans on the west bank so they don't suspect anything is coming.'

'Ah,' I said, trying to mask my disappointment. XVII Corps had neatly side-stepped the whole mess, leaving it firmly in our lap.

'How long is it, exactly?' asked Loomis. 'The unfinished section between Sains-lez-Marquion and Moeuvres.'

'Roughly 2600 yards, sir.'

Ominously, an ear-shattering crack split the sky, followed by a long roll of thunder rumbling in its wake. It began to pour. For days on end it had rained. Not continuously, but often enough and hard enough to make life miserable. Autumn was coming, and with it new misery, and another new battle – the two inextricably linked. I looked to the dug-out entrance where silhouetted against a dreary dawn light a sheet of water was streaming down over the head jamb. As I watched, a soldier dropped into the entranceway and made a dash for it; the curtain of water broke around him as he entered the dug-out. He was drenched.

'A mile and a half,' mused Loomis, oblivious to the drama at his own front door. 'That's a very narrow front to put four divisions through.'

'Yes, it is, sir. Not to mention it would be a disaster if the Boche put down a gas bombardment on our assembly areas. We'll be packed in like sardines.'

'All right,' said Loomis, with a finality in his voice. 'We'll leave crossing the canal up to General Currie. He tells me our role will probably be to follow the lead divisions, and push in the direction of Cambrai, once the canal is crossed and Bourlon Wood taken.'

'Cambrai,' I whistled. 'That means puncturing the Marcoing line and likely tackling the Canal de l'Escaut as well.'

'Indeed it does, Major. At this stage nothing is definite, but we need to get planning right away.'

'Very good, sir,' I responded. 'I'll arrange a reconnaissance. And I'll request some additional aerial photographs. Hopefully I can soon give you more information.'

Overhead there was a long whine. Not long after, the muffled crump of an explosion. The daily Boche regimen of serving up early morning cocktails of high explosive and gas had begun. It was a tiring way to begin the day.

18ᵗʰ of September, 1918
Canal du Nord near Inchy-en-Artois, France

Having spent the better part of two days in a waterlogged tent with Smith pouring over maps, drawings of the canal and hundreds of aerial photographs, I was surprisingly eager to be in the field again. It was always one thing to read the reports from the scouts, and something entirely else to see it with your own eyes. General Lipsett had taught me that. I'd been teaching it to Smith.

Which was why he was beside me now, most of him obscured by a shrub. Off my right shoulder, ensconced in green shrubbery of his own, was Captain Merston, an intelligence officer from one of the 4ᵗʰ Division's brigades. He wasn't tall, so he fit in well. Myself, I was peering through the battered Lemaire field glasses I'd "borrowed" almost a year earlier. Leaves tickled my ears, a branch rubbed painfully against one cheek as I tried in vain to wriggle into a more comfortable position. Were it not that the abundant shrubbery on the other side of the canal housed dozens of machine guns, I would have just stood up. But the young lieutenant from the scouts who was our guide had made it abundantly clear that to show but a touch of flesh was to see it shot off. He made a persuasive case.

At this spot we were only a short sprint from the canal, and a few hundred yards from the German positions further south. Luckily, this morning, it cleared up a bit and the visibility was decent. The sides of the canal were dark and greasy from the recent rain. While they weren't terribly high, it would be no easy feat scrambling down one side, crossing the canal bed and climbing up the other under a hail of machine gun fire.

'Sir,' whispered Smith. 'It's a veritable Skittle Alley. I can see at least three machine-gun nests covering the road.'

'I see them,' I replied. The small road from Inchy crossed the canal close to where we lay. The construction work in this section was not far advanced, the excavations really just started. The canal bed was shallower still where the road dipped into it before rising again on the enemy side, heading towards Sains-lez-Marquion. The Germans had constructed an earthen and brick embankment along their edge of the canal. 'We'll need to take this quickly,' I said in Merston's general direction, 'so the artillery can move across.'

'Yes, sir,' came the reply from the shrubs. 'Perhaps we should move on ourselves,' he suggested. We'd barely backed out of the greenery edging slowly towards the rear, when a machine gun began rattling, quickly followed by another. The bushes we'd vacated were seeing a nasty trimming.

We spent the rest of the day working our way down the canal at intervals in the direction of Moeuvres, squirming forward in the moist earth as far we dared, taking notes of everything we saw.

Finally, around two, I turned to Smith, Merston and the scout lieutenant. We'd temporarily retreated to the staff car on the road for a hasty picnic of sorts, our sober lunch spread out on the bonnet. 'So, gentlemen, has anyone reached any useful conclusions?' I asked, and gulped at my canteen.

True to form Smith answered first. 'The enemy bank is very well wired, sir.'

'But the trenches behind are in poor condition,' said Merston. 'And the artillery should be able to clear a path through the wire, thick or not.'

'What do you think, Lieutenant?' I asked of our guide. He was the youngest of the party, and noticeably reticent, but you didn't get to be a lieutenant in the scouts on the strength of your diplomatic skills alone.

'Well, sir, I reckon it's neither the wire nor the trenches, but what's behind them that will prove crucial.'

'Fine,' I said. 'I'll bite. So what's behind the wire and the trenches?'

'See, sir, that's the whole problem. We don't quite know. To the east is Bourlon Wood. But with all the foliage on the trees you can't make out anything. Other than to suspect it's packed with Fritzs and their Mausers. One thing I will say, is at the battle of Cambrai the British ran into all sorts of dug-outs, and other obstacles, approaching Bourlon Wood. Overgrown or not, my bet is the wood, and every tiny undulation in front and behind, is full of Boche.'

I hadn't thought of that. The battle of Cambrai. There was a wealth of information from the maps and reports of November 1917 when General Byng and the Third Army had mounted their ill-fated surprise attack. Certainly everything the lieutenant said rang true. All the photos I'd seen of Bourlon Wood and vicinity had shown a lot of trees surrounded by thick undergrowth and long grass. With little creativity required Kaiser Wilhelm could have had his summer palace there, for all we knew. 'What about patrols, then?' I asked.

'Oh, we have made patrols, sir. At night. We've even crossed the canal and gone into the first trench system. But as you know, even if we were to make it through unnoticed there's a second line 1500 yards further on.' He raised his hands in a gesture of helplessness.

Merston spoke up. 'I have a feeling we've seen all we're going to see, sir. And I have a Commanders' Conference to attend shortly.'

'Fine,' I said resignedly. I made no attempt to argue with him. 'Looks like Smith and I are going to have to dust off the archives.' At the rate things were going, my report to Loomis might not even fill a page.

Having said our good-byes to Merston and the perceptive scout lieutenant, we were soon bumping down the Arras-Cambrai road towards Vis-en-Artois and our HQ near Chérisy. The engineers had done wonders patching the holes and removing the wreckage, but I was glad it was light, particularly as I was driving. It was not a road to attempt at speed, which made it fortunate the pedal-heavy Australians were miles to the south. Once it turned dark, the road would be packed with men and material all moving surreptitiously forward. Amiens was a mere six weeks ago and already we were working feverishly to prepare our third major attack.

'It's ironic, don't you think, sir?' said Smith.

'What is?'

'We've spent the whole day reconnoitring on our bellies, and it turns out the real intelligence is to be had from a few old maps and a couple of reports, we could have examined at our desks.'

Sourly I grunted. Today's "lesson" had taken an unexpected turn.

It was going on nine o'clock when a single bugle called out. 'Not again,' groaned somebody in exasperation. The bustling activity in one of the headquarter dug-outs gave itself over to a heavy unnatural silence. The lamps were shuttered and I blew out the candle beside me. There were shouts of 'lights out, lights out,' from outside. Heine was overhead.

The heavy droning crept closer. I looked over at Smith. 'Gothas,' he whispered excitedly. The whispering wasn't intended to be dramatic, but I could see the faces of our two new clerks as they exchanged meaningful glances. Everybody in the division knew what had happened a few nights before when a party was caught in the open and a couple of Gothas released their eggs.

'It takes real courage to venture out only at night,' I muttered to Smith. 'If they'd tried this three hours ago they'd be burning wrecks on the ground.'

'I expect the Germans realize that, sir,' said Smith, absentmindedly. I looked at him. He had his head tilted to one side, listening intently. I couldn't detect any sign of fear – curiosity rather. His own close encounter with a Gotha last spring, seemed to have left few scars, at least none I could see. Sensing I'd been staring at him he looked up and a shy smile appeared. He probably thought I found this as interesting as he did; he'd questioned me endlessly about my time in the aeroplane.

In a slow buzz the bombing machines, two or three I guessed, passed by. They hadn't spotted us. Or if they had, they hadn't wanted to waste their loads. Within a minute the sound of them disappeared, and reinforced dug-out or not, the faces within brightened appreciably. Soon the lights went on, work resumed, and General Loomis finally appeared.

'Tell me,' he said, after he'd plunked himself down next to the small table we were working at. 'What did you learn today, Major MacPhail?'

I told him straight. Naturally, I'd debated adding some rhetorical flourishes and extraneous detail, to camouflage the simple fact that I could tell him precious little beyond the obvious; the path to Bourbon Wood, and later to Cambrai, was likely sown with enemy positions. I had drawn a handful of obstacles on the map to show him, from an old British trench map Smith and I had discovered. And I had an aerial photo or two with a clear shot of the wood and the Marcoing Line. I didn't feel like much of an intelligence officer I must admit. Being on "probation" didn't help my frame of mind.

'The way I see it, sir, is that whatever plan we make, it's going to be contingent on fifty different things that *could* happen in the four miles before we're even in action, including the canal crossing itself. It doesn't help, I realize, but I think we have to prepare for anything and everything. Assuming we take Bourlon Wood, and that will be tough, the path to Cambrai is not likely to get any easier.'

Loomis pursed his mouth and observed me, expressionless. He said nothing for the longest while. 'Fine, Major. Thank you. We'll talk again tomorrow.'

As he clambered out of the dug-out I looked questioningly over at Smith.

He shrugged. 'I don't know, sir. He didn't say much.'

'No,' I said. 'And that's precisely what worries me.'

CHAPTER 23

21st of September, 1918
Château de Duisans, Duisans, France

Arriving at Corps Headquarters, I found myself still thinking about the two letters that I'd received in yesterday's post, and feeling mildly depressed as a result. I was accompanied to Corps HQ by another cold, drenching shower, which only added to my melancholy.

The first letter had been from Captain Clavell of the military police.

Dear Sir,

Subsequent to our conversation of September 12th last, I felt it only fitting to inform you of the progress of my investigation. I have followed up on the information you brought to my attention.

Following my recent inquiries to the relevant French Army authorities, I have been informed that Capitaine Madelot is unavailable for questioning regarding this matter, for the simple reason he has been reported missing for more than two weeks. I am therefore compelled to inform you that this avenue of investigation must, as a result, be considered a blind alley.

I will you keep you abreast of any further developments.

Yours faithfully,

Captain Aidan Clavell

A blind alley! I'd sat fuming at my desk. If I had pilfered a King's ransom I'd be missing as surely as Madelot was. Only I wasn't missing and Madelot was. That must be obvious. Clavell couldn't see reason if it hit him on the head. But then he appeared to be working to a foregone conclusion and it wasn't hard to guess what that was. All the rest of this farce, including his inquiries about Madelot, were pure form. Frustrated, I slammed my fist on the table, the letter crumpled in my hand.

Tibbet looked up, startled. 'What's the matter, Malcolm?'

'Oh, nothing,' I responded. 'Nothing you can help with, unfortunately. Thanks for asking, though.'

'If there's anything, anything at all, let me know. I'll do the best I can, Malcolm.'

'Thanks, Paul.' Tibbett's offer was well-meaning and I was touched by it, but he was as powerless as I was against the workings of an army bureaucracy run amok. Or more accurately a certain red-capped captain on a crusade. And I didn't much relish telling him the story – I'd told Benoît, of course, simply to get it off my chest – as that would require telling the *entire* wretched story, including my narrow escape from Clavell's uncle and the court martial he had planned for me. Only one or two others, including Benoît and Smith, knew anything about that. Predictably, when he did hear of my latest predicament, Benoît was as empathetic as ever.

The second missive had been no more uplifting than the first. My mother was spending her afternoons in bed. "Old age has finally struck," she wrote with two exclamation marks. That was a fairy tale I knew, for she was barely fifty, and I'd only ever known her as an inexhaustible bundle of energy that neither flu nor family misfortune could quell. My father and I struggled to keep up. So I guessed it had to be her heart. Spotting the familiar château at the end of the drive, I willed myself to push it all from my mind.

McAvity greeted me as I arrived. For his part, he was doing his utmost to hurry me into the Château de Duisans, whilst appearing not to.

'I see you've landed once again in the lap of luxury,' I said. 'Had enough of the dug-outs?' I stopped and breezily waved my arm at

185

the ivy-clad white stone of the façade like an enthusiastic tour guide intent on a lengthy explanation.

He cut me short. 'We're expecting an important visitor, momentarily,' he said. 'I had to be here, so that's why I asked you to come to the rear headquarters.' Slowly, a thought came to him. 'What exactly are you insinuating, anyhow, MacPhail? You lot had your headquarters here not two weeks earlier.'

I shrugged innocently, bounded up the couple of steps, walked across the paved stone terrace, through the open doorway and nearly mowed down Lieutenant-General Sir Arthur Currie. Fortunately, it would have taken more than me to bowl over our Corps commander. I probably would have just bounced off. Currie stood anchored there as solidly as the bronze likeness of Robert Peel outside the Parliament buildings in London. He was wearing his best dress hat, with his tunic neatly buttoned, a thick brown belt tightened not around his waist where the number of belt holes no doubt came up short, but well above it. The general was leaning on his cane, waiting. I had a suspicion it wasn't for me.

He took my theatrical entrance in stride. 'Major MacPhail. Always a pleasure to see you. Come in.'

'Hello, sir. Thank you,' I said and crisply saluted.

'To what do we owe the pleasure?' he asked.

I motioned to McAvity, who by now had joined me.

'Ah, visiting with Major McAvity. I'm pleased to see you're well, MacPhail,' Currie said. 'Lately, I think frequently of our time at Ypres.'

'As do I, sir. Although not fondly, I'm afraid to say.'

The general nodded understandingly. 'No. They were not the best of times, were they? Have you seen the canal?'

'Yes, sir, I wanted to tell Major McAvity about my reconnaissance.'

'Now that you've seen it, what do you think?'

It was a question you could answer a myriad different ways. I hesitated, thinking quickly of Benoît's advice to watch my tongue, and just as quickly threw that to the wind. Currie was not a general with whom you had to mince your words. In fact, he didn't have much respect for those who did.

'It appears the only way to attack is across the dry unfinished section,' I said. 'While it's strongly defended – there's little question about that – with a heavy artillery barrage we ought to be able to cross the canal and the trench lines behind. An element of surprise would help, naturally. Play to the fact the Boche may not think we'd be so rash.'

'It's definitely risky,' he agreed. 'We could get caught like mice in a trap.'

'There is a lot of risk, sir. It's a very narrow gap for the entire Corps. The artillery, and particularly the counter-battery guns, will need to be in top form. And speed will be crucial. We'll have to move across and fan out as quickly as possible, before the Boche can counter-attack or bring in more artillery. And then rapidly move up our own guns to support the advance.'

'So, in your opinion – do you think we can do it?'

I looked at him. 'Yes, sir, I do,' I said, vaguely aware I'd stuck my head above the parapet like a pumpkin on a stick, and for no apparent good reason.

Currie said, 'I'm happy to hear you say that, Major, for that's precisely what I intend to tell the field-marshal, when he asks.' *The field-marshal!*

McAvity made to spirit me away.

'Hang on a moment, gentlemen,' said Currie, 'I'll introduce you to him.'

I made faces at McAvity, a surprised face; he'd said nothing about the commander of the BEF dropping by. McAvity stared ahead. His brow was moist. There seemed little point in mentioning that an introduction was redundant – for the best part of a year I'd been bumping into the field-marshal.

The field-marshal didn't keep us waiting long. His staff car purred up only minutes after mine, explaining McAvity's earlier agitation. An adjutant with an umbrella promptly ran down the steps to greet him. General Currie walked down as well, at a more leisurely pace and received a handshake that spoke of an easy familiarity. Together, the two of them sauntered back up the steps, followed by the anxious adjutant with umbrella, who couldn't quite figure out how to shelter them both. I could see his dilemma; General Currie alone didn't fit under that modest circle of silk.

Field-Marshal Haig was immaculately turned out as always, but looked unusually grey and haggard.

The welcoming committee was small. Other than McAvity and myself and a major I didn't know, the only other familiar face was Brigadier-General Ox Webber, Currie's chief of staff. Since the Amiens show we knew each other quite well. He said a few friendly words to me as we waited.

When it was my turn, I saluted, and before General Currie could introduce me, the field-marshal gently cut him off; 'Major MacPhail and I are already acquainted, Arthur.' His manner was formal, but warm, and despite myself I felt a glow in my cheeks, perhaps embarrassed at the many pithy remarks I'd made at his expense. 'Best of luck in the coming campaign, Major.'

'Thank you, sir,' and for some reason I added, 'And don't worry, sir, we'll deliver the goods.' It was a line General Currie used often. Both he and the field-marshal smiled at my impetuousness, but said nothing.

Later, alone with McAvity, I asked, 'So why is Sir Douglas here?'

'Our esteemed army commander, General Horne, is very nervous about the plan. I imagine the field-marshal is here to judge for himself,' he answered.

'And what is the plan, exactly?'

McAvity smiled. 'You know better than to ask that. Although the way you talked to General Currie I had the impression you already knew.'

'It's what I would do,' I responded. 'At least if the option of doing nothing is definitely off the table.'

'It is,' McAvity said resolutely. 'Doing nothing has been assigned to other divisions.'

'We never seem to get the choice assignments,' I muttered.

McAvity covered his mouth with his fist. He knew exactly what I meant. No, there would be no holding the line while someone else battered their way through the heart of the German defences. We were first in line for all the tough chores – us and the Aussies. They attracted their own fair share of trouble, and word had it they were ordered to smash through the centre of the Hindenburg Line.

'What's with Haig?' I asked. 'Is he sick? He looked terrible.'

'He's under a lot of pressure, Mac. The Third and Fourth Armies together with the First French are still pushing through the outworks of the Hindenburg system, but the casualties are heavy enough that the politicians are in a tizzy. And Haig is getting an earful.'

'It makes you wonder where the politicians were in '16 and '17,' I said caustically, 'when the casualties were really piling up.'

McAvity ignored me, and continued. 'The Americans and the French are taking a pause.'

'I'm surprised they were so successful at St. Mihiel,' I said. I was referring to the huge bulge in the line between Verdun and Metz that they had successfully exorcised little more than a week before. 'The Sammies did well in their first big show.'

'They did,' agreed McAvity, 'although they had a bit of luck, too. The Germans were in the midst of a retreat.'

I took a sip of my tea. 'And what's next?'

'This is very hush-hush, Mac, but our assault is to be accompanied by offensives along the entire front. That's what General Currie told me. I'm sure Haig will have more news for us today...'

'I never thought I'd say this, but I actually feel sorry for him.'

McAvity gaped. 'For Haig?'

'Yes,' I said. 'He looked terrible. He's done a lot of stupid things, I'd be the first to acknowledge that, but in the past half year... he's made all the right decisions. Even when they weren't popular ones. *Particularly* when they weren't popular ones. Like halting the offensive at Amiens when Foch was nagging at him to continue. And just as Haig seems to be coming into his own, the know-it-alls in Westminster are taking him to task. Talk about rotten timing. It just doesn't seem fair, that's all.'

'Perhaps, if it doesn't work out with Loomis, you can sign on with Haig?' said McAvity. 'Your charming ways would be a beacon of light at GHQ.'

Wearily I shook my head. I'd made the mistake of telling him about my tenuous relationship with my new general.

26th of September, 1918
Warlus, France

For the time being Loomis was revealing little of what he thought about our relationship or anything else. He was, however, keeping me very busy. I don't know whether it was a result of Haig's visit or something else, but not only was the attack on, the objectives had actually expanded. That meant yet more planning. More details to master. We were now to cross the canal, fight past three trench lines and the imposing Bourlon Wood, all the way to the outskirts of Cambrai – a huge rectangle of ground beginning with the canal on the left. *Then* we were to circle around Cambrai to the northeast, seizing the bridges over the Canal de l'Escaut, where it exited the city and headed north.

I found Benoît sitting on a small wooden bench at the back of the château. Uncharacteristically he was hunched over, staring out at the garden behind, hands clasped before him. The small château at Warlus was a lovely place, surrounded by green and a small pond out back, undefiled by the tents and Nissen Huts assembled nearby. It was only eight in the evening, but already the grounds were cloaked in a shadowy gloom, with darkness soon to follow. Apart from the distant boom of guns fifteen miles away near the canal, it was quiet.

I hadn't talked with DuBois for a while, a snippet or two at most – not long enough to call it a conversation. There was a lot I wanted to say. With some time on my hands after dinner I'd gone searching for him.

'*Salut*, Benoît,' I said. 'Long time no see.'

'Hi, Mac.' He grinned a big, toothy grin and patted the small patch of space on the bench beside him.

I sat down.

'Ça *va?*' he asked.

'I don't know,' I replied. 'Loomis wants me up with the 4th Division tomorrow. To keep an eye on their progress. And to warn him before we need to move up ourselves, I suppose. So I expect I'll be in the middle of it once more.'

DuBois nodded. 'Here we go again…' he said. He gave a small

190

laugh, although there was absolutely nothing to laugh about that I could see. Benoît could make light of anything.

'One thing I *can* tell you, Benoît, if the Boche artillery catches us while the whole Corps is lined up, waiting to attack…' I shuddered. It wasn't purely a theoretical concern; I was going to be in the middle of that mass of troops. Three of our four divisions were poised to attack, seventy-five thousand men. Thousands more from the 11th Imperial Division were to join us.

'We've arranged a counter-battery barrage,' said Benoît. 'If the enemy starts to shell our lines before the attack, our heavies will smash him. Can you guess what the call sign is?' He had a smirk on his face.

I shook my head.

'Hell.'

'How appropriate. And what's the countersign? Damnation?'

He shook his head. 'Bricks.' I looked at him dubiously.

'The Boche will wish they were bricks when we're done with them,' he muttered. Benoît's hatred of the enemy was as legendary as his appetite.

'That sounds fine,' I began to say, 'but if you lot miss a battery of whizz-bangs hiding behind a hill…'

Benoît cut me off. 'We've identified at least a hundred guns already, Mac. We've been very busy. I don't think you have to worry about that. We'll get them.'

'Let's pray you're right,' I said.

We sat in silence for a while, thinking. In my case brooding. Almost dozing in his. Benoît's face had taken on the complexion of a placid summer lake, untouched by wind or rain. Later, reflecting on it, I had it completely wrong. His languid features were mere camouflage for the swirling eddies below. He was the closest thing to a best friend I had, and I was still discovering new things about him.

'Have a look, Mac,' he said softly. He inhaled the "H" as he always did and dragged out "look" so it became "luke". On an upturned palm he revealed a dainty silver locket on a thin silver chain.

There was something tender about the way he was cradling it. 'From your family?' I asked.

Benoît beamed. I was glad for once I'd held my smart Alec remarks in check. 'Geneviève, my little sister,' he explained. 'She just turned thirteen.'

With two fingers I gently plucked the chain from his hand and placed it in mine. Carefully I pried opened the heart-shaped locket with my thumbs. Inside there was a picture of a young girl in dark ponytails, smiling broadly.

'Well,' I said, 'now I finally know who got the looks in the DuBois family.'

Benoît didn't argue. In fact, his face was bursting with pride.

'In all the time we've known each other you never *once* told me about your younger sister,' I said. 'I've heard about your mother, your father, your brother, your older sister Gisèle, your aunts, uncles. Christ, I even heard about your grocer, Dénis Lévesque. But not your younger sister?'

'*Non*,' he said, and after a pause: '*Ceux qui vous sont les plus chers…* He stopped, and glanced at me to see if I understood. Seeing my bewilderment, he explained: 'Our dearest… we keep them to ourselves.' I nodded. 'Mac, we've been through a lot, you and I. Haven't we?'

'Yes we have, Benoît. We sure have.'

'Tomorrow I'm to move up with the divisional artillery. As soon as the engineers can get some bridges built.' Restlessly he consulted his watch. I didn't have to. I knew the whole treacherous endeavour was less than nine hours away.

So that was it, this unexpected burst of sentimentality. Benoît was nervous. 'What are you supposed to do?' I asked.

'To coordinate between the archies and the forward observers. The artillery is moving ahead with the advance. And we have to keep the Boche guns under fire.'

'Ah,' I replied.

We stared out into the darkness, where the old trees and the little paths that wound between them were hidden from us, except for the rustling of leaves audible with each puff of wind. We sat like this for a couple of minutes.

Suddenly Benoît asked, 'So, what did you tell him?'

'What do you mean?'

'General Currie, when he asked you whether we could do it.' I'd forgotten I'd mentioned my encounter with old "Guts 'n Gaiters" to him.

'How do you know I said anything?'

Benoît rolled his eyes. 'Come on, Mac. I know you. You can't help sharing your wisdom, particularly when generals are involved.'

I groaned good-naturedly. 'I said we could do it.'

'And you think we can?'

'Yes, but there's a chance it could turn into the biggest disaster of the war.'

Benoît nodded and leaned against me with his arm draped brotherly around my shoulders. It was the sort of intimate, unmilitary gesture only he could get away with. 'You take care of yourself, Mac.'

'You too, Benoît, you too. Don't worry, you'll do fine. Listen, when this is all over I'll treat you to a good bottle. I've still got that 1905 St. Emilion I liberated from a dug-out in the D-Q Line.'

His eyes lit up. Once more, he was his old self. 'I'll hold you to that, Mac.'

CHAPTER 24

27th of September, 1918
Dug-out near Inchy-en-Artois, France

It began raining around 1 a.m. By 3 a.m. the troops were largely assembled, huddling miserably in shallow slit trenches, shell holes, anything that afforded a touch of cover. Not from the sheets of cold drizzling rain, but from what we all feared might come. Would a German bombardment crash down on our heads? With four divisions packed together like so many cattle in a stockyard. In the darkness you could feel the tension. It hung in the air, an invisible mist that penetrated clothing and body, all the outwardly stoic pretences, settling into the deepest corners of the soul where it lingered and festered. Which was where the pre-battle tot of rum came in. The army had presumably invented the tradition precisely for times like this. Only a chug or two of diluted rum rarely dispelled the uneasy, pulsing knot in your gut. And so it was again.

This morning the lads just wanted the show to start. So did I. They were nervous but they were ready. I chatted quietly with a few of them. After a spell, well soaked by now, I trooped back to the relative safety of a dug-out inhabited by one of the 4th Division's brigades.

12th Brigade HQ was in Slip Trench, once the Hindenburg support line, a modestly deep, well built, but now very crowded bunker 1200 yards behind Inchy-en-Artois. The village itself was no more than a thousand yards west of the canal. At this range, if the Germans did begin shelling, there was no way we'd escape their wrath.

Lieutenant Smith had accompanied me here around midnight. The new commander of our own 7th Brigade had just joined us. That Smith was along was no particular surprise. I must have looked puzzled, though, when Loomis told me Brigadier-General Clark was to be in our party. Either Loomis didn't see my puzzlement for what it was, or didn't care that he had, for an explanation was not forthcoming. Painfully aware of my status these days, I'd dumbly nodded. I was doing a lot of that recently, it occurred to me.

We were gathered in a small room at the end of a dark, earthen passageway which led to a rough-hewn staircase of a dozen-odd steps that rose into the trench itself. Under the low wood-beamed ceiling, the air was hazy with swirling blue tobacco smoke and that peculiar sensation of nervous anticipation. Brigadier Clark was seated at the rectangular table in the middle of the room. He was sharing tea with Brigadier MacBrien, the CO of the 12th, together with the brigade major and the very same intelligence captain, Merston, who'd accompanied us on our canal reconnaissance.

From an angle, I studied Clark. Despite his rank, he couldn't have been more than three or four years older than I was. Judging from the acres of bulbous forehead, shiny in the soft light, his hair had been in full retreat for years. To compensate he'd grown a neat little moustache. Clark was visibly nervous. He had these big, unnaturally round eyes, set deep back in his skull, flitting to and fro. At every lull in the conversation, he rubbed at the cleft in his chin. I suppose in his shoes I would have been nervous too. Coincidence or not, two weeks before Clark had been one of the battalion commanders in the very brigade we were visiting. To everyone's shock, the commander of the 7th Brigade, Brigadier Dyer, had left at a moment's notice. Lieutenant-Colonel Clark was promoted in his stead. Now he was commanding a brigade himself in an entirely new division. He was to lead it into battle in less than twelve hours. It was all very mysterious.

I leaned over to Smith. 'So why *did* Dyer leave?' I whispered. 'Did he fall out with General Loomis? It can't be a coincidence he left the very same day General Lipsett did. Loomis must have demanded it.'

'I don't think so, sir. That's not what I hear. They say Dyer was ill.'

'Yes,' I acknowledged, 'I did hear talk of that.'

Smith clearly heard the doubt in my voice, for he added, 'Brigadier Clark has a good reputation, sir.'

'Yes, yes he does.' I looked over at Smith. Without me saying much of anything at all, my lieutenant knew exactly what I was thinking – that some murky behind-the-scenes intrigue was rearing its head. Probably he was thinking the same thing himself, but those were the sort of roads Smith never, ever, went down. I usually did, even if I regretted it afterwards. One thing was certain, changing horses in midstream weeks before a major attack was a risky affair. It made me wonder whether General Loomis might have sent me here for an entirely different reason other than simply monitoring the 4th Division's attack and preparing our own. Perhaps he was anxious that an old hand like me keep an eye on our fledgling brigade commander?

Then Smith spoke and I was an illusion poorer. 'Of course you knew, sir, the 7th Brigade is to move through the 12th later this afternoon? That's why the brigadier is here.'

'Of course,' I quickly responded.

At a quarter past five, we climbed out of the dug-out and positioned ourselves on an embankment looking east to watch the show. The rain had mercifully stopped. But the sky was dark and overcast, the ground treacherously slippery.

Five minutes later at ZERO hour, I nearly jumped out of my skin. A battery of field guns crashed violently into action immediately behind us. The heavens lit up. To our rear, muzzle flashes of orange, violet and red merged into one. Fifteen hundred yards ahead, the detonations came so fast in succession that the horizon seemed ablaze, leaving the passing clouds above glowing in ominous hues of oranges and reds. The very ground was trembling and each of us with it. We stood watching, mesmerized. Dante's inferno had descended on the west bank of the Canal du Nord. Slowly, deliberately, it began a terrifying march across.

800 guns were bellowing. There was one for every nine yards of front, excluding the heavies designated for counter-battery duty, or shelling the crossroads and strong points. When you considered that

each 18-pounder was firing four shells a minute into those scant nine yards, you could imagine the devastation. It was an unprecedented storm of fire and steel. Even by the standards of the past few months, when every barrage somehow surpassed the one before, the effect was awe-inspiring; there had been nothing like it the entire war.

Hundreds of heavy machine guns now took up the chant, chattering angrily. A deadly hail of lead was showering down upon the German lines. A torrent of khaki-clad men pushed forward. General Currie's daring plan was on.

There was no point talking – the thunder of the battery to our rear made certain of that. Despite the light from the barrage, an acrid shroud of smoke had settled in and trying to see much of anything was a challenge. As dirt and bigger things began flying around, we retreated to the safety of the dug-out, except for Captain Merston who headed out towards the canal. We were all painfully aware the German retaliation would come here in our rear lines. There was no glory and even less sense in sticking around. We'd hear soon enough whether the canal was breached.

That didn't make the waiting any easier. But at 6.35 a.m. – I was keeping close watch – a little more than an hour after the attack began, Captain Merston returned. 'The 10th Brigade is well across the canal,' he blurted out as he burst into the room. There was a collective sigh of relief, followed by a second of silence until the room exploded in voices and Merston was spirited away to the corner, where two brigadiers and a major awaited his report. The 11th and 12th Brigades would be following closely, so understandably they wanted to know everything.

I gazed over at Smith standing a few feet away. He was wearing that lop-sided boyish grin of his and I couldn't help throwing him a smile of my own. A lot could happen. However, the first big obstacle was overcome. The German bombardment arrived a little slow and the initial fury dissipated quickly. The counter-battery lads were well on top of things. DuBois had been right about that as well. I can't say I'd ever seen them more effective. And that was likely the most important news of the morning.

Around 7 a.m., an hour and half after the attack began, the first field guns were being manhandled across the canal. To our left, 1st

Division reported they were well on their way. As to the battalions of the 4th Division, they were moving like veritable bulls of Bashan. By 7.15 a.m. they rushed the Canal du Nord Line and took Quarry Wood. Soon they were through the Marquion Line. In less than two hours we'd crashed the canal, two trench lines, and were more than 2000 yards ahead, still going strong. Only Bourlon Wood and the Marcoing Line remained.

An hour later Brigadier MacBrien stood and made an announcement: 'Gentlemen, it's time HQ moves forward. Collect your things, you've got five minutes.'

I was prepared. Since early August, hardly a reconnaissance or liaison of mine had gone as planned. Consequently, I was ready for more of the same and had made my preparations accordingly. In addition to my normal accoutrements, I'd brought along a pack stuffed with five 10-round magazines, four packs of hardtack, three tins of bully beef, some tinned milk, three Mills bombs, an extra canteen of water, plus one Lee-Enfield and a bayonet. It was quite a collection. The partridge in the pear tree I left at HQ.

'Damn,' I cursed, the loaded pack cutting into my back. I'd stepped out of yet another shell-hole and tripped almost immediately over a strand of wire. My left arm was beginning to throb. We were crossing the torn fields in the direction of the canal and I was rethinking the advantages of travelling light.

Captain Merston glanced at me. A flicker of what might have been amusement passed over his face. 'You're better equipped than the assault troops, Major.'

I gritted my teeth and pulled my pack up over my shoulders. Soon we reached the canal.

Once there, I grasped a rope line with both hands to repel down the slope. Somehow, as I stepped off the bank the rope got tangled in all the gear and, in my efforts to untangle it, I lost my footing and my grip. Rope burning in the one hand, I slid precipitously down the slippery embankment and into the waiting arms of Lieutenant Smith. It wasn't so much painful, as painfully embarrassing. My left shoulder and arm were aching by now. The others seemed preoccupied with their own tribulations.

'There we are, sir,' Smith said, helping me to my feet. He looked concerned. It was one of his endearing qualities; most others would have laughed their heads off at seeing a major on his ass.

'Thanks,' I murmured. I pulled myself together and looked around.

By this hour, it was long since light and the bed of the canal was buzzing with activity. A line of horse-drawn guns were moving cautiously through a gap in the western embankment and along a narrow, elevated track leading to the other side. Sappers were filling a massive mine crater with debris scavenged from nearby. A sergeant was urging them on. A lot was riding on the engineers; to them the task of building the tramways, bridges and roads that would carry the waves of guns and horses, and, not to forget, the thousands of shells needed to sustain our attack. Off my left, where the canal made for the hamlet of Sains-lez-Marquion, a swarm of men, long timbers swaying on their shoulders, were erecting two wooden trestle bridge frames. From the looks of it they were making good progress.

On the far side of the canal bed, a score of tall scaling ladders stood propped against the earthen wall. I made grateful use of one of them and climbed up to the eastern bank. Almost immediately, I encountered a handful of corpses in a pit next to a smouldering machine gun. The gun was a Maxim. The grey-clad forms were German. All around were blackened shell holes, shreds of wire, debris, and mutilated bodies; what the awesome tornado of the barrage had chewed up and spat out in its wake.

Not much further on I came to a line of three other bodies – ours. They lay one neatly after the other, only paces apart. A machine gun crew had survived the barrage and caught them as they'd moved along in file. They'd been too close together, drunk on the heady, intoxicating spirit of battle.

Once we emerged from the belt of shell-ravaged shrubbery and German defences, we came to a startling green vista, punctuated by the strange sight of dense white columns of smoke billowing upwards from the smoke shells. The colour of the landscape alone confirmed what we all knew, that the war had taken a turn for the better. After four years of back-and-forth fighting over tortured landscapes of muddy browns, greys and blacks, any colour was a welcome sight.

Less welcome was the dark rise, looming up a mile to the east. The ruins of an ancient village abutted it to the north. Merston caught up with me as I stood studying the sight with my field glasses.

'Daunting isn't it?'

I nodded. 'It is indeed, Captain. There's a lot of history there. The Brits had a terrible time at Bourlon Wood during the Cambrai offensive last year. They finally took it – at Field-Marshal Haig's insistence I heard – but they were forced to give it up only days later.'

'Which is why we've been pouring gas on it for five straight days, I expect,' said Merston.

'Yeah,' I said with a sigh. I lowered my glasses so I could look at him. 'I hope you fellows have more success than they did.'

We pushed on. A thousand yards to the east we arrived at a German dug-out. Further east the fall of shells and the rattle of gunfire was plain to hear. This was to be the 12th Brigade's new HQ, in the middle of the recently vacated Marquion line. 'Jesus, the stove is still warm,' I said, to no one in particular, and I snatched back my hand. 'Pity they didn't leave any food.' There were a few smiles.

No sooner did we arrive, than word came that the lead battalions had reached the village and Bourlon Wood. Which was exactly what we all wanted to hear. But an hour or two later, the good news came to an abrupt end.

'What's wrong?' I asked Merston. I'd seen him turning away from the runner, and from the troubled look in his eyes, it was obvious something was bothering him.

'Our right flank is hanging. The 63rd Division hasn't come up yet.'

'The Navy, eh? Have they run aground so soon?'

Merston looked mystified.

'The 63rd. The Royal Navy Division,' I explained. 'It's not the first time those sailors have left us hanging.' I told him about our first day at Passchendaele, eleven months ago, when the 63rd was meant to be holding *our* flank. Now we were holding *theirs*, or more specifically the flank of the Third and Four Armies who were approaching the Hindenburg Line along a vast front to the south. The only thing was, the flank was further ahead than the attack. It was not the way things were supposed to be.

'Well, there's little we can do but refuse our flank and wait till they catch up,' Merston said. 'Bourlon Wood has just become even more difficult.'

Unbeknownst to me, Clark was listening in, and he approached me after Merston left. 'What did he mean, Major? About Bourlon Wood becoming more difficult?'

I stared at him surprised. I was beginning to worry that Clark was in way over his head. Rather than voicing that concern, I simply explained: 'It's a bit of a balls-up, sir. The plan was to encircle the Bois de Bourlon in a pincer movement. The 54th and the 87th Battalions are trying to make their way around the left side and through the village, but we can't very well move around the right until the Imperials are up. As it is we're ahead of them, and we're supposed to be holding the Third Army's left. Besides, it would be a nightmare to do so. Just think what the German enfilade fire would do. Until the Royal Navy comes up, the Boche gunners on our right have nothing to do but shoot at us. As it is, simply staying put, I expect the MGs are causing havoc.'

Clark frowned. 'Yes, I see,' he said. From his expression, I wasn't entirely convinced he did. But whether he did or he didn't, I wasn't about to enquire. In my experience, generals rarely take well to having subordinates point out their inadequacies.

'I'm going to send a message to General Loomis, shortly,' I announced. 'I intend to suggest we postpone the 3rd Division's attack until tomorrow.' Clark's face darkened. 'If we leapfrog through, we'll only further expose our right flank, sir. And we'll be in no position to take the Marcoing Line. I don't think it's advisable. Not the way things stand now. Certainly not until Bourlon Wood and Fontaine-Notre-Dame are ours, and that could take a while. Unless you think otherwise, sir?'

'No. No. I suppose not,' said Clark. He knew I was right, but I could see the gears churning upstairs as he searched for a way out. Apparently he didn't find one, for after a pause, he sighed. 'I don't imagine General Loomis will be pleased.' Which, no doubt, was what was worrying our new brigadier all along.

'Think of it this way, sir. Just imagine how pleased the general will be if he loses the better part of two battalions before we even get to our starting lines.'

It proved a convincing argument. 'Right. Well, carry on then, Major.'

With that he moved off to MacBrien and the 12ᵗʰ Brigade staff – more congenial company than the sourpuss from divisional HQ.

I turned to Smith and raised my eyebrows suggestively. Smith looked back, uneasily, but said nothing. This time I didn't let it be.

'You heard it all. No sticking your head in the sand this time, Lieutenant.'

Smith paused, collecting his thoughts. 'I expect the general's a trifle anxious, sir, if that's what you're getting at.'

I sighed. 'You're probably right. I hope his nerves settle down before the division attacks. He's got a brigadiers' conference later this afternoon. That's why I thought I'd lay it out for him. We wouldn't want him proposing something rash in the heat of the moment.'

'Well, sir, if the 4ᵗʰ Division don't take Bourlon Wood fairly soon, it may not much matter.'

To which wisdom I said absolutely nothing. There was nothing to say. Without Bourlon Wood the entire undertaking was a distinctly shaky affair.

CHAPTER 25

28th of September, 1918
1200 yards northeast of Bourlon Wood, France

Smith and I needn't have worried, at least not about Bourlon Wood.

Close to one o'clock, a spray rocket to the east had soared into the air and from it showered a rain of silver and gold. It was an ostentatious display, the kind one might more readily associate with a sun-drenched Dominion Day, were it not that the Dominion was an ocean away, the sun was obscured by cloud, and this was a day dedicated to war not celebration. The 4th Division, brutally aware of the importance of its objectives, wasn't about to be waylaid by the Third Army's late arrival. Two battalions stormed around the left of the Wood and through the village. Another, the 102nd – full of big outdoorsy types from the northern forest country of British Columbia – beat its way through the trees to the south. Bourlon Wood fell surprisingly quickly. But ominously, from the village of Fontaine-Notre-Dame, 1000 yards further on and with the Bapaume-Cambrai road running down its middle, Boche machine guns were spewing fire.

While the 4th Division took right, the 1st Division fanned out to the left. The *Old Red Patch* rolled up the heavily defended villages lining the canal and raced northeast to capture the blue line on schedule, then pushed on. To think it was less than a month ago they'd battered their way through the invincible Drocourt-Quéant Line. On their heels came the Corp's recent addition, the Imperial 11ᵗʰ. Late in the afternoon, the Brits moved past on the left and pushed another two and a half miles northwards. They took the machine-gun infested heights of Oisy-le-Verger from behind and almost made it to the Canal de la Sensée.

All in all, General Currie had every reason to be pleased; he'd pulled off the canal crossing, and in the process kept his job. If there was a more daring operation in the entire war I didn't know of it. According to a whispered telephone call from McAvity, half the general staff had warned him of the consequences if the attack went sour. Which was more than a little ironic. Especially as the ones doing the warning, were virtually identical to the ones pushing for an attack in the first place. Most importantly, to my way of thinking, we'd avoided a bloodbath.

Unfortunately, early the next day the casualties began pouring in.

It was 9.30 a.m. when I once again reached the Royal Canadian Regiment's humble headquarters. I'd been with the battalion since six this morning, ever since they'd stormed out of their assembly positions on the eastern fringes of Bourlon Wood.

The dug-out to one side of the sunken road had been transformed into a twisted shambles. A handful of men were heaving at timbers. As I approached, one squirmed out of the wreckage of the entranceway. 'This is all I could find, sir,' he shouted, holding up a pile of papers.

I went and stood beside the kilted major he was addressing. 'What happened?' I asked.

'Shell hit it. Colonel Willets and a few others were wounded, and his adjutant Captain McCrae is dead, I'm afraid. General Clark told me I'm in command of the battalion. Somehow the telephone is still working.' By way of explanation he tilted his head in the direction of the dug-out where it was a sheer wonder there was anything left, let alone a working telephone.

'Rough luck,' I said, shaking my head. 'I'm MacPhail from the divisional intelligence staff. I'm here to follow the attack's progress and keep General Loomis informed.'

'Topp,' he replied. For a split second I actually thought it was a curiously worded greeting. A "top of the day" kind of thing. Then he clarified. 'Charles Topp,' he announced, and extended a hand. 'I'm not even from the RCR. In fact, I'm with the 42ⁿᵈ. After the Camerons took Fontaine this morning, my CO sent me out on a reconnaissance and I arrived in time to see the explosion. It could have been worse. A minute earlier and I don't think I'd be standing here. But now I have to figure out the lay of the land, and quickly, too.'

'Well, I can help with that,' I said. 'I'm just back from the fighting. The battalion's finally made it through the wire and they're solidly on the Marcoing Line. Not far from Raillencourt. However, they've lost most of their officers and the casualties are quite heavy. The Boche are putting up a very stiff fight. The plan is to move on to the support line. Is there anything I can do?'

'I don't suppose you'd mind heading back and keeping an eye on things? Just so I know what's going on. I can't very well go out on reconnaissance myself.'

I stared eastwards, where across a thousand yards of shell-pocked undulating land and atop the highest of the small ridges, was the last German trench line before Cambrai. At least it had been until an hour ago. 'Sure,' I replied. Under the circumstances, there was little else I could say. I left my scribbled report with Major Topp.

The Marcoing Line stretched from left to right (north to south), beginning at the Canal de la Sensée. The canal formed a natural northern boundary to this rectangle of land we were on. From the canal's edge, the Marcoing Line snaked southwards, edging along the valley of the Scheldt and the city's eastern suburbs, and on to the village from whence it took its name. The plan had been to take it yesterday. But that was not to be. By sheer perseverance, and the courage of a lieutenant named Gregg, the 42ⁿᵈ Battalion had found a way through the wire and into the trench this morning. However, the Germans were fighting on.

As I approached the crest, there was another burst of machine gun fire, this one uncomfortably close. I made a run for it and dove into the trench ahead. Startled, an officer and three other ranks turned quickly, bringing their bayonets to bear. They'd been looking down the reverse slope towards the support line 400 yards away. That's where the action was. 'At ease,' I said, and they relaxed.

'We're pinned down, sir,' said the young lieutenant from the RCR.

'We're taking heavy fire on our left from those houses at Sailly, and even more from Ste. Olle, ahead of us. The support line is heavily wired, sir. We're still trying to find some gaps. Where on earth are the Boche getting all these men from?'

'Based on the identifications we made this morning, I'd venture to say they're from the 26th Reserve Division, among others.'

'You mean that same blasted bunch that chewed us up near Boiry?'

'Yes, indeed, Lieutenant. The Württemburgers are back, rested and refreshed after a month away. I can't say I recall seeing them in the German order of battle. My guess is they've been rushed up as reinforcements.' As I said it the dreadful realization hit. This battle was going to be a meat grinder.

I'd been so focused on whether we'd get past the Canal and capture Bourlon Wood, I hadn't given much thought to the second phase, swinging around Cambrai to the northeast and capturing the crossings on the Canal de l'Escaut (Scheldt). But the enemy had. He was determined not to lose Cambrai, so that meant holding firm. That explained all the reinforcements.

Inevitably, I couldn't help thinking about all the pieces that hadn't fallen into place yesterday; the Third Army not coming up; the 4th Division being temporarily stymied outside Bourlon Wood; our attack being delayed… one thing had led to another. And that had granted the enemy the time he needed to bring in waves of reinforcements.

The lieutenant and the men were watching me. As the superior officer they probably thought I had all the answers. I didn't bother to disillusion them. 'How bad is it?' I asked.

'Bad, sir. We've lost a dozen men in the past ten minutes. I was planning to send a runner to Brigade, to let them know.'

'No, let me. I'll go. You need some support right away and I suspect they'll be more apt to listen to a major on their doorstep.'

The lieutenant nodded enthusiastically. He brushed away a long lock of curly brown hair that had dropped down from under his helmet. It seemed that at every battle the officers were getting younger. It might also have just been me getting older. On the Western Front age doesn't creep up, it races.

'Don't worry, lieutenant. Keep at it. I'll be back soon. Hopefully with the cavalry.'

I didn't run, but I did walk very quickly and after a brief pause to inform Major Topp – who suggested I simply call – I arrived at brigade headquarters, a covered trench on the north side of Bourlon Wood, panting so hard two orderlies jumped to their feet to come to my assistance.

'I'm going to send in the PPCLI,' said Clark, after I explained. 'The brigade is tasked with taking Ramillies today, and the crossings over the Canal de l'Escaut, so time is of the essence.'

'You must be joking, sir. Ramillies? That village is three miles away, on the northern side of Cambrai?'

Clark had a harried look to him. 'Yes, that's correct, Major.'

'And there's a trench line, two major roads, one rail line and half a dozen villages in between. And God knows how many Germans.'

'Well, then I suggest we get at it, Major.'

I was about to sputter a response, but short of sparking a mutiny I saw that I'd lost his attention. Clark had turned to a signaller who appeared more harried than he was. 'I'll telephone the orders ahead,' he called out over his shoulder. 'If you hurry you might catch up with them.'

'Yes, sir,' I grumbled. If only I'd taken Topp's advice and used the field telephone.

Brigade Major Styles, who I knew from way back, stopped me as I prepared to leave. 'You forgot that,' he said, and pointed at a familiar looking pack wedged into an alcove in the trench wall.

'Thanks, but I have what I need,' I said, brandishing my Lee-Enfield. 'I don't think I'll have any use for tinned milk where I'm headed.' But then I walked over to the pack, knelt down, pulled out two packages and stuffed them into my satchel bag along with the Mills bombs and the spare magazines.

'Milk, after all,' said Styles with a grin.

'No, bully beef and hardtack,' I replied, 'otherwise lunch is going to be a very Spartan affair.'

The Patricias, together with the RCR, quickly swung the tide. They rolled up the rest of the Marcoing Line in this sector and worked their way into the support trenches. The PPCLI were in foul spirits and it wasn't entirely due to sleep deprivation; their revered commander and one of the old *Originals*, Lieutenant-Colonel Charlie Stewart, had been killed only hours earlier and they were out for revenge.

After things settled down I asked around for the RCR lieutenant with whom I'd spoken. The faces were dour. A corporal responded. 'A machine gun caught him, sir. I don't think he's going to make it.' Grimly I nodded. I was strangely affected by the news, even though I didn't know the young lieutenant's name. War was like that, coldly impersonal, but then I'd looked this fellow in the eye and promised him I'd be back with help. And that was anything but cold or impersonal.

Before long, the morning's concerns were supplanted by new ones, and I appeared to be smack in the middle of them. Trouble had been a recurring theme of my time in the army, so it ought not to have been a great surprise.

The objective was the road and railway to Douai heading northwards out of Cambrai. Beyond them to the east was the high ground and the strategically located village of Tilloy. Evening was approaching, and with dusk the fields took on a soft glow, a backdrop against which the furious maelstrom of the barrage played out. Arranging it and feeding the guns took more time than foreseen, but once they roared and the attack began, initial progress was rapid. I met a steady stream of prisoners trickling back.

I trailed along behind, anxious to see if we might still make some headway at this late hour. It wasn't only Clark's first operation, it was also the general's. Loomis had been divisional commander for barely two weeks. Based on what I'd seen up until today, I had a feeling he'd want to know everything.

Three companies of the Patricias were sweeping forward in artillery formation, following a simple dirt track in the direction of the road when everything turned on its head. Rising above the boom of the guns, a harsh staccato of machine guns sounded from all around. And urgent shouting. There was the screech of a whizz-bang and then an explosion a couple of hundred yards ahead. The air was full of smoke and swirling dust. The platoon in front of me went to ground and I followed their example.

'There's two belts of wire in front of the road,' someone finally shouted. 'Look for gaps,' came the response. One of the officers, I presumed. The message was shouted forward. If there was one thing that stopped infantry dead in their tracks, it was wire. Of the handful of tanks with which we started the attack yesterday morning, none had shown up here. Without them I feared the worst.

We pressed forward, keeping as low as we could. I saw the road appear, a dusty yellow-brown trail running straight across our field of view. Ancient trees lined each side. The astonishing thing was, the trees were still there, in all their green finery. Not far beyond the road and parallel to it was the raised gravel embankment of the railway. Along its entire length I could see flickers of orange and puffs of white smoke. It seemed like every barrel the Germans had was in action, and that was a considerable number. *So much for the barrage.*

In small groups, men inched towards the line of wired fence posts before turning tail in the face of a hail of bullets. More often than not, they dragged one of their number with them as they retreated. Cutting a path by hand was suicide. There was no mistake about it; the entire western side of the road was hermetically sealed off by barbed wire, all cloaked in a hedge of green shrubbery. The wire was rusty but brutally effective all the same. The barrage hadn't touched it. 'There's nothing on the maps about wire being here,' said a voice to my left. A scout lieutenant had crawled up beside me.

'Believe me,' I said, 'it's not supposed to be.'

'Forgive me, sir, but that's small comfort,' he replied.

'Yes, I know,' I murmured. Under my breath I cursed. We'd spent days going over the maps, and photographs. *How could we have missed this?* The vegetation, of course. From above it would look like any other strip of greenery. Nature was inadvertently lending our foe a helping hand. However, this was no time for well-meaning excuses, or recriminations. They would come later. Against two dense bands of barbed wire the attack was going nowhere. And the PPCLI were getting chewed up in the attempt.

'I'm going to see if I can find a hole,' said the lieutenant. He scampered off without awaiting a reply, leaving me feeling like the infamous deadweight from headquarters, the very same one I'd always disparaged in jest. Half hour later, he was mortally wounded, searching in vain for a breach in the wire.

The uneasy stand-off lasted for almost thirty minutes, during which time the casualties steadily mounted. Undeterred by the bursts of small arms fire, parties of three or four men probed the line. The rest of us tried to keep our heads down. Then there were shouts off to my left. Others heard it too and soon it was clear what was happening. Two officers were mustering their men to move through a gap in the wire they'd found.

I ran across the field in their direction and took shelter with some others in a stand of plane trees, only a hundred yards from the road. As I studied the wire I saw it. An unmistakable gap. It was a couple of feet wide, easily enough for a man to squeeze through. Only it was too damned convenient. What were that odds that in a double line of hundreds, perhaps even thousands of yards of continuous uncut wire, this little strip, alone and unguarded, was cut?

A line of men were running for the gap.

'NO,' I shouted. And again, louder. I knew exactly what it was. They'd done the same thing in the Salient. 'STOP. It's a trap!'

Oblivious, the men rushed ahead into the gap. For a fleeting moment, to my overwhelming relief, I figured I had it wrong.

Then the TUF-TUF-TUF sounded. A refrain soon taken up by another, then another, until the air was filled with them. The file of soldiers wilted.

I lifted my rifle and began to shoot furiously in the direction of the German Maxims. It was hopeless, of course. A small handful of men backed away, most of them dragging another. Two or three made it to shelter. The gunfire tailed off.

Elsewhere, I could still hear shooting, but here the front was cloaked in a mournful silence. None of us said anything.

'Withdraw! Withdraw!' The orders, when they came, were not unexpected. The attack was turning into a rout.

The withdrawal risked becoming one too. A party of maybe thirty or forty Germans had infiltrated our left flank and were moving towards us. 'Counter-attack!' I heard someone yell. A Lewis gun began rattling. The Germans were in an extended line. While some of them fell, the remainder closed on the Lewis gunners, bombarding them with a deluge of stick grenades.

The small party of five soldiers I was with were giving it their best – to no avail. I lowered my eyes to the rifle sights and shot again.

The enemy were closer now, moving slowly but methodically, taking advantage of every shrub, every dip in the earth, every shell hole. A column of grey helmets was slowly encircling us. When they were close enough to see their faces, they began to trot. Like sharks circling in a frenzy, the smell of blood in the water.

I took aim at the closest one and shot him dead in the chest. Two to his side fell as well. At this the others began seeking shelter. In their midst, only 30 yards away, an officer raised himself up, pistol pointed in our direction, searching for a target. I could hear the rough guttural tones as he barked orders over his shoulder.

I reached into my satchel for a Mills bomb and made ready to throw it. *Damn, bully beef.* The Germans were on their feet readying to rush us. I hurled the tin as hard as I could. The officer saw it coming and instinctively ducked, hooking his pistol arm in front of his head in a reflex to protect himself. The tin bounced off his arm and onto the ground. He looked at it for an instant and I saw a smile appear. He straightened and brought his pistol to bear. There was a crack beside me. The German's head jerked back. Unceremoniously he crumpled to the ground. At that, the determination of his unit to do anything but save their skins evaporated. Hastily they began to retreat.

Once the danger had passed, I exhaled. 'Damned fine shot,' I said to the private who'd done the shooting. 'Any closer and I'm not sure we would have made it.'

'Nice pitch, yourself, sir,' said the private. 'What *was* that you threw?'

I sighed. 'Dinner.'

CHAPTER 26

28th and 29th of September, 1918
Near Sailly, France

It was late, going on 10 p.m., when I arrived back at 7th Brigade headquarters. The Patricias had pulled back. Their position was precarious, and frankly I didn't see how the division was going to meet its objectives. While I didn't have any special insight into the Corps Commander's strategy, I suspected that as long as we were thwarted here, our entire offensive was in danger. It was definitely not the news either Brigadier Clark or General Loomis would want to hear – nor General Currie come to that. Being the messenger, I was painfully aware I might suffer the consequences, even if they didn't include being shot. We'd lost far too many men today to risk thinning the ranks any further. I was exhausted, thirsty, hungry, and my feet felt like they'd been run over by a Whippet tank; not that there was any great likelihood of that. We hadn't seen a single one all day. If we had, things might have been different.

Leaving the road, just shy of an old mill, I entered the by now familiar trench. As I approached the section where brigade HQ was located, I heard raised voices. From the sounds of it tensions were running high; I'd escaped one battle, only to land in another. Reaching the dark dug-out entryway and the stairs leading down, I had no difficulty understanding what was being said below.

'We should delay, sir,' pleaded a voice, 'until we can get some tanks, or at least a decent barrage.'

'And risk losing what we have? That's one of the first principles of war, Colonel. Don't give anything away,' said another, a little peevishly.

The first voice cried, 'We don't want to do it! The PPCLI couldn't do it, and we *can't* do it.'

I descended a dozen steps into the dimly-lit chamber where Brigadier-General Clark held court. As I did so, I saw that it was the commander of the 42nd Battalion speaking, Lieutenant-Colonel Ewing. Ewing had light bushy eyebrows as thick as a pair of fox pelts, and they were furrowed together. He stood beside the lantern hanging from the ceiling. His round, expressive and usually cheerful eyes had shrivelled into pearly black beads. He looked like he was preparing to explode.

Across from him and seated, the general seemed poised to join in the fireworks. Clark's lower jaw was coiled in anticipation. The jaw was big, but the chin was weak. A deep ravine divided it in two. It reminded me of a chin that would sell you a second-hand Ford with a leaking carburetor at inflated prices.

Finally Clark spoke. 'Why not?' he snapped at Ewing, 'Why can't you do it?'

'Because there's too much wire there.'

'How do you know there's too much wire there?'

'The PPCLI told us,' replied Ewing. A captain from the Patricias, who I hadn't paid much attention to, nodded vigorously.

'I have aerial photographs,' said Clark. 'There's no wire there.'

'If the PPCLI tell us there's wire, we believe them, sir. If we told them there was wire, they'd believe us too!'

'Sir, the colonel is correct,' I began to say. 'The road is completely wired.'

Clark and Ewing both turned to look, and I could see the surprise on their faces. Perhaps they hadn't seen me slip in. More likely, there were was no other subordinate dumb enough to throw himself into the No-Man's-Land between them. It was a trick I'd never caught on to. 'Ah, it's you,' growled Clark.

'Yes, sir.'

'It's interesting you should say that, Major,' he said. 'You're in intelligence. Where do *you* suppose the information came from that from I'm talking about… the information that says there's no wire at the road?' He paused, a trifle melodramatically. I didn't need a fortune teller to know what was coming next. Clark didn't bother to wait for my answer. 'I'll tell you, Major – the INTELLIGENCE section!'

I began to mumble something about it being impossible to see the wire from the air because of the grass and the vegetation, and that there was really no substitute for reconnaissance on the ground. Clark, however, was in no mood for self-reflection, let alone a discussion. Tea was out of the question.

'Well then, MacPhail. Given your *extensive* reconnaissance today, I suggest you accompany the 42nd to help them get past it. You might as well do something useful.'

'Yes, sir,' I said, wearily. At any other moment I would have returned his fire, but I was in no shape to do anything except fall into a cot. Unfortunately, the cot wasn't to be, nor even a dry spot on the trench floor. I was heading back into action.

By the time the details were ironed out a few hours passed, and it was the middle of the night before we left. Low to the horizon, the pitch dark sky glowed a menacing red; the villages of Raillencourt to the left; and Neuville-St. Rémy to the right near Cambrai, were burning.

On the way to the 42nd Royal Highlanders, Ewing insisted I guide him to RCR headquarters, which I did, albeit with a wrong turn along the way. Once there, he woke Major Topp and promptly stole him back from the RCR, his need being greater than theirs – a sentiment I could appreciate having seen what they were up against. 'For God's sake, come along with us. We're in a hell of a jam,' pleaded Ewing. That must have struck a chord with Topp. He didn't hesitate and immediately handed over command to the captain beside him. The three of us arrived at battalion HQ past 2 a.m.

From somewhere to the east – probably behind Tilloy Hill – a German battery had begun systematically pounding the area. A regular thud of dull concussions could be heard, the flashes rudely rupturing the night and any semblance of peace. Not that the troops had much time to rest – within an hour they received their orders and moved out to the assembly area north of Sailly. It was to be another night without sleep.

Dawn broke fine but misty. The visibility was terrible. Seeing more than a few yards ahead was impossible, and would be until this heavy dew-laden veil lifted. Ewing and I squatted together in the long grass, the battalion's four weakened companies spread out before us. The men were lying on the ground, oblivious to the damp, patiently awaiting ZERO hour. 'This is no good, sir,' I said to the colonel, in a burst of frustration. I'd just finished telling him, again, what I'd observed of the terrain.

Ewing shrugged resignedly. 'Yes I know, Major. But what would you have me do?'

To that there was no satisfactory answer.

Near 8 a.m., the sun suddenly broke through. The mist vanished as if a curtain for the grand show was being drawn. Which in a way it was. A startlingly clear, bright blue canvas revealed itself, with the grey spires and chimneys of Cambrai taunting us from afar, a mile or two to our right. At the stroke of the hour came the signal from the field artillery. It was the third day of the attack.

As I feared, there were far too few guns to punch a hole through the wire. I heard it almost immediately. Of the 7th Tank Battalion, which had a handful of Mark Vs supporting the Division, there was no sign.

The Highlanders of the 42nd Battalion strode forward undaunted, in a series of long lines across the rolling fields. No one was rubbing up against their mate this morning. They'd been amply warned. The dark ribbon of the railway embankment was visible even from our starting point. Near the road were a scattering of low shelters housing enemy engineering and ammunition dumps, and rows of the same furled and rusted barbed wire the PPCLI had gone up against. Here too shrubs and grass obscured it.

'I'll let you know what happens, sir. But you need to stay behind. We can't afford to lose another battalion commander,' I told Ewing. I left him and began following the troops. The way I figured it, I was already in the midst of the attack and I had as much chance of being wiped out by a stray shell in the hole that was battalion HQ as catching a bullet during the advance. Probably I was deluding myself. But then that was something the past four years had given me a lot of experience in.

Other than explosions from the field guns, it was strangely quiet. After all the fire and fury of the past couple of days, it was uncanny not to hear a single machine gun, or even a rifle shot. The calm was unsettling. After a thousand yards, the lead troops came to the wire. And still there was nothing. *Could the Germans have pulled back?* In their kilts and their bare legs, rifles clasped at chest level with both hands, I watched the first of the Highlanders step awkwardly over the strands of rusted wire. Some were busy with wire-cutters. Kilts were caught, but carefully they pressed on. Soon, the advance section passed the initial belt of wire and began moving through the second. The next company was already approaching the wire.

Deep down I think I knew what was coming. I'd seen many strange things in this war. Because of this, I hadn't completely given up hope, and hope is what you cling to at such moments. Then the machine guns erupted and I swore. *Not again.*

There were dozens of MGs. All firing at once, seemingly from every corner of the compass. From the road, the railway, and the high ground adjoining Cambrai and its suburbs, came volleys of bullets. The men in the lead began to drop like nine-pins, one after the other.

There'd been no time to go to ground. Once the initial shock passed some tried, but most were caught in the wire, helpless. One of them caught my eye. A few bodies were hanging limply in the wire around him, but this fellow was struggling and still full of life. With the field glasses he was so close I could make out the determination written on his face. However, his determination was no match for the treacherous coils he was ensnared in, nor for the MG-08s. They'd seen him too. A long burst rang out. Horrified, I watched how his body convulsed under the spray of bullets till his head suddenly drooped. Then against all expectation, he twitched – *he was alive, by God!* I wanted to cry out. But again the gun saw him, and its cruel chatter resumed. His body shook unnaturally, a marionette in the hands of some crazed puppeteer, the ground around rippled with eruptions of dust. The gunner

216

eased off. The dust cleared. The soldier was still, his body slumped to one side, his head tossed far back. The machine gun moved on.

As did the men. Despite everything, the Highlanders kept stepping ahead, undeterred; a new desperate urgency gripping them. In snippets, barely audible amid the cacophony of battle, I heard their officers and NCOs shouting encouragement. To my astonishment the men obeyed, shooting as they went. I don't know whether it was courage, or simply following their mates, but they pushed on, the reflex of two months of uninterrupted fighting and a dogged determination that wouldn't be bent. I couldn't help thinking this was the very reason why the Canadian Corps was being thrown time and time again against the worst the Germans could offer. Only now, I feared, we were approaching the end of our rope.

I saw him struggling in the wire dead ahead, not unlike the soldier only minutes before. He was wounded I could see. But from his movements I guessed it wasn't serious. Yet his frantic struggling, the wild, unrestrained thrashing of a fish caught on a line, was going to attract attention. If he didn't calm down, the gunners would have him. But he kept at it. I shouted at him, but he didn't hear.

'Oh, damn it all,' I cussed, and jumped to my feet. I left the rifle and the field glasses where they were and rushed towards the wire. It was only thirty yards, barely a walk, but I did it at speed, keeping low. As I ran, all the shouting and blasts and clipped percussion of the MGs faded into the background. I saw only the young Highlander, his free arm tearing helplessly at the barbs that held him.

As I reached the wire I grabbed at a strand, looking to squeeze in between, and snared my hand bloodily. At the sharp pain, the sounds of battle erupted again. That was when I spotted the large iron wire cutters. Someone had dropped them in their haste. I fell prone to the ground, and fished them out from under the fence. With both hands I began to clip madly at the lines of wire.

German wire is thick. Much thicker and stronger than anything we made. I had to squeeze as hard as I could before I felt it give with a snap and the filament parted in two. Quickly I began on the next. The soldier had seen me and was staring.

'Slump. Pretend you're dead,' I shouted. 'Don't move or they'll see us.'

I heard the second strand snap. Lying on my back now, I propelled myself through the gap with my legs, and began on the next line, the cutters above me.

When I reached him, a few minutes and another fence line later, he was bleeding badly. It was worse than I thought.

'You're fine,' I assured him. 'Stay as you are. And whatever you do, don't move. I'm going to cut you free.' Which I did, with a lot of grunting, and a couple of desperate clips of the wire cutter. Then I pulled him to the ground.

'Can you crawl?' I asked.

He looked at me in a haze, but he nodded.

'Go then. I'll follow.'

When we reached the far edge of the wire, I pointed towards a crater, barely visible in the waving grass. 'You're going to have to make a dash for it. A quick run and you'll be there. I'll help,' I said. I grabbed him around the waist. While he grimaced and clutched at his side, we rose and stumbled along together.

It was a very long thirty yards, but somehow we made it and dived into the crater. I rolled over, and to my amusement saw that the hole was my very own, right down to the rifle and field glasses still lying there. Only when I looked closer, I saw the Lemaire glasses were smashed and bent, their shiny brass blackened and covered with dirt. 'Damn,' I said, softly.

The soldier looked at me puzzled, understanding nothing of this.

'It's been a tough few days,' I explained. I might as easily have kept my mouth shut.

'I guess the old Corps is done in this time, sir,' said the soldier.

I stared at him. He'd taken a bullet in the side. His tunic was torn and blood-stained, his helmet had toppled off, lines etched in his boyish face that might never disappear. But he'd live. I was certain about that. I looked to the road. Groups of Highlanders were almost up to it. 'What's your name,' I asked.

'Ron Williams, sir.'

'Well then, Ron Williams. In answer to your question I would say not yet. We're not done in quite yet. So you hang in there, we'll be needing you,' I replied. I was conscious that a voice in the back of my head had been whispering that very concern for two days running. Smith always called me a worrier. However, seeing the 42nd plunge through the wire and the machine gun fire, I'd realized something. A lot of the battalions were battered. Some had the rifle strength of a single company alone, yet despite that, the spirit of the men was alive. They were proud that *they* would get the job done. The only question was; would it be enough?

CHAPTER 27

30th of September, 1918
A dug-out 1000 yards west of Bourlon, France

The rain began after dark. It rapidly settled into a steady unremitting downpour. Huge tumblers full splashed with careless abandon over the softly rolling fields northwest of Cambrai. And through those very fields I was trudging, on my way to divisional headquarters. Off to my right, up near Sancourt where the 11th Imperials and the 4th Division were busy, the sinister white glow from a flare flickered in the sky. Occasionally the brief flash of a whizz-bang punctured the gloom. My helmet was pulled down low, my collar was up, my trench coat engaged in a valiant rearguard action to keep out the moisture. Luckily, I'd been able to retrieve pack and coat before the worst began. General Loomis had summoned me.

By the time I departed, the 42nd had secured their stretch of the Douai-Cambrai road, as had the boys from Edmonton, the 49th, to their right. The Royal Highlanders were almost on the infamous railway cutting. But their casualties bore witness to the savagery of the day; Captain Topp was hit, as were all four company commanders, and all four second-in-commands. Many of the other officers and NCOs were either dead or wounded. The battlefield itself was a mess, strewn with bodies, those for whom this place was the last they drew breath. For others, whose breath came in short painful gasps, they lay among the dead as the stretcher-bearers struggled to reach them under withering fire. It was a heavy price for a few hundred yards of ground.

I thought about this as the water drip-drip-dripped from my nose. My boots squashed their way forward, one weary step at a time. There'd been no surprise or brilliant tactics, nor sleight of hand in what we'd done. It was brutal, smashing-down-the-wall-with-your-head fighting, battering ahead and damn the consequences. That the German prisoners were streaming in and their dead lay everywhere was little consolation. Of course, the artillery had been too weak, particularly after we'd discovered the wire. But waiting to get our ducks in order would have allowed the Germans more time to prepare, or so the generals thought. I understood the dilemma and their haste to get on with it. For it was here, on these fields, that the fate of Cambrai and much more would be decided. Yet I was troubled. And dead tired. Neither of which is ideal when your next appointment is with a major-general.

'Honestly, sir? I think it was completely inexcusable to send in men without a proper bombardment,' I said in an angry burst. General Loomis was doing the asking. He and I, and Colonel Hore-Ruthven, stood deep underground, maybe 35 or 40 feet down, in a dug-out built for a hundred and more than adequate for the divisional staff. Along one side of a long rectangular room was a brazier full of coke, furiously smouldering away to keep out the chill, while a half dozen candles perched on a like number of tables strained to provide some semblance of light. Through a dark passageway at the end of the chamber the dug-out continued. Thanks to the luminous dials on my faithful timepiece I knew it was half-past twelve, and a new day was already underway. It seemed like the Borgel was the only thing about me still functioning normally.

I placed my drenched haversack at my feet and, leaning on my rifle, continued my narrative. 'The heavies could have dealt with the wire in no time, sir,' I said. 'A couple of hours to make preparations wouldn't have mattered one iota: except in the casualty count. The first day, the Patricias went in without knowing the wire was there. However, by the second day we knew, we bloody well...' I clenched my fists, and checked my mouth. I'd said enough already.

'I see,' said Loomis. He'd asked me for my impressions of the day's attack, and I couldn't help thinking he regretted it already. Hore-Ruthven looked on impassively.

Neither Loomis nor I mentioned the 7th Brigade commander Clark, even though I knew exactly why the sorry chain of events had unfolded as they had, and he no doubt suspected. Loomis appeared troubled. For a man who unfailingly preached the need for painstaking preparation, a rash rush against a wall of wire in a hail of machine gun fire was indefensible. Yet the brigade had carried it, and Loomis was not going to confide any doubts he might have about his brigadier to a lowly major. Particularly not one, I reminded myself, who was clinging to his position by his fingernails.

'How is the enemy holding up?' inquired Loomis, at length.

'They're taking a beating,' I replied, 'but they seem to have brought in every machine gun on the Western Front. In fact, we identified another new division, the 234th. That's after the 22nd, the 207th, and the 1st Guards Reserve, all in the past two days. Oh, yes, and the Württemburgers from the 26th Reserve, we can't forget about them. There are so many regiments up against us, I'm losing track, sir. The Boche are throwing in men like it was kindling on a fire.'

Loomis said, 'Well, Major, the way they figure it, their fire is in danger of being extinguished if they don't.'

'Yes, sir, that might explain it.'

'I know the losses are heavy.' He frowned. 'Are the men still up to it?'

'The battalions I saw are on their last legs or close to it. The only consolation is that ninety-percent of the casualties are from machine guns, so the fatalities are fewer. However, the men can't keep going like this, sir. They're determined, but they're losing their buddies. They feel like their luck is running out, and many of them haven't slept in two or three days.'

Loomis nodded sadly. And it was the heartfelt way he did so that surprised me. In that instant my estimation of him changed completely. I missed General Lipsett; he'd meant more to me than I realized. But Loomis was doing his best. As we all were. I had to put the past aside and get it through my dumb head that Loomis was in charge, and it was me, not him, who had to adjust.

'There is a little good news,' he said, and the deep lines around his eyes lifted.

I raised my head quizzically.

'The 9th Brigade took its objectives, including St. Olle. So that problem is dealt with.'

'That's a relief. And you're right about St. Olle being a problem, sir. Every window in that village seemed to have a machine gun in it. And the other divisions? How did they fare?'

'The 4th got as far as Sancourt, and could have gone further, but on their left the 1st Division barely moved. They're held up because the 11th Division to the north is not getting ahead.'

I cleared my throat but said nothing. It reminded me of dominos; without the first piece going down, you couldn't very well expect much from the rest. Wearily, I rubbed at my face.

Thankfully, Hore-Ruthven interjected. 'I think the major needs a rest, General,' he said in a soft tone.

'You do look awful, MacPhail,' said Loomis. 'When was the last time you slept?'

I shrugged. 'Honestly, sir, I can't remember.'

'Get some sleep. All three brigades are going in again in the morning. Every man in the rear is heading to the front. If the division is to take the crossings at the canal, it's essential we get past that blasted hill at Tilloy. Hopefully tomorrow we'll succeed. The attack begins at six. I'll see you then.'

So it was to be another bruising day of battle. The fourth in a row.

I blinked, momentarily unsteady on my feet as I fought to keep my eyes open. There was really nothing more to say. From above our heads, up the steep wooden ladder, came the sound of driving rain, vying with the sporadic shellfire to see which was louder.

'What's this!?' I asked Smith.

The attack had begun a couple of hours ago. I pointed at the well-worn map draped over a pile of papers, hanging precariously off the edge of the table. Following the show at Amiens, Smith had scavenged a large scale map of the front from somewhere and taken to meticulously updating it with each new development. It was an ambitious project, at least in the fall of 1918 when the front moved now and again. A year earlier and a child could have done it. Initially, I teased him about it. 'So, Lieutenant, I see you're already preparing for your new career on the General Staff...' But the damned thing actually proved to be useful, and everybody, from the general on down including me, consulted it regularly. One detail had caught my eye.

Smith nodded. 'Didn't you know, sir? The Fourth Army smashed the centre of the Hindenburg Line yesterday. They bore a hole through the middle. Your Aussie friends, the British, and some American divisions crossed the canal at St. Quentin. They say there were 1600 guns in the barrage.'

'1600 guns,' I repeated, in awe. 'That's twice what we had here. It must have been one hell of a fireworks display. But that's wonderful news. If the Fourth Army has broken through the heart of the German defences, well... assuming we take Cambrai... Hindenburg will have no choice but to turn his back on the rest of his line. The Germans will be forced to retreat, no question about it, just like they did when we crashed the D-Q Line.'

At that, the candle on Smith's desk flickered and went out with a sputter. Smith was nonplussed. He whipped out another from his drawer and plunged it into the still soft and smouldering mound of wax that had long since subsumed the small brass candle holder. For my part, I decided this must be a sign that I best stick with more prosaic topics, such as today's attack. I returned to my papers.

Almost immediately I again raised my head. 'The chaps at German High Command who write these orders... they obviously haven't spent much time at the front,' I declared. I waved the sheaf of captured sheets in Smith's face to remind him. He had translated those very orders only fifteen minutes before but appeared mystified at my words.

I began to read aloud: '"If you will stand fast, victory will be ours as before, for you are superior to the enemy who now only shows a desire to attack with tanks, and these tanks we shall destroy."' I cocked an eyebrow at him. 'Flowery stuff. To think the men laugh at General Currie's orders. They ought to see these. But my point *was*, our foe is obsessed with the tanks. Did you know, Smith, in three days in the field, I didn't see a single, solitary tank – not functioning that is. Despite that, we've made almost six miles, crossed a canal, beaten past three trench systems, a dozen villages, Bourlon Wood and gone up against half the machine guns Mauser ever made. And the Germans are whining about tanks?'

Smith considered this, then said, 'That may be, sir. But if the enemy are all tied up in knots worrying about our tanks, perhaps they'll be less prepared for the infantry.'

I pursed my lips. 'Perhaps,' I said, grudgingly. I had to concede he might have a point. The tanks were terrifying, especially if one was rumbling down upon you. On the other hand, our allotment of eight was expended in no time, so they couldn't have been a concern. 'Theoretically you're right,' I muttered. 'Unfortunately, the Boche following orders are less timid than the ones writing them.'

By mid-afternoon, the desperate ferocity of the fighting hinted at not so much a fear of our armoured beasts as an intention to keep the battle raging indefinitely. Our objectives were highly ambitious. The division was to move around Cambrai's northern outskirts with the 4th Division on our left, seize the railway embankment, Tilloy and the heights behind it, then the bridges at Pont d'Aire. If we could cross the Canal de l'Escaut north of the city, Cambrai's fate would be sealed. But the plan foresaw an enemy on the run. From everything I saw, the Germans were hunkering down, reinforcing, resolved to standing their ground. This was turning into a very ugly fight.

'Have you seen Benoît?' I asked, on a whim. DuBois had a way of making light of the blackest of subjects. It would be good to have a word with him.

'No, sir. He's still in the field. Yesterday, I overheard Major Tibbett speaking with him on the field telephone.'

'He'll be insufferable when he gets back, you realize,' I said with a grin. 'He never much liked the Boche, and that was before he spent four days at close quarters. Worst of all, he's had little to eat.'

Smith smiled. Our amusement was fleeting for new reports from the signallers soon landed on our table. Around us, the chamber buzzed with officers and clerks, all desperately trying to coordinate their own piece of the puzzle that was an attack not going to plan.

In front of me I had an explanation of sorts. It was a wired message from the Royal Canadian Regiment: RAILWAY EMBANKMENT IS IN OUR HANDS. 35 MGS CAPTURED AT TRAVERSE

S.20.b. PPCLI AT TILLOY. RCR MOVING ON CHAPEL. I whistled, but not because the battalions were getting ahead. As any infantryman will tell you, an entrenched position with a machine gun every ten yards is virtually impregnable: yet in one hundred-yard stretch of the railway cutting, the RCR had found 35 of them. Little wonder the plan had derailed.

Later that afternoon, after General Loomis returned from the Corps conference at 4th Division headquarters, a few things were abundantly clear. Today had been another day of bloody battering for a miserly few hundred yards of ground. Tomorrow would see a resumption, and from the absence of an invitation to accompany him, I hadn't yet gained Loomis' full confidence. In the scheme of things, being snubbed was the least important, even if from my perspective it didn't feel that way. I did, however, have a thick bacon sandwich in my hand, and that was the first halfway decent meal I'd had in days. I took a bite. I'd always marvelled at the recuperative properties of a few hours of sleep and something substantial in your stomach. But even that didn't make me any more enthusiastic about my next assignment; I was to return to the front lines the next day.

There was going to come a time when even my luck ran out. That was not me being despondent, merely realistic. I had only to look around; the past month had been very tough on us old-timers.

Smith had gone outside to catch a whiff of fresh air, but reappeared almost immediately. 'Sir! Have you heard the news?'

'They're issuing a double tot of rum tomorrow morning?'

'No, sir,' he said, smiling indulgently. 'The bulletin just arrived. Bulgaria has sought terms. They're capitulating. They're to sign an armistice.'

'Hmm,' I said, rubbing my chin. 'That is good news. Which makes it doubly a pity I haven't seen a Bulgarian in four years.'

CHAPTER 28

1st of October, 1918
East of Tilloy, France

The night had seen another bitter-cold and torrential rain, which had made the waiting just that little bit more excruciating. Battalion head-quarters, whose dignified name belied its singular lack of comforts, had nearly flooded. In the process my woollen trousers were soaked to the knee, as were my boots. I could feel my toes squishing around in socks that were reliving the hundred-year flood. In the wet misery of an approaching dawn, and yet another battle – one in which all four of the Corps' divisions were to be employed, as well as the 11th Imperials – I felt like I'd gone back in time to when I was a lowly infantryman in the mud, awaiting the "big push". So much for the crowns on my shoulders and a position on the divisional staff.

When the guns finally erupted at 4.58 a.m. sharp, their fiery tongues rupturing the pre-dawn sky, I was shivering both from the cold and the memories. Absurdly, I found it almost a relief when we finally began to tread forwards towards the wild fury of the barrage and the brutal fight that surely awaited.

The 43rd Cameron Highlanders and the 52nd Battalion were leading. I had good reason to remember both; the first from the muck of the Bellevue Spur near Passchendaele and later at Amiens; and the 52nd from… when was it now? It seemed as if an eternity had passed since mid-August when I was with Lieutenant-Colonel Foster and his men at Damery, fending off the endless waves of field-grey.

This morning I was accompanying the 116th Battalion. They were the stoic Central Ontario farm boys who had driven past Dodo Wood on August 8th. More recently, to the great relief of General Loomis, they and the 1st CMR had wrested away the suburb of St. Olle in a particularly savage fight. Now, they and I were crossing the Cambrai-to-Douai road in the direction of Tilloy. At that very moment the enemy guns began their retaliation.

'Oh, Christ, here it comes,' said the soldier in front. The ground ahead rocked and convulsed under the furious concussions of the howitzers. Explosions blanketed the length of the road and the air whined from the whizz-bangs. 'Stay in line, watch your distance, and keep moving,' roared a corporal in front. At another time we might have waited, but now we simply walked forward into the curtain of death. With each step, the next obediently following the last, it felt as if I were observing myself from afar, virtually oblivious to the chaos surrounding me. I trailed the others, one sheep in a vast flock. All around geysers of dirt and debris spiralled noisily upwards. Flashes of light sparked through the darkness. At intervals, a man would collapse when a shell fragment bore into him in a sudden unpredictable *whoosh*. But the flock moved on and I stubbornly fixed my eyes forward.

Emerging from the barrage, the air was thick with dust. But it was beginning to brighten as dawn approached. The CO, Major Carmichael, had a nasty wound on his face and was being bandaged up. Initially, he refused to leave even though his head was swathed in dressings. But finally he consented and Captain Allen took command. As we stood regrouping, a loud cheer went up amongst the men. Baffled, I turned to the man at my side. 'What's going on?' I asked.

'Don't ask me, sir, I'm from the band and the bugles,' he replied. I sighed. To the uninitiated it may have sounded more like a groan; Loomis hadn't been kidding about sending in every available man. However, I soon saw the reason for the tumult.

From where I stood, the critical high ground north of Cambrai stretched northeastwards, almost to the Sensée, looking for all the world like someone had dipped their two forefingers in ink and pressed them down on the map at a 45-degree angle. One finger of this plateau began near Tilloy, the other at Sancourt a mile and a half to the north. Far off to our left, close to Sancourt, there were long winding files of soldiers from the 4th Division in artillery formation. They were marching resolutely forward into the morning sun and onto the crucial plateau, as if no force on earth could stop them. Watching our sister division advance, it brought a smile to my face. No wonder the boys were cheering.

Moving on, we circled the smattering of broken farmhouses and other buildings that was Tilloy and the sounds of battle grew. In one of yesterday's few real successes, the PPCLI captured most of the hamlet. The Camerons finished the job not long ago. Behind the village was the pinnacle of the plateau: Tilloy Hill, its highest point at almost eighty metres. From it, within a radius of less than a mile, the Canal de l'Escaut formed an eastern boundary. To the south, startlingly close, loomed three great church towers, a factory chimney and the stone conglomeration of Cambrai. The plateau lacked the dramatic cliff-top setting of the Plains of Abraham, where the destiny of North America was once decided, but there was no doubt that the victor here would also have destiny in his hands: that of Cambrai. And with Cambrai, the fate of the German line far to the south and the north. The Germans knew all this too.

I was surprised, therefore, when a steady stream of prisoners began to pass through. I stopped several of them to examine their regimental markings and noted the numbers in my pad. There was only one conclusion to draw. The Germans had reinforced again. For weeks the intelligence summaries from GHQ implied that the Germans were teetering, their resources stretched to breaking point. Only here in the field I'd seen few signs of a manpower shortage. We'd faced a seemingly inexhaustible supply of new divisions, all intent upon stopping us.

The German officer tensed as I beckoned him over. Approaching, he threw his arms to either side, palms open like some down-at-heel, one-legged Paris merchant pleading for a sale. When I was within an arm's length, he straightened to attention, and actually clicked his heels. Taken aback at this unexpected development – heel clicking not exactly being commonplace in the Corps – and for wont of a suitable response, I saluted. It was old army wisdom: when in doubt, salute. He was an *oberleutnant*, a first lieutenant, immediately distinguishable from the single gold pips on his shoulder boards. I don't know what he thought I had planned for him, but his eyes flashed a wary, fearful look. As an officer he ought to have known better. Of course, I'd seen enough prisoners to be familiar with the wild tales of colonial savagery that infected the minds of some of our younger captives – until they had their first meal. That usually cleared away any misconceptions.

I motioned to him to empty his pockets. He did this promptly, handing me a billfold and a few folded sheets of paper. After perusing his wallet I handed it back, but stuffed the sheets inside my tunic. As to his regiment, all I had to do was read the gold numbering on his epaulettes. They belonged to a division I knew all too well. 'The 1st Guards Reserve, eh,' I said to him. He stood blinking at me. I don't think it was my Canadian accent. 'You know, we've being running up against you lot since Hill 70, and *still* you don't get the hint.' His eyes opened wide. He may not have understood what I was saying, but he did hear the tone. Every time I figured we'd seen the last of the 1st Guards, they popped up again. But the quality of the new recruits was dropping fast. I could see that too. This fellow was not like any Prussian I'd come across. He was virtually quivering in his boots. As I stared at him, he yanked off the brown leather case around his neck and offered it to me with both hands.

Reluctantly I accepted. Souvenir collecting was all the rage amongst the men. I was usually too preoccupied with whether I had another magazine for the Lee-Enfield and something to eat to concern myself with an ornamental bayonet or a *Pickelhaube* that I'd have to lug around. The thought of souvenirs, though, led me to recall something else – the burgeoning divisional pay chest we captured at Arvillers. But then the prim features of Captain Clavell flashed before me. Fortunately, on opening the case, my mood lifted. 'Ah! Wonderful! That's exactly what I need,' I said. I pulled the greenish-grey field glasses out and trained them on Cambrai. They were considerably more powerful than my old ones. Admiringly, I twisted the dual eye sights, back and forth, and they moved with a reassuring, oiled ease.

'*Danke schön*,' I said to the officer. He bowed his head, as only a Prussian can.

We walked on for half an hour in a looping curve for about a mile, in the direction of the canal. The grassy ground was flat, but undulating, and it rose steadily as we crossed the plateau. Following a narrow dirt footpath we continued up Tilloy Hill. Along the way, we encountered nothing but gaggles of prisoners under escort straggling back to the divisional cage, and the grisly site of a five man gun-crew sprawled on their backs in a deep ditch. The battalions in front had cleared the ground admirably. Then we reached the brow of the hill looking east.

It was there the trouble began. A crescendo of machine gun fire erupted. Worse, that was soon accompanied by a succession of deeper bangs and the sound of whizz-bangs whining through the air. There must be a battery close, I thought.

The men crouched low. Ahead, I could make out D Company falling back under the withering fire. 'Where are they?' shouted Captain Allen. He rounded on me. 'Can you see them, Major? We need to turn their flank before they cut us into bits.'

'Shall I go and have a look?' I offered.

'Would you?'

Which is how I ended up a couple of hundred, harrowing yards further, scrunched into a rifle pit with two others, surveying the scene with my new Fernglas 08 field glasses. And I spotted them. A puff of smoke from one of the field guns gave them away. They were in a small wood on the very crest of the hill, four or five hundred yards from us. 'Look right,' I told the soldiers, and I pointed. 'Do you see? In the wood, there. Pass the word. I'm going to inform the CO.'

It didn't take long before a hundred-odd rifles and a collection of Lewis guns were spewing covering fire. Small squads of men alternating left and right began slowly working their way up to the trees, firing as they went.

'Some of the Boche are retreating,' I shouted excitedly to Allen. Clutches of dark figures could be seen darting from the woods and disappearing down the far slope where our first objective, the village of Ramillies, guarded the canal approaches.

Allen gave the signal to advance and the better part of the battalion moved to envelop the wood. He and I followed.

The stand of trees formed a small triangular cluster, numbering probably no more than twenty, but stuffed in it we found three field guns, four machine guns and close to eighty Germans. Dozens of their dead and wounded littered the gun pits. Seeing as how the entire battalion, including the band, numbered less than three hundred, it was quite a haul.

Quickly Allen gave orders to move on. I went forward with a few sections of C Company down the slope towards Ramillies. There weren't enough men and not nearly enough officers for me to loiter in the rear. Besides, at this stage, any intelligence I might send Loomis was insignificant compared to the value of the 116th taking its objectives.

Lining the road, and behind high red brick walls, I made out the pointy clay-tiled rooves of houses and the larger curved wooden ones of barns. Out of sight, concealed by the village centre, was the canal and the crossings General Currie had sent us to secure. It was all so tantalizing close, a five minute walk.

BOOM. A shell exploded in a plume of dirt and dark smoke a hundred yards to my side, taking two men with it. Then another, not far from the first.

'Whizz-bangs,' shouted the sergeant. 'Take cover!'

Cover, such as it was, amounted to some furrows in the ground, a few larger shrubs and a couple of shallow practice trenches. It wasn't much, but fortunately a lone soldier pressing himself to the ground doesn't offer much of a target. By the time I'd hidden myself away in some tall grass with my glasses and rifle resting at my side, I figured the field guns had us at virtual point-blank range. The guns weren't in the village as I first assumed. They were on a spur of the hill just to the north of it. From there they could enfilade us at will.

The sergeant crawled up to me. 'What do you think, sir?'

'We'll be cut to shreds if we move further down the slope to Ramillies. They're firing over open sights from our left. At that range they could take out half a company with one shrapnel shell.'

'Yes, sir. That's what I thought, too.'

The problem was I couldn't readily think of many alternatives. We couldn't very well pull back a thousand yards up the hill, and then move laboriously forward again to encircle them. If there were Germans in Ramillies, they'd counter-attack in a flash. With the battalion on the move that would be disastrous.

'Look it's not much of an answer, but let's hold here and try to keep out of sight,' I suggested. 'We've got a good position in case any Boche come out of the village. We'll have to hope the 4th Division comes up on our left and takes out that battery.'

So we lay there. Only as time crept by and the occasional shell landed precariously close – one lucky round made a direct hit on an occupied hole – it was clear 4th Division wasn't coming to our rescue. Almost two hours had passed.

The grass rustled. It was the sergeant, crawling back to me on his belly. 'Sir, I sent a runner to the Captain.' Underneath the tin helmet his forehead was drenched in sweat and from his expression I knew the tidings were bad. '4th Division is held up between Blécourt and Bantigny. Our left is wide open,' he reported.

'Hmm,' I responded. Something had caught my eye to the north. It was our open flank.

The sergeant, unaware, continued, 'I think we should pull back over the hilltop, sir.'

Distractedly, I muttered, 'Hang on.' I grabbed the glasses and trained them on what I'd seen. It took me a moment fiddling with the focus, but I wasn't mistaken. Even from a mile away I could easily make out the vast swarm. They were marching west out of the canal-side village of Eswars in the direction of Bantigny and the ravine. It wasn't in our direction, for it was northwest. They were going to counter-attack the 1st and the 4th Divisions!

Any military man worth his salt will tell you that high ground is sacred. Only here, on this plateau near Cambrai, the Boche had turned that age-old wisdom on its head. For two days they'd poured regiment after regiment into the shallow ravine in the north of the plateau, and from concealed positions been raking its gentle slopes. Those were the very slopes the 4th Division was now traversing.

'More trouble,' I said to the sergeant. I told him what I saw. 'It's shame we can't pass this on to the artillery.'

The sergeant looked thoughtful. 'I can send a runner. Harris is as fast as they come. There's surely a telephone in Tilloy, and it's not much more than a mile. It'll take him ten minutes. You'll see, sir.'

I looked sceptical, but rolled on to my side and eased the map from my pocket. I'd have to make a rough guess where the column would be by the time the artillery got into action. The crossroads north of Bantigny, I reckoned. I jotted down the coordinates. 'Give him this,' I said, tearing a page from my notebook, then followed-up by scribbling a few lines for General Loomis and Colonel Hore-Ruthven. 'Here, and this too. Wish Harris luck. Tell him I'll be timing him.' The sergeant grinned and scrambled away on his hands and knees.

When he returned, the sergeant had brought orders from Captain Allen. The gist of them left me and a dozen men manning the outpost line (by my own volition it must be said), at the mercy of the field-gun battery but well able to see what our artillery was up to. The others were to rejoin the battalion and move to less exposed positions on the far side of Tilloy Hill.

As it turned out, it took the combination of Private Harris, several signallers and a lot of gunners only seventeen minutes all told. Which must have been some sort of world record. When I saw the smoke plumes erupting due north and heard the retort of our guns, I clenched my fist defiantly. 'That should dent their enthusiasm a little,' I muttered.

'Sir?' the private next to me enquired. But I didn't respond. I was too busy observing the billowing smoke near Bantigny.

The afternoon passed agonizingly slowly. When you're all alone holding the front line with a handful of others, the minute hands of a watch can seem like they're anchored in glue. The 2nd Division's 27th Battalion from Winnipeg came up in support on our left and dealt with the field-guns, but the news further north was worrisome.

Our artillery had been roaring all day. They hadn't been able to stave off the inevitable; the Germans were pouring in men with reckless abandon. Our lead domino, the 11th, had got nowhere. And the 1st and the 4th were being pushed back. Allen even thought we'd lost Blécourt, a mile and a half to our rear. That left us far out on a limb. I was perched precariously on the furthest twig of that limb.

By now it was nearly 6 p.m., the time decent families sat down for dinner together. But the bully beef was long gone, as was the hardtack. The company too was far from decent; Germans had been spotted.

'Here they come!'

A horde of them were sweeping up the slope from the direction of Pont d'Aire on our right. One group had branched off and was heading in our direction. Weighing the odds, a retreat seemed the sensible course of action. Only none of us had much stomach for retreat these days, not after all the friends we'd lost getting this far. I could see it on the faces around me. Foolhardy or not, the men were set on a fight. I grasped the polished wooden stock of my rifle and chambered a round. The man beside me did the same. 'Think of your grandchildren,' I said. 'Make this a story they'll want to hear.'

With only a single Lewis gun, we didn't have the firepower to wait and lure them in. So when the first German was only a tiny bead in my sights, I heard the first shot.

'If you shoot, make damn sure you get him,' I yelled.

'Yes, sir,' voices replied.

At first there was a cool-headed abstractness to it, like shooting prairie dogs back home, methodically taking aim at one of the distant figures and, as the retort of the round echoed in my ears, seeing him go down. But soon enough the figures became men and began shooting back. The cool-headedness gave way to an asphyxiating, dull pounding in my chest. There was no time for careful marksmanship any more. It had devolved into a fight for our lives.

'Shoot you idiots,' screamed the corporal.

And whether it was coincidence, or his words had some galvanising effect, the line of grey figures seemed to waver in the face of the storm of lead. The Lewis gun rattled on.

My heart was racing, fuelled by that heady mix of excitement and fear, my senses momentarily overpowered by the flush of battle.

Then the grey line began moving again. Towards us.

My elbows dug into the earth. Around them brass cartridges littered the ground. I fired. Reloaded. And again. There was no time to look at the others. I kept firing.

The toll we were taking was a terrible one, but still they advanced. CLANG. I snapped a glance over my shoulder. Then I looked closer. 'You're fine,' I said, to the private. 'It went off your helmet.' The helmet had an indentation in it the size of my thumb, and the private looked like he'd been hit by a bus. 'Pick yourself up, Gates! And get into action,' I admonished him, and turned back to the grassy slope.

An officer, or an NCO, appeared to be mustering the Germans for a final assault. They were a hundred yards away, out of range of our bombs. He was shouting, violently waving his arms in our direction. His men were responding.

I took aim at him, stupidly concentrating on the shiny, rounded *stahlhelm*, and fired. Miss. Then beside me I heard a crack and saw him stagger. He wilted to the ground. The soldiers of his squad checked their step and stared at him. Then I saw one drop his rifle. Others fell to their knees and dropped theirs. Hands were raised in the air. 'Cease-fire,' I shouted. 'Cease-fire.' My words were too late for a number, but of those that remained all had their hands in the air.

When it was over there was no cheer from the men. In the air hung a most sickly odour of gunpowder and what I can only describe as death. The slope, once verdant, was scarred and littered with the debris of war. On it the pride of the Imperial German Army lay dying or crippled. There were only ten of us left, and four of them were nursing wounds.

'A fine shot, Gates.' My arms were shaking. I drew a deep breath, collecting myself and walked cautiously towards them, rifle extended. Everywhere the grass lay strewn with bodies. I stared down at one. His dark blond locks had fallen onto his forehead. A helmet rested upturned a foot length from his head, the leather webbing inside bizarrely new. The lad's eyes were cold and inert, although his face had an unnerving serenity to it. Dark wet patches stained his tunic. He was wearing an Iron Cross. *Gott mit uns* (God with us) read the buckle on his leather belt.

I shook my head. The chaplains did their best to convince us that God was on *our* side. While I'm not exactly of a religious bent, that sort of reassurance is always welcome. It was, however, somewhat difficult to reconcile with this German's belt buckle. I wasn't sure how God planned on resolving it. Perhaps a roll of the dice. That's how the boys usually did it. Dear old Canon Scott of the 1st Division would have had an answer, but he was on his way to a hospital. He'd had an encounter with a shell shortly after we crossed the canal.

It had been a day of hard fighting, fierce fighting, savage fighting of a kind I'd seldom seen. A day of determined rushes; of going right when left was barred; of frantic SOS bombardments and rifle bolts so hot you needed your foot to open them. Waves of field grey had swept again and again over these rolling fields, so fresh and pristine only days before. They had come in overwhelming numbers and so they had died, in a desperate cause. Later was I to learn that the enemy had thrown 33 battalions against us this day, almost four entire divisions. None of us felt sorrow, but not a man amongst us could deny them respect. They too had been courageous.

We abandoned the advanced posts with a trail of thirty-odd prisoners, our own wounded and theirs, and pulled back to the line of rifle pits where the battalion had dug in. There I said my good-byes to the 116th. No one said much. There was not much to say after a day like today. They'd been promised relief and I needed to get back to headquarters. The division was dangerously extended, if even half what I'd heard was true. It put us in grave danger if the Germans had a mind to cause trouble. Offhand, I couldn't think of an instance when they weren't so inclined.

It was dusk, leaning towards night. I shuffled over the hill westwards, desperately trying to keep my concentration. Without a footpath the ground was rough, a sprained ankle or worse only a misstep away. As was an encounter with a stray group of Germans. But I made it unscathed.

Crossing through the village of Tilloy, I came to a track that skirted the outskirts of the suburb of Neuville St.-Rémy. There, in the cover of a barn-like structure, I came upon a small dressing station. A row of stretchers was lined up on the ground, and from an adjoining single-story stone building, the traces of a lantern's yellow glow leaked through closed shutters. A horse drawn ambulance was waiting nearby.

Closest to me, as I approached, a big man on a stretcher lay groaning. He was huge. Where one leg had once been, I saw a bandaged stump and winced. One arm was in a dressing, and his head and chest were bound in white.

Oddly, I couldn't keep my eyes off him, this giant of a man. To my astonishment the man suddenly waved at me. He had one arm in the air and was struggling to raise himself at the waist, without any support whatsoever. A medic saw it too and was hastening towards him. Walking closer I squinted, trying to make out more. The door to the building opened a crack and a shaft of light caught him. That was when I saw his face.

The shock ran through me; a current as powerful as any derived from placing a finger on a live lead. My stomach turned to mush and I felt my knees wobble.

'Oh, no,' I whispered. 'Please, God, not him...'

CHAPTER 29

1st of October, 1918
Neuville St.-Rémy, France

A pained smile lit his face as I approached.

'Benoît! Good God. What are you doing here?'

He grimaced for a second and then it passed. 'A little rest and relaxation, Mac.' At the thought a laugh came bubbling out of him, but soon turned to a hacking cough.

I grasped his free hand and squeezed it firmly. 'You'll be okay,' I said, and repeated it louder, trying to convince myself as much as him, I think.

Benoît certainly wasn't fooled. I saw it in his eyes, but he played along. 'I'll be home before you will,' he said.

'And you deserve it too. What happened?'

'A shrapnel shell,' he replied, and began to cough again. After a moment he cleared his throat and went on with his explanation. 'I was with the observers looking for the batteries on the far side of the canal, and then... you can guess the rest.' A weak smile appeared. 'I guess it's only fair after all the Boche I've shelled in my life.'

'No, it's not fair,' I said. 'It's NOT fair at all. They keep throwing us again and again at every damn German on the front. We're dropping like flies. All the old veterans from Ypres, the Somme, Vimy, Passchendaele, Amiens... They survived all that, and now they're dying, one by one. And still they throw us in, day after day. You'd think we were the only ones in the entire bloody British Army. It's not fair at all!'

Benoît looked surprised at my outburst. He'd never seen me in such a state. I'd barely ever seen myself in such a state. Offhand, the only occasion I could remember was when one of my clients, Mr. Hobson from Hobson's Hardware, came whining to me about some trivial matter. Unfortunately for him it was precisely a week after my wife had died – not that he was aware of that. Unfortunately for me, he was my best client, although after signing up that didn't matter either. On seeing DuBois, however, his huge body broken and dismembered, my cauldron had well and truly bubbled over.

'Water,' he whispered. I pulled out my canteen, screwed off the metal top, and reached out to offer it to him. He waved me away. His finger pointed at the pile of gear at his feet. *Ah, his own canteen.*

I bent down and rummaged through it, finding it almost instantly. It was bigger than mine. But he was a big fellow so he had scrounged up another. I opened it. On a hunch I took a whiff. 'No. No. Don't think you can fool me, Benoît. You're in no shape for that botch. Wait till you're patched up and I'll treat you to something decent.' I lifted my own canteen and held it to his lips. He closed his eyes and guzzled deeply. Water dripped from his mouth down into his beard and I dabbed it away with my sleeve as best I could.

'Listen, Mac,' he said. 'I want you to take this.' With his fingers he rummaged in his breast pocket and produced a thin silver chain that I recognized. He indicated that I should take it. I opened my palm and he placed it carefully it in the middle.

'Oh, I can't take this Benoît. You'll be fine. You'll be at a casualty station within an hour, and a hospital by tomorrow. They're very good you know, the medical corps. Besides, your little sister won't be pleased if she hears you've lost it. Or worse, that I have.'

He shook his head, and then winced again, in obvious pain. For my sake, I could see he was holding back the moan. 'Take it, Mac, please. Give it to Geneviève when you get home. *Oui?*'

The orderlies were lifting stretchers on to the ambulance. I stepped out of the way to make room for them as they came to collect Benoît.

'Here, let me help,' I said. It was fortunate I did, for the three of us barely managed to lift him onto the bed of the wagon beside the others.

'I want you to promise me something, Benoît. You'll fight. Fight like you've got the entire Boche army in front of you. You and I still have a bottle to drink together, *mon ami.*' I patted him gently on the shoulder.

'Good-bye, Mac.'

'Good-bye, Benoît.'

With that, an orderly slammed the tailgate shut with a clang that reverberated far too loudly – the German lines were less than a thousand yards away – and the driver shook at the reins.

I watched the ambulance slowly pull away and I waved until it disappeared into the night. After it had gone, the slow clacking of the hooves and the creaking of the wagon echoing after it in the darkness, there was nothing left but to continue on my way. Which I did, as a hollow emptiness took me in its grasp.

2nd of October, 1918
A dug-out 1000 yards west of Bourlon, France

At divisional headquarters, the identical dug-out I'd been in a very long 24 hours before, Lieutenant-Colonel Hore-Ruthven greeted me with enthusiasm. I couldn't help thinking he was never more enthusiastic than when he hadn't seen me for a spell. I might have devoted more thought to it if I hadn't felt like I did. As it was, I acknowledged his greeting as best I could, though mustering a smile was temporarily beyond my abilities. I didn't enquire where the general was; no doubt he had a lot on his mind. Understandably, Hore-Ruthven was very concerned about our situation. He'd heard all the reports and to an experienced officer like him there was no need to spell out that we had a mile-long left flank that was positively inviting Fritz to come strolling on through.

The colonel listened intently to what I had to say. Then I told him I'd heard enemy dumps being blown as I walked back and he perked up.

'What's that? Are you certain, Major? The Germans were blowing their dumps?'

'As certain as I can be, sir. It's not a sound that's easy to forget. I can't imagine what it could have been, otherwise. The fires were easily visible.'

'Very strange,' he murmured. 'Do you think they realize how worn down we really are?'

'I don't know, sir. But if they did, I don't think their first response would be to blow their dumps. Although, from what I saw, the enemy had a tough day of it as well. We can only hope they're as battered as we are.'

'Yes, although I don't think we'll rely on hope alone.'

'Sir?'

'It's been decided to put down a very heavy barrage at 5 a.m., in the event they *are* planning something.'

'That's probably wise, sir,' I responded. Something about the halting way I said it made him look at me.

'Are you feeling all right, Major?'

I looked at my feet. 'On the way back I came across Captain DuBois at a dressing post. He was in very bad shape. He lost a leg, sir. I'm not sure…'

Hore-Ruthven was silent. A pained look came into his eyes. Eventually, he said, 'I'm very sorry to hear that.' He laid a hand on my shoulder. In all the time I'd been under his command, he'd never once done that.

Tibbett went white when I told him the news. He and DuBois were as close to being polar opposites as any two people could be. Yet they had a warm and oddly symbiotic relationship. Tibbett was the direct superior of the two, and smarter than most of the General Staff put together. He spoke in complete sentences with a patrician precision that was at times painful to the ears. To anybody schooled in English, DuBois' speech in contrast, was simply painful. Grammatically painful, but wonderfully engaging. From a provincial town on the banks of the St. Lawrence River, Benoît was the gregarious life of the party, in a way which the meek, awkward and well-bred Londoner would never be. Somehow, the two of them got along splendidly. For my part, I couldn't imagine any better friends. It hadn't always been that way, at least in Tibbett's case, but war has a way of making short shrift of the social conventions and inbred prejudices that so encumber civilian life.

After I'd described what I'd seen as best I could, Tibbett asked, 'Do you think he'll live?' Naturally, it was the only question that really mattered, and one I'd put firmly out of mind on the long walk back. I hadn't dared to think about it, fearful I'd arrive at a conclusion I didn't want to.

'I don't know, Paul. I really don't. It didn't look good though. He was in terrible straits.' I sighed. 'I'm afraid...' I began to say, but the words escaped me.

'They can accomplish wonders these days, Malcolm. Modern medicine has advanced a great deal, and the medical staff is very proficient.' He looked at me through his silver wire spectacles with an almost juvenile earnestness that in other circumstances I would have teased him about.

'Yes, I know. That's what I told Benoît as well. Remember, I was at a casualty station myself not so very long, ago.'

'Of course,' he replied. 'And how *are* you doing, Malcolm?'

From a casual glance he ought to have known, but that wasn't why the question came as such a surprise. Feelings, and horror – discussing them aloud – were not something that came easily to my aristocratic friend.

I shrugged. '*Comme si, comme* ça, as Benoît would say.'

'You look a lot worse than so-so,' Tibbett responded. His eyes darted surreptitiously to one side – General Loomis was still out, and Hore-Ruthven had disappeared. He motioned me to follow. Deep in the dug-out we came to a small alcove off one of the main chambers. It reeked of must and mould. Simple wooden bunks stacked three high lined the walls. In the middle of a small table, a finger's length of candle protruded from a tin. Tibbett lit the candle and we sat down on the edge of a bunk. Then he pulled out a silver flask and set it down between us. It wasn't water, I was quite sure of that. The war had led us all in unexpected directions.

'Thanks, Paul,' I said, and I took a small swig when he offered. At first it left me dizzy, but then I felt a warm glow. I nipped at it again, a little more this time.

We talked for half an hour, perhaps longer. That is to say, I talked and he listened. Which was unusual in itself. Tibbett, for all his stilted ways, could talk up a storm when he got going. However, Benoît's plight had hit him hard too, and I think he knew I had a lot on my shoulders. I told him about the day and the ferociousness of the fighting. We talked about all the battles in the past two months, about my fear that the coming day might be worse. I even told him, briefly, about my mother. He nodded empathetically, especially when I described my ill-fated efforts to get leave. 'I'm afraid General Loomis isn't overly fond of me, so getting leave from him is out of the question. As it is, if I screw up, he'll have me in an infantry battalion in no time. And to top it off, Clavell is still out for my blood.'

He'd been about to take a drink, but at this he abruptly put down the flask. 'Clavell?'

I gulped. That was another thing I'd never mentioned to him. But with that slip of the tongue there was nothing left but to reveal the whole sordid story; from my almost court martial at the hands of Clavell's uncle in August; to the booty Rutherford and I had found at the German headquarters; the mystery of the missing French captain Madelot; and finally, Clavell's suspicions that I'd snatched the lot.

When I was done, he looked at me not with the sympathy I expected, but barely disguised amusement.

'No need to be quite so cheery about it,' I muttered sourly.

'No. No, Malcolm. You don't understand. You should have told me about this much earlier. About Captain Clavell, I mean. I rather think I might be able to help.' His eyes shone and I recognized the boyish enthusiasm that percolated up whenever some arcane subject grabbed his interest. Only this subject was my life, so his interest was welcome.

Puzzled, I raised my eyebrows but said nothing. From experience, I knew there was little point in interrupting.

'Malcolm, you must remember Lord Derby?'

Awkwardly I glanced to the side, not willing to meet his eyes. *Derby?* I racked my brain.

'Surely, you must recall him. That hockey cup of yours.'

'Oh,' I exclaimed. 'THAT Lord Derby. Edward Stanley of the

Stanley Cup. The fellow in the suit we saw at Valley Wood in August. The British ambassador to France. Of course I remember him.'

Tibbett looked at me sceptically, but continued: 'Yes, well, he's a very old and very dear friend of the family. It also happens that Lord Derby is on excellent terms with Générale Mordacq. You *do* remember him I trust?'

'Premier Clémenceau's military aide, the one with the epilated eyebrows and the waxed moustache? Yes, naturally, but I don't see how that makes any difference?'

Tibbett waved me quiet. 'I'm going to write a letter to Lord Derby, to explain. If anyone can find this Captain Madelot of yours, Mordacq can and will.'

I began to sputter.

'Malcolm, listen.'

'Mac, call me Mac. I've told you that a thousand times. All my friends call me Mac.'

Tibbett sighed. 'All right, Mac.' I could see it took an effort. 'If General Mordacq can track down this elusive captain, you think he'll have the answer?'

'Not the answer,' I said, 'the money.'

'Right. So he's the key to the entire matter. And regardless how much you've perturbed this policeman…'

'Why do you automatically assume I've perturbed him? He's the one out perturbing people.'

Tibbett looked hopelessly at the ceiling, as if the mould speckled concrete might bring deliverance.

'Okay, fine, I could have been a little more polite to him,' I grudgingly admitted.

'So. As I was saying. If General Mordacq can locate this Captain Madelot whom Clavell said the French Army couldn't find, that would be helpful. And I rather suspect if the *chef du cabinet militaire* inquires, Madelot will not be missing for long. Even if nothing incriminating turns up, Clavell can hardly maintain that you've done anything wrong with Madelot in the picture.'

'You don't know Clavell.'

'Trust me on this, Malcolm. Mac. It'll work out. Leave it to me.'

'I hope you're right. Either way, thanks Paul.' I clapped him on the shoulder. For a brief, fleeting moment, my mind had been off Benoît, and for that I was grateful.

There was a commotion and a couple of officers barged into the room, their words echoing in the near empty chamber, heading for the bunks. 'I think we should get some sleep, too,' I said. 'The barrage is in four hours. I fear it's going to be a very long day, Paul. And that assumes the Boche don't attack even earlier.'

Early that morning, as Hore-Ruthven promised, the guns thundered into action across the entire line, hoping to catch the assembling masses. We girded for battle, but nothing came.

'He's beat it,' I heard the runner say to the trio of signallers.

Rays of light were poking cautiously down the dug-out entrance. Yesterday, the artillery had gone through 7000 tons of ammunition in a single day. Accounting for the differing weights, Tibbett calculated that they had fired close to half a million shells. If I hadn't been there I would have scoffed at such a ridiculous number. This morning the artillery was at it again.

The signallers stood casually, loitering by the ladder, smoking cigarettes and awaiting orders. The runner must have known one of them.

I elbowed my way into their midst and asked, 'What's that you said, just now?'

The runner straightened, and reached to remove his helmet. 'He's gone, sir. The Hun have pulled back.'

Naturally that wasn't the entire story; that only dribbled in in the hours that followed, but the private's pithy conclusion held water. The Boche had seen enough. Where I had feared for the counter-attack that would break our weakened lines, the enemy had seen only his own shattered ranks. And so came to an end, in the early morning of October 2nd, some of the fiercest days of fighting the Corps had ever seen, and one of the worst twenty-four hours of my life.

Only Cambrai remained.

PART FOUR

CHAPTER 30

9th of October, 1918
Cambrai, France

I lowered the field glasses. 'Can you men swim?' I asked the two brawny soldiers to my side. Their physique wasn't particularly conducive for swimming, but definitely for what I had in mind afterwards.

'Yes, sir,' they cautiously replied.

'You can't be serious, Major?' said the fresh-faced lieutenant from the 5th Mounted Rifles.

'Damn rights, I'm serious,' I said. 'That bridge is blown. And even if you *can* cross it, there's a machine-gun emplacement with a line of sight right down the middle. So if you waddle your company across, we both know what's going to happen. Someone has to deal with those machine guns. I don't see many other options, Ingersoll.'

'True enough, sir. But swimming?'

'Why not? I could swim the canal myself, and I'm not in the shape these fellows are. Damn it. I'll go with them. Just make sure you get your platoon across that bridge when we give the signal. Like the dickens, Lieutenant. Like the dickens.' And before I had a chance to reconsider, I had handed an astonished Ingersoll pretty much my entire wardrobe including my Burberry trench coat, tunic, Lee-Enfield rifle, Fernglas field glasses, and an unbranded but rubbery-tasting respirator I was thankful to be temporarily rid of. The revolver I kept, as well as the Mills bombs. I debated taking off my boots, but decided against it.

The young soldiers were grinning as they too stripped down.

'Keep low,' I whispered as the three of us, still clad in far too much uniform, and with helmets tightly fastened, crept towards the banks of the canal.

I was grateful that it was so dark. Sudden cold squalls had punctuated what was otherwise a crisp autumn night, but for the moment it was dry and reasonably safe from falling shells. The trench mortars out of Cambrai had shelled us since sunset. Mercifully around midnight they fell still, but the past few hours were unsettling ones.

Plans had changed almost hourly. XVII Corps was to take the Awoingt Ridge south of Cambrai, at which time the 2nd Division was to cross the canal at Ramillies and Point d'Aire, then move east. This would complete the encirclement we'd already begun by meeting up with the divisions from the south. However, despite some initial success, the Imperials were unable to reach their objectives. They seldom did these days, it seemed. No wonder the Aussies had taken to calling them *Woodbines*, after the cheap cigarettes that burned through in a dash. So the pincer to the right of the city was left dangling, an undercut to the chin that was delayed until further notice.

Nevertheless, our generals decided the time was ripe. At half-past eight in the evening, the final orders arrived. And not long after, at 1.30 a.m. – henceforth to be known as 0130 hours according to a new decree, one I hadn't yet wrapped my brain around – the deafening drumbeat of the guns signalled the attack was on. At 3.00 a.m. our turn came. The 3rd Division was to secure the crossings into Cambrai and establish bridgeheads in the city itself. Loomis ordered the 8th Brigade's battalions to probe the enemy's position. For Fritz it was an unmistakeable signal; his long occupation was coming to an ignominious end. However, no one wished to battle through the narrow, populated streets of Cambrai – not if we could help it, which was why the plan had been to encircle the city. We had strict orders not to bombard it; the French were understandably keen to avoid another of their centuries old cities being reduced to rubble. It was a dictate the German artillery had used to full advantage. But, if all went well, that would soon end.

'Listen,' I whispered to the two soldiers. 'Do you hear that?'

We squatted near some trees lining the bank.

'It's from the fires, sir,' said one of them. Cartwright was his name. He was a hard looking fellow, but with a voice so soft it was hard not to think of him as anything other than a gentle giant. At that thought an image of Benoît passed through my mind.

Twenty feet in front, the canal coiled silently by, an inky black ribbon. The Canal de l'Escaut formed a boundary around the west and the north of the city. If we were to enter it, crossing the water was essential. On the other side of the canal, off towards the city centre, hung an orange glow from the fires. If anything, they seemed to have intensified, and what I'd heard was almost surely a muffled explosion. Here on the canal bank, the air smelled distinctly of smoke. What could the Germans be up to?

'We'll cross here,' I said, motioning. I'd picked a spot a little downstream from the bridge, reckoning that the Germans in the bunker to our left couldn't readily see us. One end of the bridge, a long, rectangular metal-box construction, with a patchwork of woven steel supports along both sides, was tilted at an angle into the water on our side of the canal. To use it would mean first climbing down the bank, and then ascending a steep slippery incline to the other side. With wet boots, and in the pitch dark, it would be a challenge. With machine guns raking it, it was a veritable deathtrap.

'And no splashing,' I commanded, 'or they'll hear us for certain. Once we get to the other side, we'll regroup, then move around the position from the rear. OK?'

Cartwright and his only slightly smaller compatriot nodded agreeably. If I didn't know better, they actually seemed to be looking forward to it. Myself, I'd instantly regretted my bravado, but in the past several days a weary fatalism had taken me in its clutches. The memory of Benoît, lying maimed by the roadside dominated my thoughts. And I couldn't shake the notion that I wouldn't survive much longer myself. To my surprise I found that I'd almost given up caring.

But now I had two soldiers, each seven or eight years my junior to watch out for. I was determined that my rash impulse was not going to cost them their lives.

We sat down on the embankment and gingerly lowered ourselves into the cold water, a few feet beneath us. Pushing off I caught a last glimpse of Ingersoll and a squad from D Company watching from the tree line. We swam three abreast. The current, such as it was, was almost imperceptible and we reached midstream in no more than a minute. Then I heard a splash. I wrenched my head around to glare at the soldier. He'd let one of his arms carelessly fall back into the water. It was the sort of mistake that could cost us all our lives.

Reaching the far bank several strokes later, I grasped at one of the wooden poles lining it to hold on. I was breathing hard, not so much from the exertion as the excitement. For a long instant, I held it in to listen. Nothing. Painstakingly, we pulled ourselves up onto dry land and crawled as quietly as we could up the bank to the trees. 'Fine, so far,' I whispered. I scanned the area of the bridge for any sign of a sentry but saw none. 'Follow me,' I said to the other two.

At the bridge's concrete foundations we paused and tucked ourselves tight alongside it. I beckoned to the two soldiers to come closer. 'Harris, right?' I whispered to the second one, 'I want you to cover us. Get up to the road once we're gone and make sure some Boche patrol doesn't catch us from the rear. Cartwright, you're with me.'

The two of us scuttled up the dirt embankment to where the road met the bridge. Again I paused to look around. Seeing nothing, we got to our feet and scrambled across. Nestled up against the right side of the bridge was a concrete pill-box.

Approaching the back of it, I pulled a Mills bomb from the satchel slung across my chest. Not long before it had housed my respirator, but now it was full with five shiny cast-iron pineapples. When a Mills bomb explodes, metal shards rip into anything within a 10-yard radius, making it the perfect implement for dealing with pill-boxes.

I saw that Cartwright was also fondling one. He had even removed the ring, although the lever was held tightly in his big hand. With a stabbing finger I indicated where we were going. Then, with my right hand aloft in a fan, I very slowly counted down from five with my fingers whilst tip-toeing down the pair of steps to a tarpaulin-covered entryway. Cartwright was close behind. As my little finger descended, I tore open the tarpaulin and Cartwright leaned passed me and flung in a bomb. We pivoted away. After a second or two there was a dull thud. I reached forward again and tossed in the grenade I was holding. Another boom. Sharp acrid smoke came billowing out.

'That ought to do the trick,' said Cartwright, grimly. He'd un-sheathed his bayonet and moved forward. I pulled out my revolver while he bent down and squeezed through the narrow entranceway. There was barely enough room for Cartwright in there, so I stayed where I was. If he ran into a survivor he'd need the room to manoeuvre. I glanced briefly into the darkness but couldn't see a thing.

'Fancy that, sir,' said Cartwright, his head suddenly emerging. 'All this trouble, and it turns out it was abandoned.' I grunted. Then I stared down at my muddied and dripping uniform.

Abandoned was a word that aptly described Cambrai. The three of us kept a wary watch as Lieutenant Ingersoll's company edged up the sharply tilted bridge in file, arms hooked together. When they'd all made it safely across, we moved further along the canal. But we didn't find much. And not a single German soldier. Reaching our objective, where the Rue Cantimpré crosses the canal, we halted. The bridge there was also badly damaged, but not so badly that the engineers wouldn't have it in operation by this afternoon.

'What do you think, Major?' asked Lieutenant Ingersoll. 'There's not a Fritz to be found.'

'Good thing too,' I said. 'What do I think? I think you should send a message back to headquarters that you've reached your objectives. The two bridges are secure. And we haven't met any opposition.' I let a long pause creep in. 'Then…'

Ingersoll and his company sergeant-major looked at me in antici-pation. 'Yes, sir?'

'*Then* I think you should move your company into the city. Straight down that road is the Place d'Armes and city hall. Let's see if the Boche have really pulled out. If they have, we certainly wouldn't want to give them an opportunity to change their minds. And if they hav-en't, better to deal with them straight away.'

'Yes, sir, but our orders are to hold the bridgehead?'

'There's a time and a place to sit on our asses, Lieutenant, but this isn't it. Trust me.'

The sergeant beside Ingersoll was doing his best to hide his amuse-ment; headquarters staff weren't usually so rough around the edges.

But even Ingersoll was smiling. 'Take the initiative, yes sir, I believe you're right.' Whereupon he turned to the sergeant to organize a party to remain behind to keep watch over the bridges.

As we trooped down the street we came to a burning building, and soon another, this one more damaged than the first. The fire's ravages had turned it into a smoking shell. The air was thick here, with a dense haze of smoke that scratched in my throat and burned the eyes. 'I'll be damned,' said the sergeant, when further on we spotted a huge pile of broken furniture and other incendiary material propped up against the thick wooden doors of a large building. 'The Hun intend to burn the entire place to the ground.'

A few minutes later, a flanking party returned to us accompanied by a couple of prisoners from the 212th Regiment. They were a rearguard and had surrendered readily. A brief interrogation, however, made clear their orders were not so much concerned with guarding as with torching anything that hadn't already been torched. There wasn't much left to do.

'It's a scandal,' muttered Ingersoll. To which I could only nod in agreement. Every window in the city was broken, every door asunder. The proud capital of Cambrai was a smoking, broken ruin. Even now, explosions were going off as a mine or a booby-trap was tripped, or some other Boche rearguard blew a house into the sky.

Ingersoll took his company off to the northeast towards the barracks and the hospital. I reached the Place d'Armes, where the ancient buildings around the square looked like those in Arras after three long years of bombardment. Emaciated skeletons of stone and mounds of smouldering rubble were all that remained. The cobblestoned square was littered with the grey stone of buildings blown, and lantern posts tilted drunkenly, witness to an orgy of demolition. Only this was not the by-product of war. It was wanton destruction.

Slowly, I walked across the vast square towards the *Hôtel de Ville*. The sun had long since risen and I caught glimpses of bright blue peeking through the dense smog. Thick black plumes of smoke rose from every corner of the city, lending the scene an apocalyptic air. Against this sullen tableau, small groups of soldiers were moving, bayoneted rifles hanging over their shoulders, gawking at the destruction.

I saw a team of engineers rush past at the double, with a horse and a wagon filled with firefighting gear plodding along behind.

The city's *Hôtel de Ville* had been transformed into the *KOMMANDANTUR*, the commander's headquarters. That I recognized it as such had less to do with my background as an intelligence officer and more with the giant white letters affixed to the first floor balcony. The sign was pretty much the only thing about the building that wasn't damaged. The façade looked as if a regiment had used it for target practice, so pocked it was by bullets.

A piano stood outside, a couple of elegant chairs strewn nearby. I picked up one of them, brought it over to the piano and sat down. Putting my feet unceremoniously onto the piano – there was nothing my feet could do that hadn't been done already – I leaned back and went to take out my notepad. But then I remembered it was in my tunic. And Ingersoll, in his haste to get across the bridge, had neglected to bring that along. Thankfully he *had* remembered my trench coat.

I sauntered over to the wrought iron fence on which a bulletin board was fastened and ripped off one of the pages. When I saw what it was about, the importance of keeping order – I recognized the word *ordnung* – I snorted. Ironically, the pages I'd captured from the Prussian officer near Tilloy described in considerable detail why order might be a real concern to the local commandant. A group of Bavarians had gotten into a row with some Prussians about divvying up the loot and an officer had been thrown on his head from a third story window. Until today, and dubious of Smith's translation, I couldn't figure out where loot came into it. I needn't have doubted him.

As a soldier passed, I waved him over and scrounged the stub of a pencil. Sitting once more, I began to write. It was high time General Loomis came to see this for himself.

'They told me you were in here.'

I turned. It was General Loomis. Duguid and a few others from the staff straggled in behind.

'Yes, sir,' I said, and saluted.

'My heavens, what happened to you?' asked Loomis, as he approached. I was standing in a house in what looked like someone's living room, or had been prior to the hurricane of the Imperial German Army sweeping through. But Loomis ignored the ravaged state of the room and gawked at me.

'I swam the canal, sir.'

His eyes widened but he didn't say anything. With a mystified look, he glanced over his shoulder at the others to see if they'd caught what I was on about. They all shrugged. I began to understand why I was the intelligence officer.

Not having any particular desire to relive my morning's adventures, I began talking. 'Have a look around, sir. The Boche have looted everything in sight. What they couldn't loot they've wrecked. It's just a normal everyday house. And now the family who owns it will have nothing to come back to. They've completely plundered Cambrai.'

'*Gott mit uns*,' murmured Loomis. He was reading the gothic letters, crudely carved into a chest-high mahogany room divider that might have been elegant, were it not for some Prussian's penknife.

'That means "God's with us", sir.'

'Does it now?'

'Yes, that's what it is says, sir. Although if I were God, I think I'd have picked a side by now, and I can't imagine it'd be the same one as the ruffians who did this.'

The general was shaking his head. 'No, indeed.' Then his voice firmed. 'I see you went ahead and captured the city, MacPhail.'

Without thinking – because for the most part I'd simply tagged along, and taking a city couldn't be a bad thing? – I gave the stock army reply, 'Yes, sir.'

Only that seemed to aggravate things. 'Unfortunately, Major, I believe the plan was that XVII Corps was to capture Cambrai. I have a feeling they'll be somewhat peeved you've done it for them.'

'Uhh,' I began. For a one-time, reputedly silver-tongued lawyer, it was an inauspicious beginning. 'I'm terribly sorry about that, sir, but…'

Then I noticed Loomis' face. He was grinning. An actual honest to goodness grin. The general was joking (a weak joke, mind, but a joke nonetheless). Sheepishly, I looked away. I was embarrassed I hadn't caught on and the bleachers behind beamed at my discomfort. But there was something about that rare expression on Loomis' face that lit up the whole wretched scene of that ransacked house.

For a couple of hours after, I felt pretty good, better than I had in days. Perhaps it was going to work out after all, with General Loomis. Then I bumped into a group of soldiers as I headed for the shattered cathedral.

'So Jack, we've taken Cambrai,' said one. 'Perhaps they'll let us shack up here for the winter, eh?' 'Fat chance of that,' muttered another. A third added, 'Forget that idea. You saw how quick the Imperials were to move in. They've found themselves some nice cushy quarters for the winter.' He was immediately challenged. 'I wouldn't worry about it too much, lads. We'll be at it soon enough a couple of miles down the road, anyhow.'

With that my pleasure at General Loomis' words faded faster than a prairie sunset. I began to think about what lay down the road. The only thing I could come up with was more Germans, and more fighting. The soldier had it right.

CHAPTER 31

15th of October, 1918
Communal Cemetery, Quéant, France

Generals Horne, Currie, Loomis and His Royal Highness the Prince of Wales, and what seemed like everybody who was anybody on the Western Front, was in attendance. There were a hundred soldiers from every battalion in the division and most of the officers. More than 1,500 men. From the 1st Division, the 8th Battalion was out in strength, for they were to provide the burial party – it had once been his battalion. General Lipsett was being buried today.

Yesterday, when I heard the news, I'd quickly sat down, a sickening numbness coming over me. Of course, it was typical Lipsett; never one to leave the danger to others. He'd gone out on reconnaissance, crawling through the grass near some infernal river with the officers from his new division, including no doubt his new intelligence officer. However, a Hun sniper had spotted them, and with the soft-spoken earnestness which characterized him, Smith informed me that the general was hit in the head. Lipsett crawled back to the wood behind but died shortly thereafter. In hindsight, seeing my ashen face, I suspect my worthy assistant realized those were details he might have spared me.

The cognoscenti said we were winning this war. They said the Germans were on their last legs, yet men I cared about were dropping around me. Despite the fall of Cambrai the fighting was still raging. All along the far side of the Canal de l'Escaut the 2nd Division and our Imperial replacements had battered through fortified villages. But the cognoscenti insisted victory was near. They said next year would bring the triumph. Of course, they'd been wrong before. Lately I'd taken to wondering if any of us would survive the year. The Americans would make the difference they insisted. Only we didn't see much of the Sammies here. At the Meuse-Argonne near Verdun, their General Pershing had stubbornly made the same old mistakes with his inexperienced troops. The very ones which had cost us so dearly years before. And the Yanks had died in their thousands. Their sheer weight of numbers carried the day, and the newspapers called it victory, which I suppose it was. It was precisely the sort of victory I feared; the one where no was alive to celebrate.

Today was dull and cold, the slowly shifting sky a monotonous dreary grey. A steady drizzle had fallen all day, and the war-torn, rolling French countryside was transformed into a truly sombre and depressing place. If ever there was a more fitting backdrop for a funeral, I couldn't picture it.

The sunken road from Quéant was lined on both sides with men for almost as far as the eye could see. Their heads were bowed, left feet a half-pace forward, rifles turned on end into the sleek dirt of the road, held upright by hands lain one on top of the other. The soldier in mourning. On the banks overlooking the road, I stood with the other officers, long rows of us. At attention, silent, with rain streaked trench coats and collars turned up against the wind, eyes oblivious to the weather and riveted on the single horse-drawn limber, atop which lay a flag-draped coffin. Paying our respects to one of Canada's most august generals, Irishman though he was. Behind shuffled the great and the good.

After the procession had passed, Cunningham gently lay his hand on my shoulder. Others did the same. Some said a few words and Duguid patted me on the back. Smith refused to let me out of his sight, although I'm not entirely sure why. Lipsett's old staff treated me as if I'd lost family. I guess they knew that ours had been a special relationship. And none had forgotten about Benoît. There was still no news about him.

When the salute finally came, I flinched. As the sound of the rifles' volley echoed away, the bagpipes began their shrill but moving homage, and the coffin was slowly lowered into the ground. Then came the lonesome, sober notes of the *Last Post*. I brushed at my eyes and was thankful for the rain.

Afterwards, little groups of officers congregated together, seeking out each other's company. I joined the familiar faces from the divisional staff. They were chatting quietly, before we all motored back to head-quarters. General Loomis was to drive back with Hore-Ruthven.

'Is it really true,' one was asking of Smith, 'what General Currie wrote in his special order? That Ludendorff sent 12 divisions against us? 12 divisions against a single corps, and only twice that many against the rest of the First Army, the Third Army, *and* the Fourth Army?'

'Yes, sir,' replied Smith, 'and that excludes the special machine gun companies we faced.'

'No wonder Cambrai was so tough,' said the officer. The others in the group nodded solemnly. Our recent losses had left no one untouched.

'What do you think, Mac?' asked Duguid, turning to me. 'Do you reckon they'll put us back into action again soon?' I could see a blood vessel pulsing nervously in the vast plains of his forehead. He was always an anxious looking type, and this afternoon he was wearing his deer-caught-in-a-hunter's-sights expression.

I tilted my head as if I needed to think about it, searching for an optimistic tack to take. Finding none, I said, 'Be thankful, we're in reserve for a spell, Archer. However, the way it looks, the whole Corps is going to rejoin the 1st Division near the Scarpe, and push north and east on Douai and beyond. General Loomis believes we have a few days to rest and refit. From what I hear, GHQ is insistent we don't afford the Boche any peace, which means we definitely won't be having any.'

'Correct me if I'm wrong, sir,' said Smith, interrupting, 'but if the Corps moves towards Douai, won't we just be smoothing out our own left flank?'

'By which you mean, where is rest of the First Army?' I responded.

It was an astute question. Our attack at the D-Q Line and Cambrai had left the rest of the First Army far behind. Now it appeared our next task was to help them catch up. Smith was the junior officer present, but as usual he'd cottoned on to the ramifications long before the others.

We were preparing to leave when a well turned-out young officer came striding up to us. He was wearing a pair of the shiniest, most stylish knee-high officers' boots I'd ever seen. I had a strange feeling I'd seen him before, although I was certain we'd never met. Then I realized I'd observed him trailing along with General Currie in the funeral procession; an adjutant most likely. Considering his rank – he wore the three pips of a captain on the shoulders of his greatcoat – he was remarkably fresh-faced, an effect accentuated by the absence of a moustache and a smooth, almost baby-faced complexion. With all the casualties, the officer ranks were getting younger by the day. His manner, however, was considerably more mature than his age suggested. Startlingly so.

'Good afternoon, gentlemen,' he greeted us. 'Might I trouble you for a lift?'

'Of course,' I said, 'it might be a little tight, but if Cunningham here sucks in his belly we should manage it. We're only going as far as the crossroads north of Quéant, though.'

'That's fine,' he said.

The staff car was one of the larger models, but even so fitting four of us on the rear bench of the Crossley was a tight fit. The officer, a thin lad, squeezed in beside me and closed the door with a clunk.

'It was a moving ceremony didn't you think?'

'Yes it was,' I responded. 'He meant a lot to us, General Lipsett. Especially to those of us in his old division. One of the finest generals in the entire army, if you ask me.'

The odd thing was the officer's accent was English, unmistakeably upper-class English. Admittedly, we still had quite a number of senior British officers, such as Hore-Ruthven, but for a new junior staff officer – and that's what I guessed he was – it was unusual.

'My condolences,' he said, after we got going. 'From all I hear he

261

was a very popular general.' For a long moment there was silence, and then he continued. 'You're all from the 3ʳᵈ Division, Major?'

'Yes. We're on General Loomis' staff.' I shifted a little in my seat so I could steal a glance at him. 'I don't believe we've ever met before, Captain. Although if I'm not mistaken, I spotted you earlier with General Currie?'

'That's correct,' he said. 'I'm recently attached to the Corps as GSO2, so I see a lot of the general. I'm forgetting my manners, though. I should have introduced myself. I'm Edward. *Major* Edward.' Seeing me eyeing his pips, he quickly added. 'New uniform's not back from the tailor, yet.'

If I'd had half my wits about me, his name might have rung some bells. But I was too busy thinking how Currie's band of staff officers was suddenly becoming rather posh. Heaven knows how McAvity was fitting in. Well-dressed decorum had never been his strong suit, any more than it was mine. 'You must have quite the connections, Edward, to land a nice position like that,' I said. That cloaked the question I'd avoided asking outright: why was an immaculate, proper young Englishman on the Corps staff in the first place?

The traces of a smile appeared, but he said nothing.

I turned awkwardly and offered my hand. 'MacPhail. Malcolm MacPhail,' I said. 'Pleased to meet you.' And then I introduced him to the others. For a talkative bunch, they'd all gone curiously mute, which left me to do all the talking. The driver's eyes kept appearing in the rear-view mirror. I wished he'd keep his eyes on the road; between the shell-holes and the rain, it was not in the best of shape.

'So, Edward. What do you make of our predicament? You're at Corps headquarters,' I asked.

'The enemy is in retreat to the south and the north. Their front is split in two, and the Hindenburg system is penetrated in two spots. Frankly I'd say the Boche are in quite a pickle. Surely you must have heard, there's even talk they're seeking an armistice?'

I grunted. 'Armistice. Right. I can't say I've seen many signs of that around here. All our local Fritzs want to do is fight from what I can see. And we've been obliging them, going on two months now. I wish I could say that I think that'll change, but perhaps you know better?'

'Well, the watchword from GHQ is to "Hustle the Hun",' he began.

I interrupted. 'Which does have quite a ring to it when you're sitting in the safety of the château at GHQ. I'm not sure the troops will take to it so readily, though.' Even to myself I sounded grumpy.

Edward nodded politely.

We chatted about this and that – he was an easy talker – and it wasn't long before we pulled up to the motley assortment of huts, tents and dug-outs that comprised headquarters.

'It's been grand speaking with you, Malcolm,' Edward said, as we clambered out. 'I ought to be getting back, however. General Currie will be wondering where I am.'

I turned to the driver. 'Private, would you take the Major back to Corps headquarters?'

'You could walk it,' I said to him, 'but it's best not to keep the Corps commander waiting. Good luck, Edward, and drop by if you're in the neighbourhood again. I'm sorry for the reception. We're a reasonably congenial bunch when we're not attending funerals.'

We shook hands and he gave a polite nod to the others.

'Pleasant enough chap,' I said, as the car pulled away.

Tibbett cleared his throat. He hadn't spoken a word in the past ten minutes; a new record for him. 'I realize you're upset, Malcolm, but I thought you'd be more circumspect these days.'

'What do you mean? I was perfectly nice to the lad.'

Wearily he shook his head. 'Mac, you know the insignia of every regiment in the German army, yet you don't know *who* that was?'

'No. But he seemed all right. Who was it then?'

'The heir to the throne. Prince Edward. You might know him better as the Prince of Wales.'

'Oh,' was all I managed. I'd never been much good at names and faces.

CHAPTER 32

16th of October, 1918
Quéant, France

When I saw him again at the staff conference the next morning, General Loomis was unusually sombre. Naturally he had the arrival of the Corps Commander and entourage to consider, but the battle was won. Congratulations and commendations were in order. That was the way the army worked, and there was little question they were amply deserved. Yet Loomis looked anything but elated. I wondered whether he'd been pondering the same thing I had, that both of the 3rd Division's first commanders were dead; Malcolm Mercer at Mount Sorrel in 1916, and now Louis Lipsett at the River Selle. Loomis was third in line, and the recent fighting was if anything more desperate than ever. Perhaps he was ruminating over his own chances.

That afternoon, despite all they'd gone through in the preceding weeks, the 7th Brigade put on an impressive show on the muddy field north of the village. For me, however, it was not the spit and polish parade, nor the sight of Sir Arthur and His Royal Highness (who waved at me when he saw me) taking the salutes of the battered 49th Battalion, the PPCLI and the others, but the late arrival of a plain manila envelope which defined the day.

It was addressed to *Major Malcolm MacPhail, MC*. Which was fairly unremarkable one might think, and truthfully most of my correspondence was similarly addressed, but for one small thing: the "MC", or Military Cross, bringing up the rear. It was true I had one. I'd won it way back in 1916, half a lifetime ago. But not even my father, regardless how proud he was of that little bauble, would go so far as to put *that* on a letter. Therefore it could mean only one thing: officialdom. Officialdom wisely stayed out of the fray when the troops were at the front. There was little point bothering someone about some trifle when the recipient might be dead by the time the letter arrived – one of the few times when good sense reared its head amongst the army bureaucrats. So an official letter was news. As he handed it over, I could see from Smith's expressionless face that he'd come to a similar conclusion. We both knew that news, in all probability, meant bad news. Neither of us were expecting a kind letter from the King.

I took the letter, unopened, and went back to my tent.

My first reaction was to breathe a sigh of relief when I saw it had nothing to do with my family. My second was to curse. The letter had come from Montreuil, which as everybody knows is General Headquarters. Underneath the scribble at the bottom, the sender's title was neatly typed. It was from the Provost Marshal, the most senior policeman in the British Expeditionary Force.

The letter was short, and spare in explanations, summarily inviting me to an interview on October 22nd at Montreuil – less than a week away – to formally respond to allegations of "theft of Crown property". Embezzlement had now become theft, I noted. Clavell was turning the knife.

I fished around in the envelope and out slid a smaller handwritten note in the spidery scrawl I'd recognize in my grave. Captain Clavell tersely informed me that he had located Lieutenant Rutherford, and even spoken with him. Rutherford had vouched for me, as I knew he would. In fact he'd corroborated my entire story. However, Clavell pointedly noted that Rutherford had declared he left Arvillers before I did – it couldn't have been by any more than a minute or two. In his absence, concluded Clavell, the German pay box had vanished "without a trace". "Consistent with these findings, and absent any satisfactory explanation as to the whereabouts of the captured booty, I must inform you that I have recommended to the Provost Marshal to lay formal charges." The letter ended with a short postscript: "You will note I have delayed proceeding with these matters in view of the evident importance of Canadian Corps operations in recent weeks."

'Jesus Christ,' I exploded. 'Am I supposed to thank him, too?'

'Everything all right in there?' asked a meek voice. A head poked tentatively through the opening.

'Hi Paul. Come in.'

Tibbett squeezed through the opening, removing his cap as he entered.

'Do you want a drink?' I asked.

'That bad?'

I snorted. 'Clavell. Why don't they assign him to us for a week? Experience the real war for a while. Then he'd be singing a different tune. Of course, there's nothing wrong with Clavell that a number 9 wouldn't solve.' The properties of the army's famous laxative pill were the stuff of legend.

Benoît would have laughed at this with a face that suggested I was taking life far too seriously. That wasn't Tibbett's way, even if the only tangible difference was that he put a more diplomatic face on it.

'Did you hear some news, then?'

I sat down on my cot and threw the two letters dismissively onto the little table. I motioned to him that he could have the chair.

Tibbett pulled it out, sat down, and began to read. I could see his eyebrows furrowing as he raced through the letter from the Provost Marshal. His head yanked back ever so slightly when he came to Clavell's note, as if he couldn't believe what he was reading. I barely believed it and I knew Clavell.

'I see,' he said, as he finished. He lay the note neatly on top of the letter and pushed them away.

'You understand my problem now,' I said. I got down on my knees and pulled at the trunk wedged underneath my bed.

'I'm not so sure,' he said, cautiously. 'This might very well work in your favour, Mac. The Provost Marshal is not about to lay charges on a decorated officer unless he's really quite certain. He'll need more than hearsay to do that. You're the lawyer. What do you call that?'

'Ah, here it is,' I said, and with a flourish held up a bottle and a corkscrew. 'Hearsay? In the legal profession we call it *circumstantial evidence*, Paul, that's what we call it.'

266

'Exactly. Circumstantial evidence.' Tibbett repeated it slowly. 'Mac, you have the chance to tell your side of the story. If I were you I'd go through it very carefully. You have almost a week to prepare and I'd be delighted to help, if you'd like. The Provost Marshal will surely see there's nothing to Clavell's allegations, not once you give him all the facts. And then that will be that. It's actually good news if you think about it.'

'Only we're a long way from a real court of law, Paul. What if the Provost Marshal simply ignores what I have to say, and sends me on to a court martial presided over by a collection of scrambled eggs who've spent their entire careers a hundred miles from the front? They'll swallow anything. Even Clavell's tortured logic. And who's to say the Provost Marshal won't do exactly that? It wouldn't surprise me if he plays bridge at GHQ with Clavell's uncle, Colonel Whatley-Wigham. Whatley-Wigham may even be a judge. I don't know who's worse, the uncle or the nephew…' There was a plop as the cork popped out. I was pleased to see I hadn't spilled a drop.

Tibbett pulled a face. 'You really ought to have more faith in military justice, Mac.'

'I would if it wasn't so lopsided. Let's see if we can find you a glass.'

'There,' pointed Tibbett. Two tin mugs were balanced precariously on a haversack in the corner.

'Try this,' I said, and poured a generous measure of wine into one of the enamelled mugs. 'By the way, have you heard anything from Lord Derby?'

'No, not yet. But he'll come through. Don't worry about that. These things take time. Although, honestly, this hearing may settle the matter long before Lord Derby's intervention is required.' Tibbett rang his finger dubiously around the rim of the mug, but then took a sip. In the time he'd been talking, I'd downed a third of mine before I even realized it. 'Oh, my. This is quite delicious, Malcolm.'

I grabbed the bottle by its neck and flipped it around to show him the label. I didn't bother correcting my name. "Mac" was never going to slide easily from Tibbett's throat, regardless how lubricated it was.

'A Saint Emilion! My father bought those by the case. I remember, as a child, I broke a bottle one time and received quite a licking. Wherever did you find it?'

'A bunker in the D-Q Line. Its previous owners abandoned it for some reason. I think they were forced to depart on short notice.'

'Mmm.' Tibbett was sipping again. For someone who'd barely touched a drop of the stuff in the first quarter of his life, he was making up for lost time.

'Let's hope it's not poisoned,' I said. Tibbett ignored me and continued staring into his mug. I took another drink, this time a sip. The Germans often poisoned the wells as they fled, but I didn't really expect them to foul their loot.

'But this is fine wine,' protested Tibbett. 'This is hardly the time or the place to drink a wine like this.'

Which, on the face of it, it wasn't. The place was a perfectly normal canvas army tent, just big enough for a cot, a few items of furniture and a lantern hanging in the middle. It was dry, only a little musty smelling, and not the most obvious locale to taste France's finest. One thing this war had taught me though; there was no time like the present.

'No, perhaps not, Paul. However, I can't think of a better occasion. Besides, who knows if we'll both be around next week?' I raised my cup. 'Let's drink one to Benoît.'

17th of October, 1918

The next morning General Loomis was back to his old self. That is to say he was peppering Lieutenant-Colonel Hore-Ruthven with questions about the finer points of the day's preparations. General Currie was returning to inspect the 8th Brigade, and later the 9th. Loomis, with his penchant for organization, was leaving nothing to chance. I'd been invited to ride along, although I sat in the front with the driver. Far enough away to miss most of the conversation, but close enough to be called upon when needed.

Loomis must have been satisfied with Hore-Ruthven's explanations for I heard his raised voice address me. 'What do you reckon, Major, will the war be over soon?'

'I wouldn't know, sir. I've been concentrating on getting through each day as it comes.' It was not the most refined answer for an intelligence major, but it was honest. However, the general's words weren't solely idle chitchat. Every day fresh rumours surfaced of an impending peace. The Germans were falling back across the entire front.

'You realize, since August, the Corps has gone up against 47 German divisions and defeated them all. That's hardly a reason to be glum. That's a quarter of the German army on the Western Front, MacPhail.'

'It's not the one-quarter we've defeated that I'm worried about, General,' I said, 'it's the other three-quarters we still have to face.'

Neither Loomis nor Hore-Ruthven responded.

Not long after, we arrived at the same muddy parade ground. As we climbed out, I found myself standing beside the general. I cleared my throat. 'Sir, there was a small matter I wanted to discuss with you.' I'd decided it was long overdue that I tell my superiors about the charges I faced. 'I received a letter from GHQ yesterday...'

He turned to face me. 'Yes, Major?'

But then a soldier rushed up and saluted. 'General Currie has arrived, sir.'

'Fine,' Loomis responded. He turned to me. 'We'll continue this later, MacPhail. I'm going to greet the general.'

Unfortunately, as so often is the case, later didn't come – at least not until it was too late.

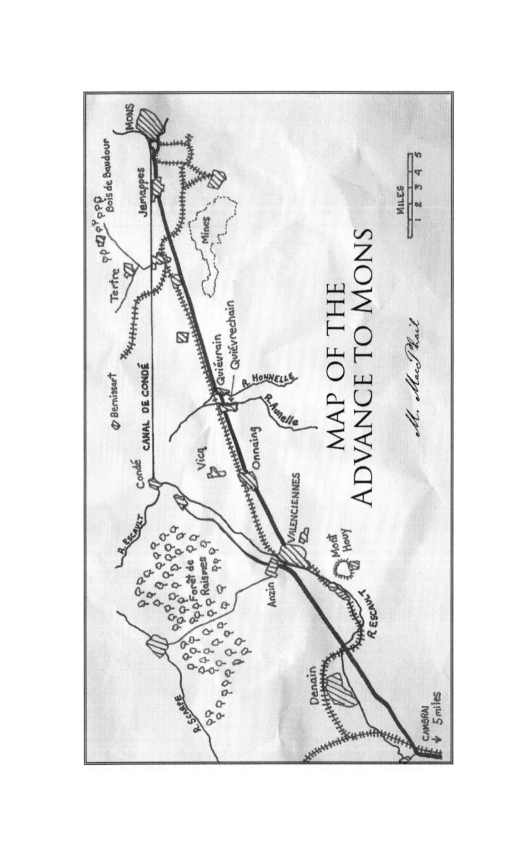

MAP OF THE
ADVANCE TO MONS

M. MacPhail

MILES
1 2 3 4 5

MONS
Jemappes
Bois de Baudour
Tertre
Mines
Bernissart
CANAL DE CONDÉ
Condé
Quiévrain
Quiévrechain
R. HONNELLE
R. Aunelle
Onnaing
Vicq
R. ESCAULT
VALENCIENNES
Mon Houy
Anzin
R. ESCAULT
Forêt de Raismes
R. SCARPE
Denain
CAMBRAI
→ 5 miles

CHAPTER 33

20th of October, 1918
Denain, France

Considering that it had been only nine days since Cambrai fell, it was a little surprising that I was on my way to Denain. This sizeable industrial town sat more than a dozen miles further east, on the banks of the Canal de l'Escaut at the tip of a huge arrowhead. Douai formed one corner of its base, and Cambrai below it, the other. A deep, broad swath of France that had been German for longer than I'd been on the continent was liberated.

Not long after taking Cambrai, the Corps pulled back, retrieving the doughty fist we'd rudely stuck into the enemy lines. We were assigned a new front, behind and a jot to the north of where we'd been, with Douai on our left. There we pushed and probed, and patrolled aggressively. But for small gains, the Germans stubbornly held their ground. That is, until early on the 17th, when the morning patrols reported that the enemy was gone.

Thus began the advance. The likes of it, both in its speed and its depth, none of us could have imagined barely a month earlier. Douai fell the very first day to patrols of the 1st Division, although the honour was to go to the British Middlesex regiment. Village after village was freed, nearly 40 of them yesterday alone. The biggest was Denain. Unlike most of the towns and hamlets we'd passed through since early

August, we encountered civilians, great numbers of them. This was mildly astonishing after the scarred and all but deserted ruins of places like Monchy-le-Preux, Boiry, Inchy-en-Artois and Cambrai, where only the ghosts of inhabitants still remained.

From Quéant, close to the heart of the D-Q Line, and now safe miles from the front, the driver and I took a road heading northeast. We crossed the Canal du Nord at Sauchy and meandered through the ruined stone desert of Oisy-le-Verger that I'd seen from the air until we came to the Canal de la Sensée, the watery east-west barrier separating Cambrai from its northern neighbour, Douai. Here the advance had begun.

At the canal-side village of Aubenchel-au-Bac we made a brief jog due north. In a traffic jam of horses and trucks, we passed slowly over the waterway on a bridge still under repair. As I gazed out the window to my left, engineers were swarming over the twisted steel supports of the blown railway crossing. Against all expectation, the war was becoming a war of movement. Feeding supplies to an army on the march was proving to be a formidable challenge.

Once across the slow trickle of the Sensée and its flooded marshes, we turned right (eastwards) and took the road along the north bank of the canal until it was intersected by the Canal de L'Escaut coming northwards out of Cambrai. There we turned left, following the northern bank of the Escaut as it curved north and eastwards. The road was in remarkably fine shape except at crossroads, or where it passed over some obstacle like a bridge or a culvert that lent itself for destruction. Entirely in character the Germans had seized these opportunities as if they'd been offered the keys to the Tower of London. Seldom was our enemy as methodical, or as meticulous, as in the path of destruction he was leaving in his wake. The engineers were busy, but the going was slow.

We drove through a succession of small villages, with names like Aubigny-le-Bac, Féchain, Wagnes, where townsfolk waved at us and, once, even threw flowers. Soldiers tend to be a tough, cynical lot, inured to their station in life, but I found my heart going out to these poor souls. Beast, grain and treasure, the Boche had stripped the land bare, leaving nothing in their rapid retreat.

Soon we arrived in Denain. 'Well, it's not exactly Paris,' I said optimistically, after we passed a succession of grimy two-store buildings that looked as if they hadn't seen a lick of paint since the last war in 1870.

'No, sir, it's not,' agreed the driver, a taciturn fellow by the name of Perry. He possessed small bones and fine features, although in this October of 1918 they were marred by an ugly crescent-shaped scar on one cheek and another above his left eye. Perry had only recently joined the divisional motor pool after an extended stay in hospital and a rest camp. It took me almost five minutes to learn that much. I eventually gave up my attempt at idle conversation and went back to staring out the window. He might not have been talkative, but Perry was a fine enough driver, which is all you really need in a driver. At the sight of Denain, however, he came to life. 'What a crowd, sir,' he said enthusiastically. Then he shook his head and his voice took on a darker edge. 'To think these poor folks have been living here all these years, with the Hun lording it over them. And now he's robbed them of everything. There'll be no peace until he makes this good, sir,' he warned. It was a sentiment I was hearing a lot.

Throngs of people in their Sunday finest crowded the street, blocking our way as we neared the centre of town. Perry leaned half-heartedly on the horn a few times, but this had no obvious effect other than to elicit a cheer from those in front. 'Let me out here, Perry,' I said. 'I'm never going to get to the church on time at this rate.' As it was going on eleven o'clock I feared I was already late. Missing my appointments was an unfortunate habit I'd picked up in kindergarten and hadn't been able to shake.

Walking wasn't much faster than driving, but the crowd at least was heading the same way I was, down the narrow street to the Eglise St. Martin. While Denain may not have been a gleaming pearl on the Escaut, its citizens exhibited a warm-hearted hospitality those in the grander metropolises could learn from. They all smiled at me enthusiastically, as if I were the one who had singlehandedly snatched the town from the Germans. Old men added a pat on the back or shook my hand as I squirmed between them. Little boys with little flags ran beside me.

'*Bravo*,' I heard, repeatedly. '*Vive les Canadiens!*'

'*Vive la France*,' I replied, with a smile, and they all cheered heartily.

At the church the modest square in front was packed. Green-patched soldiers from the 4th Division – the real victors at Denain – loitered against the windows of adjoining buildings while their comrades in helmets held back the press of women and children. A row of elderly gentlemen in shiny top hats and long black coats were lined up. Apparently they weren't the town's aristocrats, but rather its veterans: from 1870, no less. Noting their age, an explanation for the run-down state of the place came to mind. What I didn't have an explanation for was how I was going to manage my late entrance.

Height, I'd come to learn, is a mixed blessing. It was definitely no advantage running from one shell-hole to the next, overeager Württemburgers with machine guns waiting. Today, however, it had its benefits. I watched above the heads of the others as a congregation of officers, one of whom was recognizably General Currie, slowly followed the half-dozen white cloaked priests into the church. I was on time. *That was a relief.* I hadn't relished the idea of pushing open a massive, creaking oak door while the priest interrupted his sermon, and His Royal Highness, Sir Arthur, and a hundred other dignitaries craned their necks to spot the intruder.

While I needn't have worried about being late, making it into the church took all my powers of persuasion. Eventually, a stern-faced corporal accepted my explanations and let me pass. Loomis had sent me along to represent the division. 'A little church may do you some good, MacPhail,' he added, and for once that was a sentiment I agreed with. I certainly had no shortage of things to pray for.

Today's service was a Thanksgiving service. In the past four years there'd been precious little to be thankful for. I suspect that was why I'd long since forgotten the occasion. However, Denain had good reasons to think differently today. Squashed in between some officers on a pew near the back I heard nothing of the sermon, but the air was festive and alive, the choir's joyful song positively infectious. Yesterday's message that Benoît was miraculously alive and in a hospital in England (although I still couldn't help fear the worst) had buoyed my spirits. For a few blessed moments as music filled the air I forgot the war.

For the occasion, the sun even deigned a brief appearance and when we emerged from St. Martin's, I turned my face to its warmth.

Then I spotted the Prince of Wales. Despite sharing the same rank as me, he was clearly the guest of honour. General Currie accompanied him, looking fitter than I'd seen him in years. Currie seldom slept more than a few hours, so the victories must be doing him good, I thought.

With the prince and the general in the lead, we set off down the cobblestoned street lined with people. General Watson of the 4th Division and General Morrison of the artillery were close behind, followed by other senior officers, including a pot-bellied Frenchman who by the look of him had deftly avoided the shortages that were afflicting so many of his countrymen. I fell in behind.

Small flags and banners fluttered gaily, hung by their hundreds on strings crisscrossing the road above our heads, giving the town the appearance of a festival. Until yesterday there'd been absolutely no reason for festivals, and probably wouldn't be again for some time, not until the town's citizens could once more eke out a meagre living. But today they were making the best of it.

'You know, for the first time, this really makes me appreciate what we're doing here,' murmured the officer I was walking beside.

'Doesn't it?' I replied. 'When you see all these people, you realize perhaps there was some meaning to this war.' I couldn't help thinking how strange it was, when my spirits were at their lowest, I'd been sent here to Denain. Even the most battle-hardened of us couldn't help but be touched by the outpourings of gratitude. For the signs of privation were etched indelibly on every face we saw.

As we ambled along, the dignitaries stopping and greeting those along our route, a young lady in a dress of green and white chiffon – far too light for the weather – elbowed her way through the crush and ran to me, grasping me firmly around the waist. Before I could say or do anything she leaned forward, stood on her toes, and in an intoxicating mist of sweet perfume and leering catcalls from the crowd, planted a kiss. Smack on my lips.

By the time I came to, she had been swept away, only the top of her wavy blond curls still visible as the crowd swallowed her up. As she passed far too quickly from sight into memory, I brushed absent-mindedly at my lips with two fingertips. A moist film coated them. It was red... lipstick. I smiled.

In front I saw that His Royal Highness had paused and was observing me. He didn't say anything. But there was something in his expression, more than simply casual interest, or sharing a moment of amusement, which let me in on a secret: our future king had a taste for the ladies.

Finally we arrived at a square, the appropriately named Place de la Liberté, which a statue of Marshal Villars had once dominated. Villars was something of a local hero, having beaten the Dutch and the Austrians in 1712 during the War of the Spanish Succession, and liberated the town. Villars was absent without leave today, however. His bronzed figure, and the horse he rode in on, had been ripped from the imposing base and carted off to Germany. Even if Villars could be retrieved, a similar honour for General Currie was out of the question; Denain simply couldn't afford the funds for that amount of bronze.

The prince took the salute as the veterans of 1870 and the 10th Brigade marched proudly past, and when it was done the saluting party dissolved into small groups, talking amongst themselves.

'Ah, Major,' I heard, from the cluster of officers arrayed on the base of the statue. 'Come join us.'

HRH the Prince of Wales was shaking a cane at me, although that was less fearsome than it sounds. I couldn't help noticing that General Currie, who looked exceptionally formidable standing behind the lithe, rather scrawny young prince, wore a bemused look on his face. His cane though was at as his side, presumably cocked and ready to give me a swat if I stepped out of line.

'Your Highness,' I said, when I reached the prince, not knowing whether I should bow or salute, but in the event did neither. He was a major, too, after all. I began to stutter what was meant to be an apology for earlier transgressions of protocol until Edward mercifully waved me quiet.

'Don't worry about that, Malcolm. I prefer Edward, as it happens,' said the heir to throne. 'I rarely have a chance to talk man-to-man. My name too often gets in the way.'

I nodded sympathetically. Even if I'd never really had that problem, except with the odd Frenchman who equated MacPhail with a kind of unpronounceable tropical disease he'd never heard of. Out of earshot, but under the watchful eye of General Currie we traded a few pleas- antries, awkward in my case and warmly engaging in his, until he said; 'We had a visitor the other day.'

'Oh?'

'Yes, a colonel from GHQ. A very proper, distinguished-looking gentleman. Told me he'd even met me at the box at Ascot when I was a boy, although I don't recollect him. Anyhow, I happened to mention I was with the 3rd Division for a spell, and spoke with one of its officers. He asked if it was you. He even mentioned you by name. It's astonishing really, of all the men in uniform, and the colonel knew you! He seemed very interested to hear what I had to say.'

I tensed. 'Did he now?' I said. 'You don't happen to recall the colonel's name, by chance?'

'Whatley something or other.'

'Whatley-Wigham?'

The prince nodded with enthusiasm. 'Yes, that's it. So you *do* know him?'

I sighed. 'You might say that.' As I searched for an explanation fit for royalty, I paused. Suddenly, I thought of the prince's appreciative look at the mademoiselle and it came to me. I'd had quite enough of the Whatley-Wighams and extended family. This might put a tiny dent in their armour. 'It's a trifle embarrassing,' I began. I glanced awkwardly from left to right.

The Prince of Wales stared at me. 'It's all right,' he said softly, brushing at a strand of his dark blond hair.

'The colonel's taken quite a shine to me. From what I hear I'm not the first boy to have caught his interest,' I said. The prince had a puzzled look. I winked, a slow exaggerated wink that would have done any theatre troupe proud.

'You don't mean to say…!?' The prince had his mouth open and was staring at me.

I shrugged.

'But he has a wife and children.'

'I know,' I said.

The prince looked away, and I swore I saw a shiver ripple through him. No doubt he was thinking of his days as a young boy at Ascot.

'Don't say anything will you? He's a colonel at GHQ and he could make my life miserable.'

A harder look came into the prince's eyes. 'I shouldn't worry about that, Malcolm, if I were you.'

'Thanks, Edward,' I said. 'I'm glad to have it off my shoulders.'

'Yes, I can imagine. I'm so sorry.' He glanced over at the Corps staff who were preparing to depart. 'I'm afraid I must leave. In case I don't speak with you again, it was a pleasure, Malcolm.'

'Likewise,' I replied. This time I didn't offer my hand, but he did give me his.

I had a feeling that the days of the Whatley-Wigham family enjoying a pleasant afternoon at Ascot had come to an abrupt end. With any luck that wouldn't be the end of it.

I'd done everything I'd been taught not to. The sort of petty scheming and conniving that I'd been warned about since I was a toddler. And I liked the prince. He was a little gullible, of course, but I liked him. But more than I liked him, I didn't like Clavell and his uncle. I may not have helped my case one whit, but it sure felt good.

CHAPTER 34

21ˢᵗ of October, 1918
Somain, France

'Damn it, MacPhail. You should have told me about this much earlier.'
General Loomis' face had taken on the appearance of a red Very flare.
As anyone will tell you, you don't want to be two feet away when a
Very flare is ignited.

'I meant to, sir, but the opportunity didn't present itself,' I stammered.

'Well, I think you'd best take this opportunity to tell us everything,
Major.' Hore-Ruthven, to his side, nodded vigorously. He didn't appear
too pleased, either. In fact he looked downright grumpy. He'd always
supported me, first with Lipsett and now with Loomis, and I could see
this unexpected broadside from one of *his* staff officers made him look
bad. These were subjects he was supposed to deal with, so the general
didn't have to.

There'd been really no way around telling them. When I heard that
the 22ⁿᵈ of October was fixed as the day of our attack, I instantly realized
that I couldn't pick up and leave for GHQ: summons or not. So with
lead in my shoes I dragged off to my superiors. I kept my account short
and factual. No mention of a scheming Clavell, or a prima-donna uncle
with a bruised aura of superiority and a distinct dislike of me. Just the
facts. And the fact I hadn't done a thing. Which was what I had been
intending to tell the Provost Marshal in the morning.

'Well, I'm sorry, but there's absolutely no question of you going off to Montreuil,' said Loomis when I finished. 'I need you here for the attack.'

Seeing my face, his voice softened and he added, 'Look, you're a fine officer, MacPhail. I'm sure this will blow over. It's not as if you actually did anything wrong?'

Emphatically I shook my head. 'No, sir,' I said. Not that Clavell seemed overly concerned with trivial issues like what I'd done or not done. But I couldn't very well tell Loomis that.

In the end Tibbett had convinced me that a good interview with the Provost Marshal might see the end of this nightmare. As the day approached I looked forward to getting it behind me. Only I wasn't going to be able to tell my side of the story, and there might not be a second chance. I couldn't imagine the Provost Marshal was used to being snubbed when he sent out invitations.

'I'll send a telegram to explain,' offered Hore-Ruthven. He appeared somewhat placated by my explanation.

'Thank you, sir. I'd be grateful if you did.'

There was one small consolation; General Loomis had called me a "fine officer". In addition to which, if I didn't make it through tomorrow, the entire affair wouldn't matter, anyhow.

22nd of October, 1918
Forêt de Raismes, France

Six miles northeast of Denain, and less than two miles due north of the suburbs of the city of Valenciennes, lies a vast tract of hardwood trees. There are fifteen square miles of them and they are known as the Forêt de Raismes. We were ordered to move through and mop it up. At any other time in this war an order like that would have been akin to suicide. It might still be, I reminded myself.

In late October, the skies in Northern France are still dark at 7.00 a.m., and I felt better for it. I was with a party of twelve, one NCO and eleven other ranks. As the ranking officer I ought to have been in command, but that wasn't how the chain of command worked, and it was a good thing. Sergeant Miles appeared to have everything well under control and I had other things on my mind. Like what we would discover in that sea of trees cut through with clearings, ditches and roads. The Boche could have hidden two divisions there for all I knew.

The problem wasn't only getting supplies forward in this headlong advance; we were literally flying blind. We simply didn't know what we were up against. It was an uncomfortable feeling, not least because it was my job to see that we did. At first I admonished Smith, a trifle harshly I'm afraid to admit, for having collected so little usable information. Quickly I realized it wasn't his fault. For more than a week the skies were as thick as split-pea soup. In that the Royal Air Force was about as useful as a ham hock floating in its midst. Nor did it help that in this rush to close with the enemy, often no more than two hours ahead, there was no time to do anything but keep going. As long as the Germans kept running that wasn't a problem. When they stopped, however, or threw out a rearguard, we risked running off a cliff. Naturally I didn't put it like that when I briefed the general. But who, how many, and what exactly we faced, were questions for which I had no satisfactory answers. I didn't protest when the colonel suggested I go ahead with the scouts.

We crossed the main road, then over the railway, both heading north out of Valenciennes. We entered the forest proper in a loose grouping. By this time the sun was up. Under the huge oaks, beeches, and chestnuts it was still quite dark. The scouts were moving rapidly, yet there was scarcely a noise.

Reaching a small clearing, we paused briefly. I grabbed Sergeant Miles by the arm and thrust the map in his face. I pointed at the squiggled red lines drawn on a rise 700 or 800 yards ahead. 'Don't forget about those trenches,' I whispered. That was one small detail we *had* been able to find. Miles scratched at his chin and nodded. Without even consulting his compass we began veering northeastwards. His plan was to bypass them to the north and then come from behind.

Half the battalion was following in our wake. The 42nd had drawn the assignment. If we didn't hurry, the Highlanders would run straight into that position. Like bloodhounds on the scent of a fox, without a word exchanged, the scouts seemed to understand this. Our pace quickened.

The forest was not nearly as dense as I first imagined. The piles of underbrush and neatly stacked logs were evidence that the Germans were logging intensively. This made the going quicker, the risks commensurately higher.

Abruptly, Miles put his fist in the air. We halted, just short of a clearing. I couldn't see much other than a few trees on a modest rise off to our right. That had to be the position, though. The sergeant waved his arm at the squad and three soldiers raced across the open patch before disappearing in some undergrowth. In this way the sergeant marshalled his troops forward. When the others had passed, he touched me on the arm, and I ran with him across the open ground. It couldn't have been a hundred yards, but I was relieved when I slipped behind a modest oak.

Minutes later we were turning to move back southwestwards, hugging the clumps of trees that were much denser on this rear slope of the hillock. We were divided into three groups. I was with four others whom the sergeant had entrusted to me. All had their rifles cradled at hip level. A general would have called this the left prong of the attack. We had the furthest to go.

In fact we didn't reach our objective before the shooting began. A volley of rifle shots. Upon hearing them, we ran pell-mell in the direction of what appeared as a rough "H" on the map. Somehow I reached the trench first and slid down into it. It was a crude affair, not at all like those we'd encountered earlier, roughly dug with none of the finishing touches for which the Germans were known. The others followed close on my heels.

The fight, such as it was, didn't last more than a minute. We discovered a group of five crouched behind a crude log barricade looking west, at the end of one arm of the H. They were dealt with in short order. Two others we missed. We saw them sprint from the far end of the trench towards the trees, heading in the direction of home.

One of our men fired a few shots until I said, 'Leave it. You're just going to hit a squirrel. There's little enough wildlife around here as it is.'

'That's right, Mason,' said a soldier. 'You missed the bucks by a long shot, anyhow.'

We all smiled, which comes easily when your blood is still pumping madly, the fight is over and everybody is in one piece.

After this we advanced almost without a hitch through the forest. We zig-zagged along the roads and paths for the most part, heading east for more than 3 miles until eventually we came to the road in the map quadrant Q22.a, our objective for the day. It was late afternoon. Already the sun was making its retreat. I decided to press on a bit. Together with a soldier we crossed the road and plunged into the bush.

The private and I became separated from the others around this time. I figured we were only a few steps ahead. Knowing the scouts and how they'd blazoned their way through the forest, they'd be past us in no time. So Timmy Collins and I, for that's what the young private was called, pushed on.

It was our speed which proved fatal. That, and a certain dulling of the senses. Since our morning skirmish we'd encountered only a handful of Germans. We met another party of scouts, but mainly it was an endless succession of trees, fallen logs and underbrush obscuring ruts in the ground. That's why we finally stuck to the paths, where thoughts inevitably turned to other things, like dreams of a billet with a full pot and a warm bed. I ought to have known better. I was the major and it wasn't as if I was lacking in combat experience – Christ, the past two months had been nothing else. I suppose I was anxious to report to the general and Hore-Ruthven that we'd taken all the objectives, not hindered by a lack of proper intelligence.

The clearing was like every other. Reedy grass, the faded stumps of a half dozen trees. Collins stepped out, and a footstep later so did I. Then I heard the metallic *click click* of a rifle bolt. It's a sound like no other. My heart skipped a beat and my head jerked up. Ahead I saw a colour that didn't come naturally to forests in France. It was field-grey.

'Oh, shit,' I heard beside me.

Uneasily, I stopped in my tracks and stared at them.

Not a word passed. There wasn't much need for words. The thick black tube of a MG 08 was pointed straight at us. If that wasn't clear enough, four rifles were as well.

I dropped the rifle and slowly raised my hands into the air.

CHAPTER 35

23rd of October, 1918
Forêt de Raismes, France

Once relieved of our weapons, we were led to a freshly dug hole. I handed my Webley, a few Mills bombs and my Borgel wristwatch to a short, pock-faced fellow with a corporal's button on his collar. He sported a *stahlhelm* too big for his head, a sour look, and a dark brush-cut moustache that seemed to be the latest fashion with the Fritzs. I kept hoping that a party of scouts might appear. But they didn't. The Germans, however, seemed as ill-prepared for our capture as we were. They were discussing the matter amongst themselves, just loud enough for us to hear.

'What are they saying?' whispered Timmy. Timmy was from Montreal. While he might have spoken a word or two of French, he'd hadn't learned any German in the first eighteen years of his life. If things didn't take a turn for the better, both of us might soon be learning a lot more.

'I'm not sure exactly,' I said, 'but they don't seem to know what to do with us.'

A voice raised above the others said, *'Aber der Hauptmann...'* Then multiple voices spoke up, all at once. It sounded like a disagreement.

Timmy looked frightful. 'What's that?'

'Quiet,' I breathed. 'They're talking about me.' I wasn't a captain, contrary to what the Boche seemed to think, but an intelligence officer of any rank would be quite a prize. Thankfully, from the couple of words of German I *did* know (intelligence officer being one of them), they hadn't caught on. From what I'd heard until now, they spoke no more than a half-dozen words of English between them, so an interrogation was out of the question.

The discussion ended quickly. I never did learn the conclusion, but thankfully shooting us didn't appear to be one of the options. The Germans had opted to eat instead. Two of their brethren were stationed on lookout, while the others dedicated themselves to their food. They didn't bother to offer anything in our direction. From the looks of them they were ravenous.

Timmy had gotten over his nerves sufficiently, for his stomach to take over the talking. 'I wish they'd give us something to eat, sir. I'm starving.'

'Have some water,' I grunted, and passed him my canteen.

As the sun began to set I realized the corporal and his squad had no intent of pulling back. For that I was thankful. Here in the Forêt de Raismes we might have some slim chance of escape. The Germans were obviously a rearguard with orders to hold fast, although if it came down to it, the battalion would run them over and barely pause for breath. I wondered if they knew that. Of course, if that did happen, I didn't give much for our own chances. We'd be mowed down like the rest.

I took a look around. In front was the machine gun, deftly concealed behind a pile of brushwood. Either side, covering the flanks, were two slit trenches. The Germans had taken to calling them fox-holes. When I first heard the expression, I found it rather amusing. In our own small hole, which would barely fit a fox let alone two, I failed to see the humour any more. To our rear was a length of covered trench, a ditch really, which the Germans were using to rest in and store their gear, including that what they'd stripped off us. It was all very makeshift, definitely no D-Q Line.

As night fell the forest took on a life of its own. Trees creaked and groaned with each murmur of the wind. An owl – at least I took it to be an owl – made horrible screeching sounds, the kind that send shivers down your spine. The sky was clear and the air cold. The sentry was seated on a tree stump watching us carefully. He pulled up the collar of his coat. Not having coats ourselves, there was nothing for Collins and me to do but huddle together and try to get some sleep.

For a spell I hoped the soldier might doze off, but every time we so much as changed sides, I saw him straighten and clench his rifle as if he feared we'd jump him. One of us might make it, but not both. After a couple of hours watching him, as my left arm started to ache and I lay shivering on the cold ground, I gave up and surrendered to the exhaustion.

Dawn came early. Which is not to say that it was light, only that the Germans were awake. Although we weren't offered scones with jam and a hot cup of tea, a young lad did prod us with his foot, and when he saw we were awake threw us each a chunk of bread. '*Guten appetit*,' he said. I nodded gratefully, and Collins started in immediately.

The soldier stood there a few paces away, watching us eat. I wondered if he'd had as bad a night as I had. I was dead tired, cold, sore and apprehensive. This was not how I'd envisaged my war ending.

As I took a final bite of the coarse brown bread, I stared at him and noticed that I'd gotten his attention. 'Do you hear them?' I said softly. I cupped a hand to one ear and pointed forward with the other. 'They're coming. *Sie kommen*.' Collins was looking at me as if I'd lost my marbles, for there wasn't a sound to be heard.

The soldier ignored me and looked away.

'And when they arrive… *Kaputt*,' I said, '*Kaputt oder Tot* (broken or dead).' For effect I shot myself in the temple with my finger.

He pretended not to, but from the corner of his eye he was still watching me.

In a slow arcing motion, with my finger extended, I pointed westwards. 'They're coming,' I said. '*Schnell. Sie komen Schnell.*'

At this he turned on his heel and returned to the trench. I saw three of the others gather round him.

A mist had formed during the night. As the sky brightened, the line of trees surrounding the clearing was barely visible. Wreaths of fog hung almost motionless, and behind them the dark forms of the forest: a scene from Hansel and Gretel. When I was boy I'd lain awake half the night the first time it was read to me.

I turned to Collins. 'I hope you're ready,' I said.

'What for, sir?'

'We may have to make a run for it.'

Collins eyes widened, but he didn't say anything. He only nodded.

However, the soldier who was watching us from afar – Hans, one of his mates had called him – was taking no chances. I had the feeling he was more fearful of his corporal than of us. The more I saw of his corporal, the more I understood. There were six of them all told, including the corporal. That was at least three or four too many for Collins and I. Their routine was fixed; one man to keep guard; four forward with rifles and manning the MG, the corporal moving between them.

I began to whistle – loudly – the tune from the *Maple Leaf Forever*. I don't imagine the Germans had ever heard it before and I always found it to be an uplifting ditty, somehow oddly appropriate. Collins broke into a smile and joined in. Luckily. He kept a tune much better than I did.

The corporal bustled over. '*Ruhe,*' he hissed. While I didn't understand, there was no misunderstanding his meaning. And just in case we had, he pulled out a foot-long bayonet that glistened even in the mist and pointed it menacingly in my direction. Cowed we both stopped whistling.

He took a step toward me, brandishing the bayonet. He had a wild angry look to him.

'Shhh,' I whispered. I cupped a hand to my ear.

The corporal stopped, the dark intensity of his gaze softening, replaced by uncertainty.

I cocked my headed to one side. 'Did you hear that, Collins?' I said.

This time Collins played along. 'Yes sir, I did.'

'Yes,' said the corporal in a thick accent. He listened too. I knew from his insignia he was a Bavarian. '*Was ist los?*'

'*Soldaten,*' I mumbled with a shrug, and looked away.

The corporal's natural frown returned, which had the effect that his eyes narrowed and his eyebrows and moustache bristled. To say that he looked like a plum left to shrivel on a tree was no exaggeration.

I smiled at him.

The corporal cursed, sheathed his bayonet, and snarled something at the sentry. Then he rushed over to the MG.

I winked at the soldier whose duty it was to watch over us. He gave me a shy smile.

It didn't take long before actual sounds of combat could be heard. They were far off, but there was no mistaking that they were rifle shots. It was light and the attack would be on again. The Germans hurriedly began rechecking their kit. The youth, a pleasant looking fellow with fine features, fair hair and brilliant blue eyes, kept nervously looking over his shoulder.

There was another volley of rifle fire. Closer this time.

Then I saw the soldier stiffen and I quickly understood why. The corporal was heading our way.

'Look awake, Collins,' I whispered.

I stood up and made as if I was awaiting the corporal's arrival.

'*Bleiben Sie sitzen!*,' he growled. As instructions go it was clear enough; I was to stay seated. But instead I shrugged, in that universal gesture of bafflement, and looked down submissively at my feet.

The corporal quickened his pace. As he reached me, he extended his arm intending to push me to the ground.

Which was when I hit him. A left to the gut. A soft blow, but it caught him off guard and he leaned forward, winded. I followed up with a right uppercut. A hard uncompromising punch. As hard as I could manage in the circumstances. My knuckles smashed into his chin and his head jolted back. He teetered and as he did so, I snatched at his belt and pulled out the bayonet.

With my left arm I grabbed his collar in my fist. With the other I held the blade rigidly against his stomach, the razor-sharp tip just piercing the cloth of his tunic.

Behind him the sentry had regained his wits. He was standing, his rifle pointed uncertainly at us. The corporal's back was the only clear shot.

Collins was also on his feet. The commotion had alarmed the others who were abandoning their positions and moving towards us.

The corporal looked ready to say something so I gave the bayonet a sharp prod. He winced, stifling a curse.

It soon devolved into a classic Mexican standoff; me keeping a firm grip on the corporal's collar, the five soldiers of his squad spread out in a semi-circle with their rifles pointed at us. I wasn't in an ideal position. The corporal was still in shock, but that would wear off soon enough. Plus he had has hands free. There was only the threat of the dagger to keep him in line. Something was going to have to happen and fast.

'It's a shame you don't speak any German, Collins,' I said, quietly. 'So we'll have to do a little mime. Put your hands in the air like you're surrendering.'

'Sir?'

'You heard me. Do it.'

Hesitatingly, Collins raised his arms and the Germans glanced at each other in disbelief – they hadn't expected this.

'Now lower them.' Collins did.

'*Und jetzt Sie* (and now you),' I said, raising my voice. It was something Smith had taught me. '*Kamerad, Kamerad,*' I added. I said it exactly like I'd heard so many times before as some Fritz crawled out of his hole. The soldiers looked at each other. As hints go, even King Ludwig II of Bavaria would have understood and he was even madder than his cousin Kaiser Wilhelm. 'Come,' I said, 'the war's almost over. It's time to surrender. Unless you want to be back in *his* hands.' Roughly I pushed the corporal a half-step in their direction.

The corporal inhaled deeply, like he was steeling himself for something, so I pressed the bayonet hard into him. He yelped in pain, but said nothing. I could feel the resistance seep out of him. The soldiers exchanged words, then suddenly one of them threw his rifle on to the ground, muttering something I didn't understand. It was the fellow who'd brought us bread this morning. Then Hans our blue-eyed sentry did the same. After a moment's hesitation the others followed, and they all just stood there, watching us.

I took a step back and as I did so, violently yanked the corporal to the ground where he wouldn't cause any trouble. 'Collins, look after him,' I ordered.

And with that it was over.

I didn't rest easy, however, until the first soldiers from the 42nd Highlanders appeared, roughly a half-hour later.

'Smith!' I cried when I saw him, as a second group of soldiers moved into the clearing. I barely recognised him with his helmet down low and a Webley in hand, until he was right up to me.

'The colonel sent me, sir. You were reported missing…' I knew from his voice there were a thousand questions he wanted to ask.

'A few hours,' I said, 'Nothing to fret about. And already you've taken my place?' Naturally, I said it in jest, although I think Smith took it altogether more seriously.

'No, sir, but the colonel felt we needed an intelligence officer in the field. He thought I might be able to assist in locating you.'

I clapped him on the shoulder. 'Well done in that case,' I said, 'you've found me.'

'What happened, sir? You and the private went missing and you turn up this morning with six prisoners?'

A couple of months ago I would have seen this as the perfect opening for a tall tale. No longer. The overall war had never gone better, yet my own war was strewn with the sort of booby-traps the Germans were leaving everywhere. Or perhaps it was simply that after almost four years at the front, I too had succumbed to the war of attrition. 'I let my eagerness get the better of me,' I said. 'Fortunately it worked out all right.' Then seeing his face bursting with curiosity, I told him the whole story.

I remained with the battalion for the remainder of the day. The advance went swiftly, even if danger lurked behind each log and ditch, snipers and machine gunners hidden everywhere. The enemy either retreated, or were cut down in a hail of fire from the flanks. Carefully, but inexorably, the scouts pressed forward. By nightfall the entire Forêt de Raismes was in our hands, we were approaching the Canal de l'Escaut where it turned north to the crossroads village of Condé, and we were past Valenciennes to the south. The forest, an astonishing five miles in length – a terrain built for the defender and that might have reasonably held us for days, if not weeks – we had captured in little more than a day.

For some reason General Lipsett came to mind. He would have been proud. To think of all that had happened, from that brief moment only 80-odd days ago near Amiens, when he told me we were to go on the offensive. It was astounding.

But now the town of Valenciennes awaited. Across miles of inundated plains – the Germans had dammed the canal and flooded its western outskirts – my next battle would not be long in coming.

Assuming the Provost-Marshal didn't come calling first.

CHAPTER 36

30th of October, 1918
Denain, France

I wasn't wrong about the objective. But I was wrong about how long it would it take.

It was exactly a week since we'd cleared the Forêt de Raismes and we were gathered at 78, rue de Saint-Amand, a two-story, rather distinguished looking brick school in Denain fronted by a tall, imposing brick and wrought iron fence. It was a fence that made you wonder if the intent was to keep the students in, or someone else out, neither of which seemed congruous with it being a school. It was certainly not like any school I'd ever attended. However, it was the current whereabouts of the headquarters of the 4th Division. A Corps conference was underway. And the topic was Valenciennes.

'You should be thankful, Mac, we would have been in action much earlier if we didn't have to wait for XXII Corps to catch up,' said McAvity.

McAvity and I were strolling around the rather austere courtyard, kicking our heels, waiting for our superiors to conclude their discussions which began early this morning. For the first time Loomis had invited me along, although if he'd heard the impertinent questions I was asking of McAvity he might have thought twice. Somehow the general had learned of my escapade in the forest and I guessed he was secretly pleased how it turned out. Having been in the field for almost the entire war, Loomis had little patience for the scholarly types. He appreciated being able to tell his peers that *his* staff wasn't just churning out paper.

'I should have known it'd be something like that,' I said finally. 'VIII Corps on our left is also delayed. Not that I mind.' McAvity stared at me, no doubt confounded at the absence of any caustic footnote. So I felt compelled to explain. 'The weather's been glorious. Who'd have thought France had Indian summers? And at the end of October, no less. At home we'd be getting out the snow shovel by now. There are worse things to do than wait for the Imperials to catch up.'

McAvity grinned. 'From what you described this morning about the flooding, you'll be needing rubber boots a lot more than a shovel,' he said.

Grimly, I nodded. 'I could have used a pair already. I've been up to my waist these past days,' I said, 'reconnoitring how we should advance. At least with the sun, the top half of me was warm. You have to give those Boche engineers credit; they did their best. There's no way to move on Valenciennes from the north *or* the west. Not in any numbers. So from the south it'll have to be.' I paused to wipe my brow. 'Whatever did happen with the Scots, anyhow?'

Two days earlier the 51st Highland Division had attacked the dominating high ground to the southwest of the city, but were rebuffed.

'Well, they only sent in one battalion, that's for starters.'

'One battalion to take Mont Houy? That was optimistic. The Germans have 3 divisions in the area.'

'Optimistic,' snorted McAvity. 'That's one way to put it. I'll spare you the details, but the Boche pushed them out in no time. So that job has fallen to us too.'

'Mont Houy *and* Valenciennes?'

'Don't worry, I think General Watson and the 4th Division will get the assignment.'

'Oh, I'm not worried,' I said. 'I'm sure they'll find something else for us do.'

What I said was true enough. Mont Houy and Valenciennes were tough nuts, but so was crossing the Escaut north of the city. General Loomis had been extremely interested in my findings about how to do that. That was as good an indication as any to what we'd soon be doing. I'd hear shortly. As to worries, I wasn't so much worried as deeply uneasy that the Provost Marshal hadn't responded since I'd spurned his invitation for afternoon tea. The signallers got so used to seeing me they shook their heads the moment I appeared. And no one else at headquarters, including Smith, knew a thing; they all had more critical matters on their minds.

'Buck up,' said McAvity, misinterpreting my look. 'You did sign up for this, Mac.'

1st of November, 1918
Denain-Anzin (north of Valenciennes), France

To the south of us close to Valenciennes, the dark, drizzling sky suddenly erupted in light. A crashing roar shook the earth. It was deafening even at two miles away.

A watch was utterly superfluous and that was fortunate, as mine had been acting up ever since I'd retrieved it from the Boche corporal who'd pocketed it as loot. The attack was on, which meant it was 5.15 a.m. Our fourth month on the offensive was beginning.

By the early morning of November 1st two things had changed; the weather had worsened, and the Ottoman Empire had surrendered. While the latter was arguably the more significant event, I suspect the average soldier thought differently. Far from home, facing new dangers almost daily, soldiers concentrated on what was going on in front of their noses rather than a couple of thousand miles away. As the rain, now driving hard, clattered down on our helmets and soaked our pants and tunics, we were a miserable lot. And in front of our dripping noses was more water: the Canal de l'Escaut.

I'd swum that very same canal at Cambrai – the boys from the 4th CMR found this quite amusing – and had no intention of doing it again, soaked or not. However, under the watchful eye of Brigadier Draper who'd come to see for himself, Major McLean had devised an equally hair-raising scheme. Actually, he told me only that he *had* a plan. The hair-raising element I discovered later.

Directly north of Valenciennes is the industrial suburb of Denain-Anzin, a dreary ugly place strewn with telegraph poles, large factories in varying states of disrepair, cobblestone courtyards and railway sidings overgrown with grass. The canal banks were high in this section. Only a thin sheet of water covered the ground. Here we split into two parties. Lieutenant Nodwell had taken his patrol several hundred yards northwards to look for another spot to cross the canal; I suggested up by the glass works where the waterway made a small bend. On our side of the canal there were some large buildings close to the water and precious little on the opposite bank.

I remained with McLean and his group of almost twenty near the old enamel works. A couple of hundred yards south of us was the main railway crossing for the line from Douai. Several engineers were heading that way to inspect it. While I wasn't an engineer, the steel bridge was tilting at an unnatural 25 degree angle, so without the benefit of any inspection whatsoever I'd written it off as a possible crossing. That's how we ended up in the loading yard of the enamel works.

Above the loud rumble of the barrage we didn't need to shout to make ourselves understood, but nor could we whisper. The artillery was creating a terrible storm. 'Fourteen brigades of field guns and heavy howitzers,' Tibbett had explained earlier. 'Never has a single brigade enjoyed such artillery support.'

Moving through the rail yard and trying to keep low, even though it was still dark, we came to a large white sign. *Halt!* it screamed in Gothic letters, followed by twenty lines in German I had neither the time nor the inclination to decipher. The others ignored it completely. Thirty feet from the canal bank I spotted what Major McLean had on his mind.

'So this is it? This is your plan!?' I said to McLean, pointing at the flat wooden craft with two pontoons, 'A raft?'

'Yes. I thought you'd be delighted. You won't have to wet your feet, MacPhail, let alone the rest of you.' I was learning that McLean was quick on his feet and even quicker with his tongue. He'd been a lawyer in St. John. After I confessed to the same occupation, we'd sparred on the way here. Now he looked at me. 'Unless you have a better way of getting across?'

I didn't. So I said nothing.

McLean continued. 'I think it's best if I go first with a runner, to see the lay of the land.'

'You may not make it if they spot you,' I said. It was no idle worry; a few days ago some intrepid souls from the 4th Division had tried something similar and barely made it back alive.

'I know,' he replied. 'That's why I don't want to take the entire patrol.'

'I'll go with you,' I offered, a surge of guilt rising up. 'You may need some help.' At twenty-nine I felt ancient at times, but I was at least ten years McLean's junior, and I didn't have the stomach to watch him and an eighteen-year old tackle this on their own. Besides, I was the intelligence officer.

'You sure?' he asked.

I shrugged.

'Alright, then.' He turned to the squad and under the direction of a company sergeant major, soon had them carrying the raft to the water's edge. 'Quietly,' he ordered.

We slipped on to the raft and pushed off with a few cautious paddles, gliding silently through the water. The noise of the barrage suddenly seemed a long way off. The rain had turned into a misty drizzle, a thousand pins pricking the surface of the water. In no time we reached the opposite bank, perhaps 50 yards distant. McLean clambered off first. Then suddenly his paddle fell with a clatter on the stone lip of the embankment. Disconcerted, he straightened up and turned to us.

TUF-TUF-TUF.

I saw the muzzle flashes from mere yards away. 'Get down,' I shouted and scrambled ashore, pulling the Lee-Enfield by its strap from my shoulder.

McLean had his pistol out. From a kneeling position he was shooting at the German position as fast as his finger could pull the trigger. There was a cry. 'Got one,' he shouted.

'Get some help,' I yelled at the runner, and began to shoot. The raft moved away. McLean had fallen prone as well, furiously reloading his pistol. I was firing quickly, conscious I'd only brought a handful of magazines, keeping a careful bead on the place where I'd seen the flashes. The machine gun was silent for the moment – reloading. I ceased firing and everything was dark. In the distance the guns thundered. Here, the air was strangely tranquil, a tautness in it you could neither see nor hear, only feel. Then I heard the soft click as the chamber of McLean's Webley closed.

'Save your ammunition,' I whispered to him. 'We don't know how many there are. I sent the runner back for help.'

The machine gun began stuttering. Immediately we both took a measured shot. It was impossible to tell whether we'd hit anything, but the rattle ceased.

'I think they're in a ditch,' said McLean. 'Do you see Goodchild and the patrol?'

I hesitated, staring at the far bank through the gloom. 'No, not really,' I answered. 'Wait… I think I see some movement. Yes, that's them. They're boarding the raft.'

'Good,' McLean said. 'Let's cover them.' And we both started to shoot.

Without warning there was the sound of concussions and a series of flashes in front of us. 'Good man,' said McLean. Goodchild and the patrol were using rifle grenades to lay down a covering barrage.

Shortly I saw the raft bump up against the bank, laden down with men. CSM Goodchild leapt off and sprang towards us. He was followed by more than a dozen soldiers. McLean jumped to his feet.

'Follow me,' he shouted. They rushed the MG position. Quickly I rose and went in pursuit.

I was wary, all too conscious I hadn't even fixed a bayonet. But the Boche gun crew had evidently chosen life above valour, for all ten of them had their hands in the air, three of whom were wounded. There were also several bodies, although no one paid them the slightest attention.

I watched the prisoners being assembled. 'Not a bad round of shooting for a couple of lawyers,' remarked McLean, sidling up to me.

'And elderly ones at that,' I added.

'Speak for yourself, MacPhail.'

McLean had every right to feel pleased, I thought. If Lieutenant Nodwell could also cross the canal, we'd have a decent foothold on the eastern bank. The plan to encircle the city from the north would be one step closer.

In the event, the 4th Division hadn't required our help at Valenciennes. On the heels of the barrage, they swept over Mont Houy, battered the Germans in Aulnoy and Marly, and had patrols in the city by midday. 800 Germans were dead and 1800 prisoner, to only 380 casualties of our own. The enemy had sought to drive a stake in the watery ground at Valenciennes, hoping to anchor his crumbling line, but the stake was uprooted. The advance would continue.

As to Lieutenant Nodwell, I learned his story when I crossed back to the opposite bank. One of his patrol told me himself. 'He crossed the canal, sir, and thanks to him we managed to get a cork bridge across.'

'However did he manage that?' I asked.

'That was the darnedest thing, sir. He swam, just like you.'

'Did he now?' I said quietly. While it shouldn't have mattered, something inside of me felt differently.

However, when General Draper began to question me about the terrain east of the canal and Valenciennes, the feeling disappeared as quickly as it came. For Draper wouldn't just be asking. Not if there wasn't a good reason. Would he?

CHAPTER 37

4th of November, 1918
Vicq, France

Brigadier-General Draper's interest in what lay to the east was indeed more than a polite query. While I answered him as best I could, later in the field I realized I'd completely misjudged it. The flooding was far worse than I expected.

In fact, east of the Escaut, almost the only places that weren't flooded were the railway embankments, the upper floors of farmhouses and the towering mountains of slag from the coal mines. There were rich coal veins here, in fact the very ones that extended westwards to Vimy Ridge and beyond. Where there wasn't any water, there were inevitably German guns. And where there weren't any German guns, there were other German guns sited to fire there. No wonder Draper had quizzed me so long.

His men had a tough go of it, but in the past few days they'd pushed along the two railway lines and this morning were approaching the mining town of Vicq, nearly four miles from the canal. I met up with the battalion charged to take the hamlet at around 4 a.m.

The 5th CMR had chosen the drier path, the one from the south. Where the rows of brick tenement housing announced the village of Onnaing, they'd veered left along a very muddy but otherwise unflooded road. I know that because I took the same route myself. The party I was with were standing in the lee of a fair-sized building, a barn I presumed, at what had once been a small crossroads. By now it was past eight, and in theory the sun was rising. I saw only a monotonous grey sheet, until forced to lower my head as gusts of wind kept blowing a spray of water in my eyes.

The attackers came straggling back. The lieutenant reported "stiff resistance". To anyone not in the know, that is an old army euphemism for getting battered to pieces. Someone suggested an artillery programme. That struck me as a good idea and I said so. They sent a runner off to the battalion commander, whom I knew. I'd heard he'd been promoted to lieutenant-colonel. Then I heard my name.

'Here he is, sir. The prisoner you wanted to see. We captured him this morning, down the road a bit,' said the sergeant from C Company. He pushed the prisoner forward. Other than his shave, there was nothing clean about him. In a sodden grey greatcoat with a helmet a touch off-centre, he made a sorry sight. Appearances notwithstanding, his eyes told me he was a real soldier.

The prisoner looked down, studying his boots with a sullen expression. Alternatively, it might have been a look of misery. It had only just stopping raining, though it threatened again. The German's boots looked as if they hadn't seen dry land in two weeks.

'115th Regiment,' I said, grimacing, as I scanned his papers.

'Sir?'

'Part of the 25th Division,' I explained. 'One of the few first class divisions the enemy still have.'

I cleared my throat and stared at the prisoner. In my best approximation of German, I asked, '*Wie viel Bataillone* (how many battalions)?'

He must have understood for he held up two stubby fingers in response.

The sergeant groaned at this intelligence. 'Great,' he mumbled.

Two seemed to be an unlucky number today. If I peeked around the corner of the building, 800 yards east of us were the ill-matching pair of peaks that were causing all the trouble: the dark, perfectly conical slag heap of the Fosse Cuvinot that reached a hundred metres high. To its right, a smaller, irregular tree-covered mound. The former was topped by an observation post. Thanks to the morning's attack the number of machine guns guarding its slopes was no longer in much doubt. "A" Company were quite emphatic about it. I was told the latter also housed several MGs, and at least two trench mortars.

One-time major, now lieutenant-colonel, Rhoades showed up not long after. 'I've asked the artillery to do a shoot,' he said when he arrived. Sure enough, within an hour, the artillery did as they were asked. As I stared through my Fernglas field glasses I saw shell after shell bury itself in and around the pyramid of mine tailings. Each sent a geyser of rocks into the air. It looked impressive, but I was uneasy, and it must have showed.

'Not enough?' said Rhoades, glancing at me. He'd come to stand beside me.

'It's not that,' I said, 'but the tailings deaden the impact of the shells. On top of which, the bombardment isn't even reaching the far side. The trajectory's all wrong. I saw the exact same thing near Lens, at the Fosse there. Unless you get a direct hit, the defenders just brush off the dust and line up their sights again.'

'Loomis wants me take to take Vicq, Mac,' said Rhoades wearily. 'I can't do that without first taking those two piles of dirt. What am I supposed to do?'

I shook my head. 'I wish I had an easy answer for you,' I said, 'but easy never made it to this front.'

There was a silence. 'Have you heard anything about the war?' he asked. He had a hopeful tone in his voice.

I took a breath. 'You may not have heard. The Austro-Hungarians signed an armistice yesterday. And the Germans are supposedly very anxious for a peace settlement. There was a long article about it in one of the papers.'

'That's encouraging,' he said.

I shrugged. 'I suppose so. Although if I recall correctly, they were writing the same thing a month ago. And the Boche are made of sterner stuff than the Austro-Hungarians. Who's to say negotiations won't drag on forever?'

'Leaving us at *this* forever.'

'Exactly,' I said.

We turned back to the business at hand. The sooner we got on with it, the better. Back at High Command I'm sure they agreed; there was nothing like a few whacks from a club to get your opponent to see things the way you did. Only at Vicq that strategy wasn't working out as planned.

After a day of fighting, the final straw came at four-thirty. A detachment of C Company had crossed the field, pierced the wire and had a modest foothold at the bottom of the shale pile. I was watching from 200 yards away in a row of trees with the rest of the company.

CRACK. I was conscious of something flying, and something did hit my cheek. Immediately I let the field glasses fall. As I did so, out of the corner of my eye, I saw that the bark on the tree beside me had a nasty gouge driven into it as if someone had gone to work with a chisel. 'Sniper!' I yelled, and dropped to the ground. Around me the others were doing the same. I touched my cheek and saw fingertips dotted in blood. A scratch. I think I hated the snipers even more than I hated the gas. On the Western Front there was never a shortage of things to hate.

The clatter of the machine guns intensified. There was a sudden *whoosh* and an explosion near the slag heap. As the dust settled two more went off in rapid succession.

'Fish tails,' I heard someone say.

Then there was a heavier boom and a correspondingly heavier shower of debris. 'That was no trench mortar,' I mumbled to myself. I could hear our men near the bottom of the pile shouting to each other.

The lieutenant was looking around for a solution, only there wasn't one at hand. The last squad he'd sent forward had returned almost immediately, three of them with wounds.

The problem was simply no cover. Out of the trees it was as flat as Saskatchewan and as barren as the North Sea. There wasn't a single, solitary blade of grass higher than shin-level to hide behind. Nowhere in those two hundred blasted yards. And north of the fosse, it was flooded. CRACK. This time I was well behind the tree, down low, and feeling secure. But the damned sniper was still at it. Suddenly I had a thought. If he was tucked away near the observation post at the summit he could see me lying prone. A cold chill ran up my back. Quickly I squirmed left. The peak was now completely obscured behind the tree. I could, however, still see men at the bottom of the slag heap. They were digging in.

The lieutenant called over. Neither of us dared move.

'Sir?'

'I don't think there's enough of your men out there to hold a counter-attack,' I said. 'And there's definitely not enough to take it.'

'What do you suggest, sir?' he shouted.

'Pull them back. Put up as much covering fire as you can muster. And pull them back.'

The lieutenant winced. It wasn't how he'd envisaged the attack ending. Most of the officers were young fellows, not long on the front, with visions of glory still fogging their minds.

I said, 'Sometimes the best thing to do is to call it a day, Lieutenant. That's what the smart commanders do. Besides, there's always tomorrow.'

Fortunately, I mentioned the bit about second chances. I don't think he'd have gone for it, otherwise.

They waited for dusk. It took some time and more casualties, but the squad made it back. Next morning, early, they were at it again. This time the company seized the slag pile and the tree-covered mound. An hour and a half later they entered the town of Vicq. Remorselessly, the advance was continuing.

6th of November, 1918
Quiévrechain, France

A day passed. By 4.30 a.m. on the 6th, Vicq was nearly four miles to the rear. Such was our pace. The enemy was on the move again and we were nipping at his heels. The First Army directive was clear; we were to pursue the enemy with vigour. Having rained every day for a week that was easier said than done, however. The Valenciennes-Mons road was a muddy porridge, so narrow and covered in ruts that the lorries were forced to pull to one side to allow opposing traffic to pass. But it was passable, and a sight better than tramping through sodden fields or flooded rice paddies, which is how much of the ground north of the road looked. Where the enemy was fleeing to an uncertain future, our men had the invigorating scent of victory in their nostrils.

Not that I felt any of that. A dry, pasty bitterness coated my tongue by the time I arrived at the battalion. I took a swig of water hoping it would help. If ever the time arose for some sober self-reflection, I might have reflected on my "own worst enemy", as Benoît unfailingly called it. For it was thanks to my big mouth that I was once again in the field. Barely back at headquarters, I'd felt some inexplicable need to lecture the general and the colonel on what I thought the priorities should be. 'Sir, if we can grab the bridges between Quiévrechain and Quiévrain, we'll be past both rivers. Then it's a straight shot along the main road to Mons. It'll save days and who knows how many casualties,' I enthused. 'The other crossings are important, but those ones are crucial.' They asked a few questions, but mainly they just let me run. Afterwards, I suspected I hadn't told them anything they didn't already know, but it served their purpose. I barely had time to change my socks before I was heading out again. I was to ensure that it happened as we all hoped.

'Yes, I see,' said the captain at battalion headquarters. 'I thought as much when I saw the map.' Captain MacGregor of B Company was not an officer on whom you had to waste elaborate explanations. I'd barely introduced myself and mentioned the two bridges when he leapt to the same conclusion I had. I knew of MacGregor. He wasn't tall – burly rather, with a broad chin and a sincere, clean shaven face that could have graced a recruitment poster. He looked like a soldier should. He was also something of a living legend in the 2nd Mounted Rifles, having joined as a private and already the bearer of a Military Cross and a Distinguished Conduct Medal. I also happened to know something his battalion didn't; he was up for a Victoria Cross. I'd seen the papers by chance. Fascinated, I'd read of his feats a month ago at Neuville St.-Rémy. I had good reason to remember this because it was at that very spot, one day later, that I found Benoît.

'Well, you understand completely, Captain,' I said. 'I can see I won't be needed here. I'll just saunter back to headquarters, shall I?' He said nothing but a smile emerged.

The barrage went off at 5.30 a.m. Like hunting dogs straining at their leashes, the 2nd Mounted Rifles bounded ahead and I went with them. Somehow the artillery had moved up enough guns. General Currie's decision in the spring to expand the engineers when the whole war seemed to balance on a knife's edge, had been sheer brilliance. At the time not everyone thought so. But engineers or not, we needed those bridges intact.

On the map the task looked straightforward enough; take the road eastwards and keep going. First there was the small village of Quiévrechain, and immediately past the glass works the trickle of the Aunnelle crossed the road at a right angle. 400 yards further on came an almost identical stone bridge and another stream, La Grande Honnelle, after which one entered the western outskirts of Quiévrain. What the map didn't show were the German garrisons in both places. Given their strategic importance I guessed we could count on a minimum of two hundred, or perhaps even three hundred men. Of course the bridges would be wired for immediate destruction.

Captain MacGregor's plan was to barrel down the road at full speed. He'd detailed a platoon under the leadership of a Lieutenant Pye to race forward, while he followed close behind with the rest of the company and the *mopper-uppers*. I volunteered to accompany Pye. It wasn't entirely selfless devotion to duty; I figured I'd need my superiors' help when the inevitable summons from the Provost Marshal arrived. This might be a chance to chalk up some points, assuming it worked.

The barrage tore through the village. As the flash of explosions carried on eastward, we trotted along close behind in two single files, one on each side of the road moving fast. The bulk of the village was to the south, and this merely the industrial suburbs, but any of the simple houses lining the muddy thoroughfare could have housed a machine gunner. Ten minutes in, we hadn't seen any, but didn't stop to check closely. Ironically, the first soldiers we met were ours, scouts from the 78th Battalion, the Winnipeg Grenadiers. They'd come from the south. We didn't stop to chat with them either. They had their job and we had ours.

'Hold up,' ordered Lieutenant Pye, his fist raised. Puzzled I went to him, then saw what had caught his attention. A handful of men were mustering in the back garden of one of the houses. Pye obviously presumed they weren't from Winnipeg, and I concurred.

'Quickly,' he said, and chopped his hand through the air a few times for the benefit of those on the far side of the road. Not running, but at a healthy clip, we moved past. The Germans didn't notice, or if they did, they didn't do anything. Which suited me fine.

Off to our left, three big buildings of the glass works stood out as dark blocks against a horizon only slightly less dark. The barrage had ceased. I heard rifle shots from the village and the brief rattle of what sounded like a Lewis gun. We halted. Examining the terrain, Captain MacGregor rushed up to join us.

'Well?' he asked.

'The good news is I think they're intact, but the second bridge I can't tell for certain, not from this distance,' I said, handing him the glasses. 'There's no sign of the Boche.'

'Perhaps we should take a closer peek?'

The easiest way to do that was to walk down the road. However, that was exactly what a German sniper would be counting on. Instead, we slipped behind a row of houses on the right and picked our way through their gardens in the direction of the Pont du Corbeau. It was dark and nothing was moving. At a large, rather dilapidated brick shed we came to some trees. Beyond them, we saw the Aunnelle. I peered around the corner of the shed. The bridge was 15 yards to my left.

I shook my head – *no enemy* – and motioned for MacGregor to follow. We eased along the wall of the outbuilding, almost at the water's edge, trying not to accidently knock a piece of debris into the water. The bridge was definitely deserted. MacGregor crawled deftly down the bank and disappeared underneath. After a minute which seemed longer, he returned, nodding grimly. It was mined all right.

'We're going to take the bridge. Let's be quick about it,' he told Pye after we rejoined the platoon. We took one final look for safety's sake and rushed it. It was a short run, but nerve-wracking all the same. Reaching the opposite bank, the men fanned out and assumed firing positions, rifles pointed east: watchful.

I turned to Pye. 'Time for the sappers to do their work, Lieutenant.' He nodded.

I looked at MacGregor. 'How about taking a peek at the next one, Captain?'

MacGregor wasn't the sort content to twiddle his thumbs while the sappers defused the mine and appeared pleased at my suggestion. 'Why don't we,' he replied.

Funnily enough, the chickens were what first alerted me we were in Belgium. Pens of them were arraigned behind almost every house. I also spotted a pig. And a goat. Where the Boche had stripped France clean, they'd been of a milder bent across the border. Even the buildings looked better.

MacGregor and I were cautious, so it took longer than expected to reach the next bridge, a jaunt of only 400 yards down the road. It was immediately clear the grey stone crossing was intact, mined, and equally deserted. Where were the Germans?

Hastily we returned to Lieutenant Pye who reported the first bridge was secure. MacGregor gave him his new orders. There wasn't any time to lose. The Germans would send it up the instant they got wind we were so far. MacGregor gave me his hand and then set off to rejoin the rest of the company still dealing with the garrison in the village.

Pye turned to leave as well, anxious to get on with his mission. But I grabbed his arm. 'You really should leave a Lewis gunner or two,' I said. 'Just in case the Boche decide to retreat.' I pointed back towards Quiévrechain. 'It wouldn't do to lose the bridge from behind.'

He shook his head.

We made good time, but a surprise was awaiting us on the far bank of the La Grande Honnelle: Germans. In the grey pre-dawn gloom their dark figures stood out.

'Damn it,' I muttered as I put down my glasses. We were standing tight against the façade of a building, looking at them from only twenty yards away. They seemed oblivious to our presence.

'I count four,' Lieutenant Pye said.

'We'd better move quickly,' I whispered. 'Before they have time to blow the bridge...'

Which is perhaps why the plan turned out to be not so much a plan as a mad 20-yard dash with the entire platoon. For a brief instant, as we thundered across the cobblestones, the clatter of our boots sounding for all the world like a stampede of bison, I thought we were done for. Obviously the Germans noticed us, but instead of firing, they hurriedly bent down over something, while one of their number clambered down the bank. There was no need to guess what they were doing.

Panting, I roared, 'Halt!' to which they didn't bother looking up, even though I was half-way across the bridge and only twenty feet from them; two officers and two other ranks. One of them had a roll of wire in his hands of the kind the signallers used for laying out lines. I stopped as the others rushed past, raised the rifle to my shoulder and fired in their direction.

Miss.

Working the bolt back and forward, I fired again. Another hurried shot.

At first I didn't think I hit him but I must have. The man with the roll of wire dropped it and the first of the platoon stormed off the bridge. The man who I was shooting at took a rifle butt hard in the back, collapsing on the ground. The others were unceremoniously herded together.

'Phew, that was close, sir,' mumbled one of the men as I strode over.

I didn't respond. I just stared down at the roll of electrical wire. A length of it led down the bank until it disappeared into the black shadows of the bridge's underbelly.

The pounding in my head began to subside. The air had a welcome chill to it. *Click*. One of the sappers snipped the wire. Another was on his knees at the water's edge leaning underneath the stone arch of the bridge.

Pye came and stood beside me. 'Congratulations, Lieutenant,' I said.

He was glowing, but his face suddenly turned ashen. 'Did you hear that?' he asked.

'Hmm,' I grunted. 'Lewis guns.'

It was exactly as I feared. Pinned down by the rest of B Company the Germans in Quiévrechain were pulling back eastwards, across the only avenue left to them, the bridge over the Aunelle.

'Lieutenant, if you want to stay here and guard the bridge, give me a couple of men and I'll go back.'

It was as well I did. The two Lewis gun squads had set up cleverly to either side of the Pont du Corbeau, with interlocking fields of fire, able to sweep it with a hail of bullets. But the four had their hands full.

One pair was frantically changing pans, while the other fired at targets on the west bank. I guessed there were thirty or forty enemy, if not more. And they all wanted to cross. B Company was nipping at their heels and they were desperate.

'Whatever you do,' I said to the four men who were with me, 'don't miss. We may be here for a while.'

At first the Boche took absurd risks, whole groups of them rushing the bridge. But with five rifles and two Lewis guns, the toll we exacted was a powerful deterrent to dissuade the rest. They didn't give up, however. They maintained a deadly fire in our direction. More than once I heard a bullet crumble into the wall behind me. As long as our ammunition and our luck held out, we'd be okay. Fortunately, MacGregor and company turned up before either were seriously put to the test. Then all there was to do was count the prisoners.

The bridges were ours, the advance would continue. Down the road loomed Mons.

On the 7th we reached the Belgian villages of La Croix and Hensie and I received a thick pile of letters from home, the first in weeks. I read the last one first. All was well.

On the 8th we struck north across the Canal de Condé to safeguard our left flank. Along the Mons road to the east we captured Thulin, Hamin and Boissu and I received another letter and a telegram. The letter from my parents, dated only two weeks earlier, was cheery enough. Only rereading it I sensed that the uncertainty, the extra burden on my father, was weighing heavy. "We so hope you'll be home soon," it ended. The telegram was from the Provost Marshal and curtly to the point. My general court martial had been convened and scheduled. In five days. I was to report in Montreuil at ten sharp.

And on the 9th I saved Captain Clavell's life.

CHAPTER 38

9th of November, 1918
Tertre, Belgium

I had an unsettled night. I'd tossed and turned, falling in and out of sleep, disturbing visions flitting through my head. I worried about my mother and father, and while the Germans were in full retreat life here was still precariously uncertain. Then there was Clavell. He was devoting his career to ensuring that even if I somehow scraped through, my own career would end in bitter shame and disgrace. After everything I'd been through these long years, I was damned if I was going to let that happen. Yet, like Ludendorff, I didn't see an obvious means of escape.

My day began when General Loomis sent me north, across the Condé-Mons canal. He was worried about our left flank. In this war the power of man could at times seem overwhelming, but nature trumped all, something the army to its credit fully acknowledged. Which was why the arrow-straight canal from west to east had come to be the Corp's northern boundary. However, while we were racing ahead across flooded plains and rivers, through villages and past coal mines, with Valenciennes already an astounding thirteen miles to the rear, the plodding Brits north of the canal were "held up". The general decided to send in the 49th Battalion to do their job for them. I was to see they did.

'How far back is the 52nd Division, sir?' I'd asked Loomis.

'Oh, seven or eight miles, give or take.'

'I see. They're having a well-deserved rest in Calais, in other words.'

It was mischievous, granted, but he actually smiled. I saw it with my own two eyes. 'They might as well be,' he agreed.

'I thought perhaps, after yesterday, when you sent the 5th CMR across the canal to help…' I began.

'You thought wrong, Major. But if all goes well, the Imperials will meet up with our Mounted Rifles in Bernissart this afternoon.'

I whistled. 'Bernissart. But, sir, that's even further back than eight miles.'

There was one saving grace to it all and it came as our conversation concluded.

I could tell something was on the general's mind, for he gently grasped my arm when I went to leave. A softness appeared in his eyes. I'd endured the cold glassiness often enough, so this was noteworthy. 'I misjudged you, MacPhail,' he said, 'and I'm sorry for that. You're an outstanding officer and a credit to me and the division.'

'Sir?'

At his words I was temporarily bereft of my own. I may even have blushed. General Loomis was not renowned for doling out praise, let alone of the effusive variety.

'I wanted you to know.'

'Thank you, sir.'

'And one other thing. Colonel Hore-Ruthven told me of your family circumstances. He said you wished to request an extended leave?' I looked at him, not daring to speak, but I nodded. 'Well, you can have it. Once this is over, you have my permission for a one-month leave to Canada.'

'Thank you, sir,' I said, my cheeks glowing. 'I don't know what to say.' In my excitement I didn't even think to ask what "once *this* is over" meant.

'There's no need to say anything,' he replied. 'Keep your wits about you. There's nothing as dangerous as a cornered bear, I can assure you. And that's what they are, MacPhail. Don't ever think otherwise.'

I caught up with the 49th Battalion at the small hamlet of Tertre. They'd been marching for days. I'd done a little marching myself this morning, abandoning the car and driver a thousand yards shy of the canal. Crossing first a small stream, then the canal itself by clambering over a stone bridge. An over-precise German engineer had calculatingly blown it in the exact middle. On the far bank I headed northeast for a couple of miles able to follow a series of tracks, once muddy, now hard dry ruts. The weather had turned and I was grateful not having to endure the endless drizzle. Passing fields, stands of trees, and isolated farmhouses with their smattering of outbuildings, I even spied the sun overhead. I wasn't so carefree though that I didn't keep a wary eye. Stumbling upon the Boche in my lonesome was the kind of danger Loomis had warned me about. But I reached Tertre without difficulty.

Near the crossroads I spotted two officers studying a map. I slipped up to them. 'Yes,' one was saying, 'the CO wants us to secure the entire area from the Bois de Baudour down to the canal, as far east as Ghlin.'

'Ghlin,' I exclaimed. Startled they both turned and I smiled apologetically. 'I'm MacPhail from the intelligence staff, in case you're wondering. General Loomis sent me to look in on you fellows. He's somewhat uneasy about our left, as you might imagine.'

The dignified looking major responded at once. 'Sore feet aside, you can tell the general he needn't fret. As you heard, we're sending a screen of patrols east almost as far as Mons, and north from the canal to the wood. If the Boche show up, we'll know. There'll be no surprise counter-attack from here, Major. I can assure you of that. Let me show you,' he said, and he lifted the map so I could see.

For a short answer it had been a long walk.

Naturally, I didn't let it go at that – the general would want more reassurance than, "oh, everything's smashing, sir," but for every probing question of mine, Major Chattell had a convincing response. Our flank was safe enough with the 49th.

At this stage I had three choices. I could turn around and go back the way I'd come, eventually crossing the canal at the same spot as this morning. But the car was long gone, and it was a forbidding hike from there to a road where I might get a lift. The left fork led up to the Baudour forest. I had no particular desire to see that. For all the major's calm confidence, forests were exactly the places fleeing Boche would take refuge in. I chose to go right. It was almost a straight line down to the canal with the village of Saint-Ghislain on the other side. There'd be a crossing somewhere. This would bring me to a road and a car, and I wouldn't be a million miles from where the PPCLI were leading the charge today. That I did want to see. General Loomis and the colonel would be equally interested.

Apart from a smoking machine-gun nest on the north bank, Saint-Ghislain was undisturbed. The bridge had a hole in it the size of the Lochnagar Crater, but with some fancy footwork I was across. In the village a few Patricias were in evidence. However, motorized transport wasn't. When I asked them where the others were, they all pointed east. I buckled up and began walking.

At the road on the edge of town, I came across a wrinkled old man in the ditch, bent over and taking his shears to a telephone line. The Belgians had this curious belief that every wire inevitably led to a German booby-trap.

'Shoo,' I said, nicely. '*C'est le nôtre* (it's ours).' This news sent into him a frenzy of apology. He snatched off his tattered beret and began to bow and shake as if I might do to him what the Boche surely would have.

Fortunately a lorry approached. It was heading east. I waved it down, and when it slowed, patted the old fellow on the shoulder and jumped in... beside Captain Clavell.

There was a long, awkward silence, with a current running through it.

Perplexed, the driver finally spoke. 'Sir?'

'Oh, yes, thanks for stopping. Much appreciated.'

I glanced to my side. The same fussy black moustache, the identical ski slope of a nose, and damned if he didn't have his uncle's beady dark eyes. No doubt about it. 'Captain Clavell,' I said, cheerfully. 'I had you down as a traffic control man. But not knowing left from right, I see they now have you guarding lorries. What's in it? The Royal hardtack?'

I heard the driver squelch a laugh, but he soon wisely devoted himself to the road ahead.

'Hello, Major MacPhail. As a matter of fact, I was compelled to borrow a lift, as well. My motorcar broke an axle in one of those infernal craters. I left the others behind to see if they could have it tended to.'

'Really?' I said. 'A broken axle? You weren't pursuing an enemy agent at the time, I hope?'

Clavell sighed and looked away. 'Please, Major. It's been a taxing enough day as it is.'

'At least you didn't have to walk,' I mumbled under my breath.

'What's that?'

'Nothing. But why are you here? This is a very long way from the delights of General Headquarters.'

'I've been transferred to the First Army, as it happens. You fellows captured a high ranking Boche officer this morning. I was to take him into custody.'

'And now you plan to do that on your lonesome in a lorry filled with hardtack?'

'Yes, well. I can't very well...' he began to say. Then the lorry turned off the road.

Alarmed I spoke up, 'Where are we going?'

'Bridge is out ahead, sir. A little detour,' responded the driver.

'I hope the detour doesn't land us in the middle of enemy ground.'

It didn't, but perhaps as a result of that, the enemy had no compunction about lobbing a high explosive shell onto the road forty feet in front. In a cloud of dust we ground to a stop.

The driver shook his head and cursed softly. I understood why when I looked closer. The shell had completely cratered the middle of the road. We were going nowhere.

'It looks as if it's high time for some marching, Captain,' I said. 'Thanks for the ride, Private. And good luck. We'll see if we can cut through here on foot to Wasmuel.'

Here was a dismal landscape of towering ash-grey slag piles and mine heads, tall ungainly structures of wood and steel and small simple brick buildings amidst a warren of unpaved rutted roads. We were in the heart of the mines.

Clavell frowned distastefully. 'I hope you know where you're going...'

'I looked at the map if that's what you mean. You might try it sometime. It's what soldiers do.'

Clavell ignored me. I think he knew very well what I was implying. After a few minutes he said, 'The mines are in astonishingly good condition.'

'They are, aren't they? They were producing here only a couple of days ago. The coal from this region is reputedly the best in Belgium. The Germans will sorely miss it.'

'It's not all they're going to miss,' he said. I cocked an eyebrow. 'They're negotiating final armistice terms. It can't be long now.'

'Is that true?'

'That's what I hear. They're gathered in Compiègne.'

We walked in silence for ten minutes, maybe longer, following a line I figured was roughly northeast, where eventually we would arrive at the village of Wasmuel and the main road.

Peace. Would the war end before my luck ran out? The German army was crumbling, there was no denying that, but what had Loomis said about a "cornered bear"? That's what they were alright. Cornered bears can be savage, as anybody with any experience can attest.

I glanced over at Clavell. He was gazing around like a tourist. He'd have made a nice mouthful for a bear. Clavell certainly hadn't made my life any easier. War or peace, the headache he'd created wasn't going away. In a normal court of law the case against me was pretty flimsy; I didn't need to be a lawyer to know that. However, it wasn't the weak case, but the weak minds of the judges I worried about. The same ones that had made so many botch-ups during this war that they were eventually relegated to the rear, now presumably assigned sensitive tasks like manning a court martial. Thoughtfully, I reached into my breast pocket and fingered the delicate silver chain.

God, I missed Benoît. He'd always had a knack for putting things in proper perspective. I'm sure he would have pointed out he was only one of many thousands who had fallen these past months. There was definitely a certain irony that it was Benoît (a Frenchman), who was always telling me (an Anglo), not to get into a flap.

'Wait,' I whispered, and I stopped. 'Did you hear that?'

Clavell stared at me blankly.

I made the motion of chambering a rifle round. When I thought about it, since leaving the main road we hadn't seen a single soldier. I would have expected a patrol or two of ours at the very least. The surrounding villages were all on the day's objectives. I had an uneasy feeling I may have led us too far east and not far enough north. 'Follow me,' I murmured and pointed to a worn mining shack, only a stone's throw from the path.

Bent over I ran to it. Clavell followed at a more leisurely pace.

The shack was in reality a mining office, or that's what I took *Bergbaubüro* to mean, a place where miners might come to punch their time cards at the beginning and end of their shifts. On a hunch I pulled my Webley from its holster. It was a far better close quarter's weapon than the Lee-Enfield. Then I pushed down the handle and yanked open the door.

There were two of them, both officers, both in their shirtsleeves, both German. They were sitting beside each other, behind a simple wooden table facing the door. A nondescript brown bottle, a couple of glasses and two helmets lay on the table. Their tunics hung behind them. The room was bare and rudimentary and there were a handful of windows so covered in black grit it was hard to tell if it was night or day. The light they let in only accentuated the gloom. The officers looked surprised.

Quickly I entered. Clavell followed, frantically drawing his revolver as he did so. I kept mine aimed midpoint between the two officers. 'Close the door,' I snapped at Clavell.

What I couldn't figure out was why they were here. Where were their men? Had they run away? Maybe this was the defeatism I'd heard of. Or were these two simply taking a hurried refreshment to steel their nerves? The answer would have to wait for the interrogation.

Clavell was in his element. He jutted forward against the table top and faced them down. 'Come along then, hands in the air,' he said. The officers said nothing. One raised the glass he'd been holding and drained it. The other, just sat there, his hands still on his lap.

'I said hands in the air,' repeated Clavell. Then he waved his revolver melodramatically up and down like an orchestra conductor, no doubt hoping this clever mime would spur some action.

The officer with his hands under the table had been staring at Clavell, although this in itself was hardly remarkable. He was practically on top of them. When Clavell's revolver began its bobbing-for-apples trick, the officer's eyes narrowed and he stiffened.

I fired. A Webley is a powerful weapon at ten feet and the shot tore a hole in the officer's chest. As the boom echoed away, he looked down at himself in consternation. Then he toppled slowly forward onto the table with a loud thump. The bottle fell over and rolled off.

Clavell was aghast. 'MAJOR, you just shot a prisoner of war.'

'Did I? Perhaps you would have preferred I hadn't? Why don't you take a look at his hand, Captain?'

I kept the Webley pointed squarely at the other officer.

Clavell edged around the table and stooped down. When he rose his face was pale.

'He had a pistol! How did you know?' he gasped. And then more quietly, 'You saved my life.'

I shrugged.

'I don't know what to say,' he said.

Under the circumstances neither did I. I hadn't spent a lot of time thinking about it. I hadn't weighed the pros or cons, or made a well-reasoned case. I hadn't considered the arguments. Not like a lawyer would. Not that I was a lawyer these days, not anymore, perhaps not ever. It was a strange conclusion to come to, but I'd spent more time fighting than anything else in my life, so that must make me a soldier. And I'd acted like a soldier, relying on instinct and training. As a soldier I didn't regret saving Clavell, that's what you did for a fellow comrade at arms – even if he was a pompous prick.

'We've got to get out of here.' I said. 'If there are others around they'll be here in no time.'

Hurriedly I opened the door a crack, saw nothing and we tumbled out. I pointed north. We stuck close to the small buildings, piles of coal and debris and any other cover we could find. When we had to, we ran. Our prisoner moved with alacrity. I suppose he realized what would happen if he didn't.

We spotted some Germans from afar, but avoided them. A gun fight with Clavell on one side and a prisoner on the other struck me as a very bad idea. Approaching Wasmuel and safety, Clavell spoke up again. 'It's out of my hands, now. You have to understand, Major. I'm terribly sorry. I'll try to put in a good word for you, if I can.'

Heatedly I responded. 'A good word for me? That's a little rich, don't you think?' I began. Then I thought better of it; he wasn't worth the energy. I still had to get to Jemappes where the Patricias were to capture the last village before Mons. General Loomis would want to hear all about that. Mons was where we'd be heading next.

Clavell looked sheepish. 'You really didn't do it, did you, sir?'

'No, Captain, I did not.' Seeing his face, I almost felt sorry for him.

CHAPTER 39

10th of November, 1918
Jemappes, Belgium

Mons had a ring to it like no other. For the British Empire, it was here the war had begun. In August 1914, a small, hastily cobbled-together British Expeditionary Force encountered the enemy for the very first time, and held the line. But within a day they were falling back. The Great Retreat commenced, all the many miles of ignominious flight to the banks of the River Marne near Paris.

Four years and almost three months on, we were to put it right.

'I've received orders,' announced General Loomis. 'We're to continue the attack and capture Mons.' It was 10 p.m. and the general's staff stood in our new headquarters in the basement of a brewery in Jemappes, awaiting our orders; what landed on the general's desk didn't tend to stay there long.

I grimaced. Naturally Loomis saw it. 'General Currie is most anxious we capture Mons. It's a question of reputation, you understand, Major.'

'I understand that, sir, but what I don't understand is whether it's worth another life. Brigadier Clark reported they met very heavy fire trying to get into the city today.'

Lieutenant-Colonel Hore-Ruthven jumped to his aid. 'Peace is coming, Major, but who knows when, and until it does arrive we're still at war.'

'Well said, Colonel,' said Loomis. 'And seeing as we are still at war, we're going in tonight. Crossing the canals in daylight is impossible, as I think we've learned today.'

'Yes, sir. I'll get my things,' I said.

Loomis said, 'Yes, would you? I'd like you there. I'm sending in the 7th Brigade again.' Then he looked at the colonel and back at me. 'I didn't forget my promise, MacPhail. Don't you forget it either.' Which I suppose was his way of saying, "be careful".

11th of November, 1918
Mons, Belgium

The old walls of the ancient fortress city had long since disappeared, broad boulevards from the *Belle Epoque* taking their place, but the moats remained. While the moats weren't moats anymore, canals had replaced them. The Canal du Centre and a tributary of the Trouille River ringed Mons with water, as at Valenciennes, so the effect was the same. Particularly as all along the southern and western fringes of the city, the second stories of the large houses were occupied by machine gunners and snipers. They were from the 12th Division, as far as Smith and I could figure, and that's what I told the general. Not that who pulled the trigger was of any interest whatsoever to the soldier running across the canal on a plank.

At a little past midnight that soldier was me. If I had any complaints, however, I knew who to take them up with; it was my plan. So I concentrated on keeping my feet on the plank and getting off it as soon as I possibly could.

With the onset of dusk the Highlanders of the 42nd had wasted little time. The scouts had done their work and the value of a good reconnaissance proved itself once more. In the northwest corner of Mons they found a gap in the cordon of water. A thousand yards west of the city, the Condé-Mons canal split in two. One branch ran east along the northern outskirts, while the other curved right to encircle the city from the west and the south. The result was that we could cross the water early, away from the city and its gunners with only the vast expanse of the railway yards dead ahead.

'You're not going to find a better spot than that,' I said to Captain Grafftey, whose D Company had drawn this straw.

Grafftey stared at the map. 'I'm still concerned about all those machine guns, Major.'

'Remember, most of the MGs are south of us. The others are on the far side of the train tracks. That's 200 to 300 yards away. Keep left, and in this darkness you should be able to slip past them unseen.'

'And once we reach the station, we turn right into the city and roll them up from behind.'

I gave him a clap on the back. 'That's the spirit, Captain.'

Rather than accompanying the captain and his men I decided to go with a platoon south, where we'd attempt a canal crossing. But of course the bridges were holed and the scouts warned us of machine-gun nests on the far bank. I didn't bring up the possibility of swimming.

That left us in a fix. Happily, it resolved itself an hour later when we received word from Grafftey that they were at the station, working their way into Mons. 'It's now or never,' I said to the lieutenant, 'The Boche will be distracted.' Before I knew it, we were on our way.

My chest was pounding. Somewhere in the city a fire crackled, but apart from that it was deathly still. And dark. The first men had carefully lain timbers on the demolished bridge. Now there was only the shuffle of our boots on the narrow wooden plank as we crossed.

Stepping onto solid ground I breathed a sigh of relief. We hadn't heard the sound I'd been dreading, the staccato of a Maxim or the sudden crack of a Mauser 98. To my surprise Mons appeared empty. The outposts lining the canal must have withdrawn at the threat from behind. We filed through the narrow winding streets. Again, there was no sign of the enemy.

With only empty roads and a deep quiet, enlivened once by the concussions of some grenades further on in the city, the tense alertness wore off. The men began talking among themselves. One soldier dragged his rifle with fixed bayonet along the metal barred windows, creating a rhythmic clanking. Soon the whole platoon followed suit. The streets began to fill with people.

The realization that their city was free spread like a prairie wildfire. By the time we passed the great square, an atmosphere of exuberant gaiety had taken hold. An elderly woman bustled up and clenched my two cheeks in her pudgy hands like my grandmother did when I was ten. 'Les braves Canadiens,' she said. While I was still glowing from her words and the pinch on my cheeks, she conjured up a bottle and a cup from her bag and offered me the sort of drink my grandmother never had: cognac. I coughed, and with a trail of liquid fire racing down my esophagus handed back the cup, giving her what I sincerely hoped was a winsome smile.

Once through the city we headed east. The patrols had located the enemy in a line five kilometres further. The battalion began to dig in, in a series of slit-trenches and small holes. It was there around dawn, as it broke dull and dreary, that I spotted a familiar figure trotting up the road in considerable haste, coming from the direction of Mons.

Approaching the platoon his head darted from left to right and I knew he'd come for me. I waved.

Tibbett could barely contain himself. 'Malcolm! An armistice has been signed!' he blurted out.

'An armistice? You mean there's peace?' I scratched at my chin and thought about this. It wasn't what I'd been expecting. 'Are you positive about that?' I asked. 'I did wonder why there were no new orders for the advance today. But I've run out of fingers counting all the peace rumours.'

'This is no rumour, Malcolm. A message from Corps headquarters arrived at seven this morning. Duguid took it. He was duty officer. There's no mistake about it, the Germans have agreed to an armistice. It's to take effect today at eleven a.m. They're still busy informing all the units.'

Slowly, I shook my head. 'Now, isn't that something?' I said. 'I wondered if this day would ever arrive, Paul. I really did.'

'It's over, Malcolm. The war is finally over.'

Only Tibbett was not entirely correct. It wasn't quite over yet.

I consulted my Borgel. Earlier I'd synchronised it again. This was a day when time counted more than any other, and I saw that it was 10.58 a.m.

'Malcolm. Have a look!'

Beside me Tibbett slowly rose from the ditch and stepped up on to the uneven ground in front. He stood upright and began frantically waving his arms above his head, as if in distress. And then I saw what the commotion was all about. A young woman hung out a farmhouse window, a hundred yards away. Seeing Tibbett she raised her own arm, and waved gaily, shouting something that was lost in the wind.

What the hell was he doing? 'Get down, you bloody fool,' I shouted. Tibbett hesitated, but ignored me, waving with a look of unfettered joy on his face.

'Oh, no,' I cried, 'I'm not going to lose you, too.' I jumped from the ditch and leapt for him. My tackle was rough and I hit him hard. 'Malcolm...' he sputtered, his face contorted in angry bewilderment. Unprepared, his legs buckled. But as we tumbled to the ground there was a loud *CRACK*. It was a single round, and its echo seemed to go on and on, burying itself indelibly in my mind. And then it was quiet.

Frantically we scrambled back into the ditch. There we lay, winded on the cold earth. Me on top of him, until he began to squirm and I rolled off. I glanced at him. Mud clung to his face. His helmet was askew, his spectacles bent and twisted. One glass was missing. He looked like a school boy after his first schoolyard tussle. Tibbett looked up. With new eyes. Round ones full of astonishment. And I began to laugh.

He stared at me as I doubled over, tears of mirth flowing unrestrainedly down my cheeks. And then he too smiled and began to laugh. I gasped for air, my belly aching, and I made to wipe my face with a hand. Then suddenly alert I paused, and listened. Quickly I brought a finger to my mouth.

'What's wrong?' he asked, a dark shadow moving across his face.

'Listen,' I whispered. 'Do you hear that?'

Tibbett cocked his head, listening, then looked at me in confusion.

'It's quiet.' A deathly silence had fallen. A silence I'd never known in all my years at the front. There was no distant thud of a cannon, nor retort of a rifle. No buzzing aeroplanes. I saw men, but the battlefield was silent. I strained my ears and still I heard nothing.

Tibbett fished in his pocket and pulled out a silver timepiece. He held it up, a hand's length from his face and peered down his nose. 'It's 11 a.m.,' he said. 'It's the armistice.'

Far in the distance a solitary church bell began to clang.

'I'll be damned,' I said softly, and I sat up. He did the same and we looked at each other. I grasped his hand and shook it. 'Congratulations, Paul.'

'Who would have believed,' he said, shaking his head. Then his eyes narrowed and his expression turned serious. 'I wouldn't have made it without you, Malcolm…'

'Shhh,' I murmured gruffly. 'We were here for each other, Paul. One for all and all for one. That's the Corps motto, isn't it? That's how we made it. Don't ever forget that.'

Gravely, he nodded.

'But if you really insist, I wouldn't say no to a cognac in Mons.'

A smile returned. 'Nor would I,' he said. 'Which reminds me there was one other piece of good news. I clean forget to tell you. Benoît sent a postcard. He's still in the hospital in England but doing well he says. Although he did complain about the food.'

I laughed. 'If Benoît is complaining about the food, he's definitely all right.'

'They're sending him back to Canada soon.'

'That's wonderful news,' I said. 'Simply wonderful.' Then a thought came to me. 'For a brief moment, Paul, I thought you'd come to tell me the Provost Marshal had reconsidered.'

'No, I'm sorry, Malcolm. No news there. Don't worry, I'm sure it will work out.'

The parade had come to an end. The pipes had played, the battalions had marched and the 5th British Lancers who'd fought here in '14 had escorted General Currie into the city to wild applause. The Grande Place was festooned in banners and flags, and madly cheering citizens packed the square, every window of every building requisitioned by the enthusiastic folk of Mons. Even I, tone deaf at the best of times, felt a shiver run through me as this sea of people lifted their voices in unison when the bands struck up *La Brabançonne,* the Belgian national anthem. I'd laughed as the organ began and the men belted out "It's a long way to Mons", to the tune all of us knew so well.

Now it was over and the troops were dispersing. I stood with Tibbett, Smith and a few others from the division. We'd listened to all the speeches from the front row.

Toot I heard, and the low growl of a motor. I didn't look at first, the afternoon had been one great orchestra of sound, but coming closer the sounds repeated. A French motorcyclist encrusted in mud was making his way across the square. It was tough going. I watched him as he pushed his bike with his feet, the motor putting, trying to wend his way through the throngs who showed little sign of yielding, jovially patting him on the shoulder instead. At a group of our men, the motorcyclist halted, and he spoke with them. The soldiers began to look around, trying to peer over the heads of the crowd. Then one of them, an officer I knew, looked in our direction and gave a cry. Those with him all turned, their eyes soon fixed on us. Several stuck out their arms, pointing in our direction. The motorcyclist looked around trying to follow their lead. The men waved. I threw up an arm. The motorcyclist shook his head as if all was clear and headed towards us.

Clad in blue, his tall riding boots caked in dirt, a black leather despatch case was fastened across his chest. He looked like he'd driven every dirt road in France this day. Right before he reached us he leaned his motorcycle onto its stand and stepped off. Smartly he walked towards us, snapped to attention, and gave me one of the sharpest salutes I've ever seen.

'Vous êtes le commandant Mac...?' he asked, and I saw his mind and his tongue enter a No-Man's-Land over what exactly came next. I was prepared for this; the MacPhail clan, for whatever its virtues, had given itself a name wholly unpronounceable to our French allies.

'Oui, je suis Major MacPhail,' I said, coming to his aid.

'J'ai un message pour vous,' he announced. He rummaged in his despatch case and handed over a large buff manila envelope. Then he saluted again.

In return, I gave him my own best effort and thanked him.

'A votre service, monsieur,' he replied, and grinned. The end of the

war had done wonders for French morale. With that he turned on his heel and returned to his idling motorcycle.

By now the others had congregated around. It wasn't every day the French army came calling.

Tearing open the envelope I removed a single sheet of fine cream paper and unfolded it. It bore a fancy official letterhead, of which I saw nothing except the single line, *Chef du Cabinet Militaire*. It was dated November 10th.

Mon cher major, it read, *J'ai l'honneur de vous rendre compte…* (My dear Major, I have the honour to inform you…). The letter was signed, Générale Mordacq.

'Well… what is it?' said someone. 'Don't tell me you're to get the *Légion d'Honneur*,' said another, to a smattering of chuckles. I think it was Duguid.

'No. Nothing like that,' I mumbled.

At that moment, the 42nd Highlanders' band began to pipe their retreat. It offered me a welcome respite from all the attention. Except for Tibbett and Smith. They both remained at my side.

'AND?' said Tibbett. He was beside himself with excitement and curiosity.

'Wonders never cease,' I said, shaking my head. 'It's from General Mordacq. Your Lord Derby came through in spades. He appears to have related my entire story to the general. You remember I once told you I thought Mordacq looked like a detective. Well, as it happens, he's cracked the case. The French Army just arrested Capitaine Madelot. He'd deserted, and was making for Switzerland with a considerable sum of money when he was apprehended. They're interrogating him.'

Tibbett's eyes widened. 'What happens now?'

'All the information will be passed on to the British Army authorities.'

'Ah, so that will be that,' said Tibbett, grinning. 'I knew it would work out.'

'And to think I doubted you,' I said, and I too began to smile.

Smith coughed gently, as he's wont to do when he has something to say.

'What's on your mind, Lieutenant? You wanted to congratulate me?'

'Yes, that too, sir,' said Smith. 'I was just thinking, however…'

'Yes...?'

'The money that went missing was German, I believe you said?'

'A little French, but mainly German, that's right. Why?'

'Well, sir, German currency is as good as worthless. At least now it is.' A crooked little smile came to his face.

I blinked, thinking about this. Then I grinned. 'Ah! So if it's worthless...' I said slowly.

'Exactly. You couldn't very well have stolen something that's worthless, sir.'

I groaned. 'Now you tell me, Lieutenant. This has been eating at me for months.'

'If you don't mind me saying so, sir, you always did worry too much.'

Which, come to that, was probably true. But then there'd been a lot to worry about. It had been a very long war.

'You know,' I said thoughtfully. 'I think right about now, I might appreciate that cognac you promised, Paul.' I put one hand on his shoulder and the other on Smith's. 'Captain Tibbett is treating, Lieutenant. Why don't we all go and have a drink to Benoît?'

AUTHOR'S NOTE and ACKNOWLEDGEMENTS

The last hundred days seldom rates more than a brief postscript in the popular narrative of the Great War. Which is strange, as it was in those few months, from August until November, that the Imperial German Army was beaten and beaten decisively. When Germany sued for peace other factors undoubtedly weighed, but by the late fall of 1918 its generals had concluded that militarily the end had come.

My Hundred Days of War is a work of fiction. However, beyond Malcolm's own tale, it also sketches the war's final months, and those of the Canadian Corps whose feats helped bring about its end. The Corps would pay a heavy price; a staggering 46,000 of them fell, from a nominal force of 100,000. Of the Allied forces pressing relentlessly to either side on a long front, the casualties amounted to many more. It is a story the world deserves to know better.

I hope to have left an appreciation and a feeling for what it must have been like on the battlefields of Northern France and Belgium as the tide of war slowly swung. For the ordinary soldier, fighting almost daily, vague rumours of peace were far removed from his day-to-day existence.

While Malcolm MacPhail is in every respect a figment of my imagination, I have done my best to ensure that the events in which he plays a role are as true to history as I could make them. In my research I have left little to chance and, where the record is clear, I have let the times, weather, places, people and details speak for themselves. Where it is not, my imagination has filled in the gaps. Occasionally I had to take sides in the historical debate. To the profound sorrow of Malcolm, General Lipsett, was indeed transferred against his will from the 3rd Division. Most histories ascribe this to a policy of "Canadianization". The facts seem to suggest a more prosaic reason. That at least is the story I chose to tell, and the truth may never completely be known. Likewise, the ill-fated and last-minute decision by Major-General Montgomery of the Fourth Army, on the second day of the Amiens "show", to reverse earlier orders and throw the 3rd Division back into action may not have made a difference. I tend to think it did, hence Malcolm's frequent grumblings. Again, we will never know for certain.

Malcolm's final months of war are dramatic ones, although no more than the history itself. Soldiers of the 5th CMR did, for example, swim the canal at Cambrai on the night of October 9th to secure the pill-box and enter the burning city (Chapter 30). The daring crossing of the same Canal de L'Escaut three weeks later at Valenciennes, under the command of Major McLean, is the stuff of movies even if the story is taken from the pages of the 4th CMR Battalion history. My take became Chapter 36. For his actions in securing the critical bridges at Quiévrechain and Quiévrain on November 6th, as fictionalized in Chapter 37, Captain John MacGregor of the 2nd CMR would receive the second highest award for gallantry in the Empire, the Military Cross (his second). MacGregor ended the war as one of Canada's and the Empire's most decorated soldiers, holding the Victoria Cross (the highest award), a MC and bar, and a Distinguished Conduct Medal.

As for Lieutenant Charlie Rutherford, the man of the hour in the capture of Monchy-le-Preux on the first day of the attack towards the Drocourt-Quéant Line, he was to win a Victoria Cross. His deeds at Arvillers two weeks earlier (Chapter 3) earned him a Military Cross. Rutherford survived the war, one of the Empire's most decorated veterans. Interestingly, war diaries for August 9th reported the capture at Arvillers of a large pigeon wagon, 150 new machine guns and a large but undisclosed amount of cash. As far as I am aware, however, the latter was never reported missing.

Other than characters such as Paul Tibbett, Lieutenant Smith, Malcolm's good friend Benoît DuBois and his "enemy" Captain

Clavell, many of the peripheral characters were real people. As a novelist I've put words in their mouths which in most cases were not theirs (there are some exceptions where the past lent a welcome hand), and had them do things they may not have done. Where I've imagined, embellished and added in the interest of drama, I like to think it could have happened. HRH the Prince of Wales, for instance, clearly never made Malcolm's acquaintance yet had Malcolm been there, who is to know?

I can't end this note without acknowledging the help of others. In particular, I want to thank Dr. Gary Grothman and Diann Duthie, whose critical read of the first draft saved me from numerous mistakes, and whose input greatly improved the final book. My editor Dexter Petley was everything you could wish for in an editor, his feel for language being truly masterful. Finally, I'd like to thank Ian Forsdike for his dedication and remarkably keen eyes in proofing the final version.

If you enjoyed reading *My Hundred Days of War* I would be very grateful if you wrote a review online. It needn't be long, but the experience of readers like yourself is invaluable in encouraging others to discover new books (including mine).

Should you be interested in learning more and keeping abreast of new publications, I encourage you to sign up for my email notifications at www.darrellduthie.com, the virtual home of Malcolm MacPhail. Thanks very much for reading.

Darrell Duthie
Amersfoort, June 27th, 2018

Printed in Great Britain
by Amazon

56485821R00201